Blood For Blood

by

Ben Wolf

www.benwolf.com

BLOOD FOR BLOOD
Published by The Seymour Agency
2333 Barton Oaks Dr., Raleigh, NC, 27614

In cooperation with
Splickety Publishing Group, Inc.
PO Box 513
Bettendorf, IA 52722

ISBN 978-1942462002
Copyright © 2014 by Ben Wolf
Cover art by Benjamin Lucas Powell
Cover design by Arpit Mehta

Available in print from your local bookstore, online, or from the author at:
www.benwolf.com/blood-for-blood/

For more information on this book and the author visit: www.benwolf.com

All rights reserved. Non-commercial interests may reproduce portions of this book without the express written permission of the author, provided the text does not exceed 500 words. When reproducing text from this book, include the following credit line: *"Blood for Blood by Ben Wolf, published by The Seymour Agency. For more information visit www.benwolf.com. Used by permission."*

Commercial interests: No part of this publication may be reproduced in any form, stored in a retrieval system, or transmitted in any form by any means—electronic, photocopy, recording, or otherwise—without prior written permission of the author, except as provided by the United States of America copyright law.

This is a work of fiction. Names, characters, and incidents are all products of the author's imagination or are used for fictional purposes. Any mentioned brand names, places, and trademarks remain the property of their respective owners, bear no association with the author or the publisher, and are used for fictional purposes only.

Scripture quotations are taken from the KING JAMES BIBLE/KJV, which is public domain. All rights reserved.

Brought to you by the creative team at TheSeymourAgency.com,
Nicole Resciniti and Julie Gwinn, Agents
And by Splickety Publishing Group, Inc. www.splicketypubgroup.com

Library of Congress Cataloging-in-Publication Data
Wolf, Ben
Blood for Blood/ Ben Wolf 1st ed.
Printed in the United States of America.

PRAISE FOR *BLOOD FOR BLOOD* AND FOR Ben Wolf

"Action, humor, romance, and an age-old question of the soul. *Blood for Blood* is a lively new twist on an old tale. Ben Wolf goes for the jugular and dares to ask: is anyone beyond the grace of God?"

—**Tosca Lee, *NY Times* bestselling author**
of *The Legend of Sheba* and *Iscariot*

"From the moment I met Ben in 2009 I've loved his passion for stories, for people, and for stretching the envelope of what can be done in the world of publishing. It's been a kick to watch him grow as a person and as an author."

—**James L. Rubart, bestselling author of *Rooms***

"Ben Wolf has a real winner in Blood for Blood. Solid writing, believable characters, fluid pacing, and a premise that exemplifies Christian speculative fiction: Could a vampire be saved? I loved the boldness, the nonstop tension, and the well-timed twists. I highly recommend this book."

—**Kerry Neitz, author of *Amish Vampires in Space***

"I have said before and I'll say again that Ben and those like him are the future of Christian publishing."

—**Jeff Gerke, founder of Marcher Lord Press**
(now Enclave Publishing) and author

"I had brainstormed a book about the conflicts vampires face when they become Christians. Ben stole (Okay—I gave him my permission) the idea and wrote an action-adventure thriller that's worthy of my being robbed. The story and style reminds me of Ted Dekker's *Showdown* series. Ben twists the plot with so much tension—don't be surprised if your book snaps when you read the last fifty pages!"

—**Matthew Sheehy, author and victim**
of intellectual property theft

"*Blood for Blood* pulls you in from the beginning and doesn't let go. This book pulls you through twists and turns in a thrilling race to the end while dealing with the classic question: can God really save *anyone*? You don't want to miss this book!"

—Avily Jerome, Editor, *Havok Magazine*
www.splicketypubgroup.com/havok

"*Blood for Blood* is a must-read for fans of the traditional vampire. It blends timeless faith with monster lore in a thought-provoking and thrilling tale that will leave you thirsty for more."

—Benjamin Lucas Powell, horror writer and artist

"Raven's transformation gives hope to those whose lives have been deadened by life-controlling challenges in this brilliant story that shows how all things are possible through the power of the Cross. Ben Wolf intrigues us with a soulless being to demonstrate how the blood of Christ can transfuse new life into any who have lost their way."

—Susan Erlichman, Ben Wolf's mom

"Ben Wolf wields a masterful grasp on story and myth, weaving two conflicting world into a single pulse-pounding tale. You need to read this book."

—Charis Ditamore, author

"I love Ben Wolf's irreverent sense of humor. *Blood for Blood* is an exploration of a question that, while audacious on its vampiric surface, really cuts to the heart of the deepest, most human question of all: is there anyone who exists beyond the reach of God's redemptive grace? Get ready for a twisty-windy thrill-ride of an answer that only Wolf would dare to deliver."

—Lindsay Franklin, author

For Brian, Susan, and Lauren,
my first and biggest fans.

Acknowledgements

First I need to acknowledge Jesus Christ, without whom this book could not exist. I'm not just writing that because he's my personal Lord and Savior (though that's part of it)—I'm writing it because without Jesus' sacrifice, the entire concept for this book wouldn't work.

Second, I have to credit my agent Julie Gwinn with getting me to write this book. We met at the 2010 ACFW conference and hit it off almost immediately. We kept in touch because she wanted to publish me at B&H Fiction, but as a debut author I couldn't break in.

In 2011 I attended a different writers conference in Nashville and met with Julie afterward in the Lifeway cafeteria. She and I talked through the concept for *Blood for Blood* at that meeting, and within a few days I had written a long synopsis for the book. A year later I pitched it to her, officially, at the ACFW conference, but for all of our efforts, separately and together, we couldn't get it published. Vampires were just too risky for established Christian publishers.

But Julie didn't forget about me. (I'm annoying and persistent, so I made it hard for her to ignore me.) When she became an agent later this year (2014), she reconnected with me and I signed with her shortly after. *Blood for Blood*, in the form you're about to read, came as a direct result of that partnership.

Without Julie this book probably would have continued to languish on my hard drive, under-developed and inaccessible to read-ers. I owe Julie more than I can express for her help and belief in me.

Matt Sheehy also gets a shout-out, because like Jesus and Julie, without him this book would not exist. Matt mentioned his idea for a parody of a vampire who got saved at the 2009 ACFW conference, and I loved it—enough to steal it. He graciously gave me permission to hijack his idea, and I ran with it, and *Blood for Blood* is the result.

I have to extend thanks to my parents Brian and Susan for always believing in me, and, for the first several years of my professional writing career, for helping to fund my excursions into the world of fiction to the tune of several thousand dollars. Kudos also to my dad for coming up with the title for *Blood for Blood*, which is not only awesome but also opened up worlds of possibilities for symbolism within the story itself.

My Spectrum critique group deserves some credit as well. Andrew Winch, Adam Weisenburger, and Charis Ditamore let me hone my editing skills on their work, and they tore apart some of mine and helped me put it back together again. Without them I wouldn't have anyone to refer to as "you people," nor would I have the support of three very awesome, talented friends. Also, \BAM/.

I need to thank my team at Splickety Publishing Group,

many of whom served as test readers for this book and caught a bunch of stupid errors, historical and otherwise, that I corrected and thus used to improve the book.

All of my staff are incredible and without them Splickety wouldn't exist, but I especially want to thank Lindsay Franklin who grilled me on the historical issues in my novel. Avily Jerome caught a big annoying continuation error and gave me a stellar review for the inside of the book cover.

Let's not forget Arpit Mehta, the most underpaid graphic designer in the world (but at least he's getting paid something) who is responsible for the text layout of the covers and for basically everything graphic at Splickety.

Big thanks also to Ben Powell, the phenomenal artist of *Blood for Blood*'s incredible covers (back and front) and a good friend of mine.

NYT Bestseller and friend Tosca Lee generously allotted some of her valuable time to read, endorse, and help me enhance *Blood for Blood* on more in-depth levels than I knew were possible.

Kerry Nietz also lent me his authorial expertise and gave me a great endorsement, and Jeff Gerke has been a constant cheerleader and source of wisdom for me for years.

Thanks also to Ashley, who provided some inspiration for this novel and served as my first beta reader. Also thanks to Liam and Violet, whom I love, and who are two of my primary reasons to get this book out into the world.

I also want to express my great admiration for Frank Peretti, the author from whom I gleaned my great desire to write. Robert Liparulo also gets credit for writing some of the best fiction I've ever read and continues to inspire me to up my game as an author.

Last of all, thanks to everyone I didn't specifically name in this endorsement. I'm about as far as it gets from being an elephant when it comes to remembering things, so please don't take it personally if you weren't listed by name.

Most of all, I hope you enjoy *Blood for Blood*.

Prologue

June of 1850

"I don't care what you *think* you saw, Duke. I'm doin' this, and you're not gonna stop me." Uncle Murray unsheathed his military-issue officer's saber and raised it over his balding head.

"Move and I'll shoot you dead." Duke pulled the hammer back on his revolver and pointed it at his uncle's chest. Tears streamed down his face.

Uncle Murray froze, then glared at Duke. "As dead as she was just last night? Earlier today?"

"We obviously made a mistake." Duke's voice quavered, but he couldn't help it.

He glanced down at Eleanor, still alive, now at his feet next to their overturned dinner table. Her white burial dress was covered in blood. Her blood.

A wooden leg from that very table, broken in half, protruded from her chest, and her long blonde hair, now stained red, lay in a mass by her face. "She was fine before you stormed in here and stabbed her!"

Eleanor moaned.

"See? She's still alive. We can save her if we get her to a

doctor before—"

"*No*, Duke. You can't save her. That's what I'm tryin' to explain to you." Uncle Murray lowered his saber, but didn't sheathe it. "She's not human anymore, son. She's somethin' else. Somethin' dark. Evil."

Duke tightened his grip on the revolver. "She's my *wife!*"

"Not anymore, she ain't," Uncle Murray yelled back. "She tried to kill me not two minutes before you walked in. Don't you see my left arm, boy? She mangled it with her *bare hands*."

Duke gawked at his uncle's arm. In the heat of the moment he hadn't noticed how it bent in several places where it shouldn't have, and red splotches tainted his otherwise cream-colored shirt all up and down his left sleeve.

"How else do you think this happened?" Uncle Murray pointed the saber's tip down at Eleanor. "She did this to me, and she would've done far worse had I not put that table leg through her chest. I've seen this before, once, in Romania. You have to stake them with wood and cut off their heads or they won't die."

"She barely weighs a hundred pounds. You expect me to believe *she* did that to you?" Sweat snaked down Duke's forehead and onto his nose and cheeks.

"She's not human, anymore, Duke. How many times do I have to say it?"

"Put the sword down." The revolver trembled in Duke's hand. "Now."

"Not a chance." Uncle Murray raised it over his head again.

"Uncle Murray!" Duke yelled. "Put it down!"

"I'm sorry, son. You'll understand someday." Uncle Murray lunged toward Eleanor.

Duke pulled the trigger. The revolver flashed.

A geyser of red erupted from Uncle Murray's bulging gut and he staggered back, wide-eyed. "Duke, don't—"

Duke fired again.

Uncle Murray dropped the sword, clutched his chest, and gasped.

Duke shot him two more times, once more in the leg, and once in his neck. His shakiness had thrown off his aim, but it was enough to finish the job. Uncle Murray hit the floor next to Eleanor with a thud, and a pool of blood collected under his body.

Duke didn't lower his gun until Uncle Murray stopped moving altogether. Eleanor wasn't moving either. She lay on her side facing Uncle Murray's body, motionless.

The gun dropped from Duke's grip, and he dove down next to Eleanor and grabbed her shoulders—she was still breathing, but on her side, facing away from him. "Elly?"

A gurgle caught his attention, followed by a faint sucking, slurping noise. Tears rolled down Duke's cheeks.

Eleanor's eyes cracked open. Her skin was frigid, as if she'd been standing out in the cold for an hour, despite the heat wave they'd had all June.

"Eleanor? *Eleanor?*"

She moaned at first, then said in a weak voice, "Pull it out."

"Pull—what? That table leg?"

She nodded.

Duke reached for the table leg and got ahold of it, but stopped. "It'll…it'll kill you. We need to get you to a doctor."

"Please."

Duke marshaled all his fortitude and yanked the table leg from her chest.

Eleanor convulsed and howled, then exhaled a raspy breath. "Thank you."

Duke dropped the table leg and touched her shoulder. "Elly, darling, I'm going to pick you up. I'm taking you to a doctor."

She shook her head and turned away from him, toward the floor. "I don't need a doctor."

"I'm not giving up on you." Duke scooped her into his arms, but she writhed out of his grasp and back onto the floor.

"*Stop.*" Eleanor's voice hardened. "I'm already dead, Duke."

Yes, she had died. He'd been certain of it. He'd seen it happen.

A man, a phantom of a man with black hair, dark, sunken brown eyes, elongated canine teeth, and pale skin—skin the color of Eleanor's now—had attacked her in the night. Duke found the two of them in the parlor of their small house and he'd chased the man away.

At first he'd thought Eleanor had been unfaithful, but when he noticed she wasn't moving and found the two bloody holes on her neck, that thought dissipated.

She'd died in his arms, and they buried her the next day.

But now she lay before him, next to his dead uncle, whom he'd killed because of her.

And she was alive.

And…slurping.

"Elly, what are you—"

Her head spun toward him and for the first time since he'd found her atop of Uncle Murray not ten minutes earlier, Duke saw her face.

Blood coated the left side of her chin, her cheek, and caked in the hair on the side of her head by her ear. More of it tainted her full lips, and her blue eyes had a cloudy quality about them that Duke had never seen before. More disturbing still, her canine teeth now extended well beyond their original length.

Elongated teeth. Just like the man who had attacked her.

She shoved him back and stood to her feet, towering over him.

He sat and stared up at her.

She tilted her head and grinned at him, but those teeth protruded from behind her lips nonetheless. As Eleanor stalked toward him, the hole in her chest sealed up.

Duke's eyes widened. "Elly, what in God's name is going on?"

Her fingernails bared like claws, she flung herself down at him. Duke rolled away and her nails embedded in the floor.

He scrambled to his feet and backed away from her.

She hurtled toward him again, but he sidestepped her and she clung to the wall, her fangs bared, her eyes wild with murder. This was *not* the Elly he'd married, not the woman with whom he'd lived for the last three years.

She lunged toward him again and he tried to get away, but he tripped over Uncle Murray's body and landed on his back.

Eleanor, also on the floor, smiled and crawled toward him. She purred, "Where are you going, Duke? You have me back. You made a vow at the altar. Man and wife. Mr. and Mrs. Duke Flax. Remember? Don't you want me anymore?"

His fingers found something cold and metal. They closed around it. His revolver. He adjusted his grip and pointed it at Eleanor.

"Don't come any closer, or I'll—"

"You'll what? You'll shoot me like you did to Uncle Murray?" Eleanor cackled, and Duke's bones filled with ice.

She jerked toward him and he pulled the trigger. Eleanor recoiled from the shot and stared down at the bullet hole on the right side of her chest. Her mouth hung open at first, but her lips curled into a wicked smile.

She came at him again and he pulled the trigger. The bullet smacked into her forehead, but it barely slowed her down. If bullets couldn't harm her, then—

There. By his right boot. The half a table leg he'd pulled from Eleanor's body. *You have to stake them with wood and cut off their heads or they won't die.* If Duke could just reach it...

Eleanor's clouded blue eyes fixed on it as well.

Duke dropped the revolver and lurched for it, but Eleanor sprung at him, her hands aimed at his throat. His fingers scraped against rough wood, but she pinned him to the floor with icy hands before he could get a grip on the table leg.

She smiled at him with evil in her eyes and kicked the table leg away. Eleanor opened her bloody mouth and lunged toward his neck.

But she barely weighed a hundred pounds, and they were right next to the overturned table—right next to the other half of the broken leg, still attached to the bottom of the table. He pushed her back and she hissed, but he tightened his hands on her shoulders.

She scratched at him and writhed against his grip. He hefted her higher, twisted his body toward the table, and slammed her down onto the exposed table leg. It pierced through her back and stuck out of the middle of her chest.

Eleanor arched her back and shrieked, her voice breaking into three dissonant, droning tones.

Duke rolled away and forced himself to his feet. She squirmed and groped at the jagged chunk of wood protruding from her chest then reached for him, but she couldn't get to him. Duke picked up his uncle's saber and walked over to her.

"I'm so sorry, Elly." He raised the saber over his head. "By God, I'm so, so sorry."

Eleanor screamed for the last time.

Chapter 1

May of 1885 – Northern California

Hunger drove Raven Worth to the big tent revival that night, but it wasn't what made him stay. Usually in such a public gathering he'd have lurked just beyond the edge of the crowd to scan the fringes for stragglers. In other settings he'd often harvest the ones who looked the most destitute or lonely.

He could relate to them. He knew their pain.

But not that night. The crowd seemed devoid of the transients and homeless nobodies Raven preferred. Everyone beamed with happiness—they enjoyed the service, the evangelist's booming voice, and each other in a form of unity Raven hadn't seen since before he'd turned.

Then again, that was almost a hundred years ago. Sometimes it felt more like a thousand.

A few children wandered along the crowd's outer ring, not engaged by the service in the least. One of them, a small girl with hair so blonde that it seemed to glow under the moonlight, sat alone on the ground and played with a rag doll.

Raven couldn't help but stare at her.

Who would leave such a beautiful child unattended? Raven

clenched his fists. Didn't her parents know what kinds of horrors roamed the night in search of weak, vulnerable prey exactly like her? Perhaps she was an orphan, with no one to look out for her wellbeing.

A rumble in Raven's stomach reminded him why he'd come tonight. He shook off the weakness and resigned himself to his task.

She was a small girl, small and alone, but she would do. Perhaps if he could restrain himself enough she wouldn't die after he finished.

Either way, if he didn't feed, he wouldn't survive.

She's just an orphan. She has no one. No one will miss her. She'll be better off.

He stepped toward her.

The evangelist's voice thundered and the girl's head swiveled toward the stage. Raven froze in place, enraptured by her golden hair.

She stood up and turned toward Raven. Her warm brown eyes locked on his for a moment, and she smiled.

Raven's eyes widened. The blonde girl snatched up her doll, gave him another grin, and then bounded off through the crowd toward the stage.

"My sheep hear my voice, and I know them, and they follow me." The evangelist's voice filled the tent and much of the space beyond. He reached out his hand and pulled the small blonde girl onto the stage with him. "These are some of my sheep, my family."

Raven stared at the six people on the stage: the evangelist, the little blonde girl, a burly young man with red hair in his early 20s, two boys—one in his mid-teens, the other under ten—both little copies of their evangelist father, and a captivating young lady with auburn hair and dark eyes who looked to be about 18 or 19 years old.

Raven fixed his attention on her.

The evangelist motioned to her. "And now my daughter Calandra will sing for you."

Calandra. A name Raven had never heard before, even in all his decades of haunting the night.

Calandra began to sing.

> *"O come and dwell in me,*
> *Spirit of power within,*
> *and bring the glorious liberty*
> *from sorrow, fear, and sin.*
>
> *Hasten the joyful day*
> *which shall my sins consume,*
> *when old things shall be done away,*
> *and all things new become.*
>
> *I want the witness, Lord,*
> *that all I do is right,*
> *according to thy mind and word,*
> *well-pleasing in thy sight.*

I ask no higher state;
indulge me but in this,
and soon or later then translate
to thine eternal bliss."

Raven forgot his hunger. He couldn't stop staring at her.

"My friends," the evangelist said. "The apostle John said that 'if we confess our sins, he is faithful and just to forgive us our sins, and to cleanse us from all unrighteousness.'"

Raven shuddered and the hunger in his chest resurged. He'd have to find another lonely soul along the outer rim of the crowd.

A green bottle clanked on the ground to his left. A woman, middle-aged with red hair and freckles, tottered a few steps away from the crowd. She swayed like a flower in a light breeze—a drunken flower, but a flower nonetheless.

Less than ideal, but Raven stalked toward her anyway.

"Turn away from your old life, your old existence, and become a new creation tonight." The evangelist's voice split Raven's thoughts.

Old existence. It had gotten old, alright, but Raven was cursed. No one, God or otherwise, would free him from his damnation.

Raven stopped short when he noticed a thin gold band on the woman's ring finger. So she wasn't a lone soul after all. She had a husband, and probably children too. Raven's jaw tightened.

The woman leaned over and scooped up the bottle with one

hand, then peered inside. She hurled it to the ground and it shattered on a rock. Tears streamed down her face and she dropped back onto her rear-end in the grass. A few people on the edge of the crowd turned to stare at her, but a silver-haired woman started toward her.

The evangelist's voice boomed from the stage again. "Come up to this altar and meet the one who will save you from your past, renew your present, and ensure your future."

If Raven didn't go to the woman now, he'd miss his chance. He stormed toward her.

He reached the drunk woman at the same time as the old woman, who reached down and touched her shoulder. The drunk woman sobbed.

At the same time, Raven hooked his left arm around the woman's waist and helped her to her feet. "Come, now. Let's get you out of here."

The old woman clamped onto his wrist. "Do you know this woman?"

"Of course I know her." Raven stared into the old woman's blue eyes. Given the drunk woman's age and reddish hair, a stark contrast to Raven's black hair, pale complexion, and youthful appearance, only one explanation would appease the old woman. "She's my aunt."

The old woman squinted at him but released his wrist.

Raven nudged the woman who now clung to him. "Auntie, look at me."

The woman raised her green, bloodshot eyes to Raven's. Her

breath reeked of whiskey. "How do I…know you?"

Raven stared deep into her eyes, past the haze, and into her mind. He placed the lie in her head as truth, just as he had to so many other victims over the years. "It's me, Raven. Your nephew."

Through her inebriation, the woman smiled at him, in spite of her tears. "Raven. My nephew."

Raven turned to the old woman. "Thank you for your concern. I'll take it from here."

"My pleasure." The old woman tilted her head. "Can't be too careful in these dangerous times. Many a man would do a helpless woman harm in the state she's in. What'd you say her name was?"

"It's Caroline." Raven shifted his gaze from the old woman to "Caroline" and focused on her mind again. "Aunt Caroline."

"Aunt Caroline," she repeated with a smile.

Raven nodded at the old woman, then turned Aunt Caroline away from the crowd and toward the deep darkness of the surrounding woods. "I'll get her back to our farm. Good evening, ma'am."

"Good evening," the old woman said, but the suspicion didn't leave her eyes. From behind them she called, "And God bless you, and your Aunt Caroline."

Raven clenched his teeth so hard that his jaw hurt. Several steps later he disappeared into the woods with Aunt Caroline in tow.

Chapter 2

Raven returned to the revival the next night only to find that the crowd had swelled, even in spite of the gusty winds that rippled the massive tent's fabric. The music had stopped, and the evangelist had taken the stage.

Sure, he had to feed, but he also wanted to see Calandra, to hear her voice again. Even so, tonight Raven would waste no time prowling. He couldn't risk any additional unwanted attention, especially since he'd been foolish enough to come back a second night.

There. A short, round, brown-haired man with a half-week's worth of stubble on his chin. Awkward. Alone. Disinterested in the revival itself. Perfect.

Well, almost. Raven didn't feed on men if he could help it. They put up more of a struggle, and he preferred attractive prey, but tonight, in a rush, he'd make do.

"*Stop.*"

The evangelist's voice halted Raven's progress toward the man.

"Turn back." The words boomed from the stage.

Raven's gaze fixed on the evangelist, whose finger pointed

directly at him, then panned across the crowd. In the center, the massive log that functioned as the main support for the tent swayed a bit, then stopped. It wouldn't go anywhere. It had to weigh a thousand pounds, at least.

"It's not too late." The evangelist grinned, and he motioned for his family to join him onstage as he had the night before, including beautiful Calandra. The big red-haired man stood next to her, and his hand brushed against Calandra's.

Raven cringed.

"These loved ones of mine, my children—they made the choice at a young age. Tonight you can make that same choice."

Raven turned back to face his prey, but the round man had stepped within the safety of the crowd's outer rim.

"This is your chance. He made the ultimate sacrifice so that you might have life—*real* life." The evangelist extended his hands over the audience. "Will you accept that free gift tonight?"

Raven rubbed his eyes and scanned the perimeter of the crowd again. No evident stragglers. Would he have to claim one from among the crowd?

"In just a moment we're going to open the altar for anyone interested in starting a new life tonight, but first I want to pray for us." Onstage, the evangelist and his family bowed their heads.

An unsettling warmth, comparable to what he'd experienced last night when he heard Calandra's song, spread through Raven's chest. What was happening?

"...In Your Name we pray, amen. Now, if you want to be

free from the curse of sin—" the evangelist said. Was he looking right at Raven? "—if you want God to restore your soul, then I ask you to come up to the altar and receive his forgiveness tonight."

Had Raven just taken a step forward? He glanced back. He *had* stepped forward. Why?

"That's it. Freedom is within reach," the evangelist said. "Not just temporary freedom, not the charade of freedom, but real, genuine *freedom.*"

Raven's feet had moved him forward by another twenty steps before he realized what he'd done. He stopped, but he now stood in the middle of the crowd, many of whom had their hands raised into the air with their eyes closed.

What was he doing there? He'd come to quench his thirst for blood, not listen to a sermon with a bunch of Christians. Yet now he stood among them, inclined to not only continue forward to the stage, but to run up there at full speed with his arms stretched toward the heavens.

Still, an equally strong compulsion to turn back and flee into the surrounding forest gnawed at his gut. Nonetheless, Raven carved a path through the throngs of people toward the stage—the "altar," as the evangelist called it.

Within seconds he stood in front of everyone, the only person in a chasm separating the crowd from the evangelist and his family onstage. Terror wracked his body and almost ignited his will to escape, but he stood still. His frantic gaze bounced from the evangelist to Calandra to the scowling red-haired man, then to the evangelist's little blonde daughter.

When the little blonde girl grinned at him as she had last night, Raven's anxiety dwindled. He shifted his gaze back to Calandra, whose smile melted whatever terror remained in his belly.

"Thank you, son." The evangelist gave him a nod, then shifted his focus back to the crowd. "Is there anyone else who feels an impression to respond to the Spirit's prompting?"

People shuffled from behind Raven. He glanced over his shoulder and noticed about a dozen people making their way into the space around him. Raven clamped his eyes shut. They would know what he was. Someone would figure it out soon enough. No normal human had such pale skin.

When Raven opened his eyes, the red-haired man glared at him with scorn, perhaps even hatred. He had to know.

"That's it. That's it," the evangelist said. "You can all receive this free gift of forgiveness. Is there anyone else?"

A moment later, the evangelist addressed the smaller crowd that had gathered at the altar.

"Your sins can be forgiven, my friends," he said. "There are no magic words to say, but if you are willing, I will lead you in a prayer of repentance. You may repeat after me."

Raven's mouth clamped shut, and he didn't repeat the evangelist's words. He still wasn't sure what madness had urged him, a vampire, to the front of a church service in the first place.

The evangelist prayed about freedom and forgiveness.

Forgiveness? For the wrong Raven had done? How could

God ever forgive him for the atrocities he'd committed? For the death and the pain he'd created? For his complacency while he'd done it?

No, Raven would never know forgiveness. When his time came, he would join his predecessors in the deepest depths of Hell.

"I ask now that you restore my soul. Make me a new creation in you," the evangelist prayed. "Thank you. In Your Name we pray, amen."

"Amen," the crowd repeated around Raven.

He raised his eyebrow. He needed to get out of there. In the open like this, he'd made himself vulnerable to a variety of problems.

The evangelist smiled. "You've all taken your first steps into God's Kingdom, and what a joyous place of peace it is."

Raven raised his eyes toward heaven, but instead of God's Kingdom all he saw was the tent ceiling, rippling with another of the evening's mighty wind gusts. Rippling a *lot*. Unless—

Raven twisted back in time to see the tent's massive center pole waver, then tip toward the stage.

Right toward Calandra.

Chapter 3

The crowd behind him erupted with screams. Raven leapt onto the stage and positioned himself between Calandra and the toppling beam. He reached up and caught it in his hands. The stage buckled underneath his feet and he almost lost his grip, but he dug his nails into the rough wood and held on.

The beam threatened to crush him. The tendons in his legs pumped like a locomotive engine as he shifted his position so he could bear the weight on his back instead. Calandra lay on the stage beneath him with one hand up to protect herself.

Raven let out a roar and ground his heels into the wood of the broken stage with all his might, then hefted the log away from Calandra, which left her enough time to crawl out from under it. As she moved clear, her dark eyes fixed on his. In them he recognized fear, but also a hint of intrigue.

The tent collapsed in on itself. Heavy taupe fabric floated down onto the throngs of panicked people, and shrieks filled the air.

"*Calandra?*" the evangelist called from his spot on the fractured stage. He'd ended up inside the tiny tent pocket that Raven had created by wedging himself under the pole. "Oh, thank God. It's alright. We're alright."

Speak for yourself. The evangelist wasn't holding a 25-foot, 20-inch-thick log on his back.

The evangelist scurried over to Raven and drew a knife. Raven's eyes widened, but to his relief the evangelist just reached for some of the fabric and sliced a hole in it.

"Come this way, my friends. If you can't get out along the edges, follow the sound of my voice and you can get out this way." The evangelist turned to Raven. "You think you can hold it for a little longer until these people get out?"

Raven winced and his legs wobbled. He stole a glance at Calandra, shifted his left foot an inch, and hoisted the log up a bit higher. He nodded. "I don't think I can go much higher, though."

"You're doing fine, son," the evangelist said. "Just hold it there."

Dozens of people emerged from under the tent and headed toward the opening in the fabric. Not a single person passed Raven without giving him a look of fright, uncertainty, or both.

It wasn't because the tent had collapsed. It was because he, a lithe, pale young man who should have struggled to lift a hundred pounds now held more than ten times that much on his back.

After the last of the crowd passed through the slit, only the evangelist, Calandra, and her teenage brother remained in the pocket to hold the slit open. The red-haired man appeared from under some of the tent folds behind them. He took one look at Raven and grabbed a long, jagged piece of the wooden stage, sharp and pointed on one end.

"Vampire *scum*." He drew his arm back.

Raven's eyes widened. The red-haired man jabbed the makeshift stake toward Raven's chest.

"*No*, Garrett!" Calandra sprung between him and the red-haired man's stake.

The stake stopped just short of Calandra's chest, and Garrett recoiled. His face twisted with fury. "What are you doing, Calandra? I could have killed you. Get out of my way. I'm going to slay this soulless demon where he stands."

"No. He *saved* us all." Calandra glared at him. "You're *not* killing him for doing a good deed."

"If you won't move, then I'll *move you*." Garrett grabbed Calandra's arm and pulled her away, but the evangelist's hand latched onto his wrist.

"No one's slaying anyone tonight, Garrett," the evangelist said. "Now drop that piece of my stage so we can get out of here."

Garrett's jaw tensed, but he complied with the evangelist's order. He grabbed Calandra's arm and pulled her behind him through the slit.

As his teenage son climbed out of the tent, the evangelist nodded to Raven. "You can put that down now, son."

Raven managed a nod, then shrugged the log off his back. It hammered the stage and splintered another section. His relief dissipated when he sensed dozens of silent, heavy eyes bearing down on him the instant he emerged from the tent.

Towering evergreens and broadleaf trees formed the

perimeter of the forest that surrounded the throng of people. These people knew what he was, and now they'd seen his face. They would recognize him from now on. So much for hunting in this area.

"What's your name?"

Raven turned his head. "Huh?"

"What's your name?" the evangelist asked again. "I'm Luco Zambini. How do you do?"

Raven glanced at his extended hand. If he shook it, Luco would feel his cold, clammy skin. Then again, Luco had to know by now, so what did it matter?

Raven gripped Luco's hand. "I'm Raven. Raven Worth."

"Raven Worth." Luco nodded. He turned to the crowd. "Everyone, this is Raven. You can thank him for saving us all from something far worse than our tent collapsing."

Raven clenched his teeth. As if it wasn't bad enough that he'd made such a public show of himself, now they knew his name too. Perhaps he should just draw them a map to his home so they could form a posse to stake him in the morning.

"Some of you owe him your very lives." Luco showed him a sad, but genuine, smile. "I know I owe him mine, and those of my children."

The next thing Raven knew, Luco was hugging him. What should he do? Raven didn't move. For all he knew Luco meant to stab him in the back with that knife. Or maybe with a stake.

But he didn't. Luco released him and presented him to the crowd. "Will you welcome him with me?"

Raven looked back at Luco, who nodded. This had to be some kind of joke. He scanned the crowd. Raven was nobody's hero. If anything, he was the villain, and these people would agree. Their silence and confused expressions told him so.

He just wanted to get out of there, to transform and fly away.

"Do you have a place to stay tonight?" Luco smiled, shook his head. "Let me rephrase that. Do you have anywhere to go for the rest of tonight?"

Raven raised an eyebrow. "I—I don't understand what you're asking me."

"I'm sorry," Luco said. "Would you like to come over to my house, to my family's house, for a few hours? I'd love an opportunity to chat with you for awhile."

"Aren't—aren't you afraid of me?" Raven half-whispered.

Luco tilted his head. "Should I be?"

Raven scanned the crowd until he found Calandra. She held her sister, the tiny blonde girl, in her arms, and they both smiled at him. Just behind them stood Garrett, his arms folded in front of his chest, still wearing a scowl on his face.

"You could join us for dinner, if you like."

"No thanks. I'm not hungry." It wasn't true, of course. Raven hungered alright, but not for normal food.

Luco nodded, his expression stuck somewhere between sadness and concern. "If you're willing, I'd like you to come over anyway, just so we can spend some time with you."

Raven squinted at him. "Why are you so interested?"

"I won't lie to you, Raven," Luco said. "I noticed you at the altar. I'd like to talk with you about what I said tonight."

"I—I'm not—"

"Nonsense. You came up to the altar for a reason. You don't have to be ashamed of it."

Raven sucked in a quick breath.

"Look, son," Luco said. "If you hadn't come up to the altar, you wouldn't have been able to save all of those people, including my family and me, from that falling timber. I don't believe that was just a coincidence."

"I don't know about—"

"Of course you don't. That's why I'm so interested in having you over. I'd like to answer any questions you might have."

Raven paused. "What if I don't have any questions?"

"You just asked one, actually." Luco must have noticed Raven's scowl, because he put his hands up. "Alright. I'm inviting you over, and that's all I can say for now. It's up to you to decide whether you'll accept the invitation or not."

An invitation. Raven raised an eyebrow again. Luco probably knew to phrase it exactly that way—a vampire typically couldn't enter a home without first being invited. "I'll consider it."

"Please, Raven?" Calandra stood to his left, still holding her little sister in her arms.

Her eyes seemed to glimmer with hope instead of the fear Raven had seen in them under the tent. That hint of intrigue she'd shown him earlier had resurfaced as well.

He hesitated. "Alright. I can come over."

Calandra smiled, as did her little sister. "Great. I'm so glad you can join us."

Raven nodded. "I'm, uh, looking forward to it."

The rest of the congregation still stared at him.

Calandra had hoped to sit near Raven on the ride back to her family's home, but he took a seat wedged between Luco and her brother Dante at the front of the lead carriage. They had salvaged what they could and packed it into the backs of the Zambini family's two carriages and then began the trek back home.

Garrett drove the second carriage behind the first. Anthony, Calandra's younger brother, rode in the back of the carriage on top of the tent fabric as usual, and Mina, her little sister, lay asleep on her lap. Calandra brushed a blonde lock away from Mina's face.

"I told your father we shouldn't have moved here," Garrett said.

Calandra tilted her head and looked at him. "You did? Why?"

"Too much folklore around here." Garrett shook his head. "And lore is usually accurate. I told him that, but he didn't listen."

"What are you talking about?"

"*Him*," Garrett said, his voice flat.

"Raven?" Calandra's smile faded. "You don't even know him."

Garrett shook his head. "Don't need to. You know he's one

of *them,* don't you?

"Of course I know. His pale skin. Lifting that log. It's night time." Calandra lowered her voice for Anthony's sake. "I know what a vampire is, Garrett."

"Then you know he doesn't even have a soul anymore."

"You don't think God can restore his soul?"

"God can do anything, but I've never heard of anyone damned to Hell who's been redeemed."

"We're all damned without Jesus anyway."

Garrett eyed her. A familiar expression, one Garrett employed when she said something he found stupid—or if she'd somehow contradicted him. "That's not the point. He's still dangerous, especially to you."

Calandra sighed. "You think so little of me sometimes."

"Come now, Calandra. You know what I'm talking about."

She twisted to face him and scrunched her eyebrows down. "No, Garrett. I don't."

"He was staring at you the whole night."

"The *whole* night?"

"At least from the moment he stepped forward to the altar. He's got hunger in his eyes, and he wants you. I know it."

Calandra shook her head and focused on the passing scenery. Something rustled in the bushes to her left. A pair of beady eyes flickered in the moonlight and then vanished, followed by more rustling. Just a rodent of some sort. "I think you're overreaching. I haven't seen that at all."

"Give it time and pay closer attention. If you were more observant, you'd see what I'm talking about."

One of the carriage wheels hit a deep pothole. The jostle woke Mina for a moment, but she shifted in Calandra's arms and then fell right back asleep.

Calandra looked at Garrett. "More observant, huh?"

Garrett just scowled at her. "Look—I don't want you talking to him. I don't want you anywhere near him."

"What gives you the right to tell me how I'm supposed to behave around him?"

"We're courting, Calandra. It's my job to protect you."

Calandra pointed her index finger at him. "No. Until you marry me, it's my *father's* job to take care of me."

Garrett's jaw tightened. "I'm not trying to tell you what to do, nor am I trying to replace your father, and I definitely didn't want to start an argument about this. I'm just trying to warn you that—"

"So I'm just supposed to ignore him entirely? What kind of message do you think that will send to him?"

"Exactly the kind of message I want you to send: that you're off-limits to him."

Calandra smiled. "You're jealous, aren't you?"

Garrett frowned. "What are you talking about?"

"You're worried that some sleek, smooth, seductive vampire is going to swoop in and steal me away from you."

"No, no. I'm not jealous. I said I'm afraid for your life."

Garrett cleared his throat. "You don't know what they can do, Calandra. These specters need blood to survive."

"Keep your voice down, Garrett." Calandra glanced over her shoulder at Anthony, who lay atop the tent fabric with his eyes shut.

"Sorry. As I was saying, they need blood, and they can hypnotize you. Convince you to do things you'd never otherwise do. Then they'll drain every last drop of your life from your body, and you'll become one yourself. Is that what you want?"

"Raven wouldn't hurt me. I saw *that* in his eyes."

"Then you're totally ignoring what I saw, or you're missing it," Garrett said.

"Please." Calandra raised her index finger to her lips. "I asked you to keep your voice down. The kids are sleeping."

"I'm just worried about you." Garrett took her hand in his. "You're my little Italian rose. I don't want to lose you."

She wrinkled her nose at his sweaty hand, but gave it a squeeze anyway. Little Italian rose? He couldn't have made her sound more helpless if he had intended to do so. "Roses have thorns, you know. You won't lose me."

"So we've agreed that you'll stay away from Raven, and that you'll have nothing to do with him. Right?"

"I have to at least be cordial to him when we're in public."

"Cordial, yes. But you leave him alone otherwise. Understand?"

Calandra looked at the forest again and sighed.

Chapter 4

Silver moonlight drenched the Zambini family's home with an ethereal glow. They lived in a dark-colored, two-story home that reminded Raven of the house he'd grown up in a century ago. It stood on a small hill, surrounded by the forest with its back almost up against the trees.

Inside, Raven met Maria Zambini, Luco's wife. When he tried to shake her hand, she spread her arms wide and wrapped him up in a big hug. She was beautiful, an older version of Calandra but heavier. Same dark hair, deep brown eyes, and high cheekbones.

"Welcome, welcome." Her voice bounced with a rhythmic Italian accent. "I'm so glad you could join us."

"Thank you." Raven rubbed his shoulder and slouched. "I'm grateful for the invitation."

"Any time, any time." Maria escorted him over to the large family table. "Have a seat, my friend, and I'll have dinner on the table soon."

"Oh, I—um—"

"This is Dante, our oldest son." Maria put her hands on Dante's shoulders. "You can sit next to him."

Raven nodded to him, and his stomach protested. He'd rather

drink Dante's blood than sit next to him at a dinner table.

"And you already know Dante, Anthony, Calandra, and Mina." Maria stood behind another seated child, this one a younger, miniature version of Calandra, probably about thirteen or fourteen years old. "This is our other daughter, Angelica. She stayed home to help me cook for everyone tonight."

"Time to eat yet?" Luco stepped back into the kitchen with a fresh shirt on. He dipped his index finger into a large saucepan of dark red pasta sauce and slurped it off.

Maria slapped his hand. "Don't do that, Luco. How many times have I told you…"

Raven watched their mock argument, now descending into a flurry of Italian, but his mind wandered elsewhere, back to when he still had a family to argue with. Back to his mother and father, his little sister, and even his big brothers, troublesome as they were. He missed them all, but they were gone, and had been for more than twenty years. Some of them even longer.

Real silverware decorated the table, along with hand-painted porcelain plates, white in the center with pink and green flowers decorating the edges. Matching teacups and saucers accompanied each place setting, and brass cups filled with dark red liquid headed four of the settings. It wasn't blood.

"Do you drink red?" Dante grabbed one of the cups and held it out toward him.

Raven raised an eyebrow. "I don't drink…wine."

Dante frowned. "Me neither. My parents let me have a little

sometimes, but they say I'm still too young to have a full cup."

"I'm sure they only have your best interests in mind."

"Yeah. We moved here because Mama's uncle owns a vineyard not too far from here. Once I get a little older I'm going to start working there and—"

"Take it easy, Dante," Luco said. "Let our guest relax. He's had a trying evening."

And it's not over yet. Raven frowned.

"Go on and get in line behind your siblings."

"You should get some food." Garrett dropped his plate onto the table with a porcelain thunk, and a dollop of dark red sauce splattered onto the white lace tablecloth. "You must be famished."

Raven stared at him, and he noticed that Garrett didn't have a cup of wine at his place setting. "No, thank you. I'm not hungry."

"Before we eat, I'd like to say a prayer over the meal," Luco said. Once Maria and Angelica took their seats, Luco nodded to his family and bowed his head, and they mimicked his action. "Heavenly Father, thank you for your many blessings and for your protection at tonight's service. Thank you for our new friend Raven and for placing him exactly where he was supposed to be tonight in time to save us from disaster."

Raven blinked. Everyone else's heads were bowed and their eyes closed, except for Garrett, who eyed him throughout the entire prayer.

"Thanks also for this marvelous food, and for my beautiful family, whom I love. Continue to fill our hearts with your word. We love you. Amen." Luco lifted his head as his family echoed "amen," and he nodded to Raven with a soft smile.

Silver clanked against porcelain, but Raven just sat in his chair and watched the Zambini family eat. He hadn't experienced a meal like this since the night he'd met *her* 83 years ago. He stared at his empty plate.

"Don't you like Italian food?" Dante's question shattered Raven's memories.

Raven turned toward him. "No. I mean, I did—I…"

Dante slid his plate of pasta and meatballs in front of Raven. The sauce had thinned a bit upon contact with the noodles, and in a way it almost looked like blood. "Go ahead. Try some."

Except it *wasn't* blood.

"Mama's an amazing cook. I keep telling her she should sell her sauce in jars. Go ahead. Try it."

Raven swallowed the lump in his throat and reached for a nearby fork, a utensil he hadn't wielded in almost a century. After a quick glance around the table, and seeing that everyone now stared at him, Raven dug the side of the fork into one of the meatballs, cut off a sliver, and took a bite.

As with the last time he'd eaten regular food, the meatball and sauce tasted like ash in his mouth.

"It's good," Raven lied. He really couldn't tell.

"Try the pasta. She made the noodles too, and they're really good with the sauce," Dante said.

Raven glanced at Calandra, who smiled at him until Garrett

leaned forward and blocked Raven's view with his big frame.

"I bet you'll like it." Garrett wore a smirk instead of a frown.

"I'm sure I will," Raven matched him with a grin.

He dug into the spaghetti, twisted it around his fork, and wrangled enough for a big bite with plenty of sauce on it. More ash coated his tongue. It didn't matter, though. He could eat as much as he wanted and it wouldn't satisfy him.

"Good, isn't it?" Dante asked.

Raven nodded as he chewed.

Sourness tingled in his mouth, then warmth, then burning heat. Raven's eyes widened as he stared down at his plate. The spaghetti sauce was searing his mouth from the inside out.

"Is something wrong, Raven?" Luco's brow furrowed.

Raven swallowed the bite in a hurry, and it burned all the way down his throat and into his stomach. "What's in this sauce?"

Maria glanced at Luco. "Tomatoes, basil, oregano—" She put her hand over her mouth.

"Garlic?" The burning spread to the outside of Raven's lips. He glanced at Garrett, whose grin had grown.

Maria's eyes widened. She shot Luco a glare, then shook her head at Raven. "I'm so sorry—I didn't know."

"Didn't know what?" Angelica asked.

Raven clenched his teeth. He pushed away from the table. "Excuse me."

As Raven tore through the back door, Garrett's laughter filled the house behind him.

Chapter 5

Raven might as well have been sucking on hot coals. He roamed the Zambini family's back yard, searching for something, anything that would quell the burn. He finally resorted to scooping a handful of dirt into his hands, ready to cake his mouth with it, but he stopped.

The faint chatter of chickens clucking reached his ears. Off to his left a chicken coop housed about a dozen or so hens, all fenced in by a wire network about four feet tall.

His black boots pounded the hard earth and he leaped over the fence in a single bound. The chickens scattered, but they couldn't escape Raven. He drained three of them before the fire on his tongue finally stopped raging.

When he finished off the third bird, he noticed Luco standing just beyond the wire fence, watching him with sad eyes.

"I'm sorry," Raven said. "I can pay you for the hens."

Luco waved his hand. "I don't care about the chickens. Are you alright?"

Raven remembered Garrett's laughter. He lied, "Yes."

"Did their blood counter the garlic?"

"Yes, for now," Raven said. "But I'll still need to feed on

human blood tonight. Animals don't sustain me for very long."

Luco nodded. He walked to the fence gate and stepped inside. "I'm sorry about the garlic. It's my fault for not telling Maria beforehand. I should have remembered how much garlic she puts in there when Dante passed you his plate. We are Italian, after all."

"I'm sure it was an accident." Raven mostly believed it. After all, why would Luco keep Garrett from staking him back at the tent revival only to feed him garlic here?

"I know how you feel," Luco said. "When I married her, she used so much that it practically knocked me off my feet. Now I barely even notice it."

"I think I had better go."

"Are you sure? Can I persuade you to stay for a bit longer? I was hoping to speak with you about what happened tonight in the tent."

"That was nothing. Besides, if I hadn't intervened—"

"No, no. You misunderstand me. I'm referring to your response to my altar call. You were the first person to step forward."

"Oh. That." Raven still held the dead hen in his hands. He tossed it behind him and it landed near the other two he'd killed. "That was nothing too."

"Nothing?" Luco's dark eyebrows raised. "That wasn't nothing, son. That was an important step, both for you and for everyone else in that tent."

"If you say so." Raven glanced at the moon. "I really should go."

Luco caught him by his wrist. "Wait. Please, just indulge me for a few more minutes."

Raven clenched his teeth and glared at Luco.

Luco released his grip. "I'm sorry. I shouldn't keep you here if you don't want to stay."

Raven squinted at him. He saw no trace of malice in Luco's brown eyes, and something about him set Raven at ease.

"I know you're hungry, but I'd appreciate just a little more time with you if you're willing. I'd hate for us to part ways on such a sour note."

Raven sighed. "Go ahead."

"It's like I said before—I believe your appearance at our revival wasn't just coincidence. I believe that God has a plan for your life. I believe he wants to save you, and—"

"I don't have a soul left to save."

Luco shook his head. "I wouldn't lean too heavily on what you've been told about your condition. If I understand God's Word and his promises correctly, then mortal man cannot even begin to comprehend the vastness of his grace and forgiveness."

"You forget that I'm not mortal. My soul is gone."

Luco raised his finger. "Actually, you're immortal because you're cursed. You forfeited your soul when you turned, and you received immortality. Either way you're still bound to the covenant you made with sin."

"I did *not* choose to become a vampire." Raven's voice hardened and he clenched his fists. "Someone else chose that for me."

"My last statement wasn't about you becoming a vampire."

Raven tilted his head, but relaxed the tension in his hands. "I don't understand."

"You may not have chosen to become a vampire, but we've all sinned. We're all cursed, Raven. There's only one way to break that curse." Luco pointed back to nowhere in particular. "It's by the blood of Jesus Christ."

Raven raised both of his eyebrows.

"Jesus gave his life and—"

Raven held up his hand. "I'm familiar with the story. I find the imagery unsettling. Do you have *any* idea what I've been doing every night for the last 83 years?"

Luco nodded. "I apologize if my presentation has been poor, but you must understand that the Gospel is offensive to many people of many different cultures around the—"

"*Especially* to us."

"Yes, especially to vampires. Everything about being a vampire is thoroughly opposed to following Christ, but I promise that if you allow him to, God can save you. You just need to be willing to give your soul back to God, and then he will give you eternal life."

Raven shook his head. "You don't know what you're saying. I just told you I already have eternal life. I'm immortal, remember?"

Luco smiled. "I'm afraid you're confusing a curse with a miracle. Yes, you're immortal, but you don't have eternal life. A vampire can be killed and his soul will be damned forever, but a man with eternal life can die and his soul will live for eternity."

Raven eyed him. The hunger flared in his chest. He needed to go soon, or Luco might become his next victim.

"Immortality is a curse," Luco continued. "It's a condition of a fallen man in need of redemption. You have to drink human blood in order to prolong your existence. Eternal life is a miracle, and it too comes by blood. God made a way for us to be forgiven for our sins—vampire or not—and as a result, we can live forever with him in paradise."

"I'm still not sure I understand the difference."

Luco put a thick hand on Raven's shoulder. "Don't worry. You will, in time."

Raven wasn't sure of that either.

"I'd like to invite you to come back inside with me. We'll keep the garlic far away from you, and we'll treat you as a member of the family, not as a vampire."

"Maybe some other time, but for now I have to go." Raven hopped over their four-foot wire fence and stared at the line of trees that framed the back of Luco's yard.

Luco nodded. "Is your mouth still burning?"

"It's starting to."

"I understand. What are you going to do?"

Raven stopped, turned, and just looked at him. They both knew the answer to that question.

Luco returned his gaze and his voice dropped into deep, firm tones. "Raven, if you want to change, to stop doing this, then you don't have to go out there tonight. God can help you change your ways. Put your old flesh to death. Fight your craving for human blood."

A part of Raven wanted to believe Luco was right, but he couldn't.

He needed blood.

Without so much as another word, Raven faded into the darkness of the surrounding forest and left Luco alone under the moonlight.

Calandra shuddered as Raven melted into the shadows of the trees that encircled her house. Such dark power frightened her, yet when she watched him, intrigue filled her stomach. Raven was so mysterious and elusive, so different from everyone else she knew.

"Witchcraft and sorcery," Garrett said. He'd been sitting next to her at the kitchen table the whole time, reading his Bible between intermittent glances out the window. "He's there one minute and gone the next. Like a sneeze in the wind."

What a terrible analogy. "I wonder where he's going."

"Does it matter? We're never going to see him again, not after your mother practically poisoned him to death with her sauce— which, I might add, was hilarious."

Calandra glared at him. "That was *not* funny, Garrett."

He chuckled. "If you say so."

She studied his sharp facial features, vibrant red hair, and light brown eyes. He may be handsome and strong, but he could sure behave like a fool sometimes. "He was our guest. I wish you had treated him better. He didn't deserve to have you laugh at him, especially over something that could have killed him for all we know."

"He's fine, Calandra."

"I hope he doesn't think all Christians behave like you did. Sometimes you're unbelievably thoughtless."

Garrett just shrugged with a dumb half-smile on his face.

"I don't know how you think you can be a pastor with that kind of attitude."

Garrett's smile twisted into a frown and he scrunched his eyebrows. "You should watch what you say. When we're married, you'll have to show me more respect than this."

The back door opened and Calandra swallowed her response. Instead, she just scowled at Garrett, then she turned to her father. "Is he coming back?"

"I don't know. Would you gather the rest of the family together, please?"

Calandra nodded. Two minutes later, everyone sat in the spacious family room near the fireplace, which radiated soft, golden heat into the room.

"Raven is gone," Luco said. "And I don't know if he's coming back or not."

"Good riddance," Garrett mumbled.

"No, Garrett. It's not." Luco stared at him with a correcting look that he usually reserved for scolding his children. "A better response would be to pray that he overcomes temptation and is delivered from evil. He needs Jesus just like us, and he's exactly the type of person Jesus would spend time with if he was walking around nowadays."

Calandra had to bite her tongue to keep from sticking it out at Garrett.

"Papa?" Mina tugged on Luco's pant leg. "Can I pray for Raven?"

Luco smiled. "Yes, Mina. Of course."

As Mina prayed in a way that only a child could, Calandra asked God to look out for Raven tonight.

Traveling as a wolf always invigorated Raven. Perhaps it was the thrill of knifing through the forest on all fours, dodging trees, bounding over exposed roots, and ducking under low-hanging branches. He tore through the woods, feeling the cool earth under his padded paws. He breathed deeper, ran faster, saw farther. It was a succulent sensation that surpassed the savagery of pursuing a victim, and for a moment, at least, his mouth wasn't burning.

Light flickered in the distance, a distinct yellow tone against the moonlight that cascaded through the trees and splashed the ground in silvery-blue patches below. It had to be man-made, probably from a house. Perhaps Raven would find a victim there.

But Luco had said that Raven should avoid drinking blood, that he could stop. How was that possible? As a vampire, drinking blood was not just part of his curse, it was central to his condition. He would cease to exist if he stopped.

He'd tried twice before, the first time not long after he'd turned. He lasted two nights before he finally succumbed to the thirst, and he ended up draining two humans of *all* of their blood, which in turn transformed them into vampires. By the time it was over, he'd actually done more damage than if he had just fed as usual.

The second time he pursued animal blood as a substitute. Much like the three chickens he'd bled dry tonight, animal blood never truly satisfied him, and he eventually wound up attacking humans again.

But if he could stop somehow…

No. Entertaining such dreams was hopeless. The only God he'd ever known was one of vengeance and retribution. He was part of the reason Raven had to endure this curse in the first place, so why would God change his mind now?

Tonight Raven would feed. He had to, especially after the garlic.

A gunshot split the night from the direction of the yellow light, then another, and then a woman screamed. Raven skidded to a halt, panting. What had happened?

A third gunshot sounded. The woman's screams ceased.

Only one way to find out. He sprinted toward the light.

Chapter 6

Raven straightened his spine and adjusted the collar of his black coat as he stood at the tree line in human form. Even after 83 years of transforming into bats, wolves, mist, and more, his clothes never managed to end up quite where they'd started before he transformed.

There, in the middle of an opening in the trees, a two-story Tudor-style home with a smoking chimney cast patches of golden light into the midnight sky. Raven studied the sight from the safety of the shadow of a large conifer, watching and listening.

Another a ruckus sounded inside the house, something like the clatter of small metal items crashing down onto a wooden floor and the shattering of porcelain plates.

The front door flung open with a crack that reverberated off the trees, and four men filed out of the house with burlap sacks over their shoulders. Even with his keen vision, Raven only got a glimpse of one of their faces, his bushy handlebar mustache, and his big nose.

"Let's get out of here," one of the bandits said. "The woods are creepier at night."

"Afraid of the dark?" a second bandit, not Mustache, asked.

"No. Afraid of what's in it," said Bandit One.

"Don't get superstitious on me," Mustache said. "There ain't nothing in them woods that can't be killed with a knife or a bullet. Anything else you may have heard is just a story someone made up to scare kids into behaving."

The second bandit guffawed. "Didn't work so well on us, did it?"

"No, it did not." Mustache grabbed the second bandit by his shirt. "But if you keep laughing like a hyena in heat, someone's gonna hear you."

"What's a hyena?" the third bandit asked.

"As if your gunshots didn't already signal the nearest neighbor of our presence." Bandit Two brushed Mustache's arm away. "I bet you woke everyone in a two-mile radius."

Mustache shook his head. "She deserved what she got."

Raven raised an eyebrow. So they *had* killed a woman, or at least shot her.

"Besides, it's 1885. The war may be long over, but everyone out here owns a gun, and everyone goes hunting. Neighbors probably thought it was just some hunter bagging a deer."

"At midnight?" Bandit One asked.

"Hey, what's a hyena?" Bandit Three asked again.

Mustache grabbed him by his shirt and yanked him close. "*Shut up.*"

"Whatever you say, *boss*," Bandit Two said. "Let's just get out of here."

They disappeared behind the house then returned to the front, each of them riding a horse. Mustache's horse reminded Raven of a fluffy white cloud—at least from what he remembered. He hadn't actually seen a daytime cloud in decades.

The bandits disappeared down a trail, swallowed by the forest.

After a moment of solitude and stillness, Raven stepped into the open, into the moonlight. If a neighbor did happen to appear, Raven could vanish easily enough. He stalked over to the front door, now attached only by its bottom hinge, and stepped inside the home.

"I don't understand," Anthony whispered in the darkness. "Raven's a vampire? What does that even mean?"

Dante shifted to face Anthony's bed so he didn't have to keep craning his neck to talk to him. "It means that he drinks blood, he only comes out at night, and he really, *really* likes girls."

"What?" Anthony asked. "You're making that up."

"It's true."

"He didn't drink any blood tonight," Anthony said. "I think you're lying to me. People don't do that sort of thing."

"You're only seven. You don't know what I know about the world."

"I'm almost eight. That's a long time."

"Yeah, but I'm almost fifteen. I've seen more things. Trust me—Raven drinks blood."

Anthony didn't make a sound for almost a minute. "I still

don't believe you."

"Want to know why we have three less chickens wandering around our coop?"

More silence. "No."

"Well, I'm going to tell you anyway." Dante propped himself up on his left arm and fixed his gaze on Anthony. "After Raven tasted Mama's pasta sauce—which had garlic in it, which vampires can't stand—he had to do something to get rid of the flavor, so he ran outside and sucked all the blood out of three of our chickens."

"I don't want to hear anymore." Anthony covered his head with his blanket.

"Are you getting *scared?*" Dante asked.

"No." Anthony didn't hesitate that time.

"Then why are you hiding under your covers?"

A pause. "It's warm under here."

Dante snickered. "You're a funny kid, Antonius."

A head emerged from under the blanket. "Don't call me that. It's not my name and you know it."

"Yeah, I know. I only say it because it bothers you."

"It *doesn't* bother me." Anthony receded into his blanket cave again.

"Then why are you hiding again?"

"I said it's warm under here."

Dante shook his head. "You know, you don't have to be afraid of Raven."

"Who said I was afraid?" The covers muffled Anthony's

voice.

"I'm just saying you don't have to be, not that you are."

"Good. Because I'm not."

"I bet I could convince him to drink your blood, though."

The covers pulled back again. "*Mooooooommm!!*"

"Alright, alright." Dante chuckled. "I'm sorry. I'll stop and you can go to sleep."

Anthony glared at him. "You promise?"

"I promise."

"Good." He retreated back under the blankets. "Good night, then."

"Good night." Dante rolled over and faced the door instead of his brother. "Antonius."

"*Mooooooommm!!*"

Raven's nose tingled. The odor of a recent gun blast still lingered in the air, intermingled with the unmistakable scent of freshly-spilled blood.

The house's front door led directly into the home's kitchen. Broken porcelain and glass covered the floor, along with an occasional piece of polished silverware. The bandits must have taken the rest of it.

A light haze hovered in the air of an adjacent room, one with a fireplace. When Raven walked in, a trail of dark blood called to him from the wooden floor. Yellow flames casually engulfed a stuffed chair, a blaze now too big to extinguish without a lot of water and a lot of people to fight it. He didn't have much time before the rest of the house caught fire.

Near the fireplace, the remains of a book smoldered next to a puddle of boiling blood on the floor. Someone had been shot there.

Raven followed the trail toward a narrow staircase where bloodied footprints ascended the stairs. In the second floor hallway, sporadic red handprints tainted the white plaster walls. Raven peeked into two spacious bedrooms before he finally found the victim in the third.

She'd been shot once in the left leg, once in her shoulder, and once in her chest. Her plump body lay in a crumpled heap in front of a dresser and next to a bed, motionless. Raven stared at her vacant blue eyes, set into a round, middle-aged face. Her mouth gaped open.

Raven shook his head. With violence like this, why did vampires even exist? Mankind created enough carnage without the undead stalking the night.

Thick black smoke began to filter into the room from the hallway. Raven needed to move.

He stole over to her, sank his fangs into the artery in her neck, and drained every last drop from her body as the flames swelled around them. The ceiling creaked and collapsed behind him as he leapt out a nearby window and vanished into the night.

Chapter 7

When Raven showed up at the tent meeting the next night around 8:30, Calandra could barely contain her excitement. Garrett hadn't scared him off after all.

There was no question in her mind that it was him. Even from the opposite end of the tent she could see his black hair, pale skin, and dark clothing. He radiated mystery.

Calandra's thoughts had revolved around Raven all day, mostly because she knew she might never see him again after everything that had happened last night. The thought of having to forget him had only sharpened her focus.

She recalled the fervor in his bright green eyes as he'd hefted the pole onto his back. The look he'd given her had seared a permanent impression in her mind. She could have stared back into those eyes forever had the situation not been so adverse and had Garrett not intervened.

Raven had done more than save her life that night.

She shook her head. What was she thinking? Garrett was courting her, and they would soon be married, probably within a year. Or two. Eventually.

Whatever the timeframe, her attraction to Raven stemmed

only from the intensity of a near catastrophe, nothing more. She couldn't let such fleeting emotions ruin the relationship she'd built with Garrett over the last year and a half.

No, Raven Worth. As intriguing as you are, I am already spoken for. She bit her lip. *Mostly.*

"Calandra?"

She spun on her heels. Her father and Garrett approached from behind.

"Are you ready to go on and sing?" Luco asked.

They all stood backstage, but they used that term loosely. The only thing separating the stage—now half of its original size due to the falling tent pole—and the ground on which it sat was a dark red curtain. It stretched across a horizontal pole suspended by two vertical poles, and a small staircase in the middle led up to the stage.

She nodded. "Yes, I'm ready. Father, Raven's here."

Luco smiled, but Garrett frowned. Of course.

"That's great news, sweetie. Hopefully he'll stick around after the service so we can talk to him."

Garrett huffed. "Yeah. That would be *great.*"

Calandra eyed him.

"You'd better go onstage," Luco said. "The audience is expecting you."

A melody turned Raven's head. Calandra's voice filled the tent and the warm night sky beyond with another hymn. Raven had never taken an interest in hymns, even before he'd turned, but now the music moved him. Something changed inside of him when Calandra sang—somehow everything about Raven's existence seemed less bleak, less dismal.

Her voice made him feel alive.

Raven caught himself checking the central tent pole for wobbles, but it seemed sturdy and unmovable. Good. He'd almost been staked for saving everyone last night. No need to repeat the incident if he could help it.

What's more, someone had already mended the slit Luco cut in the tent fabric to help the crowd get out. Now it amounted to nothing but a thin scar, barely visible so high above Calandra's head.

Calandra's song ended and she vanished behind the red curtain, replaced by Garrett, who spoke about the unconditional love of Jesus Christ for twenty minutes. Perhaps it was his bland, monotonous speaking voice, or perhaps it was because Raven knew him in person, but Garrett just didn't wield the same kind of charisma as Luco when he spoke.

Three or four people came up at Garrett's first call, then many, many more once Luco came up to pray and made a second call, but Raven didn't make any move toward the altar until the service concluded. When he did, he found himself drawn toward Calandra and Luco, both of whom smiled and waved at him.

A hulking form severed his line of sight. Garrett. "Where do you think you're going?"

Raven swallowed to give himself time to still his nerves. "I'm going up to the stage to see Luco and—"

"Not Calandra." Garrett extended his hand.

Raven stared at it. Was he supposed to play nice? Pretend Garrett and he were friends when they utterly despised each other? "Yes, Calandra too. Excuse me."

The outstretched hand went to Raven's chest as he tried to pass. "You're not going to shake my hand?"

"Do I have to?"

"You seemed to have such good manners last night. I had hoped you would show me the same courtesy."

Raven squinted at him, then took Garrett's hand in his own. "This better?"

Garrett smirked, then pulled Raven forward and wrapped his other arm around him in a one-armed hug—but not a friendly one. Dragon's breath filled Raven's ear. "You stay away from her, understand?"

Raven exhaled anger through his nose and clenched his teeth.

"I don't want to see you anywhere near her, or so help me God I'll put a stake right through your black heart. I would have done it already if it wasn't for Luco."

Perhaps Garrett didn't realize that as a vampire, Raven had the strength of ten men and could crush Garrett's hand with one firm squeeze.

"Glad to see you two are becoming friends." Luco patted them both on their backs. "I knew you'd come to terms eventually."

"Yeah. We understand each other, don't we?" Garrett released Raven and stepped back. He reached to put his arm around

Calandra but she dodged him and stood closer to her father instead. Garrett frowned, first at Calandra, then at Raven. He repeated, "*Don't we?*"

Raven bit his tongue, then smirked. "Yes. Garrett apologized for his behavior last night. He assured me that if he ever behaved like that again, he'd take an extended vow of silence much like Christian monks of history have done."

Garrett's eyes widened. "Well, I don't know about all of—"

"That's a great idea." Luco gave Garrett a playful elbow to his ribs. "Calandra certainly wouldn't be dismayed if Garrett kept quiet for awhile."

She smiled. "Not in the least."

Garrett glared at Raven.

Luco hooked his arm around Garrett's shoulder. "I admire your dedication to the faith, Garrett. I'm going to hold you to this promise, even if it means I have to preach every night we hold an event."

"But I didn't—"

"Are you coming over for dinner tonight, Raven?" Luco released Garrett.

Raven glanced at Calandra, who smiled. Then he looked at Garrett, who glared at him and shook his head almost indiscernibly. "I'd love to."

Garrett's eyes doubled in size and fury. "I don't know if that's—"

Luco waved his hand. "Nonsense, Garrett. Jesus said, 'as ye

have done it unto one of the least of these my brethren, ye have done it unto me.'"

Calandra smiled at Raven again, and something flipped inside his stomach. What was *that?* He glanced down at his belly.

"Do you mind helping us pack everything up tonight?" Luco asked.

Raven looked at Calandra. "Not in the least."

When they arrived at the Zambini family's home about two hours later, Mina charged toward Raven and leapt at him. She wrapped her arms around Raven's left leg and squeezed it tight. Anthony and Angelica came out of the house too, but they just stared at him.

Calandra must have noticed the distress on Raven's face. "Easy, Mina. At least let Raven get in the door before you knock him over. It's not polite to tackle our guests."

Mina didn't let go. She looked up at Raven with a toothy smile. "But I like him."

"We all like him, Mina." Luco snuck around Raven and stepped inside the house. "But we can't block the doorway. You can't tie him down forever, you know. He has to eat at some point."

"But—I like him," Mina repeated.

Raven's only contact with children since he'd turned was when he hunted them—quite the opposite of one clinging to his leg because she was happy to see him. A chasm inside Raven split open, a reminder of how alone he'd truly been over the last several decades.

But now someone *liked* him—and not just one person, but a whole family. It felt—

"Mina," Maria's stern voice sounded from the kitchen. "Don't make us tell you again."

"I'll get you later, though." Mina's brown eyes flickered. She let him go, then scampered over to her place at the table and climbed into her chair.

A jolt to the back of Raven's right shoulder broke his focus. Garrett walked past him, and his livid blue eyes locked on Raven's. "Excuse me."

Alright, not everyone in the family liked him, but Garrett didn't count, at least not yet. Not until he married Calandra, anyway.

At the table, Raven tried to pass on dinner again, but Maria assured him that she'd made a special plate just for him, one devoid of garlic. He acquiesced when Luco nodded at him from the other side of the table.

They ate in silence, unlike the night before when everyone had wanted to talk with him. Luco must have explained to them who Raven was, and now they feared him.

Garrett shot him a glare after almost every bite. Dante concentrated on his plate, but Anthony stared at Raven wide-eyed for most of the meal. Calandra gave him an occasional smile but broke eye contact right away, and Maria smiled at him, though it seemed half-hearted. Only Mina and Luco seemed truly happy to have him around.

"Do you like the cheese sauce we made?" Angelica finally

asked.

Raven looked down at it. "I haven't tried it yet." He hadn't tried *any* of it yet. "I—I still don't have much of an appetite." When everyone at the table looked at him, he added, "But I'm going to try it anyway, of course."

As the Zambini family returned their attention to their own plates, Raven picked up his fork and plunged it into his salad. He put a dark green leaf in his mouth and chewed. It didn't taste like anything but a piece of soft soot, as did the pasta with the cheese sauce.

They sat at the table after dinner and talked for awhile until something heavy landed on Raven's lap.

"Why don't you lead our nightly devotions, Raven?" A familiar smirk cracked Garrett's lips.

Raven glared at him until he realized what Garrett had dropped on his lap—a humongous leather-bound Bible with a gold cross embossed on the black cover. Heat spread under its weight and began to boil Raven's skin under his clothes.

With a hiss and a sharp recoil Raven flung the book across the room.

Chapter 8

The book smacked a wall and crumpled to the floor in a heap of leather and paper.

Raven jumped to his feet so fast that his chair tipped over and smacked the floor. His hip hit the table and rattled the few glasses and porcelain plates that hadn't yet been cleared. He staggered back against a wall on the opposite side of the room from where the Bible had landed.

He patted his lap and the bottom of his coat and the burning subsided, then he glared at Garrett. He almost extended his fangs, but with the children still in the room he managed to restrain himself.

"Garrett!" Calandra yelled. "What are you doing?"

He shrugged. "Just trying to encourage Raven in our faith. Reading the Bible is essential to developing a relationship with God."

"Quit playing dumb." She held her hand out to him, palm open. "You know they can't tolerate Christian symbols."

Garrett shrugged again. "I thought it would be a nice step of faith for him."

"Usually steps of faith are at either God's discretion or at that of the person taking the step, not someone else's." Luco's eyebrows arched down. He stood and approached the Bible.

"Papa, I'm scared." Mina peeked at Raven from behind Maria's flowery dress.

Should he apologize? Should he say something? Mortification flooded Raven's emotions, but he found himself unable to move or speak.

He hadn't realized it until that moment, but there had been no crosses or Christian symbols of any kind in either of the two tent meetings he'd attended. Luco hadn't even used a Bible when he spoke. Perhaps that's why Raven could approach the altar as freely as he had.

That golden cross on the Bible seared his mind's eye and ignited him with fury at Garrett's insolent behavior. He couldn't go near that book again.

Luco stared down at the Bible. As he reached for it he hesitated, as if unsure of how to salvage it without further wrinkling or creasing its delicate pages. The way he picked it up by its spine in one hand reminded Raven of a mountain lion picking up a cub with its teeth.

He turned to Raven with the book in his hands and smiled. "Raven, take a seat, please."

Raven swallowed hard, but snatched a chair from the table and sat down near the wall. As Luco stalked toward him with the book, the candles on the hearth flickered, then extinguished. Smoky ghosts danced where the fire had just been.

"Don't be afraid of this book," Luco said.

Easy for Luco to say. He wasn't a vampire.

"Yes, it is 'quick, and powerful, and sharper than any two-edged sword,'" Luco said. "But this is also a book of life, of hope, and of love."

"Don't." Raven's eyes widened.

Luco didn't stop advancing. He extended the book toward Raven.

Raven shifted to the side abruptly, and his shoulder knocked a painting from the wall. Its frame smacked on the floor. "Don't…please."

Luco paused. "I'm not going to drop it on your lap, and I'm not going to force you to take it. I'm just going to hold it out for you, and you can take it if you want to. Do you trust me?"

"I barely know you." Raven's fangs extended behind his lips—he couldn't help it anymore. He would attack Luco if he had to. He hoped it wouldn't come to that.

"That's not what I asked."

Raven glanced at Maria, then at Calandra. They stared at him, of course, but he noticed encouragement in each of their eyes. When he caught a glimpse of Garrett, he only saw disdain.

Wind howled outside and rattled the house's windows. The flames in the fireplace dwindled, and the entire room darkened.

The black book hovered at Raven's eye level, and its golden cross shined in what light remained. Abhorrent, yet appealing. Repellent, yet revelatory. Offensive, yet alluring.

"Do you trust me, Raven?"

Raven studied Luco's brown eyes and loosened the tension in his jaw. "I trust you."

"Then take the book in your hands."

Raven hesitated until he remembered Garrett's raucous laughter last night. Garrett would *not* have another laugh at his expense.

He reached for the book and set it on his lap. The instant he touched it, the fire in the fireplace swelled to its previous size and the howling wind faded.

Raven's fingers burned, but he could tolerate the sensation. "What do I do now?"

Garrett folded his arms in front of his chest and chuckled. "You've never read a book before?"

"Never read the *Bible* before." Raven didn't even look at him.

Luco smiled. "I'll help you. Open the book as close to the middle as you can, then look at the top of the page. What do you see?"

Raven complied. "It says Psalm 41."

"Psalms is one of the books of the Bible, and you're at chapter 41. Page back a few and find chapter 23."

A few pages back, Raven found Psalm 23. "I have it."

"Would you care to read it aloud for us?" Luco pulled another chair up next to Raven and peered over his shoulder.

Raven raised his eyebrows, but started reading. "The Lord is my shepherd; I shall not want. He maketh me to lie down in green pastures: he leadeth me beside the still waters. He restoreth my soul: he leadeth me in the paths of righteousness for his name's sake.

"Yea, though I walk through the valley of the shadow of death, I will fear no evil: for thou art with me; thy rod and thy staff they comfort me. Thou preparest a table before me in the presence of mine enemies: thou anointest my head with oil; my cup runneth over. Surely goodness and mercy shall follow me all the days of my life: and I will dwell in the house of the Lord forever."

Silence enveloped the room except for the faint crackling of the fire in the fireplace. Raven closed the Bible and drank in the words he'd just read, especially the "He restoreth my soul" part. Could God really do that?

After a long moment he asked, "This may sound strange, but was the author of this passage a vampire too?"

Garrett guffawed. "King David, a *vampire*?"

"*Enough*, Garrett." Luco faced Raven. "Don't worry about him. Tell me, what do you mean?"

Apprehension seized Raven's stomach, but he continued anyway. "I know we've existed since ancient times, so I was wondering if the author—if King David was a vampire."

"What makes you think he could have been a vampire?"

"He said that the Lord restored his soul. Did that mean he didn't have one, like me?"

"I'll admit that I never made that connection, but I see where you're coming from."

"You do?" As Raven said it, he realized that Garrett had said it with him in unison. They exchanged a furtive glance and then both refocused on Luco.

"I do. I think it would be more accurate to say that God was in the process of restor*ing* his soul, not so much that He had already restored it." Luco smiled. "But I don't think he was a vampire."

Raven didn't say anything. He just looked down at the Bible's cover. That made sense, but—

He stopped. He was running his fingers over the golden cross. It wasn't burning him or repelling him. What?

"It's not affecting me anymore." Raven looked at Calandra, who smiled at him. He turned to Luco, who nodded. "I—I don't understand."

"I think this is a sign, Raven. I don't believe it's just a coincidence." Luco placed his hand on Raven's shoulder. "I think God is reaching out to you."

God? Reaching out to a vampire? Why would he do that?

"Your existence no longer needs to be defined by your vampirism. Do you want to remain a vampire, or do you want to give God a chance to set you free?"

A decision. Black and white. Luco couldn't have framed it any better.

But Luco didn't understand what it really meant to be a vampire—the lifestyle, the extravagance, the mind games and manipulation, and blood, blood, blood. Raven had fed on thousands of people in his time and some of them had died and become vampires as a result. In effect, Raven had damned them.

Just as he'd been damned when *she* turned him 83 years ago.

But Luco said there was a way to be free of all of that, free of his curse. Raven found Calandra's eyes, and she smiled and gave him a slight nod. Just the sight of her filled his chest with hope. If Luco was right, and he could live a normal life, what did he have to lose?

Raven nodded. "What do I need to do?"

Luco's smile widened. "We'll do it like we do it in our tent meetings. I'll pray a prayer, and you repeat after me."

Raven repeated Luco's prayer, word for word, in front of his family and Garrett. More than once the idea that the words meant nothing crossed his mind, and the occasional glances he stole at Garrett's smug face reinforced the notion, but he finished the prayer nonetheless.

"Amen," he echoed Luco. "So…what happens now?"

"Now you go out and walk in your new faith, starting by not feeding tonight," Luco said. "You're being sanctified, Raven. Your life is changing. God is restoring your soul, one piece at a time."

Quiet lingered in the stillness of the room for several minutes until little Mina broke the silence. "Can he at least have dessert now?"

A half-hour later, Raven said his goodbyes just before Mina and Anthony headed off to bed for the evening. When Mina gave him a big hug, his stomach roiled. Just a few nights ago he had intended to drain her dry.

Luco and Maria embraced him as well, but everyone else just stood there except for Garrett, who shook Raven's hand with that familiar disdain in his eyes.

As the Zambinis and Garrett went inside the house, Raven sensed the forest calling to him. He still had a few hours before sunrise, but he still hadn't eaten. Well, he'd eaten, but he hadn't *fed*.

Then again, would he need to? According to Luco, he shouldn't. Perhaps the normal food he'd eaten would provide him with some nourishment after all. Even if the food wasn't enough, maybe he'd be able to switch to animal blood and avoid preying on another human for his susten—

"Raven?"

He turned and raised his eyebrows at the sight of Calandra standing behind him, alone under the moonlight.

The perfect prey.

He shook the thought from his mind. "Yes?"

"I just wanted to invite you to our baptism tomorrow night."

"Baptism? As in, with water?"

"Yes, of course." Her smile lit up the night.

Raven savored a long look at her. Barefoot, soft, tanned skin, long dark hair, and curves that could derail a steam engine. Too bad she was mortal. Though he could certainly do something about that…

"No." He said it aloud before he realized it.

Her smile faded. "Are you sure? I'm getting baptized for the first time tomorrow, along with Dante and Angelica. You should come."

Raven shook his head. "Sorry. I wasn't saying no to you about the baptism. I was saying it to myself."

Calandra eyed him. "I don't understand. What do you mean?"

"I—" Perhaps he should just avoid her entirely so as not to risk harming her.

Yes. He would keep his distance for her sake. And that started with a dose of honesty about why he intended to do so.

"I—I was resisting the urge to—feed. On you."

Dead air hovered between them.

"You—you want to bite me?" She didn't recoil as Raven thought she might. Instead she stood her ground.

"Yes," he replied. His gut twisted with shame. "I prefer to target beautiful young women like you."

Calandra's cheeks reddened, but whether it was because Raven had called her beautiful or because she feared him, he did not know.

"Why do you seek out young women specifically?"

Raven diverted his gaze to the bright moon overhead. "I wish I knew exactly why. I only have theories."

"Which are?"

He locked eyes with her. He could have put her in a trance right then and there, just by pushing thoughts out of his mind and into hers, but he restrained himself. "I think it hearkens back to the first vampires who strictly pursued prey of the opposite gender except in desperation. I imagine they went after prey that they found appealing."

"So you find me appealing?"

Raven swallowed.

"It's alright. You don't have to answer. I don't want to make you feel uncomfortable."

He just gawked at her.

She smiled at him again. "Although I didn't know until this moment that a vampire could blush."

Raven's eyes widened. He was *blushing*? How long had he been doing that? He touched his cheek. Could vampires blush, or was this a result of his conversion? He hadn't had a reflection for eight decades, so he had no way to know.

Calandra chuckled. "I'm just giving you a hard time, Raven. I know I shouldn't since you get enough of that from Garrett already, but I couldn't resist. You looked so vulnerable."

Vulnerable? This was certainly a switch.

"Look, Raven," Calandra said. "I know you're used to people being afraid of you and avoiding you, or even trying to harm you because you're different. None of that matters to me. I'm only concerned about one thing."

A thousand possibilities filled Raven's mind. He stared at her. "Which is?"

She tapped his chest with her forefinger. "Your soul. Who you are. I'd rather risk a few uncomfortable moments of being around you than lead you to believe that we don't want you around because you're not like us. It's more important for you to know who Jesus really is than for me to worry about you harming me."

"Alright...I guess?"

"Besides—" Calandra grinned at him. "—I have Jesus too. He's more than able to protect me from you if he has to."

Raven scoffed. Maybe Jesus could protect her from him, but maybe not. "Your father said the same thing."

"I bet he did."

"I'll tell you what I told him: if you say so." Raven rubbed his forehead.

"Well, don't let me scare you away, alright?" Calandra put her hand on his shoulder. "Stick with this. You'll need good friends if you're going to grow in your new faith."

So much for avoiding her for her own good. Raven nodded. "I'll try."

"So how about it?"

"How about what?"

"Will you come to the baptism tomorrow evening?"

"I thought you said it was at night."

She nodded. "It is, but we start the baptisms in the late evening."

"I can't be there until after sunset."

"Of course," she said. "We'll wait for you so you can get baptized too, if you like."

"Me?"

"Yes, you." She kept smiling. "Baptism is something that

every follower of Christ can partake in."

"What will I have to do?"

She shrugged. "Nothing, really. Just show up to the river and my father will baptize you."

"That's it?"

"We'll have a potluck dinner here at the house to celebrate after that."

"I see." Raven nodded to her. "I guess I'll be off, then. Have a good night."

"Wait." She took hold of his hand.

He stared down at her hand, warm against his frigid skin. So nice.

"I never got to thank you," Calandra said. "For saving my life last night."

Raven shrugged. "I couldn't let such a beautiful voice meet such an ugly end."

Her eyes indicated that she knew what he'd really meant. So much for hiding it.

She squeezed his hand and smiled at him. "You're sweet. Come to the baptism tomorrow night, and wear a robe. I'll see you there."

He nodded and let go of her hand. Raven lifted his gaze and stretched his arms toward the night sky.

A shadow passed over Raven, and then he was gone. Only a dark mist remained, and it dissipated into the night air around her.

Calandra shivered and rubbed her shoulders, then she turned back toward the house.

There, in the window, Garrett's scowling face and sullen eyes awaited her.

The moment she stepped through the door, Garrett clamped his large hand around her forearm and pulled her back outside. "Can I talk to you for a minute?"

As if she had a choice.

In the cool darkness of the outdoors, she folded her arms and waited for Garrett to speak, but he didn't. He just stood between her and the door, mimicking her disinterested expression.

"What do you want?"

Garrett cleared his throat. "You don't have something to say to me?"

She eyed him. "What are you talking about? You brought me out here."

"How about an apology?"

Calandra glanced over Garrett's shoulder, then back at his eyes. "For what?"

"I thought we agreed that you would stay away from him."

"Are you two alright out here?" Maria poked her head through the nearest window on the porch.

"Yeah, Mama. We're fine," Calandra replied. *Mostly.*

"Alright. Just checking. Don't stay out here too long. You know how your father and I feel about you two being out here alone."

Calandra glanced at Garrett, who just stared straight ahead, his brow furrowed. "We won't, Mama."

"We're all going to bed now. I'd prefer if you two were inside within the next ten minutes or so, otherwise there won't be anyone to watch you."

Garrett's jaw tensed. "We will, Mrs. Zambini. Do you mind if we finish our conversation first?"

"Sure, sure. Go ahead."

"In private, Mama?" Calandra motioned toward the door with her head.

Her mother hesitated, but nodded. "Ten minutes. And I'm leaving this window open."

"That's fine." She nudged Garrett. "Where were we?"

"I said—" Garrett exhaled a long breath. "—that we agreed you'd stay away from him."

"I *never* agreed to stay away from him."

Garrett raised his eyebrows. "You most certainly did. We were riding home from the tent meeting and—"

"And we agreed that I would be cordial to him in public."

"But not that you'd run after him like a tigress in heat."

"*Excuse me?*" Calandra's chin dropped. "What exactly are you insinuating?"

Garrett's eyes narrowed. "No. You're not going to twist my words against me."

She released a mirthless laugh. "I don't have to. You're doing fine on your own."

"You're behaving like a child."

"And you're behaving like an imbecile."

"Do *not* speak to me like that."

"Then don't compare me to a wild animal on the prowl for a mate." Calandra put her hands on her hips. Garrett hated when she did that, but she didn't care.

Garrett sighed through his nose. "I—I didn't mean—it's not like that."

"That's *exactly* what you meant." She stormed around him toward the door, but he grabbed her by the wrist. "Let go of me, Garrett."

"I'm sorry," he said. "I didn't mean to insult you. You know how much I care for—"

"I said *let go*." She stared steel into his light brown eyes until he released his grip. She wrenched her arm away and headed for the door.

"Just stay away from him, will you? I don't trust him," Garrett called after her.

Calandra shook her head as she shut the door behind her. She would do as she pleased, and Garrett would have to accept it.

Chapter 9

Luco could have fallen asleep the instant his head hit his pillow, but Maria had other plans.

"What do you think of Raven?" she asked as soon as the room fell into darkness.

"What do you mean?" He could feel the sleep encroaching under his eyelids.

"I mean what do you think of him?"

Luco exhaled. "I like him. I think he's a good kid."

"He's older than you are, you know."

"Not by much."

Maria whacked his shoulder. "Enough of that."

"I know, I know." Luco chuckled. "Does he bother you?"

"Yes," she whispered.

"Is it because he's a vampire?"

"Yes."

Luco rolled on his side and faced her. "He won't be one for much longer now that God's Word has taken root inside of him."

"I know, but—still. This is new territory for me." She gave his hand a squeeze.

"He's not the first lonely soul we've invested in."

"This is different."

"Is it?" Luco rubbed his nose. "We've taken in all sorts of strays in our twenty years of marriage. Gamblers, thugs, alcoholics, criminals, opium-addicts—"

"But never a vampire."

"You're right. Never a vampire. But is he really so different than anyone else we've tried to help?"

Maria didn't answer right away. "He is."

Luco squinted at her face in the darkness. "You really think so?"

"I do."

"Why?"

She shifted in bed to face him as well. "He's a *vampire*. He's more of a threat to our family than anyone we've ever interacted with before. What will the congregation think?"

"I think this is the perfect time to welcome a person like Raven into our church and into our family, especially with all the lore in this area. The congregation may not like it initially but in the long run they'll see how great of a need there is for this type of ministry. It's part of the reason we decided to move here to begin with, remember?"

"I remember," Maria replied, her voice quiet.

Luco tilted his head. "Are you worried that he'll hurt the kids?"

"I don't know what I'm worried about. I just can't help but wonder what he's thinking, what he might be plotting behind our backs."

"I don't think he's plotting anything."

She nodded. "Maybe not, but he's still a vampire. He didn't even have a *soul* a few nights ago. Perhaps inviting him to stay over so soon isn't the wisest choice. Maybe he needs more time to grow. Maybe we need more time to adjust."

"I hear you." Luco wrapped his arms around his wife and pulled her close. "I won't make any decisions about Raven staying with us until you're ready."

"No, go ahead and invite him to stay with us. I think by the time he makes his decision we'll be ready to accommodate him."

Luco released his embrace and looked into her dark eyes. "Are you sure? I don't want to pressure you into anything that you're not comfortable with."

Maria sighed. "It's just that I'm worried about Calandra."

"Calandra?" Luco squinted at her. "Are you worried that Raven is taking a liking to her?"

"Actually," she said. "I'm worried *she's* developing feelings for *him*."

"Really?"

"I think so. I heard her and Garrett arguing about him tonight before we went to bed. I don't think things are going well. Don't get me wrong—I really like Garrett and all, but I have a feeling he can't compete with Raven for Calandra. Whatever the case, Christian or otherwise, I won't allow a vampire to pursue our daughter."

"You're assuming Raven is interested in her."

Maria raised her eyebrows. "Luco. Our daughter is beautiful, smart, and caring. What's not to like?"

"I'm not disputing any of that, but I haven't seen even the smallest indication that he's pursuing her."

"Neither have I, but I could see him developing an interest in her."

Luco shrugged. "Maybe. We'll worry about that when it happens."

"I think we should worry about it now. What if Raven moves in and—"

"Garrett's already living with us, and we haven't had any problems."

"You didn't let me finish."

"I'm sorry."

"But you hit on my point. What if Raven moves in and develops feelings for Calandra? What kind of conflict do you think that will cause for Garrett? What kind of conflict will it create between him and Calandra?" she asked. "Is that really something we want to risk?"

"I don't know if I'm keen on the idea of Calandra and Garrett marrying any time soon anyway. They're both so young, and Calandra is headstrong." Luco squeezed Maria's thigh. "Like her mother."

"Don't you blame that all on me, *marito*. I've seen you preach. You're as fiery as I am, or more."

"I know. As for Garrett, he's still learning how to become the man God wants him to be. He's come a long way since we found him two years ago, but I don't want him marrying our daughter in the near future. Sometimes I wonder if I should have even consented to letting them court in the first place."

"But Calandra insisted," Maria said. "And so far their courtship has remained transparent and they've followed our rules."

"True."

"I just can't help but wonder if bringing Raven into our home will ruin their chances."

"Or perhaps it's just the kind of adversity they need to face to solidify their relationship, if in fact they will marry someday." Luco rubbed his forehead. "I think we need to have a family meeting about this before we make any final decisions."

Maria nodded. "I agree."

"Let's give everyone some time to adjust to all of these recent changes, Raven included. We can have a meeting in a couple of weeks or so, during the day." Luco rolled onto his back and closed his eyes. "Agreed?"

"*Buono. Grazie.*" Maria gave him a squeeze and snuggled closer to him.

---

30 Miles West of the Zambini Family's Home

"It's just beyond this hill, Harry," Mick said.

"I'll bet it is," Harry mumbled. Together with Steve and Jim, he followed Mick toward the next job. A rich old widow's house, Mick had said. An easy score, he'd said. The best kind.

Liar.

They rode on horseback toward a narrow path where the hill crested. Harry fiddled with the end of his thick handlebar mustache between his index finger and his thumb, then he unsheathed his bowie knife without a sound. He drew his arm back.

"So when we get there, the plan is to—*ghk!*" Mick's body contorted and he dropped from his horse onto the hard earth below. Harry's knife protruded from his back.

"Holy—what the hell did you do that for, Harry?" Steve asked, his eyes wide.

"Five years of knocking off stagecoaches, trains, homes, and banks, and you still squirm at the sight of violence, Steve?" Harry dismounted and stepped toward Mick's writhing body. "Sometimes I wonder if you're in the right line of work."

Mick moaned.

"Shut up, Mick." Harry pulled out a cigarette, stuck one end in his mouth, and lit the opposite end with a match. He bent down and wrenched the bowie knife from Mick's torso, and Mick yelped again. A push from Harry's boot rolled Mick onto his back. "You shouldn't have crossed me."

Mick mumbled something unintelligible.

"What'd he say?" Jim asked.

Steve shrugged. "I think he said—"

"He's begging for his life." Harry blew a plume of smoke into the cool night air. "But it won't save him."

Mick moaned again. "Plsss… Don't—"

Harry pressed the sole of his boot down on Mick's throat. "Too late for that. You earned this."

"What did he do?" Steve asked.

Harry glared at him and tightened his grip on his knife. "I wish you'd quit trying to stall for him. This is happening, no question."

Steve put his hands up. "That's not what I'm doing. I just want to know what he did."

"Why don't you and Jim go have a look over that hill?" Harry motioned toward the crest with his head. "But get off your horses, and be *quiet* about it. We can wait, can't we Mick?"

All he got for an answer was a sputter.

Steve eyed him then glanced at Jim, who nodded. They dismounted and peeked over the hill. It wasn't long before they both returned to Harry, their eyes rich with surprise.

"It's dark, but I made out at least ten men in a posse waiting for us. Probably a few more in the trees waiting to cut off our escape." Jim rubbed his nose. "They must want us bad."

"They do. Mick here sold us out." Harry exhaled the smoke through his nose. As a kid he'd seen his uncle do it, and Harry thought he looked like a dragon. When Harry started smoking three years later, he adopted the habit as his own. Now *he* was the dragon.

"How did you know?" Steve asked.

Harry smirked. "Can't tell you that, boys. Gotta keep my secrets. Never know when one of you might be next."

Mick coughed.

Harry removed his foot from Mick's neck and gave him a swift kick in his ribs. "Was it worth it, Mick? I hope they promised you a lot of money. I hope it was worth your *life*."

"What are you going to do with him?" Steve asked.

Harry gave them a twisted smile. "Put him on his horse."

Marshal Flax checked his pocket watch and frowned. "I don't know why they're late."

"Maybe something happened?" Bill Jenner, his newest Deputy, shifted his rifle in his hands—for the third time.

"Will you cut that out?" Marshal hissed. "You're making me nervous."

"Sorry. Just eager, I guess."

"You shouldn't be. This isn't your first ambush."

"I know that, but—"

"But what?"

Jenner swallowed. "But it's Harry Deutsch. You said he's the worst criminal in the county, maybe in the entire state."

Marshal raised an eyebrow. He supposed he couldn't fault Jenner for his nervousness, given their quarry. Still, with a dozen able men in hiding plus Jenner and himself, not to mention a man on the inside of Harry's band, the odds weighed heavily in their favor. "Harry Deutsch or not, we're bringing him in tonight."

Jenner looked at him. "And if he resists?"

"Keep your eyes on that hill, Deputy." Marshal exhaled a deep breath. "If he resists, we do what we have to do."

Something rustled to Jenner's left. Marshal tried to get a glimpse, but Jenner whirled toward the noise and raised his rifle.

"Easy, Jenner." Marshal put his gloved hand on Jenner's shoulder. "It's only Friedrich. Keep your eyes on that hill."

As Deputy Friedrich approached, Jenner swallowed again. Though he came highly recommended from three counties over for his considerable size, strength, and capabilities as a Deputy, Jenner seemed especially prone to erratic behavior tonight as if he had a constant stream of spiders crawling up his back.

"Sorry," Jenner muttered. "Still a bit on-edge, I suppose."

"Don't mind him, Friedrich. Go ahead."

Friedrich nodded. He removed his hat and ran his gloved fingers through his silver hair, then popped the hat back on. "There's been some movement beyond the hill crest, Marshal. We think it's Deutsch and his men."

Jenner twitched again and stared at Marshal.

"What did I tell you about that *hill*, Jenner?" Marshal pointed at it.

Jenner nodded. "Sorry—sorry."

"Quit apologizing and watch that hill. If you see movement, tell me."

Jenner nodded again.

Marshal turned back to Friedrich. "Any sign of our contact?"

"Mick?" Friedrich shook his head. "Not yet."

"What makes a man do the things Harry Deutsch has done, anyway?" Jenner spat on the ground near his boots, but he didn't look away from the hill. "Raping. Murdering. Stealing. He might as well be an animal instead of a human."

"He's not human," Marshal said.

That turned Jenner's head, and he stared at Marshal, his blue eyes wide.

"But he's not an animal either. He's worse. He's a monster, plain and simple."

Friedrich nodded and folded his arms. "No question about it. His soul's as black as tar."

"But how does a man get that way?" Jenner asked. "We all turned out good, but he didn't? Maybe a bad upbringing?"

"You watching that hill?"

Jenner shifted his attention back to it. "Sorry."

"He's got a point, though, Marshal. How *does* someone become like Harry Deutsch?"

Marshal shook his head. "No one knows for sure, but if you ask me, some people are just rotten at their core from birth."

"Marshal," Jenner said.

Marshal sighed. "There had better be something coming over that hill, Deputy."

"There is," Jenner whispered.

Marshal turned his attention toward the hill, and sure enough, a dark form materialized against the backdrop of the forest. "Jenner."

"Yeah?"

"Don't let him out of your sights, you hear?"

"Right."

The form took the shape of a man on horseback barreling down the hill straight at Marshal and Jenner's position.

"Stop where you are!" Marshal called into the night.

The horse and rider charged forward with abandon and disregarded the marshal's second and third orders as well. A gunshot split the sky from the forest beyond the hill, and everyone ducked behind their cover.

"Jenner, put him down."

Marshal had barely finished his sentence before Jenner's rifle spewed fire. The rider reeled back from the bullet's impact. As the horse continued to gallop toward them, the rider slumped forward, but he didn't fall off the horse's back. When the horse finally slowed to a halt at the bottom of the hill, Marshal's posse converged on its position.

Marshal stood up and rounded the barrier. "Jenner, keep your eyes on that hill. This may not be over."

"Got it."

No question the young man could shoot straight—even on-edge as he was. Maybe Jenner would prove to be an asset to the county after all.

By the time Marshal arrived, Friedrich had already assessed the situation. "Mick. Dead."

Marshal cursed under his breath. "How?"

Friedrich shrugged. "Jenner's bullet didn't do him any favors, but from the deep knife wound in his back, I'd say we just put him out of his misery. He may have been dead before he even came over that hill."

"They knew we were coming. Deutsch found out about Mick."

Friedrich nodded. "Looks that way. No way they'll show now. Should we go after them? They might still be right over that hill."

"It's a big hill. By the time we charge over it, they could already have a half-mile lead on us," Marshal said. "Plus their horses will have more steam left than ours. They won this one. I think we'd best accept that."

Friedrich sighed.

Jenner patted Friedrich's shoulder. "I know what you're feeling. We'll have another chance. Best thing about criminals is that they keep giving you more chances to catch them."

Friedrich, Jenner's senior by at least 20 years, frowned at him. "If you say so, kid."

Marshal eyed the hill. Jenner had a point, but after a few dozen crimes, half of them murders, each "chance" Harry gave them meant more collateral damage and more destroyed lives if they couldn't bring him in.

Marshal didn't want to extinguish the new kid's fervor, but catching Harry Deutsch was going to be much harder than Jenner thought.

Chapter 10

Calandra's insolence bothered Garrett for the early part of the next day, but he'd managed to make things right with her by midday with a bouquet of wildflowers and a penitent heart.

As usual, she melted at his gestures and finally proffered the apology he knew he deserved. She even expressed her determination to remain faithful to him and not provoke him to anger, just like a good wife would. Soon they would be married, he'd assured her, and then these pithy troubles would no longer bother them.

He whistled and smiled while he helped Luco make preparations for the baptism that night. Whenever congregants approached to be baptized, Garrett greeted them with a grin and shook each of their hands with genuine gladness, then he assisted Luco in baptizing them in the moonlit river.

That didn't include Calandra, of course, whom Garrett didn't touch since they weren't yet married. Luco baptized her on his own without any trouble.

She'd been the last one to receive the baptism that night, until a dark form materialized from the woods at the opposite side of the riverbank. The vampire. He wore a robe not dissimilar to those that the baptizees wore, except for its color: black.

Garrett shook his head. "Can you believe that? He has the audacity to show up to a baptism in a black robe."

Luco just shrugged. "We're wearing purple robes. What difference does it make?"

"But we're ministers of the Gospel. We're supposed to look different than everyone else."

"We still look different than Raven."

"It's offensive. He's mocking the gift of Jesus with his attire."

Luco raised an eyebrow. "'Offensive?' 'Mocking the gift of Jesus with his attire?' I'm not aware of any baptismal dress code in the Scriptures. Are you?"

Garrett didn't have an answer for that one, no matter how hard he thought about it.

"How about this one?" Luco said. "'Come unto me, all ye that labour and are heavy laden, and I will give you rest.' It's my understanding that Jesus wanted us to come as we are. That's exactly what Raven is doing."

"But he's wearing *black*. He looks like he's going to a funeral."

Luco smiled. "You're very astute, Garrett. He *is* going to a funeral. You know as well as I do that baptism is an important symbol of that very thing."

Garrett frowned at Luco. This was *not* how he'd expected this conversation to go.

"That's an excellent observation, by the way." Luco rubbed

his chin. "I think we ought to have black robes for everyone from now on."

Garrett turned toward Raven again to hide the scowl on his face. No matter how hard he tried or what he did, Garrett just couldn't convince Luco and Calandra how dangerous Raven was. They had no idea what Garrett had seen, or what he'd done to stop it from happening again.

Garrett just hoped it wouldn't cost someone's life—someone's *soul*—in order to get Luco to realize what a horrible mistake he was making by allowing a vampire to walk among them.

He sighed and clenched his fists, his eyes focused on Raven. He alone would protect the Zambini family, especially Calandra, from Raven.

Raven stood at the water's edge. When Calandra had invited him to attend last night, he hadn't processed the notion that the baptism would take place at a river. A flowing body of water.

According to the Old Lore, vampires couldn't cross flowing bodies of water, and most wouldn't even enter such water. Yet there he was, perched at the water's edge. A few dozen people occupied the opposite riverbank, and Luco and Garrett stood right in the middle of the river which came up waist-high on their bodies.

He couldn't do it. If he entered the water and tried to cross to the other side—well, honestly he didn't know what might happen.

Raven scanned his side of the bank. Maybe if there was a boat or a small raft somewhere, then he could use that to—

"Raven."

He knew that voice, and he locked eyes with Calandra.

"I'm so glad you could make it." She waded toward him, past a surly Garrett and her smiling father. "Come on in. The water's actually warmer than it looks, once you get used to it."

Raven swallowed. "I forgot that I—I can't."

Before he could turn away, she grabbed him by the hand and gave it a small tug. "There's nothing to be afraid of."

He studied her eyes, full of life. Calandra's hair was still damp from her own baptism, and her wet white robe clung to her shapely form.

Raven shook his head. "We can't cross flowing bodies of water."

Calandra eyed him, then the river. "Says who?"

Raven shrugged. "It's in the Old Lore. It's a rule far older than I am, probably dating back to the ancients. I once heard that it goes back to a legend from ancient Egypt where the river waters once turned into blood."

A smile cracked Calandra's lips. "That's a story from the Bible, you know."

Raven tilted his head. "It is?"

She nodded. "Moses, through the power of God, turned all the waters of Egypt into blood. It's in the book of Exodus. If you remind me later, I'll show it to you."

"So the Lore is true, then."

"I don't know if it's true or not, but I believe that Bible story is true. So what happens if you try to cross the water?"

"I have no idea. No one I've ever known has tried it, and I've never heard what's supposed to happen to a vampire who tries," Raven said. "The only message I ever got was 'don't try it.'"

Calandra shook her head. "Sounds like a bunch of nonsense to me. Come with me."

She pulled on his hand, but he recoiled and shook free from her grip. When she turned back to him, he said, "I'm sorry. I can't."

"Yes, you can." She extended her hand toward him. "Trust me. Trust God."

Raven raised his eyebrows. "I don't know…"

"That's the point of faith, Raven. You don't know." Calandra smiled again. "Now, will you come with me?"

He sucked in a deep breath and then nodded, but he didn't move.

"Raven."

Water sloshed over his feet and crept up his black leather boots to his ankles.

"Open your eyes. Nothing is happening," Calandra said.

Not yet.

They waded farther into the river, and the water reached his knees. It felt warm against his frigid skin, probably far warmer to him than to Calandra. So far nothing had happened. A current this light couldn't harm him.

Perhaps Calandra was right. Perhaps nothing would happen after all.

Under the moonlight, he noticed Calandra's reflection trailing her on the surface of the rippling waters, but when he looked for his own, it was nowhere to be found. What did that mean? Luco had said God would restore Raven's soul, but he still couldn't see his own reflection.

In mid-step, Raven's left foot slipped from its place on the riverbed, and he stumbled, but quickly righted himself. Had a fish collided with his ankle or something? Or had the current picked up as he approached the center? That made sense. With less resistance from the riverbed, the current would naturally move quicker in deeper waters, right?

The water crested just above his knees when he lost his footing again. This time he toppled forward and had to catch himself on the riverbed with his free hand. Water splashed his face, but he adjusted his steps and continued. He released Calandra's hand and went down again right away, somehow soaking himself in only about two feet of water.

"Are you alright?" Calandra asked.

Raven ran his fingers through his wet hair and pulled several long black strands away from his face. "Yes. I just tripped."

Had he tripped? Or had the current tried to sweep him away?

Calandra extended her hand again.

Raven struggled against the current, but he managed to make it to his feet. He waved Calandra off. "I'm not doing so well. Maybe it's better if I don't hang on to you. I don't want to take you down with me on accident."

She continued toward her father and Garrett as if the strong current didn't even faze her, yet Raven continued to struggle against the waters. With each additional step, the flow grew more volatile, more capable of washing Raven away. All around him the waters brewed with swirls of white foam as the river swelled to rapids.

Calandra turned back and smiled at him, even as the waters pummeled him and ignored her. By the time he made it to Luco, Calandra, and Garrett in the middle of the river, the current had increased into waves that splashed up to Raven's chin. Despite Raven's evident struggling, neither Luco, Calandra, nor Garrett reacted to the increasing waters. How were they oblivious to what was happening?

Garrett stood there, glaring at him, while Luco and Calandra smiled. None of them showed the slightest hint of concern for his wellbeing, even though the river fought to yank him away. Now he knew why vampires couldn't cross flowing bodies of water—God's Creation itself opposed them.

Was this baptism worth risking his existence?

Upriver, something changed, but not for the better. A massive swell tumbled downriver as if a nearby dam had broken and spewed the wrath of a thousand converging rivers right at them.

Raven turned back to Luco, who showed no concern that all four of them were about to be crushed by Nature's fury. How was it even possible? Couldn't he at least see the sheer terror on Raven's face?

As the tidal wave approached, Luco held Raven's arm.

"Raven, are you ready to make a public confession of your faith?"

He stole a glance at the surf plowing toward them, now only about a hundred feet away and closing fast. He swallowed, and though he didn't know why, he replied, "Yes."

Luco moved him into position.

The tumult closed to fifty feet.

What was he thinking? He should be charging back to the water's edge to get out of there before the river pulverized him.

Garrett didn't move at all, so Calandra stepped forward and put her hand on Raven's back. "It's alright, Raven."

Over her shoulder, the waves thundered to within twenty-five feet of them. They were all going to die.

"I baptize you in the name of the Father—"

Fifteen feet.

"—the Son—"

Less than ten feet. Raven's eyes widened.

"—and the Holy Spirit," Luco said.

The swell crashed down on them as Luco and Calandra submerged him underwater.

Chapter 11

Strong hands pulled Raven above the water's surface, and the thunder of the tidal wave faded to the distant swish of rushing water. Raven coughed and shook his head. He wiped the water from his face and brushed saturated locks of black hair from his cheeks.

When Raven finally opened his eyes, Calandra was smiling at him, and so was Luco. Calandra still looked damp, but Luco was dry from the waist up with the exception of his arms. Had the tidal wave somehow missed him? He turned to Garrett, whose face bore the same scowl as before Raven went under. He was dry from the waist up as well.

"What happened?" Raven asked.

"We baptized you," Garrett said, his voice flat.

Raven swiveled back to Calandra and Luco. "That's it?"

Luco smiled. "That's it."

"How do you feel?" Calandra asked.

"I don't know," Raven replied. The tidal wave still echoed in his memory.

When he looked at the other side of the river, he realized it wasn't the tidal wave making the sound. There, crowded near the river's edge, the congregation applauded him. Some even cheered.

He picked out Maria, Dante, Angelica, Anthony, and even little Mina, who clung to Angelica with a huge smile on her face.

None of them showed any indication that the river had threatened to wash Raven, Luco, Calandra, and Garrett away. Had Raven hallucinated the entire scene?

If he'd been hallucinating, then why had he struggled against the accelerating current to get to the center of the river? It made no sense.

Raven rubbed his eyes again just to be sure. When he opened them, he saw no tidal wave, only Calandra's smiling face. Instead of a potent hunger for her blood in his gut, a comfortable warmth filled his chest.

Luco patted his shoulder. "Welcome to our congregation, Raven."

Raven stared at the faces of the people planted at the edge of the river. Instead of the mixture of confusion and fright he'd seen when he'd wedged himself between the stage and the toppling tent pole, he saw hope and happiness.

The people appeared devoid of fear, but they weren't in awe of him, either. Instead, he was in awe of them.

Calandra clasped Raven's cold hand and pulled him behind her toward the shoreline. "Come, now. We get to eat, and that's the best part."

She stole a glance back at him, but his face showed only amazement. In the few days she'd known him, she hadn't seen him smile once. At that moment, she made it her mission to get him to do so. Together they stepped out of the water.

They traversed the moonlit woods with the rest of the crowd, some of whom engaged Raven in conversation about his experiences with Christianity thus far, and some of whom avoided him entirely. Several wanted to discuss his intervention two nights earlier when the tent pole fell. Mina ran up to him and didn't let go of his leg until he picked her up and carried her along as he walked among the crowd.

Calandra smiled. Everything was—

Garrett. Oh, no.

She'd run off with Raven again and left Garrett behind, even after apologizing and promising not to do such things anymore. She'd been careless again, and she was certain she had hurt him. Calandra excused herself from the crowd and hung back until she found Garrett haunting the back of the group.

"Why are you back here?" she asked.

"Someone has to keep watch, make sure nothing sneaks up on us in the dark."

"Garrett, I'm sorry," she said. "I've been thoughtless and inconsiderate to you again. I shouldn't have gotten so involved with Raven's baptism. It wasn't my place to do so."

Garrett raised his bushy red eyebrows. "Do you really mean that?"

Calandra nodded. "I'm so very sorry. Please forgive me?"

He didn't say anything at first, but then he took her hands in his. "I forgive you. You have a big heart, and I know you were just trying to help Raven. I can't stay mad at you for that."

Calandra beamed. Sure, Garrett could be a little brusque, a little ornery at times, but he always managed to impress her in the end.

"I do my best."

"We'd better get going so we don't get lost on the way back home," Calandra said.

Garrett shook his head. "Don't worry about that. I know these woods inside and out. You're safe with me."

Calandra eyed him and released his hands. "Even so, you and I shouldn't be out here alone. Come, now. Let's catch up to the others."

"I'll be right behind you," Garrett said. When she showed him a look of confusion and concern, he added, "Like I said, I want to make sure no one sneaks up on us in the dark."

"What if someone sneaks up on you?"

He shrugged. "I've got God on my side. I'll be fine."

Calandra scurried away and caught up to the back fringe of the crowd. Garrett strolled after the group, brooding in the darkness.

They may not see who Raven really was, but Garrett did. And he would do something about it.

Chapter 12

A fabulous array of Italian entrées, delicious desserts, and warm, savory bread tempted Raven's palate. After the baptism, Raven reluctantly tried another bite of the feast that Maria and Angelica had prepared for the congregants. Surprisingly, it didn't turn to ash on his tongue.

Somehow Raven could taste it all. Every bite was a new sensation, a new adventure. What's more, he ate enough of everything that he even felt full afterward, a feeling he'd not experienced since before he'd turned—a feeling almost as satisfying as when he'd consumed his fill of blood.

Human life packed the inside of the Zambini house and spilled out onto their lawn, which Luco and Garrett had lit with a variety of scattered oil lamps and torches under the moonlight. No longer a specter haunting the fringes, Raven moved through the crowd as one of them.

It seemed as though everyone wanted to talk to him, but their erroneous notions of the glamorous, thrilling life of vampires churned his stomach. They had no concept of the countless people he'd killed and turned, of the lives he'd ruined, of the atrocities he'd committed because of his curse. They just didn't understand. He hoped they never would.

The crowd didn't begin to thin until late into the night. Raven stood in the Zambini family's kitchen with half a glass of what Maria called "lemonade" in his hand. He'd drained four of them in the last fifteen minutes, but he slowed down when he noticed Garrett eyeing him from across the room.

Raven couldn't help it, though. He hadn't tasted anything like it in almost a century.

A hand touched his shoulder.

"Are you enjoying yourself?" Luco asked.

Raven nodded. "Everyone is very friendly, and I can taste the food a lot more than I could last night."

"Does it seem to fill you up?"

"I don't think I'll need to drink any blood, if that's what you're asking," Raven replied.

Luco smiled. "I'm happy to hear that. The size of the crowd didn't bother you, did it?"

"No, I'm alright," Raven said.

"Good. I don't want you to feel overwhelmed."

"I'm not used to crowds, but this was actually kind of nice. I don't feel as—" Raven hesitated. Could he say it in front of Luco? "—alone."

"I know what you mean." Luco squeezed his shoulder. "I didn't always have a family, you know. It wasn't until I found Christ that I realized I didn't have to wander this world on my own. When I found a community like ours, that was the first time I really knew I belonged. That's what you need."

Raven nodded. "It's a good feeling."

"It sure is." Luco smiled again. "Look, I've been meaning to talk about something with you. Maria and I spoke, and we'd like to offer you a place with us. In our home. Long-term."

"Like the arrangement you have with Garrett?"

Luco nodded. "Something like that."

"Hm." Raven sipped his lemonade, then took a big gulp.

"I understand it's a big decision, but at the very least, can I persuade you to stay with us for the rest of tonight and throughout the day tomorrow? Think of it as a test to see whether or not it will work out."

"Uh…" Raven glanced at the sky through a nearby window. Luco's offer was kind, but… "I think I'd better get home, actually."

"Where do you live?"

Raven glanced out the window again. "East of here, maybe in the next county. I never really thought to look for it on a map, so I'm not sure exactly how far it is. It's hard to keep track of distance when you're flying overhead or running on all fours to avoid roads."

Luco laughed. "That's alright. Should you take us up on our offer I'm sure we can find our way there with a horse and cart."

"Where?"

The voice came from behind them, and Raven turned. Calandra stood there next to Garrett. She smiled, but Garrett displayed the same old sullen frown and narrowed eyes.

The sweet excitement in Raven's chest dropped into the pit

of his stomach, now sour with disappointment at the sight of Calandra's hand clasping Garrett's. It shouldn't have bothered him, though—she and Garrett were courting, and Raven had only known her for two nights.

Still, even a welcoming crowd couldn't quell some types of loneliness.

"My home," Raven said.

"And where is that?" Garrett asked.

Raven squinted at him. "Nowhere near here."

Garrett raised an eyebrow. "I'd be very interested to see where a vampire lives."

"You're not missing anything." Raven scanned the room and realized that only he and the Zambini family, half of whom littered the family room furniture with their sleeping, motionless bodies, remained from the once-burgeoning crowd. "Well, I should go. It will be morning soon, and you know how that goes."

"No, I don't." Garrett stared at Raven, his jaw as hard as the disdain in his light brown eyes. "Enlighten me."

"Garrett." Calandra scowled at him.

"Don't worry about it." Raven held up his hand and set his empty lemonade glass on the dinner table. "I'm leaving."

"When will we see you again?" Luco asked.

Raven turned back. "When's your next tent meeting?"

"Tomorrow night."

"I guess I'll see you then."

Luco, Calandra, Garrett, Dante, and Maria followed Raven

outside. He waved goodbye to them again and then extended his arms in the shape of a cross. After a moment of stillness, he opened his eyes and glanced back at them.

The Zambini family members stood there, watching him. Garrett folded his arms.

Why hadn't he transformed into a bat? He should have been mid-flight already, soaring through the cool night air toward his home beyond the forest. Instead, he stood there with his arms outstretched like an imbecile because nothing was happening.

Maybe he should morph into a wolf instead. He tipped forward onto the ground and caught himself on all fours, ready to thread his way through the trees on nimble, padded feet. Again, nothing happened. He remained in human form.

Had he given up his shape-shifting powers in the river? Was that part of what he'd sacrificed for eternal life?

Raven snuck another peek back at the Zambini family. They all smiled at him, minus Garrett. Did they realize what he was trying to do? What he could no longer do?

Back on his feet, Raven faced them, his cheeks warm. "Well, I'm done stretching. I'll see you all tomorrow night."

They nodded and waved at him, and Dante said, "Bye."

Luco eyed him, and Garrett did too. If Raven couldn't shift into a bat or a wolf then mist was definitely out of the question. No sense in even trying.

He turned to the forest and walked in, just like any normal human would.

Raven's casual pace became a sprint when he noticed the first rays of sunlight creeping through the trees as he traversed the forest. If the sun rose while he was still outside…

No, he wouldn't let it happen. He'd make it back to his home in time. He was close.

Wasn't he?

He didn't know for sure. The scenery had blown by so quickly when he'd traveled this path—if he was even on the right path—as a wolf. Flying overhead as a bat or as mist was even easier—he'd just head east and look for his home from the air and make course corrections while en route.

This was different. Much harder. And now, due to his new faith and his baptism, much more dangerous.

Three nights. That was all it took for him to give up one of his greatest, most useful vampiric powers in exchange for the restoration of his soul. Three nights.

Now, as the third of those three nights drew to a close, Raven wondered if the same God into whom he'd been baptized would allow the sun to reduce him to a mound of ash and dust.

Luco had said God was merciful. Raven would soon find out.

The heels of his boots plodded the hard earth as he ran. The next thing he knew, he toppled forward and landed facedown on a bare patch of ground. Raven looked back and saw his left foot ensnared by a thick exposed root from a towering oak tree.

Dirt caked his lips, and he spat out what little had found its way inside his mouth. No time to lament his soiled clothes—not with the sun rising so soon. He recovered his footing and continued.

He recognized a pear-shaped boulder and a nearby rocky crag in a small opening between the trees, both landmarks that confirmed he was on the right path. Just a few minutes later he reached a familiar clearing.

The top of his mansion jutted above the tree line. He would be home soon—hopefully not too late.

Only the clearing and a garrison of trees separated Raven from his home, and he traversed them both with speed and precision. There, towering in front of him, his old mansion beckoned him to enter and sleep the day away.

But as he knifed through the trees he realized that the entire mansion, including the front door, was already drenched with golden morning sunlight.

Raven stood in the shadow of the trees. He couldn't stay in the forest all day. Eventually the sun would loom overhead and burn him up around noon. If he dug into the ground or hid under something to avoid the sun, then he risked being found by someone.

Worse yet, fatigue had begun to set in. Whenever he'd tried to stay up during the day, he couldn't. Tiredness overwhelmed him and he had to sleep. He *had* to. If he didn't make it home soon, he'd be sleeping in the woods instead.

Really, he had only one choice: charge forward. If he circled to the back door he'd have to run across an even longer stretch of sun-soaked lawn to get there. He had no idea how fast sunlight could turn him to ash, but it didn't matter. If he didn't make it inside, he'd perish anyway.

Front door it was.

Raven's strong legs propelled him forward. Twenty more steps and he'd be safe.

The burn started on the back of his neck and spread down his back to his legs.

Ten steps to go and he was running through a blazing oven.

Five and he realized he didn't have time to open the door.

He lowered his shoulder and slammed into the door with all of his might. The hinges shrieked and the door thudded to the floor, kicking up a plume of dust. Raven rolled away from the sunlight that poured several feet into his home.

That's when he noticed his robe had caught on fire.

Raven's flesh boiled under his seared skin as he rolled around on the floor. He clawed at the robe and tore off one of the sleeves, searing his hand in the process. He ripped the rest of the robe from his body and flung it away. The robe landed near a grand, curved staircase in a smoldering heap.

Raven cringed and stood to his feet, bare-chested, his body a patchwork of pale skin and charred black burns, but he'd survived. His front door had not, but perhaps he could repair it after today's sun set. In the meantime, he propped it up in its spot in the doorframe to fill the empty space, careful not to expose himself to the sunlight again.

Raven headed toward his basement door. He locked the door behind him with a key hanging on the inside and descended the archaic staircase into the darkness.

The black labyrinth of a basement could consume an unwelcome guest in no time, but Raven knew his way through the maze and the series of doors, all with heavy locks and corresponding keys that only he could access. Finally he arrived in the basement's innermost chamber where his walnut-brown coffin beckoned him to come and rest.

Rest.

He locked the final door and hung the key on a nailhead, then crawled into his coffin. The plush red pillowing inside had long since faded and torn, but it still made for comfortable sleep. He closed the coffin's heavy lid and darkness swallowed him.

Perhaps he wouldn't move in with the Zambini family right away after all. Sleeping in a coffin felt so nice.

A lone soul stood at the edge of the forest that surrounded Raven's mansion. He'd stalked the vampire's footsteps from the Zambini family's home and he'd seen Raven go inside. Now he knew where Raven lived, a piece of information that could prove useful in the future.

He knew these woods, and he'd remember this location. He evaporated into the forest as silently as he'd emerged.

Chapter 13

Marshal Flax reread the chicken-scratch note in his hands for the fourth time since he'd received it that morning.

Marshal Flax,

In light of recent events I felt obligated to send you this letter. Perhaps you are familiar with the Zambini family. They hold nightly tent meetings for religious purposes in places throughout the county. The nature of their meetings does not concern me, and it is not the purpose for this letter.

There is no easy way to say this, so I will just say it plainly: the Zambini family has welcomed a vampire into their house on multiple occasions, and I believe they will soon allow him to live in their home.

I trust that you will look into this situation at

your earliest opportunity for the protection of our community.

Regards,

A Concerned Citizen

A *vampire*? Living with the Zambini family? Someone was fooling with Marshal's imagination. It was some sort of sick joke. Worse than sick—*depraved*.

Marshal had never met the Zambini family, but the few people he'd talked to since receiving the letter had only said good things about them. Sure, they lived to promote their faith, but they had never done anyone any harm.

Quite the contrary, folks in the community said they'd heard of dozens—maybe *hundreds* of people whom the Zambini family had helped in some way or another, all within just a few months of living in the area, and not just in religious ways either. They actually went out and helped people by giving away money, or feeding people, or taking in the occasional stray—

Marshal looked up. What if the author of this note was telling the truth? What if they actually had taken in a vampire? A *real* vampire?

He'd faced death dozens of times in his line of work. He'd seen violence that would churn most men's stomachs but didn't so much as faze him. But the combination of this note and a 35-year-old memory made Marshal shudder.

He'd already made plans for the next week or so, plans that involved following up on some leads regarding Harry Deutsch's whereabouts, so the letter would have to wait. Still, hoax or not, that shudder wouldn't leave him alone. Marshal would personally visit the Zambini family's home soon to see if there was any truth to the letter.

"Get out of my sight." Harry spat on the floor at the feet of a large, gruff man with a thick brown beard and a wide-brimmed hat.

The man gave a slight nod, then turned and headed straight to the door. Maybe he wasn't right for Harry's crew, but at least he followed orders. Within seconds, the door shut behind him.

"Another miss?" Steve scooted his barstool closer to Harry's.

Harry nodded at Steve, then at the bartender, who refilled Harry's shot glass with whiskey. "Another imbecile."

"Jim's an imbecile too, but you keep him around." Steve tilted his head to his left, toward where Jim stood with a busty barmaid under each arm, laughing.

"He's also the most loyal man I've ever met," Harry said. "Aside from you, of course."

"Are you drunk already?" Steve asked.

Harry raised his eyebrows. "What makes you ask that?"

"You only compliment me when you're drunk."

"I guess I'm drunk, then."

"You really expect to find and correctly assess a man's

qualifications to fill Mick's spot while you're drunk?"

Harry shrugged, then nodded at the bartender again. He drained the next shot glass and said, "I was drunk when I recruited you."

"Don't remind me. You threw up on my boots. You were drunk when you hired Mick, you know. Your success ratio isn't very good."

"Found Jim when I was drunk too." Harry chuckled. "Two out of three ain't bad."

"If you say so."

"Hey." Harry pointed a finger at Steve. "Mick was trustworthy until he got a better offer. Well, he *thought* he got a better offer. I bet he'd have changed his tune if he knew he'd end up with my bowie knife in his back."

Steve huffed. "I sure would."

"Planning to betray me too?"

Steve shook his head. "Not a chance. I may not favor violence like you and Jim, but I'm smart. I'd never get away with turning on you, no matter how good the money was."

"You got that right." Harry noticed a set of steamy blue eyes sizing him up from across the room. He returned the favor, then leaned in near Steve. "If I can't find a man to join us, how would you feel about a lady?"

Steve scrunched his eyebrows down. "You're not serious, are you?"

Harry laughed, perhaps a little too loudly, but he didn't care.

"You don't like the idea?"

"Not unless she's smarter than the three of us combined, can outshoot us, will work for free—" Steve glanced over his shoulder at the girl Harry was ogling. "—and if she's ugly as the devil's rear-end."

"What?" Harry snarled at him. "Why on God's earth would you say *that*?"

"Because a girl like that would actually be of use to us, and she wouldn't be a distraction. You have enough of those already."

Harry waved him off, then nodded to the bartender again. He slurped the whiskey down to the very last drop in his shot glass and tossed it over his shoulder. He savored the sound of it shattering on the stone floor behind him then motioned toward the girl with his head. "If she isn't what we're looking for, I think we'll fly as a trio instead of as a quartet. Have a good night, Steve."

Steve caught Harry's arm and anchored him in place. He may not enjoy violence like Harry did, but he was just as strong. "You know every job will be that much more difficult with one less body."

Harry cast a pair of long glares at both Steve's hand and his eyes, then he yanked his arm free from Steve's grip. "Think of it this way: one less man means a three-way split on the take."

"If you say so. No more train jobs, though. We don't have the manpower."

"We don't need to do train jobs anyway. The pickings are ripe enough here." Harry winked at the blue-eyed vixen in the corner. "Oh, yes. Very ripe indeed."

He started toward her again, but Steve caught him by his arm a second time.

"What are you talking about?"

Harry clamped his free hand around Steve's throat and shoved him against the nearest wall. "If you lay a hand on me again I'll cut it off and put it in your coat pocket before you even have a chance to complain about it."

Steve gulped. "Sorry."

Harry let him go, straightened his coat, and cracked his neck. "There's an evangelist nearby, maybe a half-day's ride south of here. Just moved into the county a few months back. I hear he takes in a fine sum of money from his parishioners every time he holds a tent meeting. Saving it up to start a church or something equally as noble."

"How often does he bring the money in?"

"Almost every night. He takes off one night per week, usually Mondays."

"So we hit him on a Sunday night, then?"

Harry nodded and grinned. "He should have a whole week's worth of cash just sitting around. Maybe more. Even if he doesn't it'll still be a quick, easy score. Ain't like a preacher and his family are gonna offer much resistance. Goes against their faith, after all. We'll head out there in a few weeks, once the heat from Mick's death cools off."

"Won't need four guys for that."

"That's why I'm in no hurry to find someone else." Harry

glanced at his prey in the corner. "Now if you'll excuse me, I have a thorough interview to conduct."

Three weeks passed and summer's approach expanded the hours of daylight so the Zambinis didn't see Raven as much, including that night at dinner. Luco cleared his throat and leaned over the table. "Now that we all have full bellies thanks to your mother's and Angelica's fine cooking—"

"And mine!" Mina displayed her tiny, toothy smile and the small sprig of broccoli that stuck between two of her front teeth.

"Yes, and yours, Mina. I'd like to hold a family discussion about Raven and his future in relation to our family," Luco said. "It's been a few weeks since he first showed up at our tent meeting, and now we're reaching a turning point in our relationship with him."

"Is Raven gonna stay with us?" Mina asked. "I really like him."

"That's what we're here to talk about." Luco scanned the family room and his eyes met those of each of his children. "I've intentionally sent Garrett on an errand because I didn't want his opinion affecting our decision. After all, this is our house, and he is still just a guest here, at least until he marries Calandra. Also, whatever we decide, I'd like to be the one to share the news to him. Any questions so far?"

A few heads shook, and Maria smiled at him. They had discussed this issue again last night, and she had expressed a sense of peace regarding Raven joining them as a semi-permanent guest.

"How would you like to have Raven come to live with us?"

Mina raised her hand. "I do."

Dante and Angelica nodded.

Anthony said, "I do too, but isn't he a vampire?"

Luco glanced at Maria, who shrugged. "Yes, he is. Do you know what that means?"

"Yes. Dante told me."

Luco eyed his oldest son.

"You never told me not to." Dante leaned back in his chair.

Luco squinted at him. "You've got me there, I guess."

"What's a vam-pire?" Mina asked.

Anthony's eyes lit up. "It's basically the same as a real person, except—"

"That's not what matters," Luco said. "It just means he's different than us."

"He doesn't seem different," Mina said.

Luco smiled and knelt down in front of her. "No, he doesn't, does he? I suppose that's my point. Raven is like a lot of other people we know in so many ways, but the fact that he's a vampire makes him different. If Raven comes to live with us, our lives will have to change to adapt to him being a little different than us. Are you ready for that type of change?"

Calandra folded her arms. "I'm worried about what Garrett will think of this. I know he's a guest too, but I can't help but think he'll be upset about Raven moving in."

"I know what you mean, and that's why I wanted to talk to

him in person, alone, about this." Luco glanced at Maria, who gave him a slight nod. "He's learning how to minister to people. Part of that is living Christ's example and following his commands. This is an opportunity for us to both help Raven and for Garrett to model his faith. My hope is that he can use this experience in the future when he's a minister."

"I don't know." Calandra shook her head. "If I know Garrett, he won't like this one bit."

Luco nodded. "Like I said, I'll worry about Garrett. I'd rather know what *you* think."

"What about the congregation? What will they think if we take in a—someone like Raven?" Calandra asked.

Luco glanced at Maria. "I'm not so concerned with what the congregation will think. We'd be setting a good example for them, and they'll either accept it or they won't. I'm more concerned with whether or not you feel safe when Raven is around."

"He doesn't bother me or frighten me. I don't think he'd ever hurt me, or any of us, really." She bit her lower lip and looked at the ceiling. "So I guess I wouldn't mind if he stayed with us."

"That's not the type of answer I need, Calandra." Luco touched her shoulder. "I need a yes or a no. If any one of you objects to him staying with us, then it won't happen. Understand?"

The kids nodded and murmured in the affirmative.

He focused on Dante. "So let's go around the room and you can give me your decision. Dante, what'll it be?"

"Is he going to have to share a room with Anthony and me?"

Luco glanced at Maria again. "We haven't figured out all of the logistics yet, but he won't be staying in your room."

"Then I vote yes," Dante said.

"Me too," Anthony said.

Luco chuckled. "At least we know what's important to you guys."

"Well, I already have to share with Antonius here."

"It's *Anthony*," Anthony said. "How would you like it if I called you 'Dantonius?'"

Dante shrugged. "That actually sounds pretty good. Go ahead."

Anthony's head swiveled to Maria. "*Moooooommmm?*"

"Easy, guys," Luco said. "We're not here to argue about your names, your room, or anything except Raven living with us. Stay on topic."

Anthony pointed at Dante, who sat back with his arms folded. "But—"

"Stay on topic," Luco repeated. "Angelica?"

"I like Raven. He's nice, and he always compliments my cooking when I help Mama." She smiled a big, beautiful smile that reminded Luco of Maria. "I vote yes."

"What about you, Mina?"

She gave an exaggerated nod. "I like Raven too."

"Alright." Luco grinned and refocused on Calandra. "It's all up to you, Calandra. What's your decision?"

She bit her lip again.

Chapter 14

Wood creaked in the darkness as Raven pushed the lid of his coffin open.

Another day's been slept away; another night to hunt our prey.

But no longer—that urge had become anathema to him now that he'd decided to live for Christ. He'd traded immortality for eternal life, and he no longer needed blood to survive—at least so far. Perhaps his new faith and reliance on God really had set him free.

Sometimes—actually most of the time—he still didn't believe it, even after almost a month. Then again, a month with Jesus wouldn't erase almost a hundred years of vampirism. It all seemed so much harder and more confusing when he was alone with his own thoughts. Doubt bombarded him, and guilt churned in his gut.

You're not forgiven, his thoughts whispered. *You're the same as before, only weaker than ever. Your soul is damned and there's nothing you, Luco, or even God himself can do about it.*

This place, its darkness, the deep shadows—none of it supported his new faith. Neither did sleeping in a coffin. It was all too familiar.

Suffocating.

Raven let the coffin's lid slam shut behind him. He stormed toward the innermost door, twisted the skeleton key in the lock, and ventured into the labyrinth of his dark basement. He didn't stop until he flung the basement door open and stepped onto the marble floor on the ground level of his mansion.

A stark ray of orange sunlight knifed through a crack between the thick curtains that covered the towering windows on the west wall. Raven recoiled back into the darkness the instant the sunlight touched his skin.

See? You're no different. You haven't changed. You sleep all day and haunt the landscape every night. You're a monster. A menace.

He'd awakened too early, but not by much. From the extreme angle and color of the light he knew night would fall soon, and dusk even sooner. Until then he'd have to reside within the shadows, in the presence of his own dark thoughts.

———

"You *can't* keep including him." Garrett yanked on a large rope and then secured it to the ground via a thick wooden stake. "He's too dangerous. We've done our duty. He's converted, and we baptized him. I think it's time he moves on."

Luco shook his head. "I disagree. He's shown a clear willingness to accept instruction and to grow in his faith since his conversion. We're called to make disciples as well as sharing the Gospel, Garrett."

"But he's still a vampire at his core."

Garrett pounded the stake into the ground with zeal as if it was Raven's chest. Sure, he probably shouldn't think like that, but Raven didn't have a soul anyway. He was a demon in dead human skin, a threat to Garrett and to the Zambini family.

If only they could see what he saw, what he'd seen before. Then they'd understand.

"He may not be drinking blood anymore, but he's still nefarious," Garrett said.

"Nefarious? What about him do you find nefarious?"

Garrett leaned close to Luco. "Haven't you seen the way he looks at Calandra? His eyes are always full of animalistic lust around her. I find it very unsettling."

Luco chuckled.

"What are you laughing at?" Garrett's grip on the mallet tightened. "I'm being serious and you're laughing at me."

"I'm sorry, Garrett. It's just that I haven't seen anything of the sort."

Garrett glared at him. "Then why are you laughing?"

"I think I know why you're so adamant that he stays away from Calandra." Luco tugged a piece of the tent fabric and secured it.

"And what is that?"

"Perhaps it's best that you discern that on your own."

Garrett pointed the mallet at him. "But you *have* noticed him interacting with Calandra."

"Not in the way you're thinking. I don't think he's doing anything questionable in relation to my daughter. If he was, I'd have noticed, and I would've already taken action to ensure that it stopped." Luco resumed his work. "But like I said, I haven't seen anything of the sort."

Garrett scowled. *Maybe you're not paying close enough attention.*

"And trust me." Luco nodded to the mallet in Garrett's hand. "I would bring the hammer down on him faster than you could blink if I thought he was compromising my daughter. At this point, I still have far more reason to protect her than you do. She may be your wife someday, but she's always been and always will be my little girl. That's a bond no man will ever sever, and I assure you that Raven hasn't so much as hinted that he's trying to do so."

Garrett shook his head. "I disagree. He keeps staring at her. I don't like it."

"Have you talked to him about it?" Luco asked.

"What?" That was the last thing Garrett wanted to do. "No. Why would I?"

Luco raised an eyebrow. "The answer is obvious. He might not even realize what he's doing, and he certainly doesn't know it's making you uneasy. You should talk to him."

"Well—I've talked to Calandra about it."

"That was my next suggestion. What result did that yield?"

"Not much. She resisted at first, then sort of agreed, but now I feel like she's becoming friends with him, even though I explicitly told her she wasn't to associate with him or even speak to him. Plus you keep including him at every—"

"You *told* her?" Luco raised both of his eyebrows and squared his body toward Garrett. "You mean you didn't ask?"

Garrett tilted his head. "No. I told her."

"I'm surprised she didn't haul off and knock you unconscious right then and there. If I tried to give an order like that to Maria she'd thrash me so bad I'd have a bump on the back of my head for a month. Italian women do *not* like to be bossed around," Luco said.

Out of respect for Luco, Garrett restrained himself from rolling his eyes, but he folded his arms anyway.

"A little advice for you: don't try to *tell* Calandra anything. Ordering her or any other woman around isn't going to get you the result you want." Luco pointed his index finger at Garrett. "And for the record, just because you're courting her does *not* mean you get to marry her. Even if you do end up married, I won't allow you to speak to my daughter that way."

"I'm not trying to order her around." Garrett extended his hand toward Luco. "I'm just trying to look out for her. But even though I talked to her about it—multiple times, in fact—she still won't leave him alone."

"That's why you should talk to Raven. You may make more progress with him."

Garrett clenched his jaw. *Or not.* "Yeah. Maybe."

"Whatever you decide to do, don't become jealous. It can

lead you to some very dark places, and you might end up doing something you'll regret."

"This would be so much easier if Raven would just leave." Garrett tightened another rope around a tent stake and smacked the stake's head with his mallet. *It would be easier if I was pounding the stake into Raven's chest.*

"You can't hope for that," Luco said. "He's basically a part of our family now, just like you, and he's making real progress. I could even see him walking around in daylight within the next six months if he to continues to follow Christ. Maybe less."

That was *not* what Garrett wanted to hear. He scowled.

"I'd think that you of all people would know what it feels like to be ostracized, alone, and friendless. When we first found you, all you cared about was where your next drink came from, and look at you now. You haven't so much as touched alcohol in over a year."

Garrett bristled at Luco's reminder of his past. Had he done the things Garrett had done, had he seen what Garrett had seen, Luco would have sought comfort where he could find it, too. For Garrett it had been the bottle.

"You and I both know there's a big difference between drinking blood and just plain drinking."

"Is there? Both were life-controlling addictions, and you both overcame them with Jesus' help. How is his sin any different than yours?"

Garrett frowned. He could argue this all night if he wanted, but Luco knew the Bible better than Garrett probably ever would.

Luco would always have some sort of response that Garrett couldn't refute, and, like it or not, Luco had the moral high ground because he'd elected to show Raven God's mercy instead of God's justice.

It just wasn't worth the effort. He wouldn't change Luco's mind no matter what he said.

"I'm sorry if you don't like it, but at some point you're going to have to accept that Raven is being sanctified, just like you were. Sure, the process may look a bit different, but that's part of what makes it so wonderful. God is restoring and cleansing Raven's soul. As a pastor you need to receive all people. Jesus spent a lot of his time with sinners, tax collectors, and other lowly, undesirable people. We need to follow His example."

Did Luco really mean to compare Garrett's drinking to Raven's forfeiture of his soul? There was no comparison. "Jesus didn't have to deal with any vampires wandering around."

Luco shrugged. "We don't know that for sure, but even if you're right, he died on the cross for all of them, just like he died for you and me. We're called to show that love to all people, not just the ones we like."

Garrett bit his tongue.

"I think you should go talk to Raven about your concerns. I imagine he'll want to set you at ease." Luco motioned toward the road. "Go on. The sun is setting. By the time you get back to the house, he'll probably be there. Take one of the wagons. Dante, Anthony, and I can finish up here, and when you're done you can bring the wagon back so we can load everything up at the end of the service."

Garrett frowned again but decided he might as well take Luco up on his offer, so he mounted the wagon and steered the horses toward the road. When he arrived back at the Zambini family's house, the sun had already disappeared beyond the horizon, and the last few rays of light peeked over the edge. Raven would arrive soon if he hadn't already.

Either way, Garrett still didn't want to talk to him.

He found Calandra inside the house. "Good evening."

She smiled at him. "Good evening, Garrett. I thought you were setting up the tent with my father and brothers."

Garrett cleared his throat. "I was, but he sent me back here."

"Why? Is something wrong?"

"Oh, no. Nothing's wrong." Garrett sighed. "Alright, there is something wrong."

Calandra started to say something but the front door opened and Raven walked inside. She smiled at him and it churned Garrett's stomach. "Good evening, sleepyhead."

Raven nodded to them both. "Good evening, Calandra. Garrett."

"Did you sleep well?" she asked.

Garrett rolled his eyes. Calandra had forgotten about him already. He tugged on her arm. "Would you excuse us, Raven? We need to talk."

"Easy." She wiggled out of his grasp. "You're hurting my arm. I was talking to Raven, you know."

"It's alright, Calandra." Raven glanced at the kitchen. "I need to eat breakfast anyway. I'll catch up with you at the tent meeting."

"Thanks," Garrett said. "But we don't need your permission."

Outside, she began chastising him for his behavior, but she didn't get very far.

"Just stop, will you?" Garrett growled through gritted teeth. He pointed at her. "I'm sick and tired of *your* behavior. You're always spending time with Raven and never with me. I just watched him eye you like a wild dog sizing up a piece of venison. This has to stop, Calandra."

She folded her arms. "I don't know what you're talking about."

Garrett wanted to curse, but he restrained himself. "Don't pretend with me. You have consistently violated my trust when you said you wouldn't."

"Is this about Raven again? I thought we were past this."

"It's about *us*, Calandra," Garrett said. "Not about him."

"He needs a friend right now," she said.

"You can't be that friend. You're a girl, I'm courting you. It's not appropriate for you to be close friends with someone of the opposite sex."

"Maybe I wouldn't have to be so close with him if *you* would do it instead."

Garrett shook his head. "Whether or not I'm his friend has no bearing on your relationship with him. You're just using it as an excuse to put the blame on my shoulders instead of admitting that your friendship with him is inappropriate."

"We talked about this already." Calandra rubbed her forehead. "Three times. Remember?"

"Then I'm obviously not getting through to you." Garrett leaned against the outer wall of the house. "You even apologized for spending too much time with him, for getting too involved. Now, when I tell you that I think you're still spending too much time with him, you get angry and offended. What's *really* going on, Calandra?"

"I don't like what you're insinuating." She turned away from him, and the moonlight accentuated her high cheekbones and soft face.

"Why?" Garrett's voice rose. "Because I'm right?"

"It's because you're wrong. Dead wrong."

"*Dead* is the key word. It's what you'll be if you keep spending time with him."

Calandra stared at him, her mouth open. "Did you just threaten me?"

"No. I *warned* you. Raven is dangerous. He wants to drink your blood and kill you. I see the same lust in his eyes every night and it terrifies me. I don't want to lose you."

"He's harmless, Garrett," she said. "Aside from those chickens he killed after he ate Mama's pasta sauce, have you ever seen him hurt anything? Or anyone?"

Garrett hadn't considered that. "No, but I bet he had

something to do with the woman they found dead in her smoldering house a month back."

Calandra shook her head. "There was barely anything left of her or her house. No one knows who did it. Besides, we've all heard reports of bandits wandering around and attacking homes. It's much more likely that they're responsible."

"Even so, are you willing to take that chance?"

"Garrett." She spread her arms wide. "What are we arguing about?"

"I'm sick of you spending so much time with Raven and not with me, alright?" Garrett glared at her. "I see you walking around, hauling him behind you with his dead hand in yours. You hang all over him every chance you get."

"You don't know what you're talking about." She folded her arms and looked away.

"Then *he* might as well be courting you."

She turned back and eyed him. "Is that really how you feel?"

Garrett nodded and his stomach twisted even tighter. He'd finally found a way to get through to her, so he'd follow this trail as far as it led. "Yes. You've forgotten about me."

Her angry gaze softened. "I didn't mean to make you feel that way."

Had he won her over? Maybe his lighter approach was working. "You barely ever hold my hand, but you run around hand-in-hand with him all the time. I keep wondering how long it will be until I catch you kissing him, or worse."

Calandra raised her eyebrows and shook her head. "No, no. It's nothing like that."

Then why are you blushing? "You haven't given me reason to believe otherwise. We've been courting for over a year now. It seems like we'll never get married, even though I've asked you repeatedly—"

"That's a totally different subject, Garrett." Calandra folded her arms again. "I promised you that I'd accept your proposal when I know my father approves—"

"I'm sure he does." Well, sort of. Probably not after their most recent conversation, but… "I can go ask him right now if you want."

"—and when I feel I'm mature enough to handle marriage." When Garrett frowned at her, she said, "I'm only nineteen years old, Garrett. You're already twenty-two. You're more ready for marriage than I am, so be patient with me, please. It won't be much longer."

"Then why don't we set a date? At least we'll know how much longer we have to wait."

Calandra shook her head. "I can't do that right now. I'm sorry."

Garrett glared at her and clenched his jaw tight.

After a deep sigh, she said, "Look, I'm sorry if I've given you the wrong impression. I'll try to spend less time with Raven, and I'll spend more time with you. Is that what you want?"

"It's exactly what I want." Garrett gave her a half-smile. "For now."

She took his hand in hers. "The rest will come in time."

In time. Sooner, rather than later, he hoped. "You know, you're very pretty."

Calandra blushed again. "Thank you."

The knot in his stomach morphed into an urge that swelled in his chest. He wanted to reach out, take her in his arms, and kiss her, but he couldn't. Not until they were married.

Through gritted teeth, he said, "I need to get back to the tent. I'll see you there tonight."

"Alright." She gave his hand a squeeze and let it go. "See you then."

He hopped on the wagon and guided the horses back to the road.

None of this would have happened if Raven hadn't shown up and gotten involved in their lives. Before Raven's arrival, Garrett was certain that Calandra would agree to his proposal within a matter of weeks or maybe a couple of months at the most, but now her desire to marry him seemed as distant as the crescent moon that hovered overhead.

Twenty minutes later the wagon arrived back at the tent. Luco greeted Garrett with a smile and the horses with some water. "Well, how did it go? Did you see Raven? Did you talk to him?"

How could Garrett answer that without lying? "We sorted things out."

"Good." Luco offered his arm, but Garrett hopped down from the wagon on his own.

"And I think it will have a positive impact on how soon Calandra and I can get married."

Luco chuckled. "Oh, I wouldn't worry too much about that."

The same message from both father and daughter. Had they already talked about it beforehand? "Why do you say that?"

"We still have some time before I allow you to take my daughter from me. I have plans for you in the meantime."

Garrett swallowed. More ministry? Some kind of test to ensure he was worthy of Calandra's hand in marriage? He almost didn't want to ask. "Like what?"

"Well, since you and Raven worked things out, I figure that when he moves in he can share a room with you."

Garrett's eyes widened.

Chapter 15

The next night, Raven showed up at the tent meeting in the early evening, not long after the sun had set. He'd agreed to show up a bit earlier to help Luco and his family set everything up, and they'd agreed to start a bit later so he could join them for the entirety of the service. When Raven arrived, Luco approached him from the tent.

"Good evening, Raven." Luco smiled. "Glad you could make it."

"My pleasure. What would you like me to do?" Raven asked. "I haven't lost any of my strength yet. Do you need me to move something heavy?"

"Actually, I don't. We're working on securing the tent right now, so that's what I need help with. Why don't you come with me?" Luco led Raven over to one of the tent's corners. He bent down and scooped up two tools, then turned back to Raven.

In his hands, Luco held a large mallet and a thick wooden tent stake. Raven's heart beat faster.

After staring at them for a long time, Luco extended them to Raven, which quelled the mounting tension in his chest. Wide-eyed, Raven took them in his hands.

"I need you to secure these ropes to the ground so the tent

doesn't collapse. Make sure they're nice and taut. I'll send Garrett over to help you. Come find me when you're done." Luco patted him on the shoulder again, glanced at the mallet and the stake, and then walked off without so much as acknowledging Raven's confusion.

Raven stared at the tools for even longer than Luco had. Surely Luco realized the effect that these particular items would have on a vampire. They meant death for a second, final time. A quick trip to the damnation that awaited those whose souls are forfeit. Pain and suffering for the rest of eternity.

Now Raven held them in his hands, the wood rough against his palms, ready to secure a tent erected and dedicated to Almighty God, the everlasting enemy of Satan and his followers. Mallets and stakes both killed vampires and furthered the work of Jesus Christ. Similar tools had also nailed Jesus to a cross.

Raven didn't want to fathom how many vampires had been slain over the centuries by tools just like these. The idea set him on edge, but it didn't disturb him nearly as much as considering that perhaps this exact pair had been used to kill a vampire at some point. And how many more vampires would perish in the future because of these very tools?

"Hey," a gruff voice called from behind him. Garrett, also gripping a mallet and a stake. "Are you going to help or not?"

Raven nodded. "Lead the way."

"Good," Garrett said. "We don't have all night."

He turned toward the tent but didn't see Raven raise his left eyebrow. All night was *exactly* what Raven had.

There, at the base of the tent, Raven pulled one of the ropes taut, crouched down to line up the stake between a pre-tied loop in the rope, and swung the mallet.

Marshal Flax was waiting for the Zambini family when they arrived at their home after the evening's tent revival. As they got out of their wagons, Marshal scanned the large family for the supposed vampire.

He ruled out the children immediately. Children couldn't be vampires, right? They were too innocent. Certainly such an abomination couldn't befall a child. He hoped.

No, not the burly red-haired man. He didn't have the look of a vampire—more like a lumberjack. Neither did the young man, probably in his early teens. Even from a distance he could have passed for a younger version of his father.

What about the daughters? He hadn't considered that the vampire might be female—if it even existed in the first place, of course. But no, the letter had identified the vampire as male. Besides, the daughters resembled their mother too closely.

Marshal's eyes locked on another young man who stepped off of the wagon. Except for the little blonde girl and the red-haired lumberjack, the young man's hair color trended the same as everyone else's, but even under the moonlight his pale skin contrasted against the rest of the family's healthy tones.

"Can I help you?" the father asked.

Marshal broke his stare at the pale young man and focused

on the Zambini father. "Good evening. Name's Duke Flax, your County Marshal. How are you all doing this evening?"

"Luco Zambini." Luco shook Marshal's hand. "This is my family. What brings you to our home so late this evening?"

"From what I hear it's the only time I could actually catch you in person, what with your tent meetings every night." Marshal shifted his stance. "Nice home you have here. From what I understand, you haven't been here for long. How did you come to live here, anyway?"

Luco glanced at his wife. "My wife's uncle owns a vineyard north of here. He's done well and he's helping to support our work. If you ever want a good bottle of wine, I'd be happy to introduce you to him. He works wonders with this Californian soil."

"I'll keep that in mind."

"Would you like to come inside?" Luco put his arm around his wife. "I can ask Maria to put on some coffee for us while the children tie up the horses."

"Thank you for the offer, but I'm afraid I have to decline." Marshal nodded to Maria and touched the brim of his Stetson. "It's mighty late, and my bed is calling to me, so I'll be straight with you: I received an anonymous letter a few weeks ago concerning your family."

The kids glanced at each other, as did the lumberjack and the pale young man, but Luco kept his eyes forward.

"Regarding what?"

"This isn't about your tent meetings. Far as I know, you're

not breaking any laws or even agitating anyone. In fact, everyone I talked to had nothing but good things to say about your family."

"Then what's this about?"

"I'm getting to it, Reverend." Marshal held his hands up. "You're not in trouble. I'm merely investigating a rumor—well, more of a legend, actually. A bit of folklore. Probably just a figment of someone's overactive imagination."

Luco shook his head. "You've lost me."

"Remember that letter I received?" Marshal stopped when he noticed the lumberjack rubbing his forehead. "You alright, son?"

"Huh?" the lumberjack replied. "Oh, yes. I'm fine. I just have a headache. That's all."

"Right." Marshal squinted at him.

"Garrett, why don't you go inside and rest?" Maria offered.

"No, no. I'm fine." Garrett folded his arms. "I'd like to know what this is about."

As if you didn't already. Marshal had found his "Concerned Citizen."

"In this letter I received, an anonymous source wrote that you had—you're not going to believe this—" Marshal chuckled. "—a *vampire* living with you."

The pale young man's eyes widened, then shrank to normal again. Bingo. Marshal's heart quickened, but he couldn't be sure. Not yet.

"It's true," Luco said. "He's right here, actually. Raven, quit skulking around in the darkness and introduce yourself to the marshal."

Raven swallowed hard then took a few tentative steps toward the front of the group. He extended his hand to Marshal. "Raven Worth."

"You're a vampire? Really?" When he shook Raven's frigid hand, Marshal regretted the skeptical tone he'd used—and he regretted ever coming to the Zambini house.

"Really."

"And, uh—" Marshal cleared his throat. "—you live here?"

Raven shrugged. "I do now. They took me in. We were actually just about to retrieve my coffin so I can move in."

Everything inside of Marshal screamed for vengeance, for retribution. Such a creature couldn't be allowed to live, not after what his kind had done to Marshal so many years before. If only he'd had a stake in his hands, he'd—

Marshal closed his eyes to fight off the flood of memories drowning his calm. He clenched his fists. "So—give me one reason why I shouldn't arrest you right now."

Luco stepped between Marshal and Raven. "I'll give it to you, Marshal. Raven's been attending our meetings for quite some time now, and he's given his heart to the Lord. In other words, he's on the path to not being a vampire anymore."

Bull.

"Look, Reverend, I've been to my fair share of church services, and I've never heard of anything of the sort. You sure you're Catholics and not some weird cult?"

"Actually, we're not Catholic, but we are Christians."

Marshal squinted at him. "But…you're Italian."

Luco smiled. "They don't always have to go hand-in-hand, Marshal."

"If you say so."

"I'm positive. We follow the whole Gospel of Jesus Christ—*all* of it. We believe that it doesn't matter who you are or what you've done. It only matters who Jesus is and what he's done for us." Luco motioned to Raven. "Raven accepted God's forgiveness through Jesus Christ and his soul is being restored bit-by-bit. He's becoming less of a vampire every day and more of who God wants him to be."

"You really believe that—" Marshal almost used a colorful word, but he censored his tongue for the Zambini children's benefit. "—stuff?"

Luco stared into Marshal's eyes. For a moment it seemed as if he'd peered into Marshal's very soul. "Marshal, I have to believe that God can restore anyone's soul, be they vampire or plain old humans like everyone else."

Marshal squinted and stepped closer to Luco. "There's something very familiar about you, Reverend. Have we met before?"

Luco shook his head, then stopped and tilted it instead. "Come to think of it, I saw you in front of your offices across the street from the mercantile in town back when we moved here a few months ago. I've seen you a few times since then as well, but I'm usually in such a rush that I haven't taken the time to introduce myself."

"You're right." Marshal nodded. Not the stuff of legendary conversations, for sure, but at least it took his mind off of the vampire issue. "I recognize you now. You visit the mercantile at least once a week to buy canned goods. I know just about everyone in the area, and you were a new face. I just never knew who you were."

"Now you know." Luco smiled.

Marshal glanced at Raven again. Hard to keep his mind off of vampires with one standing right in front of him. Oh, to slay him and avenge her death—by proxy, of course. Raven wasn't actually the culprit. Same dark hair and pale skin, but his eyes were green.

No, the one Marshal wanted had brown eyes. Dark brown eyes. Even so, they were all the same. Probably. "You're sure he's harmless? He's found religion?"

"He's found his *Savior*. There's a big difference between the religion of Christianity and a relationship with Christ."

"It all looks the same from where I'm standing."

"Then we're not doing a good enough job of showing you who God is," Luco said. "Calandra, could you hand me my Bible from the seat on the wagon?"

Marshal put up his hand. "Some other time, perhaps. Right now I just need to know one thing." He pointed at Raven. "Is he dangerous?"

Raven glanced at Luco, then back to Marshal. "I haven't tasted blood for a month, now. I used to drink it every night, but I don't need it anymore. I know it sounds impossible, but it's really happening to me."

"You don't seem too happy about it."

Raven lowered his head. "When you've caused as much hurt as I have in my lifetime, there's not much to be happy about."

Luco wrapped his arm around Raven and smiled. "Give it time, son. Paul promised in Philippians 1:6 that 'he which hath begun a good work in you will perform it until the day of Jesus Christ.' In other words, God's not done with you yet."

"That's touching. It really is." Marshal rolled his eyes, stole a glance at Garrett, then refocused on Raven. "Look, if I receive any more complaints, I'm going to have to come back out here, and none of us wants that."

"You shouldn't have to. I want to change," Raven said.

"If you say so. Don't make me regret not staking you to the ground tonight," he said.

When the girls gasped and Luco's eyes widened, Marshal knew he'd taken the conversation too far. Oh, well. He had suffered because of Raven's kind, and offending these people wasn't high on his list of concerns at the moment.

"That'll do for tonight, folks. I'm off. You have a pleasant night."

"Thanks for stopping by," Garrett said.

Marshal eyed Garrett until he turned away, then he leaned in close to Raven. "Not a peep from you, hear me? If I have to come back out here, I won't be nearly as nice next time."

Raven nodded.

As Marshal Flax rode away, Raven's stomach rumbled. The old craving for blood had returned, but not nearly as powerful as it once was. He hoped that some of Maria's cooking would alleviate the lust in his belly.

He also hoped he wouldn't have to see the marshal again.

"The marshal's gone, Harry," Jim whispered. "He rode off back toward town. Do we go in now?"

Harry shook his head. He needed a cigarette, but he knew better than to risk even the tiniest bit of man-made light in the darkness, not with the marshal so nearby. "No. Be patient. We have to wait until the time is right. You brought your bandanas?"

Steve held his up, and Jim replied, "Yeah. What do you mean 'wait until the time is right?' Why don't we go in now?"

"Because the men are leaving. No need to rob a place with three grown men inside when we could just wait until they go. As soon as they leave, *then* we go in. Less resistance that way."

"How do you know they're leaving?" Steve asked.

"Overheard one of them tell the marshal something about retrieving a coffin. Didn't make out much more than that." Harry broke open his double-barreled shotgun to check the ammunition, then eased it shut again. "We only need a few minutes anyway, but I imagine it will take them at least an hour or so."

"Maybe someone died," Steve said.

"Or maybe someone's about to." Jim chuckled.

Harry caught Steve's frown, but he grinned anyway. "Maybe. Hush, now. I don't want to give ourselves away until we waltz through their front door."

Maria's garlic tomato sauce still burned Raven's mouth like a hot pepper, but not nearly as bad as it had that first night at the Zambini family's house. Even so, Raven dared not try any more. No need to drain another three chickens if it burned him again. Better stick to the special foods Maria had made for him.

"You're making progress, Raven," Calandra said.

He indulged himself with a long stare at her soft face and big smile. "If you say so."

"You are," she said. "You're not drinking any blood. You just tried some garlic and it didn't hurt you. You'll be walking around in daylight in no time."

Raven almost choked on his noodles. "Let's not get ahead of ourselves."

"I'm serious," Calandra said. "It could be any day now."

"Maybe," Raven said. "But I doubt it. I think that's probably a long way off. I can't even see my own reflection yet."

"In time, you will," Luco said. "Calandra's right. You're heading the right direction."

"I don't know. I feel like I'm missing something. I feel like I somehow need to make up for the wrong I've done as a vampire."

Luco shook his head. "Jesus died for your sins. His blood

covered your transgressions. He atoned for your sins so you wouldn't have to."

"His *blood*," Raven repeated. "I still find that ironic that His blood is supposed to keep me from drinking everyone else's."

"Blood for blood, Raven," Luco said. "His blood is the substitute for all of ours, yours included. Blood for blood."

Raven poked at his pasta with his fork. "But it didn't cost me anything. I'm cursed, damned, and immortal, and somehow God can just fix all of that with no consequences on my end? It sounds too good to be true."

"Don't misunderstand the Gospel. If you think this ought to cost you something, then you've got the right idea. When you claim Jesus as your Savior, he claims you for himself. The caveat in Christianity is that you aren't actually getting your life and your soul back. You're handing them over to Jesus. There's that element of sacrifice you're looking for."

"I don't feel like I've sacrificed anything that I wasn't already eager to get rid of, though," Raven said.

"Don't worry about that. In time, you'll see differently. We all do."

Raven nodded. "So when are we going to pick up my coffin?"

"It's not too late to go tonight, is it?" Luco asked. "I'd rather do it tonight than tomorrow. You know by now that I like to take Monday as a day of rest, so if we can retrieve it while the sun's still down, then we should."

"I agree," Raven said.

"Dante can stay here with the girls so there's a man in the house," Luco said.

Dante smirked. "Do I get a gun?"

Luco raised his eyebrows and sat back in his seat. "What are you planning on doing with it?"

"Shoot it." Dante quickly added, "If I have to."

"We'll see, son. You know where it is if you have any problems, but I expect most of the surrounding wildlife will continue to leave us alone." Luco turned to Garrett. "You ready to go?"

Garrett nodded and muttered. "Better to get it over with."

Raven still wasn't thrilled about Garrett joining them to get his coffin, but at some point he would have to trust and forgive him, even in spite of Garrett's ongoing disdain. Besides, with his coffin removed from his home, it would no longer matter if Garrett knew where he lived.

And if Garrett still wanted to stake him, from now on he'd have to do it in broad daylight in the Zambini family's home. Even he wasn't that brazen.

"Alright." Luco wiped his mouth with a cloth napkin and stood up. "Let's go."

As the men hitched two of the horses to an empty wagon, Harry barely breathed. Almost ten minutes after they were out of sight, Harry felt a tap on his shoulder. It was Jim.

He mouthed the words, "Ready yet?"

Harry nodded. He pulled his bandana up so it covered most of his face. "Come on."

The thunder of snapping wood and the screech of twisting metal wrenched the wet dish from Calandra's hands, and it shattered on the floor. Three armed men burst through their front door, and her mother and siblings shrieked.

Terror gripped Calandra's chest. She gasped, and then she began to pray.

Chapter 16

Before Calandra could stop him, Dante rushed the one in the middle, but the bandit clocked him in the forehead with the butt of his double-barreled shotgun and Dante dropped to the floor, motionless.

"Dante!" Maria started toward him but froze in place when the lead bandit pointed his shotgun at her.

Calandra's heart hammered. *Oh God, no.*

"Don't you move," the bandit growled.

"Harry, don't. That's not why we're here," one of the other bandits said.

"I'm not going to kill her, Steve," Harry said. "As long as she cooperates."

Maria swallowed hard, then gave him a slow nod.

"What do you want?" Calandra asked, her fists clenched. She wished she could help Dante, but that wasn't going to happen.

The bandits wore dark, rustic clothing, and bandanas covered the lower halves of their faces. All of them wore sidearms strapped to their belts, and each one carried either a shotgun or a rifle.

Harry cocked his head to the side and tilted his shotgun up toward the ceiling. He strolled over to her. "Well, well. Aren't you a pretty one?"

She turned her head away and Anthony clung to her side. Angelica held Mina, who appeared ready to burst into tears at any moment.

"We're here for the money, of course," Steve said.

"What money?" Maria asked.

"Don't play dumb," the third bandit said. "We're here for the money you all took in for your tent revivals this week."

Maria scowled at him. "Would you like me to get it for you?"

Harry finally broke his lustful stare at Calandra to focus on Maria. "Lead the way."

He leveled his shotgun at her again. For an instant, Calandra thought she might be able to grab the weapon and wrench it away from him, but the idea faded with another hellish glance from Harry in her direction.

Who was she kidding? She couldn't rip a heavy shotgun from a grown man's grip. Even if she could, the other two still had guns of their own.

While her children remained silent, Maria retrieved a tan clay jar from inside the kitchen. She pulled a thick cork out of the top and held the jar out to Harry who took it and looked inside.

"This is everything?"

"Did I say it was everything?" Maria drove her hands into her hips.

Calandra raised her eyebrows.

"You're a feisty one, aren't you?" Harry chuckled, and his

gaze shifted to Calandra again. "I can see where your daughter gets her tenacity."

Maria seemed to ignore the comment. She reached behind the cupboard and pulled out a thick, yellowed envelope that Calandra had never seen before. She opened it, revealing dozens of bills lined up in one neat row, then she handed it to Harry. "That's everything. Will you please go in peace?"

"Did you hear that, Jim? She said 'please.'" Harry tucked the envelope full of bills into a pocket inside his coat. "I guess you do have some manners after all."

Maria didn't say a word. For once in Calandra's life, she hoped her mother would keep quiet.

"Well, I suppose it's time we headed on out. Huh, boys?" Harry headed for the door, but stopped for another long, lecherous stare at Calandra that made the skin on the back of her neck tighten. "Then again, it would be a shame to leave the family's greatest treasure untouched, wouldn't it?"

Calandra's heart plummeted into her churning stomach. She shook her head. "No—you can't. Please."

Harry tilted his head to the side again. "Not so confident now, are you, my sweet?"

"I'm not your 'sweet' or anything else." Calandra bit her tongue. If he liked her because she was feisty, then perhaps she'd better just shut up. "Please—please don't do this."

He stepped forward, his shotgun aimed right at her chest. "Doesn't look like you got much of a choice."

"Don't," Maria pleaded. As soon as she stepped forward, Harry pointed his shotgun at her. She clasped her hands together, much like when she prayed. "Don't, please. She's my daughter. *Please* don't do her any harm."

"Oh, I'm not going to hurt her." He stopped, then he glanced up at the ceiling. "Well, maybe a little bit, but that'll be incidental."

Calandra swallowed and tried not to look so wide-eyed. In her mind she prayed, begging God to save her. With her father, Garrett, and Raven gone, God was the only one who could.

"Naw, I'm not gonna hurt you, precious." He took another step toward her.

Calandra matched his move but backed into a wall. So much for trying to run away.

"But I do intend to *thrill* you." Harry leaned close and sniffed her hair. He reeked of cigarettes, horses, sweat, and yesterday's alcohol. "You smell nice."

Calandra closed her eyes. This couldn't be happening.

"I'll bet you've never been with a man before, being the daughter of a preacher and all." Harry puckered his lips and made a kissing noise. "Or am I wrong? Do you have a *dark side*?"

She shook her head and tried not to let her tears escape her clenched eyelids, but they streamed down her cheeks anyway.

"Jim," Harry said.

"Yeah, boss?"

"How about you hold her for me, and then I'll hold her for you?"

Maria fell to her knees in the middle of the kitchen. "No, no—please don't! *Please*."

Steve stepped forward. "We don't have time for this, Harry. Who knows when the men will—"

"And Steve, you get to stand guard. Watch the rest of the family, here. If you happen to see any of the men, come get me."

"Harry, we—"

Harry pointed a thick finger at Steve's face and a slew of profanity shut him up. "Do as I say, or so help me I'll narrow our team down to two this very night."

Steve scowled, glanced at Maria, who continued to beg for her daughter to be spared, and then nodded.

"Please don't!" Maria pleaded, her face wet with tears. She groped Harry's coat. "Please. Take me instead. Not my daughter."

The blow Harry delivered to Maria's face could have knocked a horse off of its feet. Her body skidded across the hardwood kitchen floor until she came to a stop against the cupboard.

Calandra gasped. "Mama!"

"Shut up, or you're next." Harry hissed so hard that tiny specks of his spittle hit her in the face. "Come on."

Calandra struggled against his solid grip, but to no avail. She wept, Maria wept, and her siblings wept as Harry pulled her toward her own bedroom with Jim following close behind.

Chapter 17

Harry leaned his shotgun against the doorframe and shoved Calandra down on her bed. He yanked off his coat in a hurry and smirked. "Jim, hold her."

Jim obliged him, but Calandra kicked and screamed with everything she had.

"You were right, Harry," Jim said. "She *is* a feisty one."

Two points of sharp pain pinched Calandra's cheeks. When she opened her eyes, Harry's face was right there, blocking almost everything else out. His big hand gripped her chin, and his fingers dug into her skin just above her jawline.

"Now listen here, missy," he said. "This ain't my first time, but I know it's yours. Trust me when I say that if you don't fight, this will be much easier for all three of us."

No other words would have made her want to resist him more. She writhed like a snake, twisting and contorting her body, all the while yelling her lungs raw.

SMACK. Calandra heard it before she felt the deadening sting on her left cheek.

"I said *calm down*." Harry leaned into her field of vision again, this time his eyes ablaze with scorn. "If you don't cooperate,

I'll hit you again, you hear? I've got no qualms about it. The longer you fight this, the more I'll take my time. Your choice."

Fabric ripped. Her dress. He'd yanked one of her sleeves down from her shoulder to her elbow, then the other.

"No!" she cried. "Stop it!"

He didn't stop. His hands seized the bust of her dress and rent it straight down, sending buttons skittering across the floor and exposing her undergarments.

"No!" She tried to kick, tried to roll and twist and thrash, but nothing worked.

Helpless. She was helpless. *God, please.*

Harry unbuckled his belt.

Oh, God—please help me!

Something thudded above their heads.

Harry recoiled, but Jim's grip didn't loosen. "What the hell was that?"

"I don't know." Jim wrenched Calandra back down on the bed when she tried to sit up. "Quit moving around."

Clop. Clop. Clop. Clop. Hoofbeats on the roof?

No. Too light to be hoofbeats, but too heavy to be a small animal. Was someone on their roof?

Had someone come to save her?

"Do you hear that?" Jim asked.

"Shut up. Of course I hear it."

"What is it?"

"I said *shut up*. Let me listen."

Calandra listened too. She needed to know what was happening even more than the bandits. She needed to know if she was about to be saved.

More clops.

"What's that sound?" Steve called from the other room.

"Will everyone just *shut up*?" Harry roared.

"Sorry." Steve shot a glare at him.

"Get in here, Steve. Now." Harry re-buckled his belt and backed away from Calandra to retrieve his shotgun. He picked it up, opened the break action, then locked it back in place. "Jim, pick up your rifle. We've got company."

The three of them formed a loose circle, no longer focused on Calandra whatsoever. Harry stared out the window into the dark forest around the house, Steve watched the door to the room, and Jim alternated his nervous eyes between Calandra and the roof.

For almost a full minute they stood in those positions, but the sounds had ceased.

Jim finally broke the silence. "What's going—"

"Shh!" Harry hissed. "Quiet."

A whispering wind filled the room, but the window remained closed. The wind blew through Calandra's hair and rippled the bandits' clothing. They cast frantic glances in every direction, including at Calandra as if she'd somehow caused the sensation.

A second bluster extinguished the candles in the room as well as the light from the adjacent family room, and the entire house plunged into darkness. If not for the moonlight shining through

Calandra's window, she wouldn't be able to see anything at all.

In that moment, Calandra knew who had come to save her. She just hoped he knew what he was doing.

Cries erupted from the next room. Calandra recognized those of her siblings and even a startled peep from her mother.

"Shut up in there!" Harry called over his shoulder. The ruckus stopped. He muttered, "Boys, if this goes south, we're leaving through that window. If you can get to the horses, fine. If not, run, and we'll meet up at the usual spot."

"You got the money. What if you get caught?" Steve asked.

"Worry about that when—*if* it happens." Harry sniffed the air. "For now, we've got bigger problems."

"Like what?" Jim asked.

Harry shook his head. "I don't know. Something as bad as us. Maybe worse."

"Worse?"

"*Quiet.*" Harry lowered his shotgun and pulled something from his pocket. A match flickered to life in his hand, but the next instant it went out.

SNAP.

Steve screamed.

His shotgun clattered to the floor and he clutched his left arm, now horribly bent and contorted like the twisted branch of an old tree. He fell to his knees, dropped down to his side, and writhed.

Standing in Steve's place, his green eyes raging, Raven clenched his fists.

Chapter 18

Jim raised his rifle, but by the time he pulled the trigger Raven's left hand had pushed the barrel up toward the roof. The gun delivered its payload and tore a small hole in the ceiling, and a shaft of silver moonlight filtered into Calandra's room.

In one swift, brutal move, Raven wrenched Jim's gun back down and twisted. Jim's arm jerked with a loud crack, and he screamed. A powerful blow from Raven's right fist sent Jim hurtling through the bedroom window. The glass shattered.

Jim continued on an upward trajectory until his back connected with a tree branch and he came to an abrupt stop. Calandra gasped and diverted her gaze when she saw the branch protruding from Jim's chest. He hung there, skewered like a piece of meat, and just as dead.

Raven's green eyes flashed again, this time with a look Calandra hadn't seen since she first laid eyes on him.

Bloodlust.

Raven moved fast but Harry's shotgun roared and Raven flew back like a washrag destined for the laundry hamper. He hit the wall with a sickening smack and sank to the floor, leaving a trail of dark blood on the wall behind him. Then he stopped moving altogether.

"*Noooo!*" Calandra cried.

"Get up, Steve! We're out of here." Harry extended his hand to his injured companion, but Steve didn't get up. "*Come on*, Steve! Let's go. *Now*."

"I—I can't," he said through gritted teeth. "My arm is—"

"I don't care about your arm! Get up *now* or I'll leave you here."

A dark form, perhaps a shadow itself, rose along the wall where Raven had slumped down.

It was Raven. Blood saturated his white shirt, but he was still alive.

Harry clenched his shotgun and fired the second chamber at Raven's bloody chest, but this time Raven didn't go down. The shot sent him staggering back against the wall again, but he immediately started toward Harry. On the way Raven gave Steve a fierce kick to the back of his head and put him out cold.

Harry's eyes widened and he growled. He dropped his shotgun, yanked his revolver from its holster as he stepped backward, and pumped a round into Raven's torso. Then another. Then another.

By the time Harry would have fired his fourth shot, Raven closed the distance and clamped his fingers onto Harry's arm. He gave Harry's right wrist a sharp jerk, and a loud pop sounded, but it wasn't a gunshot. Harry yelled and clutched his destroyed wrist, then swung his left fist at Raven's head.

Raven blocked the swing with his right forearm and latched his left hand on to Harry's throat. Soon, Harry's boots no longer touched the floor. Raven held Harry in the air with one hand, all the while staring at him with hatred in his green eyes.

"Don't, Raven!" Calandra pleaded.

It was too late.

Raven sank his fangs into Harry's neck. Harry seized as if he was shivering in extreme cold, but with a useless right wrist, Raven's right arm locking Harry's left in place, and a mere one tenth of Raven's strength, Harry didn't stand a chance.

"Raven, stop!"

It only took a few seconds. Harry's eyes rolled back and his skin faded from a healthy pink to a dead pallor.

Harry dropped to the floor. He twitched three times, then he stopped moving entirely.

Raven turned toward Calandra. His white shirt and coat were shredded, and dark blood covered his pale chest and lean midsection. It looked like tar in the moonlight. His green eyes still glistened with fervor, but the bloodlust seemed to have faded. Still, the blood on his lips, cheeks, and the tip of his nose made him look like a rabid dog who'd just killed a rabbit.

She wanted to look away, but she'd already seen too much.

His deep, quick breaths and unbroken stare shook her from the inside out. Then he started toward her.

Chapter 19

Luco staggered through Calandra's bedroom door and stopped only two steps inside, gawking at the carnage in the room.

Raven stepped closer to Calandra. She tried to calm her rumbling heartbeat but Raven's hellish eyes wouldn't allow her any measure of peace.

When Luco put his hand on Raven's shoulder, he stopped his advance and blinked. His gaze darted around the room, lingering the longest on Harry's still body. He blinked again, then refocused on Calandra. His eyes had lost their ferocity.

In unison with Luco, Raven asked, "Are you alright?"

She opened her mouth to speak, but nothing came out. Her gaze drifted up to the hole in the ceiling from Jim's rifle blast.

"Calandra?" Luco asked.

"I—I don't know."

Luco stepped toward her, then stopped when she recoiled. "Did—did they—"

She shook her head. "No. They didn't touch me. Raven stopped them. He saved me."

But had he really? If he'd saved her, then why did she now fear him more than she had the three bandits?

Luco sat next to her and put his arms around her, and they wept together for a long time, as long as she needed. Thank God for her father.

When they finally stopped, Luco eyed Raven.

"Are you alright?" He examined Raven's bloody appearance.

"I'm fine." Raven smeared his hand from his chest down to his belly and wiped a pale streak in the blood that coated his skin. "I guess I'm still immortal after all. I'm not hurt."

Raven wiped the blood from his mouth with his other hand. Calandra began to weep again at the realization of what had almost happened to her, but her emotions sharpened into empathy for Raven's failure and fear of what he really was. He'd regressed. He'd taken the fight too far. He'd fed on human blood again.

Maybe Garrett had been right all along.

When she glanced up at him again, Raven said, "I'll go get the other one down."

"Get who down? From where?" Luco asked.

"The one in the tree." Raven motioned toward Calandra's broken window. "He's dead."

Calandra curled over the side of her bed and vomited on the floor at the thought of Jim with a branch sticking out of his chest. This all had to be a nightmare. Just a bad dream. She'd wake up soon.

No. She wouldn't.

Luco rubbed her back. "It's alright, Calandra. Let it out. Don't be ashamed."

She thought she might bring up some more of her dinner, but it never came. Calandra glanced at Raven again. She'd just thrown up in front of him—an embarrassing display, but she didn't care anymore. After seeing what he was truly capable of, she despised him. Forget whatever fledgling romantic feelings she'd harbored for him. She could never love someone so violent and destructive.

"I'll leave now," Raven said. "I'm sorry."

"You saved my daughter—my entire family. Thank you." Luco stared at Harry's motionless body on the floor and swallowed. "We'll talk about everything else later."

As Raven turned to leave he passed Garrett, who eyed him. His eyes wide, Garrett surveyed the brutality and the destruction in Calandra's room. He put his hand to his mouth and murmured, "God Almighty..."

Calandra followed his line of sight to the scene outside her window, where Raven tugged on Jim's ankle as he hung from the tree. Both Calandra and Garrett turned away. Garrett stared at the wall and inhaled in deep breaths through his nose, then exhaled them from his mouth.

His gaze shifted to Calandra in a moment of calm. "Are you alright?"

She sighed and closed her eyes. "I wish everyone would stop asking that."

Garrett wore a sour mask when she finally made eye contact with him again. She knew she shouldn't have responded in such a harsh tone, but at the moment she didn't—

SNAP.

All three of them jumped, then looked out her broken window again. Jim's body crumpled to the earth in a limp heap at Raven's feet. Calandra's stomach swelled with nausea again. She turned away and sucked in desperate breaths to quell her impulse to wretch.

By the time she recovered, Raven had reentered the room, now covered in even more blood, probably from Jim.

Death surrounded her. She clenched her eyes shut.

"Luco," Raven said.

Calandra opened her eyes, took one glance at him, then had to look away.

"The leader. I—I drained all of his blood."

Luco sighed, but nodded. "I know. We'll talk about it later."

"What about Mama?" Calandra snuck a glance at her father, whose kind face warmed her from the inside out. "Is she alright? She was hurt after that—that *monster* hit her."

"Don't worry about her," Luco said. "She's sore, but she's tough. She'll be fine. I had wanted to stay with her, but she insisted that I tend to you instead."

"What about the rest of—"

"I'm sorry to interrupt—" Raven pointed to Harry's motionless corpse. "—but if we don't get him out of here and take the necessary precautions, he's going to turn into a vampire."

Everyone focused on Raven.

"What are we supposed to do?" Calandra asked.

"You don't have to do anything." Garrett held up his hand. "You've been through enough tonight. The cleanup is going to get messy, and you don't want to be a part of that."

It figured that Garrett would tell her what she could and couldn't do, even now. Nothing out of the ordinary there.

"We need to make sure he stays dead," Raven said. "Otherwise he'll become *un*dead."

No one made a sound.

"I can take care of it, but after what I did, I have a feeling I may need some help with the garlic. And I'll need an axe, or something else sharp enough to—"

"Please." Calandra shook her head. She put one hand on her forehead and one in the air. "Don't say anymore. I don't want to be sick again."

"I'm sorry," Raven said.

"I'll help you take care of it," Luco said.

"No. No way." Garrett stepped forward. "You take care of your family. I'll handle of him. I'll fetch the marshal too. Doubtful he heard all the gunshots from so far away, but he'll want to know we're alright and who these men were."

"*Are.*" Raven nodded at Steve. "This one's not dead. He's just unconscious."

Luco centered his body in front of Raven's. "Tell me now, Raven. Did he see you bite Harry? Did he see you drain him?"

Raven shook his head. "No. I put him out before it happened."

"Then as far as he knows, this other bandit, the one you bit, is dead."

Garrett squinted. "Of course he's dead."

Luco looked at Garrett. "I'm saying that he's dead, but all this other fellow and the marshal need to know is that he's gone, out of the picture, right?"

Raven nodded. "Right. The marshal couldn't handle a real vampire. I mean, one who isn't like me, anyway. It's better if we dispose of him ourselves, the way it's supposed to be done, and bury his head separately when it's finished."

Calandra shut her eyes again and winced.

"I'm sorry, Calandra. I shouldn't be so graphic around you."

She nodded but still didn't look at him.

"Speaking of which, you ought to clean yourself up and get your story straight before I fetch the marshal." Garrett nodded at Harry's body. "I'll take care of this."

Raven shook his head. "No. You'll need my help. I know the process to—"

"Look." Garrett held up his hands. "This isn't my first time doing this, alright?"

The room filled with cryptic silence.

"What are you talking about?" Calandra asked.

Garrett's eyebrows twitched, then his brow furrowed. "I mean what I said. This isn't the first time I've killed a vampire."

"You've never mentioned this to me, Garrett." Luco put his hands on his hips and glared at him.

"What can I say? When I was seventeen, a couple dozen people from our town and some surrounding towns disappeared. I lived in a rural community with a small population. Small enough that you'd notice if someone just vanished. And they did."

Calandra's eyebrows raised and she stared at him. This was news to her.

"We eventually discovered the cause, and my father took me on a hunt with a few other men from our village back in New England. We found an entire coven of them and—" He glanced at Raven, then shrugged. "—and we solved the problem. They didn't bother us anymore after that—we didn't leave any of them around to bother us. No more disappearances."

Calandra hadn't seen her father so angry in years.

"Now you know what drove me to drink, Luco. After what I'd seen, what I'd done, it was my only escape." Garrett's jaw hardened.

"Garrett," Luco said. "Go take care of this. You and I are going to have a serious discussion about this later on. Raven, get cleaned up. The marshal will have some questions for you when he arrives, no doubt. Go now, both of you. Don't make me say it again."

Garrett nodded. He clamped down on Harry's legs and hauled him from Calandra's room, and Raven hooked his arms under Steve's and carried him out by his torso.

The moment she could no longer see them, Calandra began to weep again.

Luco moved to her side, wrapped his arms around her again, and held her to his chest, all while whispering soft, safe encouragement into her ear. "It's alright. You don't have to be afraid anymore. The danger is gone. Those men can't hurt you anymore."

Calandra shook her head and sniveled. "It's not them I'm worried about."

Chapter 20

"After you cut off his head, you need to stuff his mouth with garlic and—"

Garrett put his hands up. "Easy, Raven. I said know how this works."

Raven stared at him. As if he didn't have enough reasons to be wary of Garrett before, now it turned out that Garrett had hunted and killed multiple vampires only a few years earlier. The fact that Garrett knew what he was doing didn't make Raven feel any better about living under the same roof as him.

"I suppose you do."

"Look." Garrett put his hand on Raven's shoulder and gave him a half-smile. "I don't want you to worry about that part of my life. That was a long time ago. People change."

Raven raised an eyebrow. Five years wasn't that long ago, especially to an immortal.

"Come, now. Ease up." Garrett twitched his forearm and shook Raven's entire body. "You've got nothing to worry about from me."

Had Raven changed? After sucking Harry's life away in a matter of moments, Raven wasn't so sure he'd changed after all, except for a twinge of guilt that twisted in his stomach. Whether or not that came from draining Harry or from the knowledge that he'd let Luco and his family down—despite saving them—he still felt remorse, something a vampire shouldn't feel about any victim, especially one as twisted as Harry.

As far as Garrett was concerned, well, Raven had no reason to trust his sincerity about being a different person than the vampire killer he was a few years earlier. The only thing he *did* trust was Garrett's ability to finish off Harry once and for all.

One murderer to another.

Even so, if Raven wanted it done right, perhaps he should just do it himself. He shrugged Garrett's hand off of his shoulder. "Maybe I had better take care of this after all."

Garrett shook his head. "Not necessary. I'll handle it. Go get cleaned up."

Raven sucked in a deep breath.

"Trust me," Garrett said. "I'll take care of this."

"You're sure you know what to do? Because if you miss even one step—"

"I've been prepared for this type of situation since the night I met you."

There was no mistaking the steel in Garrett's cold brown eyes. Raven nodded.

"Just help me get him into the back of one of these wagons," Garrett said. "I'll take care of the rest."

With Steve tied up, gagged, and conscious again, Raven headed to the bathroom and locked the door behind him. Given the night's excitement, he wouldn't have time to head back home to retrieve his coffin or even a change of clothes. He and Luco would have to make a separate trip to bring it over some other night.

No sense in trying to salvage his ruined shirt—not that there was much left to salvage anyway. He slid his fingers between the soiled white linen and his skin and peeled the shirt from his body, then dropped it to the floor. Crusty, sticky dried blood, some of it his, some of it Jim's or Harry's, had caked on his torso.

He dipped his hands into the porcelain water basin atop the counter under the mirror. The once clear water turned pink as he rubbed the blood from his hands, and then his chest and stomach. He glanced at the green-eyed barbarian staring back at him from the oval-shaped mirror, then he used a nearby rag to wipe off his torso, his arms, and his—

Raven lifted his head and stared at the mirror. He could see his reflection.

He'd been using the mirror to clean himself for the last few minutes and hadn't even realized it. What did that mean? He'd drained Harry dry not even an hour earlier, yet now he could somehow see his reflection? It didn't make any sense.

Raven took two steps back and looked at his entire body for the first time in nearly a century. He hadn't put on any weight, as far as he could tell. Apart from the dried blood and the pale skin, he appeared healthy. Not muscular, but definitely lean, lithe, and limber. What he didn't have in size he made up in definition from his shoulders down to his abdomen.

He continued to wipe his body, and the water in the basin darkened with each dip. Upon closer inspection he found small scars where Harry's gunshots had struck him, but nothing more than that. Now, finally clean, he dropped the rag in the basin and gazed into his own eyes again.

Familiarity. That handsome green-eyed devil reminded him of someone he'd known long ago, before decades of violence, murder, and pain became his life. But he saw something else in his eyes: a primal quality, both unrecognizable and frightening.

You're not changing. You're still the same sick, twisted monster that you've been for the last 83 years. Your reflection proves it.

Blood still stained his lips—he'd missed it when he was cleaning himself off.

You'll never be truly clean. You don't even have a soul. Even if you did, it would be permanently tarnished. You're beyond salvation. Your soul is forfeit.

Raven shook his head and clenched his fists. He willed the voice to leave him alone.

Your soul is forfeit.

He slammed his fist into the mirror and a spiderweb of cracks sprawled throughout the glass. Eerie laughter resounded in his head.

Even in spite of his disjointed visage in the broken shards, Raven saw guilt written on his face. Soul or no soul, he'd done the wrong thing by killing Harry the way he had. He'd passed his curse on to another. He'd damned Harry's soul.

Your soul is forfeit.

For the first time in almost a hundred years, tears stung the corners of Raven's eyes.

"I came over as soon as I heard." Marshal Flax shook Luco's hand. He hadn't expected to end up at the Reverend's home again so soon, but from the sound of things the trip might be well worth his time. "This is Deputy Bill Jenner and Deputy Sam Friedrich."

Luco shook their hands too. "Thank you all for coming at such a late hour."

"No problem," Jenner said through a yawn. Marshal elbowed him and he straightened up. "What?"

"Get out some paper and take notes while I talk with the Reverend. Understand?"

"Yeah, sure." He removed a notepad from his pocket and patted his other pockets for a moment. "Umm…"

"What's wrong?" Marshal asked.

"I don't have anything to write with. Sorry… it was dark when I put my uniform on. I was trying not to wake my wife and—"

"Here." Friedrich extended a pencil to him. "Make sure I get that back, Jenner."

Jenner nodded and took it from him. "Ready."

Marshal refocused on Luco. "The young man who resembles a lumberjack?"

"Garrett."

"He showed up at my house and told me what had happened. I told him not to wait for me, and he disappeared into the woods along with the wagon he was driving while I went to retrieve my deputies. Where is he now?"

"I couldn't tell you," Luco said. "I have no idea."

"Garrett told me that he thought one of the bandits may have escaped. Do you think he went after him?"

Luco shrugged.

"If he did, there's a good chance he's in real danger. If these are the bandits who've been roaming this area over the last few—"

"I wouldn't worry about Garrett." Luco's tone matched the hardened expression on his face. "He can take care of himself."

Marshal huffed. "He's a big man, but I'm concerned for his safety. I hope he's not doing anything foolish, especially in light of the situation. He said none of you were hurt?"

"That's not entirely true. My wife and oldest son both took hard hits to their heads, but they're alright now. He should have said that no one was *seriously* hurt."

"He also said one of the bandits was killed."

Luco nodded.

"How did that happen?"

"I did it," a voice behind him said.

Marshal swiveled on his heels and stared into a pair of sullen green eyes. "Ah, the vampire. I should have guessed."

Raven frowned at him.

"Tell me what happened."

"Three men came in after we left."

Marshal held up his hand. "Wait. Who's 'we?'"

"Luco, Garrett, and me."

"Where were you headed so late at night?"

Raven glanced over Marshal's shoulder. "Does it matter?"

Marshal squinted at him. "You got something to hide?"

"I just don't see how it's relevant to what hap—"

"It's relevant if I *say* it's relevant." Marshal stepped forward and encroached into Raven's space. "*Vampire*."

Raven diverted his gaze and swallowed. "We were going to fetch my coffin."

Jenner was still writing. "From where?"

"From my home."

"Which is where?"

Raven clenched his jaw tight and shook his head.

Another step forward and Marshal stood face-to-face with Raven. "I asked you a question, *boy*."

"Marshal," Luco said. "Perhaps that detail isn't pertinent to what happened tonight?"

Marshal shot Luco a glare, but stepped back and folded his arms. "Tell me what happened next."

"We were about ten minutes out when I realized I had forgotten something. I left Luco and Garrett in the wagon and took a shortcut through the forest to get back. When I arrived, I saw them inside through one of the windows. They hit Maria, grabbed

Calandra, and headed toward her bedroom. I knew I had to do something."

"Why are you wearing different clothes?"

Raven cocked his head to the side and squinted. "What?"

Marshal stared at him. "Why are you wearing *different clothes* than when I saw you earlier tonight?"

Raven started to say something, then stopped. "You wouldn't believe me if I told you."

"Try me." He glanced at Jenner again. Still taking notes, and Friedrich stood next to him with his arms folded, not nearly as tired-looking as Jenner.

A sigh filled the cool night air. "One of them shot me and ruined what I was wearing."

Marshal furrowed his brow. "You seem alright to me. Where'd he hit you?"

"My chest, my stomach, my—"

"Whoa, whoa. Wait a minute." Marshal put his hands up again. "How are you even standing in front of me right now? Was he using a slingshot?"

Raven shook his head. "The first two shots were from a double-barreled shotgun, probably a 12-gauge. Then I caught three or four from a revolver in my—"

Marshal cursed, then turned to Luco. "Excuse my language, Reverend, but your friend here is the biggest liar I've ever met. Does he know it's a crime to obstruct my investigation?"

"I'm not lying," Raven said.

"Bull—" Marshal bit his tongue. "You're lying."

"You'd be the first to point out that I'm a vampire, Marshal," Raven said.

"Don't give me attitude, *boy*."

"I'm serious," Raven said. "He shot me. I can bring you the shirt if you—"

Marshal drew his pistol and pointed it at Raven. "Why don't we try a field test instead?"

Raven recoiled a step and raised his eyebrows, but he didn't move after that.

"Marshal, take it easy." Luco started forward from behind Raven.

"You think you're so special, so invincible." Marshal pulled the hammer back on his revolver. "Let's find out."

"Marshal—"

"*Shut up*, Friedrich." Marshal gave him a look and a tone he normally reserved for convicted criminals.

Friedrich closed his mouth and exhaled a deep breath.

Raven shook his head. "Just because it won't kill me doesn't mean it won't *hurt*."

Marshal tilted his head. "Pretty sure of yourself, aren't you?"

"You're not going to shoot an unarmed man," Luco said. "Isn't that against what you believe?"

"You have no idea what I believe." Marshal knew he shouldn't do it, but that made him want to all the more. His finger tightened around the trigger.

Chapter 21

Marshal wanted to do it to ease his pain. To claim his vengeance, even though he knew bullets could never grant him what he sought. He'd tried before, but guns couldn't slay a vampire.

And they couldn't bring her back.

"I saw it happen," a female voice said from behind him.

He peeked over his shoulder. Luco's oldest daughter stood ten feet behind him, between the Zambini family's house and the marshal.

"One of them shot Raven twice with a shotgun and then a few more times with a revolver," she said. "I thought they had killed him, but he got up and kept coming."

Moonlight reflected off of a tear running down her cheek.

"They were trying to rape me, but he saved me." Her gaze flitted to Marshal's revolver, then back to his eyes. "I think you should put the gun away."

She was right. He'd acted foolishly. If for no other reason than the ineffectiveness of his bullets, Marshal sighed then holstered the revolver. "I'm sorry. I shouldn't have done that."

Raven nodded at him.

"So, you went in after them, and then what happened?"

"I immobilized one of them, who is still alive inside," Raven said. "And I sent the other one through Calandra's window. He hit a tree, and it killed him."

Marshall pursed his lips. "And I assume this was in defense of yourself?"

"He had tried to shoot me."

"Good enough for me."

"What happened to the third bandit?"

Raven glanced at Luco, then refocused on Marshal. "He's the one who shot me. After I rendered the other one unconscious, Harry shot me and—"

"Harry?" Marshal's heart thumped faster in his chest. "Harry Deutsch?"

"I don't know. I only heard his first name." Raven's attention shifted between Marshal, Jenner, and Friedrich.

Marshal stepped toward him again. "Who else? What other names did you hear?"

"The guy we have tied up is Steve," Raven said. "The other one, the dead one, is—*was* named Jim."

Marshal wanted to whoop, but he stopped short. "Harry's the one who escaped, isn't he?"

"He's gone," Luco said.

"We need to get Steve to talk," Marshal said to Friedrich, who nodded. "Bring him out, will you, Friedrich?"

"I can show you where he is," Luco said. They left together.

Marshal turned back to Raven. "You sure there's nothing else you want to tell me?"

Raven shook his head. "Steve's arm is broken pretty bad. You probably should get him to a doctor soon."

"Good to know." Marshal nodded. "That it?"

Raven stared at the dirt, then back up at Marshal. "If you find Harry, his arm is broken too. His wrist."

Marshal nodded. A moment later, Luco stepped out the house's front door. Friedrich followed him and hauled a disheveled, whining man behind him. He deposited him at Marshal's feet.

"Well, well," he said. "If it isn't Steve Huggins. How're you feeling, Steve?"

A slew of profanity tainted the air. "My arm is killing me."

"Better than what happened to Jim." Marshal glanced between Luco, Calandra, and Raven. "You three can go. We'll take a look around after we're done with Steve, here."

They went back inside the house, leaving Marshal alone with Jenner, Friedrich, and Steve.

"Alright, Steve. Where's Harry?"

"Go to Hell."

Marshal smirked. "You still taking notes, Jenner?"

"Yep." Jenner scribbled on the notepad with Friedrich's pencil. "I just wrote that Steve wants you to go to Hell."

Marshal rolled his eyes. "Keep writing. Friedrich, come here. I need your help with something."

Friedrich complied and stood behind Steve.

"He's not tied up anymore, but I'll wager he's not going

anywhere with his arm as mangled as it is. Every step probably means a jolt of pain, doesn't it, Steve?"

Steve glared at him.

"Grab him, Friedrich."

"What?" Steve's eyes widened when Friedrich gripped his good arm and twisted it behind his back. Steve yelped. "Let go!"

"Oooh, that arm looks gnarly, Steve." Marshal rolled up his sleeves. "It'd be a shame if Friedrich had to break your other one too."

"Stop—please," Steve said. "I don't know anything. I *swear*."

Marshal leaned over and flicked Steve's injured wrist with his index finger.

"Ow! Cut that out!" After a river of profanity, Steve tried to squirm out of Friedrich's grasp, but to no avail.

Marshal flicked it again.

"Please—please stop," Steve whined. When Friedrich gave him a gratuitous twitch, he bared his clenched teeth and swore again. "Come on—I don't *know* anything."

"Forgive me if I don't believe you," Marshal said.

"I'm not lying, I *swear*." Steve moaned. "I didn't see him go. I was unconscious."

Marshal shook his head. "That's not what matters, Steve. I want to know where he's gone. Where I can find him."

Steve laughed, then he cursed a third time. "Are you trying to get me killed?"

Marshal gave a slight nod to Friedrich, who wrenched Steve downward and pushed his face into the dirt.

"*Aagh!* Stop!"

"Where will he go, Steve?" Marshal asked. "You spill it, we'll protect you. No turncoat interaction like Mick. Just you, in jail, under guard every hour of every day until he's caught. You play nice and we may even let you out of jail once we get him."

"I can't—"

Friedrich kicked Steve's broken arm and he screamed.

"You actually have tears in your eyes," Marshal said. "The hurt can stop as soon as you tell me where your rendezvous point is."

"I—" Friedrich wrenched Steve forward. "P–promise me you'll take me to a doctor."

Marshal and Friedrich exchanged glances. "First thing in the morning."

"Tonight." Steve said it with far more authority than he could actually command. Another shake from Friedrich and he said, "Alright! Tomorrow morning—tomorrow morning is fine."

"Give me a location, Steve."

He swallowed hard, and lowered his head. He mumbled something.

"What was that?" Marshal patted Steve's broken arm again. "Speak up. I didn't hear you."

Steve bit his lip and tried to recoil, but Friedrich held him firm. "Head south along the river. There's a camp setup about a quarter mile west from the four boulders stacked in a row."

"That's a little vague. Can you be more specific?"

The look on Steve's face probably would have been more heartbreaking if he hadn't been a ruthless bandit. "It's near a cave."

"How about the name of the cave?"

Steve closed his eyes and set his jaw. "It's the Blue Snake Cave."

Marshal whacked his arm again, and Steve yelped. "You think I don't know when you're lying to me? I've served this county for almost forty years and earned more gray hairs in the process than you've taken breaths throughout your miserable life."

Friedrich smirked.

"Tell me the name of the cave." Marshal grabbed Steve's left wrist and started to twist it. "Or so help me God, I'll make sure you never use this arm again."

Steve screamed, then let loose an incoherent stream of profanity-laced nonsense.

Marshal tweaked Steve's wrist again. "The cave. *Now*."

"Badger! Badger's Cave." Steve whimpered. "Please let go!"

"Did you get that, Jenner?"

"Yep. Badger's Cave. Got it."

Marshal let him go. "Friedrich, you and Jenner get him up on a horse, and then you take him into town. Jenner comes with me to the rendezvous. Forget about the preacher's house for now—tonight we're going to bring in Harry Deutsch."

Chapter 22

Raven had Calandra's room swept and scrubbed with an hour to spare before sunrise. While the bloodstained rug on her floor would eventually need to be replaced, the room was at least habitable for the time being, even if only Raven would inhabit it.

With all the shattered glass and broken wood from the window cleaned up, Raven shut the thick drapes in Calandra's room and moved her large armoire in front of the window. He even patched the bullet hole in the roof with an old rag.

A knock sounded behind him. Garrett stood in the open doorway.

"Is it done?" Raven asked.

Garrett nodded. "He's gone."

"Good."

"Look." Garrett stepped into the room, closer to Raven. "I know you and I don't exactly get along, but…"

Raven folded his arms and leaned against the wall. What was going to come out of Garrett's mouth this time?

"…I want to thank you." Garrett bowed his head and stared at his shoes. "If you hadn't gone back, who knows what might have happened to Maria and the kids. Or to Calandra."

Raven nodded. "I did what you would have done, I'm sure."

Garrett shook his head. "No, you did more than I would have done. I would have tried to intervene and failed. I guess the fact that you're a vampire is what saved us in the end, huh?"

"If you want to look at it that way."

"Don't get me wrong." Garrett held his hands up. "I definitely would have taken a shot at saving everyone, but I'd probably be dead on the floor if I had. And Calandra would have—"

"It's alright." Raven waved his hand. "You don't have to say anything else. I understand what you mean."

Garrett smiled and shrugged. "You saved her, Raven. You saved my future wife from being raped by that scum. I don't know what I would have done if that had happened—I doubt I would have married her if those scoundrels had violated her."

Raven's eyebrows went up on their own and he had to clench his jaw shut to keep from ripping into Garrett. How selfish was he? Calandra getting raped would have been infinitely worse for her than for Garrett. What an arrogant—

"I don't know how I'll ever be able to repay you for that." Garrett gave him a half-smile.

Raven stared at Garrett's extended hand. He wanted to take hold of it and crush it into powder. Garrett was lucky to have a girl like Calandra, "violated" or not. Only a fool would entertain thoughts of leaving the woman he loved during such a troubling, difficult time.

"But of course that's all *hypothetical* since they didn't

actually touch her." Garrett must have read the anger in Raven's eyes.

"Right. Hypothetical." Raven shook Garrett's hand. "I'm glad I was able to help Calandra." *But for her sake, not yours.*

"Me too." Garrett released Raven's hand and scanned the room. "Get some rest, will you? Tomorrow—excuse me, *today* is going to be tumultuous."

"I'll try." Of course, he wouldn't even be awake while the Zambini family tried to move on after such a horrendous scare. How he would sleep without his coffin—if at all—was another matter entirely.

"Good night." Garrett turned and walked out of the room, leaving Raven alone in the darkness.

"Night," Raven called after him. He glanced up at the ceiling. "This had better work."

"You sure?" Marshal Flax still had his revolver out. As far as Harry Deutsch was concerned, Marshal wouldn't take any chances.

"Yep. No one's inside." Jenner emerged from Badger's Cave with a fiery torch in one hand and his own revolver in the other. "The cave is barely a cave, like you said. It ends about twenty feet in, and there are no secret paths or anything that I could see from inside. So if he's not in there, and he's not at the camp—"

"Then either Steve lied to us, or Harry decided not to come back here." Marshal still didn't holster his pistol. "There's no sign of any recent activity at the camp. No smoldering coals, fresh ashes, leftover food. No tracks either. He never came here."

"I bet he's got a dozen locations just like this one scouted out. He's probably at one of those, just biding his time until he can show his face again." Jenner tossed the torch behind him. It landed on the dirt and illuminated the mouth of the cave.

"Or he could be on his way down to Mexico. Or heading up to Canada. Or to Australia for all we know." Marshal eyed his gun, sighed, then slid it into its holster.

"I think we ought to go back and press Steve again. I could break his other arm if you like. Or maybe a leg."

Marshal chuckled. "I appreciate your zeal for the job, Jenner. You may yet get a chance to flex those big muscles in the service of our fine county here, but I think we both deserve a little sleep. We did just bring in one of the three most notorious bandits in the region."

"And another of the three is dead." Jenner elbowed Marshal's arm. "Not bad for a Sunday night, huh?"

"You're kind of coarse when you're tired, aren't you?" Marshal smirked and put his hand on Jenner's shoulder. "I think I'll be able to tolerate you after all, Jenner."

"That's very kind of you to say, Marshal."

"Now let's get out of here and get some sleep. We'll have another chat with Steve in the morning before we take him in to see the doctor."

The next evening, Raven awoke just as refreshed as if he'd

spent the entire day in his coffin. Apparently he didn't need it after all.

Over the next week Raven continued to sleep apart from his coffin, but he still avoided forays into the sunlight. He tried it once—he'd waited until just after sunrise and then extended his hand through one of the house's windows, but the sun seared his knuckles black within seconds.

Though he couldn't go outside during the day, he occasionally tried to stay up and function during daylight hours, but each time he only wore himself out. The familiar unmanageable fatigue would sweep over him within an hour—sometimes much sooner—after sunrise. It was so potent that he literally had to crawl back into the thorough darkness of Calandra's room where he would sleep for the rest of the day.

He prayed often and read the Bible nightly, but none of it seemed to make a difference. No matter how much he did for God, Raven still couldn't break free from the remainder of his curse. His hope of walking in daylight again seemed beyond impossible.

"At least you're still strong," Garrett would say. "Got to be happy about that."

Garrett didn't understand. He never would. As much as Garrett scraped against Raven's grain, Raven hoped he would never know the suffering, the pain, the *hunger* of vampirism.

Even though Raven had overcome garlic, flowing bodies of water, holy relics, not seeing his reflection, and sleeping apart from his coffin, the thirst for blood still raged inside of him every moment. He'd trade his enhanced strength in an instant to be rid of that bondage.

"God's not done with you yet, Raven," Luco said to him again and again. "I believe that someday you'll live as one of us, free to enjoy the sun shining overhead."

Raven hoped he was right.

Someone tapped Raven on the shoulder. He spun on his heels and found Calandra standing behind him. He nodded to her. "Hello, there. How are you this evening?"

"I'm well. Thank you for asking." Calandra broke eye contact with him and stared at the cool earth beneath their feet. "I—I need to talk to you about something."

Raven stopped working the tangle in the rope he held in his hands and focused on her.

"I never—" She looked up at him, then diverted her gaze again.

He let the rope slip to the ground and took her hands in his, though he probably shouldn't have. Garrett would disapprove if he'd seen the interaction. "It's alright. You can talk to me."

When she smiled at him, something in his stomach fluttered. "I wanted to thank you."

"For what?"

"You know why." Calandra squeezed his hands. "If you hadn't come back I may have been killed, or worse."

Raven nodded. "I did what I had to do to protect you."

Calandra's brown eyes flickered with mischief.

"And the rest of the family," he added. "I couldn't let them get hurt either, you know."

"I knew what you meant, Raven." Calandra released his hands and her smiled faded. "But that's not all I wanted to talk to you about."

The flutters in his stomach turned to poisonous barbs that pricked his insides. "Very well. What else?"

She sighed. "You saved me, but you killed two men to do it."

Raven closed his eyes. He knew this was coming.

"One of them was accidental. I doubt you planned for Jim to fly through the window and hit that tree branch the way he did—" She hesitated. "—but the way you killed Harry—"

"I know," Raven said. "It's been bothering me too."

"It was the most horrifying thing I've ever seen."

He shook his head and took his turn staring at the ground. "I know."

She touched his shoulder. "No. You don't get it."

Raven's gaze met hers again and he swallowed the lump in his throat.

"By the time you finished with him, I was more afraid of *you* than I ever was of them, even when they were trying to rape me."

Guilt, his new friend, swelled in Raven's chest.

"Look, I know you've been a vampire for almost a century." Calandra's tone had softened a bit. "I can't even imagine how difficult it must be to try to control your impulses to hunt, kill, and feed, but—" She sighed. "—seeing that for the first time changed me, and it changed my opinion of you."

Raven stared into her dark, beautiful eyes.

"I don't know if I can trust you anymore," she said.

He shrugged. "I don't know why you would have in the first place. Garrett certainly doesn't. I'm a vampire. We're cursed, wicked creatures. That's part of why I wanted to keep my distance from you in the first place."

"Now you're just trying to play to my sympathies," she said. "I'm not trying to upset you or offend you. I'm trying to heal our friendship."

"I want that too," Raven said. "But I don't know what you're asking of me."

"I want to be able to trust you again. I've trusted you with my life from the moment you wedged yourself between me and that tent pole. You saved my life then, and you saved it when the bandits showed up, but when you killed Harry the way you did, all of that went out the window."

So did Jim. No, he shouldn't think like that. It wasn't funny. Well, kind of—but still.

"If we're going to be friends, and if you're going to live with us, then I need to be able to trust you."

"And if you don't, then I'll have to leave, right?"

She nodded. "It won't be me forcing you out, though. If I'm uncomfortable around you, my parents will notice, and they might send you away. I don't want that to happen."

He raised an eyebrow. Should he push it? "And why is that?"

Calandra tilted her head to the side. "You're my friend. I feel like you understand me better than anyone else. I don't want to lose that relationship."

"Even more than Garrett?" Raven asked.

"Well—" She stole a glance at the night sky. "—that's a different issue. You don't need to concern yourself with my relationship with Garrett."

"If you say so."

"Just what do you mean by that?" She put her hands on her hips.

Uh-oh. Not good. Raven swallowed. "Nothing. Just agreeing with you."

"It sounded like more than an agreement." She failed to stifle an encroaching smile. "Are you trying to get involved in my courtship?"

"No, no. Just agreeing with you, like I said." Boy, she was cute when she got feisty. "I don't want to get involved in any of the conflict."

Her mouth hung open for a moment. "Conflict? What *conflict* are you seeing?"

Raven put up his hands. He hoped he hadn't caused an actual rift between them by joking around. "Sorry. Poor word choice. I think I'd better just stop talking now."

She nodded, her anger clearly feigned this time. "I think you're right. You'd better watch yourself."

"I will. Sorry."

"You know I'm toying with you, right?" she asked.

"Yes, I do." Well, he did now, anyway.

"Then why aren't you smiling?"

Raven sighed. "When you've taken as many lives, destroyed as many families, and lost as many loved ones as I have over the last century, you might have a hard time finding things to smile about."

Now it was Calandra's turn to stare at the dirt. "I'm sorry. I didn't think—"

"No, no." Raven touched her shoulder and she looked up at him. "I owe you an apology. Again. I probably came off as a little too blunt, too harsh. I shouldn't have laid a century's-worth of woes on your shoulders. I'm sorry."

The next thing he knew, she wrapped her arms around his torso and squeezed him in a big hug, which he gladly returned.

When she finally let go, he asked, "What was that for?"

She smiled at him. "I have my friend back."

"You never lost me in the first place."

"I don't think I ever told you this, but not long after we first met I made it my goal in life to get you to smile. I haven't seen so much as a smirk from you since then. Now that God is setting you free from your curse, I expect that will change," she said. "And I'll see that it does."

Raven lifted an eyebrow again. "Good luck."

"Well, I'd better get back to helping Papa set up that curtain on the stage. He's lost without me."

"That's the truth. I don't know what he'd do without you." Raven bit his tongue. He could have easily said the same about himself.

"You're sweet." She trotted away but turned back. "I'm going to get you to smile. Don't fight me on that one."

"Give it your best shot," he called after her. If anyone could do it, it would be her. Or perhaps little Mina. Hard not to smile at a child as adorable as her, though Raven still hadn't.

"Oh, and one other thing," she said from a few yards away.

"Yeah?"

"I'm taking my room back. You'll be sharing a room with Garrett from now on."

Raven's eyes widened.

Chapter 23

Rooming with Garrett actually didn't cause Raven as much grief as he'd expected, and Garrett also seemed unfazed by the change.

"I knew this was coming," Garrett had said their first night in the room. "Far as I can tell, as long as you're asleep during the day and I'm asleep most of the night, it'll be pretty hard to get on each other's nerves."

Garrett was right about that. Most of the time they got along just fine—until one night after a tent meeting and dinner when they both occupied the room at the same time.

Raven had lit a small candle and perched it on a stand so he could read the Bible at the wooden desk nestled in one of the room's corners while Garrett slept. There was that passage again, the one Luco had asked him to read at the house after his second night at the tent meeting. Psalm 23:

The Lord is my shepherd; I shall not want. He maketh me to lie down in green pastures: he leadeth me beside the still waters. He restoreth my soul: he leadeth me in the paths of righteousness for his name's sake. Yea, though I walk through the valley of the shadow of death, I will fear no evil: for thou art with me; thy rod and thy staff they comfort me. Thou preparest a table before me in the presence of mine enemies: thou anointest my head with oil; my cup runneth over. Surely goodness and mercy shall follow me all the days of my life: and I will dwell in the house of the Lord for ever.

"Any chance you'll be done soon?" Garrett's deep voice filled the void of silence.

"Am I bothering you?" Raven asked. "I can leave."

"No, that's alright. I don't mind you reading the Bible." He cleared his throat. "That candlelight is getting on my nerves a bit, though."

"I should leave, then. I've still got a few hours left until daylight, so I won't be sleeping any time soon. I'll go." He pushed his chair away from the desk and closed the Bible.

As Raven stood up to walk out of the room, Garrett sat up in his bed. Candlelight illuminated his hairy, burly chest. "You still worry me, you know?"

Raven stopped. "What do you mean?"

"We're rooming together, and I'm getting used to you and all, but I still don't trust you."

More of the same. Garrett would never change his opinion. "I doubt you ever will. Good night, Garrett."

"Don't walk away from me when I'm talking to you." Garrett's voice rumbled like thunder in a stormy sky.

"I'm leaving so you can sleep. I'm taking the candle with me so it doesn't bother you. Isn't that what you want?"

"No. I want you to stay here and listen to me since you're

already keeping me up."

Raven turned back and faced him. "I don't like your tone."

"Are you in love with Calandra?" Garrett's brown eyes reflected the flickering light of Raven's tiny candle.

Silence lingered between them.

"You *are*."

"No, I'm not," Raven said. "I'm not in love with her."

Was that true? At the very least he felt attracted to her. But love? They were friends, and he certainly cared for her, but he didn't *love* her. He couldn't. She was courting Garrett, and pursuing her that way wouldn't be right. No, they were just friends.

They had to be just friends.

"I don't want you to lie to me, Raven." Garrett lit a line of candles atop the shelf mounted to the wall above his bed. Dancing tongues of fire illuminated the room. "I want the truth."

"We're just friends," Raven said. "I don't want to come between you two."

Garrett gave a mirthless laugh. "You've already done that and more."

Raven swallowed hard. "I'm sorry. I didn't mean to."

Why was he apologizing? It's not like he'd done it on purpose.

"You're sorry?" Garrett repeated. "That's not good enough. You singlehandedly set our marriage date back by at least a *year* because you showed up to our tent meeting that night. Maybe longer than a year. I should be helping Calandra and her family with wedding plans right now, but because of you, I'm not."

"What do you want me to say?" Raven asked. "I already apologized."

"I said I want the *truth*." Garrett stood to his feet, a peach-toned hulk clad in only a pair of red flannel pajama pants. He towered over Raven by several inches. "Why are you still hanging around here?"

"It's not for Calandra."

Garrett cocked his head to the side and tightened his jaw.

"It's *not*," Raven repeated. "I'm here because I haven't had a family in almost a hundred years. Everyone I knew died shortly after I became a vampire from a plague that swept through the region where I lived. I only survived because I had been turned."

Garrett didn't so much as blink.

"I've lived the last eight decades mostly alone. Going out, hunting, killing, feeding, and then coming home, always more miserable than the night before. When I saw a chance to break out of that cycle and become a real person again, I took it. I'm sorry if that's interfering with your *marriage plans*."

"I could care less about your conversion *or* your past." Garrett stepped into Raven's space. "All I want to know is if you're attracted to Calandra or not."

Raven sucked in a quick breath through his mouth, ready to speak, but he hesitated.

"Tell me the truth, Raven." Garrett's eyes narrowed. "Don't take this moment for granted. Tell me the truth."

"I—I'm attracted to her," Raven started. "But that's the extent—"

Garrett grabbed two fistfuls of Raven's shirt and shoved him against the wall. The Bible in Raven's hands fell to the floor with a thump. "I knew it. I *knew* I should have staked you the first night you showed up at that tent meeting."

"Take it easy, Garrett!" Instinct sent Raven's hands to Garrett's wrists. "I just told you that it isn't like that at all. I'm not pursuing—"

Garrett shook Raven and shoved him against the wall again. "Nothing you can say will change my mind. *Nothing*. I should have staked you like I staked Harry, like I staked those other vampires when I was seventeen."

"Keep your voice down." Raven clenched his teeth to keep from snapping Garrett's wrists. "I have no intention to ruin your relationship with Calandra. I never have."

"I don't believe you." Garrett shook Raven again.

Raven exhaled a furious breath through his nose. It was all he could do to keep his wrath contained. "Let go of me, Garrett."

"You're a wedge. You're trying to come between us. You want her for yourself."

"I don't want anything to do with her," Raven hissed. Whether it was true or not didn't matter. He just had to get the huge, white-skinned, red-haired gorilla in front of him to calm down. The old hunger surged through Raven's body. He squeezed Garrett's wrists and said slowly, "Now let me go."

Garrett's jaw tightened and he jerked Raven against the wall again. "Or what? What are you going to do, you undead *demon?*"

Raven locked eyes with him. He couldn't do it. He couldn't kill Garrett, or even hurt him. It didn't matter if Garrett had initiated the confrontation. If Raven retaliated he'd make enemies of everyone he'd come to call his family. He had to control himself.

But Garrett didn't have to know that. "If you don't, you'll end up like Harry. Now let go of me."

Maybe Garrett saw the bloodlust in Raven's eyes, or maybe he'd just gotten his point across. Either way, he released his grip on Raven and stepped backward. "I'm watching you, *vampire*. You're not going to get away with this."

"I'm not trying to get away with anything," Raven said. The moment Garrett released him, Raven's thirst dwindled to little more than a low rumble in his core, a miserable, yet manageable begging for another taste of human blood.

Garrett pointed a thick finger at him. "You'd better not, or I'll stake you in your sleep, so help me God. Just like I did to Harry."

Raven blew a long, belabored breath through his nose as he bent down to pick up the Bible. "I'm going to go, Garrett. I'll sleep somewhere else during the day."

Right after Raven shut the door behind him, Garrett's muffled voice said from the other side, "Stay away from Calandra."

Raven shook his head and headed for the soft couch in the middle of the living room.

"It's been well over two weeks, Steve." Marshall Flax puffed a plume of smoke from his mouth, courtesy of the pipe in his left hand. With his right he tried to flatten an archaic crease in a map of the county surrounded by a few neighboring counties. Several red circles with matching scribbles dotted the map at random points. "We haven't heard a peep from Harry Deutsch since the night we brought you in. Where is he?"

Steve rubbed his broken arm, now set between two splints and in a sling hanging from his shoulder. All four had crammed into Steve's cell for the meeting along with a table and some chairs.

"I've given you literally every haunt and hideout we've ever been to for miles in every direction," Steve said. "Every bar we frequented, every boarding house we slept at, every campsite where we pitched a tent. Harry's long gone, Marshal. That's the only explanation I have for you."

Marshal eyed Jenner, who stood guard at the door and shrugged. Friedrich, stationed next to him with his arms folded, shook his head. He refocused on Steve. "I wish I could believe you, but I can't."

"You said yourself that no one you've talked to has seen him, and it looked like all of our campsites have been deserted for quite some time. What more do you want?"

"I want Harry Deutsch's ugly face in my jail cell—" He slapped the table with his palm and Steve flinched. "—or his head on this table."

"For the record," Friedrich said. "Everyone we talked to said they hadn't seen him, but that doesn't mean it's true. You know they all heard about the last man who ratted Harry out."

"Mick?" Steve asked. "Harry didn't like Mick in the first place. Thought he had a big mouth. His betrayal only gave Harry an excuse to get rid of him."

"Either way, the locals know he's dead," Friedrich said.

"Not my fault if they won't talk to you," Steve said.

"It may not be your fault, but that doesn't mean it isn't your problem." Marshal puffed on his pipe again, this time blowing the smoke into Steve's face. "You're our best lead, Steve. By far. You don't help us and I'm not sure we can guarantee your safety anymore. Who knows what might happen to you?"

"There's nothing you can threaten me with that Harry wouldn't already do if he found out I talked. The way I see it, I'm already a dead man."

"Hmm." Marshal smirked, then set his pipe on a steel ashtray on the table. "You're right. You probably are a dead man."

Steve sat there with a smug expression on his face.

"But there are two things you haven't considered. First, we can certainly make your time here in our jail either more comfortable or much, much less comfortable. You get my meaning?"

Steve shook his head. "You can't scare me Marshal. You can hurt me and torture me all you want because no one's looking over your shoulder now, but when I get into that courtroom, things are going to change around here."

Marshal smiled. "Second, when you get into that courtroom,

you can either have us as advocates for your prompt release—probably after a short stretch in a federal prison back east—if you cooperate, or as your opponents if you don't. Help us catch Harry Deutsch and you won't have anyone to fear anymore. Not us, not Harry. You'll practically be a free man again."

"I've been *trying* to help you catch Harry." Steve's voice cracked. "But I've told you everything I know. I swear."

Marshal stared into Steve's eyes for a long time, and neither of them looked away. Finally, Marshal leaned back in his chair and locked eyes with Friedrich. "I think he's telling the truth."

Friedrich shook his head again. "He's a liar. They all are. Don't let him fool you."

"I don't know," Marshal said. "He's not desperate anymore. Seems we've tapped our resource and he's got nothing left for us."

"I disagree. Give me a chance to find some new ways to motivate him." Friedrich cracked his knuckles. "I bet I can squeeze a few more drops out of him."

"Maybe," Jenner said.

Marshal stared at him. "Maybe what, Jenner?"

"I think I have an idea."

Marshal glanced at Friedrich, then back to Jenner again. "Let's hear it."

"Well, we haven't been successful in finding Harry, right?"

"I thought you said you had an idea," Marshal said.

"I do."

"Then why are you asking me rhetorical questions?"

"I—well—"

"Just get to the idea, please." Marshal waved his hand.

"Alright." Jenner held his hands out in front of him. "What if—since Harry would already kill Steve for all the information he's given us—what if we make that information public?"

Friedrich's face twisted with confusion. "What would that do?"

"Well, Harry would have to know that someone talked, right?" Jenner glanced between Marshal and Friedrich. "Since Jim is dead and he already killed Mick, he'd figure that Steve is the one who told us everything."

Marshal smirked again.

"I don't understand," Friedrich said.

"It's simple," Jenner said. "If Harry's still around, he'll come for Steve. He'll want to kill him for talking, just like he killed Mick for trying to sell him out."

"Not bad." Marshal rubbed his chin. "That could work."

"What?" Steve gawked at them. "You want to use me as *bait*?"

Marshal chuckled. "Sorry, Steve. You haven't left us with much of a choice."

Steve's eyes widened. "But—he'll *kill* me if he finds me."

"You just said you aren't afraid of dying anymore. What changed?"

Steve's mouth hung open, but no sound came out.

"Good work, Jenner," Marshal said. "I'm impressed."

"Thanks, Marshal." Jenner wore a big smile.

Marshal pointed a finger at him. "Don't let it go to your head, son."

Jenner's face reset to stoic. He nodded, then shook his head. "I won't, sir."

"How do you propose we make this public?" he asked. "Post bulletins in the towns?"

"I think we ought to do that, plus we should run a story in all the local papers with Steve's likeness. That way Harry will know for sure who betrayed him, and it will protect anyone else who may decide to give us information if we put all the blame on Steve."

"You—you can't do that," Steve said. "He'll *kill* me."

"We've already established that, but thanks for the reminder," Marshal said. "Jenner, go make it happen. Have Friedrich read the article before you distribute it, though. You have the most atrocious spelling I've ever seen."

"Yes, sir. Sorry, sir."

As Jenner and Friedrich left the cell, Marshal winked at a bewildered Steve. He picked up his pipe and the ashtray, but left the map and a pencil on the table. "You go ahead and make a note of anything else you may have forgotten. Remember: you help us catch him now, he won't be able to come for you later on. Have a nice day."

Marshal stepped out of the cell and locked the door behind him. He reveled in one last glance at Steve's forlorn face before he stepped out of the cell block.

Chapter 24

"Aren't you supposed to be helping your mother with dinner tonight?" Luco stepped away from a group of people to speak to Calandra, who had just shown up at the tent meeting for the first time that night. "I thought you had a sore throat. What are you doing out here?"

"I started to feel better, so I wanted to come and help out, at least with packing the tent when we're finished for the evening." She coughed into her fist and glanced around the tent meeting, but she didn't see Raven anywhere.

Luco rubbed her shoulder. "I appreciate your zeal. I'm sure the Lord does too, but neither of us want you to risk your health when you don't have to. You're sick, and you ought to be at home helping Mama, or better yet, resting in bed."

"But you pray for people at these meetings all the time and they get healed from worse ailments than my pitiful cold." She coughed again. "I figured I could still help. I don't feel sick."

"There's a time for serving the Lord by doing his will, but there's also a time for serving the Lord when you're at rest. That's the type of service you need right now."

"But—"

"No excuses, Calandra. I want you to turn around and head home, please."

Calandra started to say something but a voice behind her broke up her words.

"Hey, what are you doing here?" Garrett walked up to her and touched her forehead with the back of his hand. "You feel warm. I thought you would be home, resting."

"I was just explaining that very thing to her, Garrett," Luco said. "Thank you for reinforcing my point."

"But I feel fine," she said. "All I want to do is help out, even if I can't sing tonight. Besides, Mama and the kids went to town to pick up an order from the mercantile this afternoon and they aren't back yet. I was all alone in the house, bored and hoping I could help."

"You should be content to just rest and relax," Luco said.

Calandra turned to Garrett. Maybe he would side with her.

"I'm sorry, but I have to agree with your father on this one. I'd feel horrible if you got even sicker and couldn't help us in the future. The sooner you get home and get some rest, the sooner you can come back out here." Garrett glanced at Luco. "Right?"

"Right. Let's get you home." Luco scanned the crowd. "Where's Raven?"

Garrett set his jaw. "What do you need him for?"

"I'm going to have Raven escort her home. It's not safe on the road this time of night. Frankly, I'm a little upset that you came out here alone in the first place, Calandra."

"Sorry."

"You don't need to find Raven," Garrett said. "I'll take her home. I know these woods, and I know how to protect her. I'll make sure she gets home safe."

Luco spotted Raven and waved him over. "No, that's not a wise decision. She just said that Maria and the children aren't at home, and it would be inappropriate for you and her to be alone for so long unsupervised."

"It wouldn't be for *that* long," Garrett said. "We're almost done here anyway. And besides, you'd rather entrust her to a vamp—an *ex*-vampire? How do you know *he* won't try something?"

"He has no motivation to try something. He's not courting her. You are."

Garrett folded his arms and laughed. "So you don't trust me? After all this time, and you still don't trust me to be alone with her?"

Calandra shook her head. She hated being put in the middle of these kinds of situations. "Look, it's fine. I can just go back by myself—"

"No," Luco and Garrett said in unison.

"I trust you, but I want both of you to live above reproach. I don't want even the slightest reason to question the nature of your courtship," Luco said. "Surely you understand that."

Raven walked up and nodded to Calandra, followed by Dante, who said, "What are you doing here, Calandra? I thought you were sick."

"She is," Luco said. "She needs to go home, and I want

Raven to take her."

"What?" Raven's gaze flitted between each of them. "I don't know if that's—"

"Why not have Dante take her back instead?" Garrett said. "We don't need him to help pack up, and he knows the way home too."

"Sure, I'll do it," Dante said. "Let's go."

Luco caught Dante's shoulder before he could escape. "Easy there, son. No offense, but I need someone a bit older to take her home."

"What do you mean by that?" Dante folded his arms and lowered his eyebrows.

"Don't take it personally, but between you and Raven, only one of you is impervious to bullets, knives—pretty much violence of any kind with the exception of wooden stakes."

"I could get her home safely, dad," Dante said. "I know I could."

"I know you could too, but for the sake of my aging heart, I'd like Raven to take her home. I'll feel better knowing she's with him," Luco said. "After all, I need your help here at the tent meeting after everyone has gone."

Dante gave an exaggerated sigh. "If you say so."

"Really, I don't mind if Dante or Garrett takes her home," Raven said. "I don't want to cause any trouble."

"Nonsense." Luco shooed Raven's words away with a wave of his hand. "You take her and she'll be perfectly safe. Garrett,

Dante, and I will stay here and continue to minister until everyone has gone, and then we'll meet you at home after everything is packed up."

"Really, Papa, I'll be fine without—"

"*No.*" Luco's voice hardened. He glanced between Garrett and Dante, then landed his focus on Calandra. "Raven is going with you, and that's final. Garrett is here to learn and experience ministry, Dante is too young, and I need to stay to make sure everything is taken care of. My decision is final. Do you understand?"

"Yes," Calandra said.

Luco turned to Garrett and Dante. "What about you two?"

They both nodded, but the scorn hadn't faded from Garrett's face.

"It's settled then. Raven, you and Calandra may go."

They walked along the path together, but separate. Raven didn't want to risk even brushing up against her for fear that he might incur more of Garrett's wrath. Or worse yet, that he might decide he enjoyed contact with her.

Bare branches cast harsh, jagged shadows along the ground like a thousand spider legs reaching out to grab them, but mostly they outlined the edges of the path. The moon drenched the walkway with silver light so bright that they hadn't needed to light the torch Luco gave them in case it got too dark.

"How did you become a vampire?" Calandra asked, the first words either of them had spoken since they'd left the tent meeting about five minutes earlier.

Raven looked at her as they walked. The moonlight reflecting off her dark hair had a bluish tint to it. She was beautiful—so much that Raven had to look away to keep from staring too long. "It's a long story."

"It's a long walk home," she said. "I'd like to know, if you don't mind telling me."

What could it hurt, exhuming a few painful memories for the sake of conversation? "It's not a happy story."

"Like I said, if you don't want to tell me—"

"No, no. I'll tell you. I'm just warning you that it's not the type of story that makes for pleasant conversation."

She caught him staring at her again. "I can handle it."

Wasn't *that* the truth. After what she'd seen him do, his story might seem as tame as one of her father's tent meetings. He sighed. "It was a Tuesday night. I had just turned twenty."

April of 1802

Raven's older brothers had gone out for the evening, probably carousing with their friends in town again. He had left the rest of his family—his father, mother, and his younger sister—to go outside and check on their cow, Bella. She'd been mooing something terrible for the last few minutes or so by the time Raven got outside.

In his hand he held a blazing torch, but he had to hide it behind one of their sheds because it only seemed to disturb the cow even more. There, in the foggy darkness, he stroked Bella's nose and neck until she finally calmed down.

"Everything alright out there, son?" his father called from inside the house.

"Fine, dad. Bella's just spooked at something."

"Good thing that's all. We can't afford for her to come up short on another day's milk," Raven's father said through the window nearest Bella's pen. "Take care of her, will you?"

"I'll check her out. Don't worry about it."

Bella's milk provided just one of many sources of revenue for the Worth family. They also raised chickens, pigs, horses, goats, and a variety of crops, but Bella held a special place in their hearts since she was their only cow.

Raven felt something rough under his fingers as he stroked her neck. "What's that, Bella?"

He found two small indentations—no, *wounds* in her neck. Had she leaned against an exposed nail in her fence or something? If she had, then Raven would be sure to have a word with his brothers about it. They handled maintenance around the family farm. Stray nails fell under their jurisdiction.

The lights inside the house went out. His parents and little sister were probably going to bed. His brothers hadn't returned home yet and probably wouldn't for several more hours, even though it was only a Tuesday night.

Well, with the lights out now he couldn't get a good look at the marks on Bella's neck. "Bella, I need to relight the torch, alright? I need to see what happened to your neck."

He retrieved the torch from behind the shed and brought it over. Bella mooed in protest, but Raven calmed her with a few more strokes on her nose. Upon closer inspection he saw that the marks were worse than just marks.

They were holes—deep ones, but only two. Too precise for her to have leaned against an exposed nail. He wondered if one of his idiot brothers had been careless and hit her with a rake or something.

Either way, he couldn't just leave them like that. If he didn't clean the wounds and patch her up she might get an infection, and then they might lose her.

Raven started back toward the house, then stopped when he heard a strange sound, almost like a whimper, coming from the far side of the fence. He stood still and listened for a moment.

He heard nothing else, so he continued on. Probably just the wind, or perhaps one of the animals had escaped. If it was the latter, he should probably go have a look, but not until after he tended to Bella's—

There it was again, only this time more of a whisper than a whimper. It almost sounded like someone had said his name into the darkness. He craned his torso to peer around the corner of the fence, but he just didn't have a good angle. He moved a few steps closer, then he dismissed it as his imagination and turned away.

"Help me." The whispered words hit his ears the instant he turned his back.

Ice flowed through Raven's veins. Had he really just heard

that?

He took a tentative step closer to the corner of the fence, now less than five yards away, but he still couldn't see around it. The fence stood four or five feet high, was made of adjacent wooden boards with less than an inch between each one, and didn't offer him anything even close to a line of sight on who—or what—might be just around the corner.

Fog hung in the air, wispy like the smoke from a dying fire at a deserted campsite. Raven could only see about twenty feet ahead of his position. Beyond the fencepost a dark haze cloaked the majority of his family's land—several hundred acres of wide open space with a smattering of small shelters for the different types of animals they raised. All familiar territory, even in the blackest night. Still, something else could be out there.

One of the animals had escaped, he told himself. It had to be. Probably Hector, their wily black stud. He'd gotten out three times already in the past two weeks. Smart horse. He'd found a way to nudge the gate on the fence so it opened, giving him free reign of the property.

"Help... me."

The only problem was that for all his mischief, Hector couldn't speak.

Raven stopped, now little more than six feet from the corner.

"Please...." The voice sounded airy and feminine—almost *alluring*. Definitely not Hector.

Raven extended his torch into the foggy night. If someone

was there and needed help, he would help, of course. He just wished the situation didn't sour his stomach so much. Then again, why be afraid? He was a healthy young man who could outrun both of his older, stronger brothers. Plus, he had a torch.

He didn't hear anything as he approached the corner and peered around. Seeing nothing, he rounded the angle and took a few steps forward, the torch in his left hand, the fingers of his right hand running along the rough wooden fence boards. After several more steps he convinced himself that he'd imagined the voice.

Bella mooed from her spot inside the fence, back toward the house, a reminder that Raven ought to be fetching her some bandages instead of chasing voices on the wind.

When he turned back, a body lay at his feet.

Chapter 25

Raven's stomach tried to leap out of his belly. He staggered back and almost dropped his torch. What was going on? Who was she, and how did she end up at his feet—where she hadn't been three seconds before?

She was alive, but curled up and shivering in the cold autumn night on the ground. Long blonde hair covered her face, and sheer dark fabric clothed her body.

Raven took a deep breath to slow his hammering heartbeat then bent down next to her. "Are you alright?"

"Help me," she moaned. Her voice didn't match the ethereal quality of the words whispered on the wind, but there was no other explanation for what he'd heard. "Please."

Her identity didn't matter. She needed help. Raven touched her arm. "Can you stand?"

"I—I think so—" she said.

Raven helped her to her feet with care, and finally got a good look at her: high, accentuated cheekbones, vivid hazel eyes laced with a touch of mystery, thin red lips, and a lithe, shapely figure. Beautiful, but in a unique way.

Alluring.

"What are you doing out here?" Raven gratified himself with a lingering look at her exquisite form—to ensure she was uninjured, of course. "Are you hurt?"

"No." She locked eyes with him. "I'm not."

Raven swallowed and stepped back, but found he didn't want to look away. He blinked hard and shook himself out of the moment. "What—how did you get here? What are you doing?"

She didn't move. She just stood there, staring at him. Given Raven's engagement to Kristen Hannigan, the daughter of the Worth family's nearest neighbors, prolonged stares at or from any woman weren't a good idea, especially one as intriguing and mysterious as this one.

"I don't understand what's going on." Raven's gaze darted from her eyes to anywhere and everywhere else. He knew that if he met those eyes again, those dragon eyes of hers, he wouldn't be able to stop looking.

"Don't be afraid." Her voice blossomed into the wispy, enticing tone he'd heard in the wind. "I won't hurt you."

Raven set his eyes on hers.

"That's right, handsome." She stepped toward him, her red lips curved in a cunning smile. "You're perfectly safe with me."

Safe—and in profound danger. But it didn't matter. Her seductive gaze had numbed him to everything else. Within a few seconds, the rest of the world faded to black, leaving only the dreamy, sultry figure drawing closer to him.

Her body swayed to a slow, unheard rhythm as she

approached. The sheer black fabric—basically a lacy robe that didn't split all the way down—parted in a deep gorge that stretched from her neck down to just above her navel, yet concealed enough to keep Raven interested. The remainder of the fabric flowed down her legs, aside from a gratuitous slit that ran up the left side almost to her hip.

Kristen, his red-haired beauty, resurfaced in his memory for an instant, then vanished as this new creature extended her hand to touch his chest. Her fingers slipped under his jacket and unfastened the buttons on his shirt.

Raven sucked in a sharp breath. Her hand felt like an icy snake slithering up his bare skin from his chest to his neck. She pulled him close, against her equally frigid body, and pressed her cold lips on his.

Raven drank in her touch, though it sent shivers to his fingertips. He dropped the torch, wrapped his arms around her, and delved deeper into her embrace, into her kiss.

Her affections progressed from his lips to his cheek, to his jawline, to his neck. He tilted his head back and to the side to accommodate her kissing, now accompanied by desperate, passionate clawing at his shoulders and chest.

A sharp pain jolted him from his trance. He pushed her away and clutched his neck. Blood streaked his palm—and tainted her lips.

"What the—"

"Don't be afraid." When she smiled, two elongated fangs protruded from behind her lips. "I won't hurt you."

She'd just *bit his neck*, yet she said she wouldn't hurt him?

"You know you want this," she whispered as she ran her hands down her torso.

He *did* want her, but he knew he shouldn't. This wasn't right. Yet despite the warning that echoed in his chest and the bloody wound on his neck, he stared into her captivating hazel eyes—eyes like a dragon's—and stepped toward her once again.

No kissing this time—she went straight to his neck. He gasped at the second pinch, then confined her torso in his arms once again. They fell to the earth, Raven on his back, the temptress on top of him, draining his life away one gulp at a time until everything went black.

Raven awoke in darkness and confusion with fragmented memories of what had happened. He lay on his back, unable to sit up due to something heavy above him. Thick walls enclosed him on both sides, and only a few inches of space separated his head and another wall, and his feet and yet another wall. Soft pillows padded his silent prison.

He screamed.

He howled and yelled until his voice ran hoarse. He banged on the ceiling not more than six inches above his face, but no one came to set him free.

He would die in that space. He was certain of it.

Raven flattened his palms on the ceiling and pushed with all of his might. To his surprise, the ceiling not only moved, but moved easily—until it thumped against something above it.

What?

Though the left side wouldn't budge, he managed to wedge his arm through a crack in the ceiling's right side. He felt the smooth top of his prison with his fingertips, then the rough, gritty surface of the next layer of incarceration.

He slid his arm back in, rotated his body to lay facedown on his soft pillows, and braced his back against the ceiling. With all his might he pushed up with his hands and legs and maneuvered his position to get more leverage.

Something heavy scraped against something heavier as he heaved against the ceiling. Finally a loud crash sounded, like a boulder impacting the bottom of a mountainside. He was free—though still engulfed in darkness. Raven sprung up and wandered around, only to find four more walls boxing him in.

Was this Hell? A place of eternal darkness that just kept growing and growing with each new level he encountered? Filled with coarse stone and mazes? For a moment he desired to return to his first prison, small and safe, but thought better of it.

His fingers caught on a lip in one of the walls. He traced it with his index finger down to the floor, then back up and around in a rectangular shape. A door? A passageway of some sort, perhaps? It felt like stone, just like the rest of the walls.

Where would it lead? To a deeper circle—or square—of eternal punishment?

Only one way to find out. He pressed his palms against the rectangle, anchored his feet to the ground and struggled against the stone. It budged, but not by much. After several more shoves and pushes, the wall dropped away and slammed down onto the ground. Glistening silver light poured into the doorway.

Raven rubbed his eyes as they adjusted to the light, then he stepped through the frame. The scent of grass and leaves filled his nostrils. A cool wind caressed his face and his long black hair. If this was Hell, he could probably get used to it.

A black canvass hung above him, dotted with pinpricks of light that surrounded a large, glowing orb. The sky, the stars, the moon. He remembered them. Perhaps he wasn't dead after all. He turned back to look at his cage.

If he wasn't dead, then why had he just broken out of a crypt?

He squinted at the name engraved into the stone over the doorway he'd forced his way through: WORTH.

What? His family's mausoleum? But why?

His brothers. They must have played a joke on him. Raven didn't know how, but they had somehow managed to stuff him inside a coffin inside a stone box inside the mausoleum. In black dress clothes too, just like he'd been at a real funeral. Not a humorous prank, and certainly in poor taste. He'd get them back, though.

At least he knew the way home from here.

Raven arrived at his home that evening just after dinner, or at least that's what he gathered from a quick peek inside the window near Bella's pen. Strange—Bella wasn't there. He hoped she was alright.

He walked up to the front door, opened it, and stepped inside.

"Well, I'm home, finally," he said to his family.

No one said a thing. They all just stared at him with their mouths gaping open, their eyes wide.

Chapter 26

"I said 'I'm home.' Don't look so surprised, especially you two." He pointed to his two older brothers, Robert and Rodney.

Their hearty laughter, which he had grown to hate when it was at his expense, didn't pour from their mouths as he expected. They just exchanged glances with each other and their parents.

"Raven!" Sandra, his seven-year-old sister, ran to him. "You're back, you're back!"

He swept her up into his arms and squeezed her against his chest. "Hello, Sandra. It's good to see you too, my angel."

"Brrrr, it must be cold out there. Your skin is freezing." She pulled away from him and flipped her dark brown hair from one shoulder to the other.

Raven shrugged. "It didn't seem too bad to me. Are you getting sick?"

"No, silly. Maybe *you're* getting sick."

"I don't know about that. You feel lighter to me." He set her down and faced his mother. "Has she lost weight?"

His mother dropped the ceramic bowl in her hands and it crashed to the floor. It broke into several large pieces and strawberries tumbled across the hardwood. "God in Heaven…"

"Mama? What's wrong?"

He bent down and started to pick up some of the pieces for her, along with some of the strawberries. They looked so red and juicy, and his stomach rumbled with hunger. He wiped the dust off of one with his sleeve, pinched the stem between his fingers, and bit into the fruit, but instead of succulent sweetness he tasted dry, bitter ash. He grimaced, but swallowed the bite anyway.

"Ugh—these strawberries are terrible. Where on earth did you get these?"

"From our very own farm, silly." Sandra's green eyes twinkled. "Mama and I picked them today."

"What is this?" his father asked from behind him. "Some kind of sick joke?"

Raven whirled around. "It's alright, Papa. They're just strawberries. I didn't mean anything by it."

His father, a big man in his early fifties with black hair just like Raven's, shook his head. "I'm not talking about the strawberries. I'm talking about the *imposter* standing in my house, pretending to be my son."

Raven tilted his head. "What? What are you talking about? Papa, it's me, Raven."

"No, you're not. It's not possible."

Raven swiveled and faced his mother. "Mama, what's he talking about? Why is everyone acting so spooked?"

She didn't answer. She just put her hand over her mouth as tears rolled down her cheeks.

"Robert. Rodney." He focused on his brothers. "You've had your fun, now quit acting. I never expected you'd get Mama and Papa in on this."

They just shook their heads like their father had.

"Enough, you two. They all know by now that you somehow tricked me and put me in the family mausoleum in a coffin. Not funny. You could have ruined my nice clothes. You can't imagine how hard it was to get out of there."

"That stone covering had to weigh at least seven hundred pounds," Robert said.

"More like eight or nine hundred." Rodney cleared his throat. "How on earth did you move it?"

"The mausoleum door weighed well over a thousand. It took six men to move it in place after we sealed you inside," Robert said.

"You got *six* men to seal me in there? You two and a bunch of your dumb brute friends?" Raven eyed his father. "Papa, don't tell me you went along with this."

His father shook his head again. "You're no son of mine. You—you're—"

"I'm *back*," Raven finished for him. "I'm back. Rob and Rod played a joke on me and stuffed me in a coffin in the family mausoleum. It was a bad joke, and you'd better believe they'll get what's coming to them."

All three men shook their heads.

"So you're really going to keep lying to me, even when I'm standing here in front of you?"

"We buried you in there alright," Rob glanced at Rod. "But it wasn't a joke."

Raven squinted at him. "What—what are you talking about?"

"Raven, you died last night, and we buried you this afternoon."

"Alright, enough," Raven said between chuckles. "You can stop the charade. I'm obviously not dead. I'm standing here in front of you, free from today's escapades. Sorry I missed my share of work for the day, dad, but you have Rob and Rod to blame for that."

"You were dead when we found you last night." Rod motioned toward the door. "Just lying outside of Bella's fence, dead. Two large holes in your neck. We figured some wild animal got you or something."

The holes in Bella's neck. The whispers on the wind. The blonde-haired girl in the sheer robe with those vivid dragon eyes. Her icy skin against his. Kissing. Pain in his neck.

Darkness.

He remembered it all.

"No—it wasn't a wild animal. It was—" He stopped. He couldn't tell them, of course. They'd think he was out of his mind. "I'm confused."

"You're supposed to be dead," Rob said.

"Don't talk to it," Papa said. "That's not your brother. That's something else. Something evil."

Raven put his arms out. "Papa, how can you say that? I'm standing here, alive. Obviously I'm not dead. What more proof do you need?"

Papa shook his head again. "You're dead. I saw it with my own eyes."

"And now you're seeing me with your own eyes again." He turned back to his mother. "Mama, tell them I'm not dead, will you? This isn't funny anymore."

She didn't move, except to pull Sandra close to her as she quivered.

"Papa, wha—" Raven stopped when he found a musket pointed at him.

"I want you out of here, *demon*." Papa raised the gun barrel to Raven's face. "And don't you ever set foot on my property again, or so help me God I'll make sure you stay dead this time."

Raven glanced at his brothers. "Alright, this has gone too far. You two made your point. Can we all please stop pretending now?"

"Get out. Now." His father shifted his grip on the gun, then centered it at Raven's chest.

"Papa, I'm *not dead*. I'm right here. Don't you see that?"

"Then why are you so pale?" Sandra asked from behind.

"What?"

"She's right," Rob said. "You look like a walking carcass, like you haven't got a single drop of blood in your veins."

Raven glanced at his skin. It looked a little whiter than usual, but maybe they'd just rubbed flour all over him or something. "Toss me that hand mirror on the couch, will you? I'll wipe it off, right now."

Rod complied, and Raven caught the looking glass in his left hand, then gave his brothers a scowl only a scorned younger brother could give. He held the mirror up to his face, then adjusted it. He twisted and contorted it, but for some reason it wasn't reflecting his image.

"What is this? Another joke?" Raven asked. "Why can't I see my reflection?"

Papa's eyes widened again. "Is it true, Gina?"

Raven turned back. His mother had been standing in the same spot behind him ever since he walked inside the house. She had seen it too.

She nodded, and her face crumpled with fear and sorrow.

A gunshot split the air and a spike plunged into Raven's ribs. He dropped backward and hit the floor.

Chapter 27

Raven clutched his torso and wheezed while the rest of the room exploded with shrieks and hollers. His brothers charged their father and ripped the gun from his hands while his mother and sister screamed at the sight of him lying on the floor, bleeding.

"He's a *demon*," his father kept repeating, even as he struggled against his sons. "He's a Godforsaken demon!"

The pain spread throughout Raven's entire body, even to the tips of his toes and fingers, but it dissipated just as fast as it began. He lifted his head and gawked as the bloody wound under his fingers sealed up. The blood stopped flowing, and he gasped a deep breath of air. When he stood to his feet, the room fell as silent as the crypt from which he'd escaped not a half hour earlier.

"See?" Papa broke the silence with a yell. "I told you he was a *demon*."

No reflection. Unharmed by gunshots. Pale skin. Woke up in a coffin that night.

Raven was starting to believe it too.

"I think you need to leave," Rob shouted over the ruckus as he and Rod tried to hold Papa back. "I don't know who you are, but you're obviously not our brother anymore. Get out of here."

"But—"

"Just leave before we change our minds. The next time he tries to kill you, it might work, alright?" Rod yelled. "Don't ever come back here. Never."

This wasn't happening. It *couldn't* be happening. He was dead—yet somehow living, breathing, and possibly invulnerable? Impossible.

"Get out, *demon*," Papa growled. "Or I shall smite thee again!"

Raven shook his head. This wasn't real.

A soft hand touched his shoulder. His mother's. Tears still streamed from her green eyes.

"I know you're my son," she said between snivels. "Somewhere in you is my son. But—you're *not* my son. Please—please go. Let us mourn him, the son we lost."

Raven felt his own tears welling up behind his eyes. "Mama—"

"*Please*," she pleaded. "Please go. You can't stay here. You have no place here anymore."

Raven clenched his jaw tight. Tears seeped from the corners of his eyes and crawled down his cold cheeks. Without another word he turned, stormed through the front door, and left his family behind forever.

1885

After his story, Calandra didn't say a word for a long time as they walked. When she finally broke the silence, she said, "I'm so sorry, Raven. No wonder you've taken to our family the way you have."

Raven nodded and looked away. He hoped she hadn't noticed the fresh teardrops streaming down his face. He feigned a cough and wiped them away, even though it was probably too late to hide them.

"There's more, if you'd like to hear it." Raven stared into her deep brown eyes for a long moment, definitely longer than Garrett would have liked.

Calandra gave him a sad smile. "Only if you want to tell me."

April of 1802

Kristen would understand. She would realize it was really him and not a walking corpse. She would see that he was really alive, that someone had made a mistake, and that they could live their lives together just as they had planned.

He would even tell her of his infidelity. She needed to know. He needed to be forthright about it, as it had led to his "death" and burial. Kristen would understand, though. He was attacked and harmed against his will. She would understand.

The night would linger for several more hours, judging by how dark it was. The trek to the Hannigans' house wouldn't take more than twenty minutes at a leisurely pace, but Raven didn't want leisure. He ran almost the entire way, venting heartbreak through his pumping legs and arms, and he arrived within just a few minutes.

A sole light still shone through Kristen's window on the

second floor. Perhaps avoiding her parents, at least for the time being, would work in his favor. Many nights past he'd considered paying her a visit via the tall oak tree just outside of her room, but he hadn't yet. A sturdy branch stretched almost to her windowsill, an easy route to access her room.

After a few glances around, Raven climbed into the tree and peered into her room. Kristen lay in her bed, her eyes closed. A candle flickered on the dresser next to her.

Raven dug his fingers between the window and the frame, careful to lift it with as little sound as possible. He swung his left leg over the windowsill, pushed off of the branch with his right, and landed in her room with a thud.

Kristen stirred and opened her eyes. She saw him and sucked in a breath to scream, but Raven sprang forward and clamped his hand over her mouth. She grabbed his wrist. Fear swirled in her blue eyes, then she stopped moving altogether. Her eyes widened, then narrowed, then widened again.

"It's me, Kristen," Raven whispered. "Don't scream, alright?"

She didn't move for a moment, then gave him a slight nod. When he pulled his hand away from her mouth, she said, "Raven? Is it really you?"

He nodded. "It's me."

She stared at his torso and she sat up in bed. "What happened to you? Are you alright?"

"Oh…" The gunshot from his father's gun. The blood

glistened on his black shirt. "It's nothing. Not my blood on the shirt. It's from Bella, our cow. She has two strange marks on her neck—"

Kristen leaned forward and wrapped her arms around him. They shared an embrace, long and warm.

"But—" She pulled away from him.

Raven knew what was coming next.

"—you're *dead*." The candlelight flickered in her blue eyes.

"No, I'm not." His tone conveyed more frustration than he would have liked. She didn't deserve harsh words, not after all that had supposedly happened. "I'm alive, and I'm here right now, in your room."

She reached out and touched his face, then pulled her hand back. "Your face is freezing, and when I hugged you it felt like hugging a piece of ice. Is it cold outside?"

He sighed. Not that again. "I don't know why I feel so cold. You're not the first person to say that to me tonight."

"I don't understand."

"Don't worry about it."

"No, I mean I don't understand what happened," she said. "I was at your funeral."

Raven's heart dropped. The last of his hopes that his brothers were playing an elaborate trick evaporated with her admission. He'd had a funeral—a real one from the sound of it—because his family thought he had really died, all after his encounter with the young blonde-haired vixen outside of Bella's pen.

There was no way Kristen would have attended a fake

funeral for him, and not even his tricky brothers would take a scheme so far as to affect her. They knew that no matter what, she was considered off-limits. No exceptions.

"Kristen, I—" He sighed. "I don't know what happened. I don't know why my parents buried me. I don't know why everyone thought I was dead. I'm obviously not."

"Obviously." Kristen nodded. "Your brothers found you laying by the cow pen. Don't you remember anything?"

Raven sucked in a quick breath and looked away. He did remember. "Yes. But if I tell you, you have to believe me. Every word."

Kristen shrugged. "Why wouldn't I believe you? You've never lied to me before."

"I'm just warning you—you're not going to like what I have to say."

"I have you back. That's what matters right now." She smiled and took his hands in hers. "You can tell me."

With a heavy sigh, Raven told her what had happened last night, starting with checking Bella's wounds and ending at his blackout with the blonde-haired girl on top of him, gnawing on his neck. When he finished, he read the hurt on Kristen's face.

"Did you kiss her in return?" she asked.

He had. To say he hadn't would be an outright lie. He'd not only returned the blonde-haired girl's affections, but he'd done so as willingly as he'd ever done anything in his life.

"Yes," he said. "I did."

Kristen turned her head away, but Raven could sense her struggling to keep from crying. His confession of infidelity had wounded her even deeper than his "death."

"I'm so sorry, Kristen," he said. "It was like she had me under some sort of spell. I barely knew what I was doing, or what she was doing to me."

Kristen folded her arms. "I bet it was real hard to look away, given what she was wearing, and how she threw herself at you like a common prostitute."

Raven bit his tongue. "You do realize this woman almost killed me, don't you? Do you really think I willingly participated in *that*?"

She glared at him. "From the way you just described it? Yes, I think you did."

Maybe she didn't understand after all. Raven touched her shoulder, but she shifted away from him. "Kristen, you have to believe me."

"Why would you even tell me a story like that? Are you trying to say you don't want to marry me? That you want to break off our engagement? If that's what you want, just say it."

"No, that's not it at all. I don't want to lose you."

"You're not far from it right now," she muttered.

He dropped from the bed to his knees in front of her. "Whatever I have to do to make this up to you, I'll do it. I swear. I don't want to lose you. I love you."

The scowl didn't leave her face, but she held eye contact with him for a long time. "I want to trust you, but I can't. I feel like I don't know you anymore. You're not the Raven I knew. There's something different about you."

Raven shook his head. "No. I'm not different. I'm the same person I was when I saw you yesterday afternoon, before she—before any of this happened."

Kristen's jaw tightened and a vein in her neck bulged. Raven locked onto it, and he found himself unable to look away. The experience reminded him of how he couldn't help but stare at the blonde-haired beauty last night.

"I think you should leave, Raven."

Base, primal hunger ravaged him from the inside out, different from anything else he'd ever experienced. Sure, he'd needed to eat before, but this feeling surpassed that of even his biggest appetite. He didn't just need to eat—he had to *feed*.

"Raven," Kristen said. "Did you hear me?"

He met her gaze. "Huh?"

She rolled her eyes. He hated when she did that. "I said you need to leave. Now."

That vein still protruded from her neck. It pulled at him from the inside. Oh, to taste Kristen's blood on his tongue—

What?

Raven blinked and shook his head. Blood? Absurd. He needed food. Meat, bread, cheese, vegetables, fruit. Not blood. Not human blood. Definitely not Kristen's blood.

"Why are you looking at me like that?" Kristen's eyes

narrowed. "Stop it. I don't like it."

"Like what?" Raven watched the vein disappear under her skin as she moved away from him. "Oh, it's nothing. I'm just hungry, that's all."

"I bet you're *hungry*, alright." She folded her arms again. "But don't think you're going to get the same thing from me that you got from your little blonde friend."

"Wouldn't dream of it." No, Raven had something else in mind, something inexplicable, something diabolical. Something totally unimaginable.

He wanted to drink her blood. That's what he craved.

"You're behaving strangely. I want you to go."

Raven stared into her eyes. "No. I'm not leaving."

Kristen raised her eyebrows. "What did you just say to me?"

"Do you want me to repeat myself?" Raven asked. "I said I'm not going anywhere."

Not until I drain every last drop from your body.

Where did *that* come from? Maybe Kristen was right—maybe he should leave. He should go, otherwise he might hurt her.

No, he *would* hurt her.

"I'm sorry," he said. "I need to go. I'm sorry."

"That's what I just said."

He had to get out of there. Now. Raven stood to his feet and hurried to the window. He glanced at her once more over his shoulder. "I'm sorry, Kristen. For everything."

He leapt through her window and into the tree before she

could respond. His feet hit the earth and Kristen's voice, now a harsh half-whisper, sounded from above.

"Raven," she called down to him. "Where are you going? What's wrong?"

He turned back and saw her shapely silhouette in the window. Emotion and hunger swelled in his belly. He wanted to charge back up that tree, take her in his arms, and consume the life flowing through her veins.

"I can't," he said. "I need to go. I can't stay with you or—"

"Please," she said. "I'm sorry for the way I behaved. I was just mad at you. I know you didn't mean to be unfaithful to me. Please come back up."

Raven swallowed, then acquiesced. He knew he shouldn't go up, but his hunger drove him into the tree and through her window once more. Back in her room again, Kristen stood before him, wearing only a flannel nightgown and probably not much underneath it from what Raven could tell.

"Come over here, Raven." Kristen didn't have nearly the incapacitating allure that the blonde-haired girl had, but that didn't stop Raven from taking her in his arms and kissing her.

She didn't resist him, which was good, especially since they had only ever kissed a handful of times before that. Raven pressed his body against her and drank in her warmth. He hoped he could direct his hunger into his passion for her, but he didn't last long before he moved his lips to kissing her tantalizing neck.

"Raven—" Kristen applied pressure to his chest with her

palms. "—maybe we should slow down."

"No," he said between nibbles. He retreated to her cheeks, then back to her lips in an effort to avoid sinking his teeth into the vein in her neck.

"Really—" She pushed him away. "—we need to slow down. We're not married yet."

She couldn't tell him what to do. She couldn't stop him. He wouldn't allow it.

"I don't care." He moved close again.

"Then you need to leave." Kristen shoved him back, hard, and put her hands on her hips. Her eyebrows arched and she glared at him.

Not this time. He stared into her blue eyes, his brow furrowed. "I'm not leaving. You don't want me to leave."

"What?" She raised an eyebrow. "I don't—want you to leave?"

Raven shook his head. "No. You don't."

"I—don't." Kristen's countenance neutralized and her hands drooped to her sides.

He stepped toward her, and the thirst flared in his gut. "You want me to stay with you."

"Yes, I do." She nodded.

Why she now wanted to comply, Raven didn't know, but it didn't matter. He reached his hands out to her and said, "Come to me."

Kristen walked into his arms, and he held her close, kissing her again, this time on her neck. Something tingled in his gums on his upper teeth, and the next thing he knew he'd bit her neck. She gasped and convulsed once, but Raven anchored her in place with his arms. She couldn't escape even if she wanted to.

"Raven—" she moaned.

Warm liquid metal tanged his tongue and slid down his throat like smooth, but bitter honey. He drank and drank until she fell limp in his arms and slumped to the floor in a crumpled heap, her eyes vacant and cold.

Raven stared at her for a long time, unsure of what had just happened. She lay there, unmoving, with two deep holes in her neck encircled by a mouth-sized ring of blood.

Had he—*killed* her?

The ravenous hunger in his stomach had faded to nothing, now that he'd consumed his fill of her blood. Her *blood*. What had he done?

What had he *become*?

A light tapping sounded at her door, then a muffled voice with a thick Irish brogue. "Kristen? Are you alright?"

Her father, Patrick.

Raven's eyes widened. He wanted to run, leap out her window and disappear into the shadows, but his legs wouldn't move.

The doorknob turned, and her father stepped inside.

Don't see me.

"Kristen?" Patrick gasped and froze in place, then charged to her side. "God Almighty—what's happened to you?"

Raven watched the entire scene unfold, but Patrick somehow hadn't noticed him, even though he stood no more than a few feet from Kristen's lifeless body. Patrick hollered until Kristen's mother Shannon also appeared in the doorway, her eyes wide with shock. Together they wailed and wept over her and repeatedly checked her for signs of life but found none.

Though Raven didn't fully realize what he'd done or why he'd done it, he understood enough to know that he'd taken their daughter from them forever.

1885

Now only about a mile away from the Zambini family's house, Calandra stopped and stared at Raven. "You killed her?"

He lowered his head. "Yes."

"But—from what you described, you did the same thing to her that you did to Harry, and he turned into a vampire. Why didn't she?"

"I never said she didn't." Raven stared into Calandra's eyes.

"She—she *did* turn into a vampire?"

Raven looked away again. "To my everlasting regret, she did."

Calandra stepped toward him and touched his shoulder. "What happened to her?"

"Kristen—" Raven sighed. Why he'd decided to dig into his past for Calandra, he didn't know. "—killed herself."

Chapter 28

"She became a vampire, just like me, and she killed herself. She couldn't handle it." Raven shook his head. "I couldn't handle it either, but I couldn't bring myself to commit suicide over it. Instead I took the coward's way out and survived, hunting those around me, draining their blood little by little, often several people in one night."

"You turned them all into vampires?"

"No, no. That's not how it works." Raven motioned with his head toward the path, and started walking with Calandra at his side. "If a vampire attacks a person, the victim only turns if that vampire drinks all of their blood. This can happen all at once like it did with Harry and Kristen—and me—or slowly, spread out over time in multiple attacks. All in all, I've only created a few vampires in my lifetime, and all of them have been destroyed, their souls damned to Hell for eternity because of me."

"Don't say that, Raven," Calandra said. "You couldn't help yourself. You were under a curse, and you're free from all of that now."

"I know." Raven shrugged. "Sometimes I just don't feel very free."

Calandra took his hand in hers and gave it a firm squeeze as they walked. "You will. Give the Holy Spirit time to work that out for you. In the meantime, just follow God. He'll take care of the rest."

Raven stared down at her hand. It warmed his frigid skin, but he knew Garrett wouldn't like it. Then again, Garrett wasn't here. "I'm sure you're right. You sound just like your father sometimes, you know that?"

She smiled at him. "I *am* his daughter."

They walked hand-in-hand for another moment until they caught each other's eyes again. Raven's heart fluttered and Calandra's face flushed, then she pulled her hand away from his and walked a half-step farther away from him with her arms folded.

The moon still loomed over them, but the forest's canopy had thickened, so Raven pulled out a match and lit the torch Luco had given them. It ignited to life and warm yellow light illuminated their path.

"I'm sorry," Raven said after a long pause. "I shouldn't have—"

"No, it was me. I grabbed your hand. I let it linger there for too long." She didn't make eye contact with him. "I don't want to give you the wrong impression."

The wrong impression? What other impression could she have given him?

"It's fine. I know you and Garrett are happy together, and I don't want to come between that." It was a lie, but a necessary one.

"Did you ever see that blonde vampire again?" Calandra

asked.

Raven sighed.

"Forget I asked."

"No. I'd like to tell you."

"Really, you've been forthright enough for one night if you don't want to keep talking."

"I have, but I want you to know." He lost himself in her deep brown eyes for a moment, then he refocused on the path ahead of him.

"Alright." Her voice was soft and clear.

"She also has to do with Kristen's death."

April of 1802

While Kristen's father wailed from her room on the second floor, Raven made his way out of their house unseen, or so he'd thought. Guilt mocked his footsteps as he walked down the gravel path under the moonlight, but he stopped when he heard a scuffle behind him.

He whirled around, ready to face a gun-wielding Patrick Hannigan. Instead he found a slim female figure with blonde hair, sheer black clothing, and steamy hazel eyes. The temptress from last night. The one responsible for everything that had transpired since then.

Raven didn't even think. He flung himself at her in a rage, ready to tear her apart with his bare hands, but she sidestepped and smacked him in the back of the head with her fist. He dropped to the earth, more stunned at her speed than by the blow itself.

When he looked for her again, she was gone, replaced by a thick mist that smelled like a mixture of sweet morning dew and stale death. Laughter—unmistakably her voice—sounded all around him.

"Who are you?" Raven asked aloud into the night air. His head swiveled in all directions but he couldn't determine where she'd gone.

"You have so much to learn," she said from behind him.

Raven stumbled to his feet, several steps away from her. After what she'd done to him, he had good reason to keep his distance. He clenched his teeth. "Who are you?"

She stood there, one hand on her hip, and laughed again. "My name is Vanessa. What's yours?"

Raven hurtled at her again, but she laid him on his back with one swift blow to his gut and then another to his chin. He moaned, not from the pain but from the embarrassment and the hurt inside of him.

"You might as well give up." Vanessa showed her elongated fangs in a toothy smile. "You have no idea what I'm capable of, or what you're capable of, for that matter. Now are you going to tell me your name or not, Mr. Worth?"

Raven stopped. "How do you know my last name?"

"I stopped by your property again tonight and found your family's mausoleum. I figured you'd have the same last name since you lived with them. Do you have a first name?"

Why should he tell her? She was his enemy. An enemy with a British accent that wasn't there during their first encounter. "It's Raven."

"*Raven?*" she said. "That's a cunning name even for a vampire, much less a human."

He tilted his head. "A what?"

"A vampire." She rolled her eyes and sighed. "Don't you know what a vampire is?"

"Look, I don't know *anything* about what's going on here. All I know is that I found you last night, we—you *attacked* me, and then I woke up tonight in a *coffin*." Raven stepped toward her, his fists clenched. "What did you do to me?"

She matched his step with one of her own. "I have granted your greatest desire."

Hurt? Pain? Violence? Excommunication from his family? A murderous thirst for human blood? He didn't desire any of those things. "Which is what?"

"It's the same thing every man wants: immortality."

Not only was she dangerous—she was a lunatic too. "You're not making any sense."

"You died last night, Raven. I know. I killed you."

"What?" Raven tensed his jaw. "You—"

She held up a hand. "Tonight you were reborn, a new creation. You're neither living nor dead, but *un*dead. You must feed on the blood of the living to sate your thirst. You've felt it already, and you've already quenched it for the night, haven't you?"

Raven slung a barrage of profanity at her. "Kristen is *dead*, and you're talking to me about this? I should kill you next."

Vanessa put her hand to her mouth. "Oh, I see—she was your lover, wasn't she?"

"Not my lover. My fiancée. We were going to get married and—"

"And you just drank her blood, didn't you?"

Raven stared at her, his eyebrows arched down. "Yes."

"You killed her."

He didn't want to think about that. "Yes."

She smiled. "Take comfort, my friend. Your fiancée can still be your bride, but now for the rest of your unnatural existence, all because you passed along the gift that I shared with you."

"I killed her." Tears pushed against the corners of his eyes. "She's dead. I killed the woman I love."

"If you really loved her, why were you so eager to kiss me? To hold me? To run your hands all over—"

"*Stop.*" Raven pointed his index finger at her. "You tricked me. You cast a spell on me or something. I would never betray Kristen knowingly. You're a witch."

She scoffed and put both hands on her hips. "I am *not* a witch. I'm a vampire."

"This is all your fault," Raven said. "You're the reason Kristen is dead."

"Wrong again." Vanessa advanced closer to him. "*You* killed her. You alone."

"But you made me into what I am," Raven growled. "You're the reason."

"You could have run from me. You could have turned and hurried into your house, but you liked what you saw, and you wanted a taste." She outstretched her arms and moved her pelvis a few inches toward his. "So I gave it to you."

"No. You bewitched me."

She laughed. "There's no doubt about that, but there's nothing I could ever do to any human that would take away their powers of choice. I know I'm *very* convincing, but I also know that somewhere deep inside of you, you made a choice to engage me last night. It cost you your life as you know it, but in return you received a chance to live forever."

"But I have to drink blood in order to stay alive?"

"And you can't go out in the daytime. The sun will kill you. You also can't cross flowing bodies of water, can't come into contact with holy relics or items, can't see your reflection in mirrors and the like, can't cross the threshold of a home except by invitation—"

"I just climbed through Kristen's window on my own."

She glanced back at the house. "You must have been invited in at some point as a human. It probably carried over."

"I don't believe this."

"Well, you'd better start, because you're going to be a vampire forever, or until someone kills you." Vanessa studied at her pointed fingernails.

"You just said I was immortal."

"Yes. Unless you die." She rolled her eyes again. "You can die from the sun, which I mentioned, but also from wooden stakes."

"How?"

"It's all in the Old Lore. If someone puts a stake through your heart, that will kill you. If they pull it back out, it'll be as if nothing happened to you, except you'll feel weakened until you get some more blood."

Vanessa started to circle him. Her dragon eyes scanned him up and down, and he cringed.

"Someone has to stake you, cut off your head, and then stuff it with garlic to really finish you off, though. Otherwise you can come back after being staked for weeks, months or even years at a time. But you'd better hope that doesn't happen to you. If you don't like drinking blood now, you don't want to wake up after having been staked for a long time. Your appetite grows with each day that passes while you're in stasis like that."

Raven wanted to strangle her, but he didn't want to end up in the dirt again either. "So what if I don't want to be a—a—"

"A vampire."

"—a 'vampire' anymore?"

She smirked at him. "Too bad for you. Once a vampire, always a vampire, or until someone kills you. But don't think that dying's a reasonable way out, either. When you die as a vampire, you're damned forever." She glanced at the sky. "Well, you're already damned forever, but dying seals the deal."

Raven stared at her, mouth open. "What happened to the 'choice' you were talking about?"

She shrugged and ran her index finger down his chest until he swatted her hand away. "You've already made it."

The sound of approaching hoofbeats reached Raven's ears. He turned his head to look, but couldn't see anything.

"Come, now." Vanessa tugged at his hand. "Time to go. No need to get caught out here in the darkness when someone arrives to try to help that poor girl you killed."

Raven yanked his hand away. "I loved her. She was everything to me."

"Keep telling yourself that, if it helps you cope. You'll eventually realize that it's much easier to take life and do what you need to do to survive if you develop some apathy. Or even better, some malice."

He shook his head. "I'm not that kind of person."

Vanessa took a long look at the Hannigans' house, then she refocused on Raven. "If you say so. Stay and get killed if you want, but if you don't hurry, we won't have time."

"Time?" That inflamed his curiosity. "For what?"

She smiled. "You'll see. Come, now."

Raven savored her luscious shape as she walked away but wished he'd never indulged himself in the first place. Someday, he vowed, he would make things right with Kristen, but today was not that day. He followed Vanessa into the darkness.

Chapter 29

Vanessa led him, of all places, to his own home, which only stirred up the hurt and the anger inside of him.

"Why are we here?" he asked, ready for another shot at bashing her brains in.

"We have to get your coffin out of the mausoleum. Every morning before sunrise you have to return to your coffin in order to rest. It protects you from the sun and rejuvenates you from any injuries you've sustained, life-threatening or not."

Raven dabbed at the gunshot scar on his torso.

"What happened?"

He cringed. "My father—he shot me when I tried to come home."

Vanessa smirked. "Don't worry about that. It happens to almost all of us at some point."

Raven glared at her. He didn't want to share any camaraderie with her if he could help it.

"Besides, that's not life-threatening. You could get shot a thousand times and not die from it. Probably didn't even hurt for very long, did it? Someone drives a wooden stake through your heart, though, and that's a different story. I don't know why it is, but wooden stakes just sap us of our energy," Vanessa said.

Raven raised an eyebrow.

"Blades can only kill us if we've already been staked. I don't know why I'm telling you all of this right away, though. It's not like anyone will be staking you any time soon, as long as we get your coffin out of here."

"And if we don't?"

"I'd imagine your family will be the first ones out here trying to find a way to kill you for a second time, especially since that gunshot didn't do anything to you."

Raven wanted to disagree, but she was right. Papa's gunshot and accusations of Raven being a demon resounded in his memory. "There's no way just you and I can carry that coffin by ourselves. And besides, where would we even take it?"

"We're taking it to my home, where it—and you—will be safe." She winked at him, which he didn't like. "As far as carrying it—trust me on that."

Trust her? This woman had seduced him, killed him, turned him into a vampire, and then blamed him for all of it. How could he trust her in *anything*?

Still, she seemed to know what she was talking about, and he couldn't go back home or to the Hannigans' house. Whether he trusted her or not, he didn't seem to have much of a choice but to follow her lead for now.

She led him to the mausoleum and pointed to the thick slab of rock that had been placed over the entrance. "How did you manage to get that open?"

Raven stared at it for a moment then matched her gaze. "It wasn't easy. I had to shove, and shove—"

"Try again."

"What?"

"Becoming a vampire doesn't make you deaf, you know."

Raven tilted his head.

"I said 'try again.' Try lifting that slab off the ground."

"Are you serious? I barely got it away from the door in the first place."

She put her hands on her incredible hips and raised an eyebrow until he complied.

Raven bent down and wedged his fingers between the slab and the grass, not expecting anything to happen when he lifted, but the slab moved upward as if it weighed only a tenth of what it should have. He staggered backward and let the slab drop to the ground with a loud thud, then he gawked at Vanessa.

She laughed. "Don't look so surprised. You're a vampire now. You have the strength of ten men."

"Then why was it so heavy when I was trying to get out this evening?"

"You hadn't fed yet."

Raven shuddered. The blood—*Kristen's* blood—had granted him additional strength? "So I shouldn't have any trouble carrying my coffin out. Is that what you're saying?"

Vanessa just smiled at him. "You're not as dense as you

pretend to be."

He gritted his teeth. "I don't appreciate how you've been talking to me."

Her countenance soured. "I don't care what you do and don't 'appreciate.' You're *indebted* to me, remember? I granted you the gift of immortality. You should be worshipping at my feet right now, but instead you're whining about my choice of words."

Raven didn't see things that way. She may have given him immortality, but it was *not* a gift, considering what it had already cost him. As far as being indebted to her, he disagreed with that too. *Getting even* better described what he wanted.

"As a matter of fact," she said. "I don't appreciate the scowl you're wearing on that handsome face of yours. Why don't you put on a happier expression before I do it for you?"

Raven bit his tongue. "I'll go get my coffin."

About a minute later, he emerged from the crypt with his coffin balanced between his shoulder and one arm.

She gave him a slow, deliberate clap. "Now do you trust me?

Raven sighed. "Lead the way."

"Not so fast, Killer."

"Don't call me that."

She raised an eyebrow and smirked again. "Touchy, touchy. Set the coffin down on the ground. We—well, *you* need to move the slab back in place."

"What does it that matter? I may be stronger, but hefting this thing onto my shoulder wasn't exactly easy. It's big and awkward."

"Cover the crypt to give us more time to get out of here. That way, when your family comes to stake you tomorrow during the day, they'll have to haul the slab away first. With only three men at home, they'll have to get help from your neighbors, and with your little Irish lover dead, I don't think slaying a vampire will be too high on their list tomorrow. It all buys us more time."

"Do *not* talk about her that way." Raven lowered the coffin to the ground.

"Like I said before: the sooner you develop some apathy, the sooner you'll adjust to your new lifestyle. Now put that slab back, and follow me."

1885

"She took me to the forest and led me to a secluded mansion."

"A mansion? You live in a mansion? Where did it come from?" Calandra asked.

"A group of vampires immigrated here following the Spanish who arrived first. The mansion belonged to them, but, over the course of time, Vanessa killed them all off, and she took the place for herself."

Calandra nodded.

"It took almost half the night to get there with that coffin on my back, but we made it before the sun came up. It's where I've lived ever since. Your father and I have been meaning to go to retrieve my coffin from there to bring it back to the house, but we haven't had a chance to yet," Raven said as they continued to walk down the forest path. "I guess I don't need it anymore, though."

"I don't think you need it anymore, either." Calandra smiled. "I'm glad you're making progress. And glad you're staying with us."

Raven nodded. "I am too."

A bit of golden light twinkled between the trees. They were almost home.

"I hated Vanessa for what she'd done to me, and for what I'd done to Kristen," Raven said. "But she taught me how to be a vampire. She taught me the Old Lore, how to morph into a bat, a wolf, and mist. She helped me refine my powers of persuasion, seduction, and temptation."

Calandra cleared her throat. "Not something to be proud of."

"No, certainly not. I'm just giving you a point of reference."

"What happened to Kristen?"

Raven's chest flared with hurt at the sound of her name. "The next night, she became a vampire, just as I had the night before. I went to her gravesite as soon as night fell. Her family didn't have money to build a mausoleum like ours. I found her gravestone and dug up the loose dirt so she could get out.

"She—she seemed to understand what had happened at first. I explained some of the basics of being a vampire to her just like Vanessa had done for me. When I told her that now we could literally be together forever, that calmed her down, but—"

When he didn't continue, Calandra asked, "But what?"

He shook his head. "Vanessa showed up."

Chapter 30

April of 1802

"Who is *that*?" Kristen asked.

Raven swiveled his head and saw Vanessa, clad in an embellished, bright red version of the sheer black dress she'd worn last night. She leaned against a monument to a fallen soldier, complete with a statue of a horse and rider on top.

"You—what are you doing here?" Raven's fists clenched.

Vanessa just smiled.

"That's her, isn't it?" Tears formed in the corners of Kristen's eyes. "That's the woman you kissed."

Raven refocused on Kristen and shook his head. "This wasn't supposed to happen. She's not supposed to be here. I—"

Kristen pushed him away and ran into a nearby thicket of trees, sobbing even as Raven called after her.

"Let her go, Raven." Vanessa's blood-red lips pursed together as she stepped toward him. "She's got to find her own way now."

"You—" Raven grabbed her by the shoulders. He couldn't even think of an insult powerful enough to encompass all of her treachery.

"Ooooh, I like when you play *rough* with me." Her airy words dripped with lust.

He shoved her back, but she didn't go down. Raven cursed again. "Get away from me. I don't ever want to see you again."

As Raven started to follow Kristen's path, Vanessa called, "You're wasting your time with her."

Raven paused. "No, I'm not. I love her."

"She's weak. She can't handle this. She made a choice, and she can't follow through with it," Vanessa said. "She's not like you. Not like me. We're different. Stronger."

"You don't know *anything* about me." Raven pointed his finger at her face. "She means everything to me, and I'm nothing like you."

Vanessa smirked. "Whatever helps you sleep at sunrise."

Raven charged into the thicket after Kristen.

Raven searched for her all night, but he'd never been much of a tracker. He tried to look for signs that she may have left behind—footprints, pieces of torn clothing hanging on the tips of scraggly branches, anything that might indicate where she'd gone. He tore through the forest, stopped at her home, then stopped at his own home to try to locate her, but she'd vanished like cool mist in warm sunlight.

Sunlight—the sun would rise soon, and he needed to be back in his coffin before that happened or else it would kill him, at least according to Vanessa. But Kristen would die too if she didn't return to her coffin before sunrise. He had to find her, but he never did.

He resigned himself to returning to her gravesite and waiting for her there. He'd explained the necessity of avoiding sunlight to her already, and for now he could only hope she would return to the safety of her coffin before it was too late.

As the night waned, Raven finally gave up and zipped high above the forest, traversing the vast distance between the cemetery and Vanessa's mansion as a bat, just as he'd learned from her after arriving at the mansion last night. He made it to his new home just in time to avoid the first of the sun's deadly rays.

The next evening he returned to Kristen's grave, which he found still exhumed. Near the loose soil a large pile of chalky grey ash lay with the top of a thick wooden spike protruding from one of the sides.

Raven wept over her remains. He wished his tears could bring her back to life, but they didn't. Instead, he paid her the honor she deserved and scooped as much of her ashes into the coffin as he could, then reburied it.

But he kept the stake.

"Welcome home." Vanessa lounged on a burgundy sofa in the decadent parlor of her mansion, this time clad in a lascivious ivory dress.

Beautiful as she was, the sight of her twisted Raven's stomach. He didn't respond. He just headed toward the door that led to the lower levels of the mansion where his coffin awaited.

"Did you find your girlfriend?" Her voice chased him into the hallway.

He stopped. A pang of guilt stabbed him, accompanied by anger. He turned back toward her. "Don't talk to me."

Vanessa's eyes shimmered and she gave him a greedy smile. "Wait—is she *dead*?"

Raven clenched his fists. "Don't say another word."

"She *is* dead!" Vanessa squealed. "How magnificent."

"I swear to God, I'll—"

"God?" She tipped her head back and laughed. "Oh, Raven. God has nothing to do with it. *You're* the reason Kristen is dead and damned for all eternity. Not God."

"I said don't talk to me or I'll—"

"Or what?" She stood to her feet, her hands out, palms outstretched. "What can you possibly do to me?"

Raven touched his side and felt the hard wooden stake he'd tucked in the waistband of his trousers. If she saw it, she'd know what he intended, and he'd fail to avenge Kristen.

"Just—don't press me, alright? In two days' time I've lost everything dear to me because of you."

"You can blame me all you want, but like I said before, it's you who made the choice to succumb to me, you who made the choice to feed on Kristen. Her death is *your* fault," Vanessa said. "And her own."

"I refuse to believe that." Raven shook his head.

She shrugged and stalked closer to him. "I guess I can't fault you for wanting to blame me. After all, I didn't choose you at random."

Raven froze in place. "*What?*"

"I noticed you about a week ago." Vanessa drew nearer to him. She ran her fingers down his chest again, but he stepped back. A sinister smile cracked her red lips. "I saw you tending to your animals on the farm and I knew I had to have you."

"What do you mean, you 'had to have' me?" Raven's jaw tightened.

She leaned in close to him, her lips precariously close to Raven's neck. "I mean what I said. I wanted you all to myself. I studied you. Your patterns. Your family. I bit your cow because I knew you would notice, then I baited you into my trap. You came to me, just as I knew you would. You know the rest."

Raven recoiled and glared at her.

"But the next night when you disappeared from your crypt before I could get to you, I figured you would head to see your fiancée." Vanessa moved closer again and kissed his cheek. Raven's spine stiffened. "Vampires prefer to attack members of the opposite sex in the first place, and given your close relationship and proximity to her, I knew she would be your first target. Since you had no idea what you were getting yourself into, I knew you'd kill her too."

Raven pushed her back and walked away. "That's enough."

She stepped into his path again. "Of course, I couldn't have her living as a vampire with you for the rest of eternity, so I decided to show up at her gravesite last night—"

"Get out of my way," Raven said, his voice lined with steel. One more wrong word from Vanessa and he wouldn't restrain himself any longer.

"I figured my appearance would drive her away, but I never dared hope that she would actually *die*. Now you really are mine forever. This is even better than I had planned."

That did it. Raven shoved her away with so much force that Vanessa soared through the air and struck one of the walls with a loud *thwap*. Plaster cracked from her impact and trickled to the floor in tiny white pieces, but she recovered without so much as an indication of pain. An inspired smile parted her red lips.

Raven felt no remorse for her or for his brusque action. Vanessa wasn't just a beautiful woman with a whiplash tongue—she was an undead monster who had both designed Raven's demise and achieved the total destruction of his true love as well.

He pulled off his coat, careful to conceal the stake underneath it as he did. He knew he wouldn't succeed in killing her tonight, so no need to risk revealing it to her. After he tossed his coat—with the stake inside of it—to the floor, Raven charged toward her.

Vanessa blocked his first blow with her forearm and delivered a quick punch to his gut, then followed with a knee to his face that laid Raven flat on his back. She grabbed him by the leg and hurled him into a wall, and the plaster and wood gave way as he passed through the wall. He landed on his back in an adjacent room as ornate as the one he'd just left.

By the time he recovered, Vanessa had leapt on top of him and pinned his arms down. "That wasn't very nice, Raven."

He strained against her grip, but couldn't break free. "You can go to Hell."

"I'm sure I will, someday. In the meantime, you're *mine*."

Raven writhed, but she held him down. "Let go of—"

"Not until you decide to behave yourself." She lowered her face near his and caressed his cheek with her own until he recoiled from her touch. "You may have the strength of ten men, but you haven't fed yet tonight, have you? Or last night? You haven't fed since Kristen, have you? That was two nights ago. You won't get strong unless you drink blood every night."

Vanessa kissed him on his lips. He sputtered and tried to turn away, but she shifted and anchored one of his wrists down with her left leg so she could grab his chin with her left hand and hold his head in place.

"Come now—don't pretend you're not enjoying this." She kissed him again. When Raven bit her lip, she recoiled, then slapped him. She dabbed her lip and stared at the blood on her fingers. "Playing rough, are we?"

"I'll never give in to you," Raven said. "I *hate* you. I always will. You might as well kill me now."

"And end all the fun we're having? Nonsense." She kissed his cheek. "You've just had a difficult night. That's all. But don't worry—I have a present for you."

Vanessa got off of him and stepped toward a closet door in

that same room. She pulled the door open and revealed a young, rotund brunette with skittish brown eyes and terror streaked across her face. A strip of taupe fabric stretched across her mouth, and her hands were tied behind her back.

Now on his feet, Raven gawked at her, and the hunger swelled in his chest. By the look of her, she hadn't been in there for very long, but Raven could only imagine her fright at being tied up, gagged, and locked in a closet. "What is this?"

"Dinner," Vanessa replied.

Raven found the idea sick, twisted, and horrific, but at the same time he *needed* to feed on her. His hunger drove him forward. He needed to attack the girl and drain her dry, just as he had with Kristen.

Vanessa caught him with her hand on his chest. "Not so fast, Raven."

Now she wouldn't even let him feed? What control over him *didn't* she have?

"Tonight you're going to learn some dining etiquette."

"What are you talking about?" The wide-eyed brunette recoiled at Raven's advance, but Vanessa didn't loosen her grip. Part of him couldn't believe he wanted to do this, but another part completely understood. "Give her to me."

"One step at a time, Raven. You have to pace yourself with your prey. You can't just kill every one of them, you know. The more vampires you create, the more competition there will be for future meals."

"What am I supposed to do, then?"

Vanessa wrenched the girl's head to one side with her other hand. "Have a bite, but don't drain her. You have to learn to hold back, to spare her life."

Raven hesitated when the poor girl whimpered, but he succumbed to his hunger and sank his fangs into her exposed neck.

1885

As they walked inside the Zambini family's house, Raven noticed that Calandra's countenance had darkened again.

"I'm sorry," he said. "This isn't a pleasant subject. I'll stop. I won't tell you anymore. You get the point by now."

She shook her head and reclined on the couch in the living room. "Don't be sorry. I asked, after all. Besides, now I want to know how you managed to escape Vanessa. You can't just end the story there."

"That's not pleasant subject matter either." Raven looked around the room. "Besides, we're the only ones here. Don't you think it would be better if I waited outside?"

"No." She waved her hand. "I trust you. You won't hurt me or try anything. That's why my father sent you instead of Garrett."

"I thought he trusted Garrett."

"It doesn't matter either way." She bit her lip. "I don't."

"You don't?" Raven raised an eyebrow. Interesting bit of information. He savored some of the possible implications then tucked the nugget away for safekeeping. "Why not?"

"He's too eager to get married, which makes me wonder what his real motivation is. Sometimes I feel like he really loves me, but other times I feel like he just wants to get married so he can control me." Calandra's brow furrowed. "Please don't repeat any of this. The only other person who knows is my father. I can't trust Dante or any of the other kids, and even Mama is a bit too vocal on issues like these, so we haven't told anyone else."

"I promise I won't say a word."

"But enough about me. What happened to Vanessa?"

"You sure? Like I said before, it's not a nice story."

"You *have* to tell me. This is all so unbelievable to me. It's almost as if you're describing the customs of a foreign people."

"We're not far from it. Vampirism didn't originate in the Americas, you know."

"Oh really?" She rolled her eyes.

"Are you feeling better, by the way? It was kind of chilly out there. I hope the night air didn't aggravate your symptoms or—"

Calandra stared at him. "Quit stalling, will you? Get on with the story."

"Alright, alright. Sorry."

Raven sat on the couch next to her—but still far enough away so as to avoid questionable contact. For good measure he snatched a pillow from behind him and set it on the couch between them. A chastity pillow, of sorts.

"I lived with Vanessa for several years, always waiting for an opportunity to avenge Kristen's death and my own damnation as well, but Vanessa was smart. Too smart. She ensured that I only had minimal freedom. Sure, she taught me how to shape-shift and use my other vampiric powers, but I was really nothing more than a slave to her.

"Deep down I think her infatuation with me sprung out of her own past, of which I'd only gleaned bits and pieces. I think perhaps I reminded her of someone she'd loved long ago, so she decided to take me as her own." Raven shifted in his seat. "Whatever she wanted, she got. Men are carnal, base creatures, as you know. She used every God-given tool at her disposal to tempt and seduce me into doing her bidding, and usually it worked. And when it didn't, I had to play along anyway for fear of getting thrashed again.

"She never taught me how to fight, but I took enough beatings that I eventually picked up a few things in the process. I couldn't ever get close to winning, though. It seemed as if I would never get a chance to drive Kristen's stake through Vanessa's heart.

"She made sure I didn't even have a hint of privacy while living under her roof. She knew every inch of her mansion, all the nooks and crannies, all the hiding places. I didn't get away with anything. The only reason she didn't ever find the stake was because I had hidden it off the property, in a tree at a certain spot in the forest. Only I knew where that tree was, and she had no idea what I'd been plotting for the last ten years.

"Finally, I came up with a plan that had to work, a plan that meant either her life or my own, but in order to pull it off, I knew I would need help." Raven stared at Calandra. "So, help is what I got."

Chapter 31

"He won't show, Marshal." Friedrich sat back with two of the four legs of his chair in the air. "It's been weeks since you put out those posters. He's long gone by now, and I suspect he won't come back."

"He'll show," Jenner said. "There's no way he would ignore what we put up. He's probably just planning, trying to figure out the best time to come for Steve. If I were a betting man, I'd—"

"No way. Not a chance. He's not coming back," Friedrich said.

"Both of you knock it off, will you?" Marshal Flax rubbed his forehead and leaned back in his chair. Why they had to bicker so much, he didn't know. "I have a bad enough headache as it is."

"Sorry," Jenner said. Silence filled the room until he added, "I still bet he'll show, though."

"I said to be *quiet*," Marshal said. "I'm trying to think."

"Think about what?" Friedrich asked.

"We haven't heard so much as a murmur about Harry's whereabouts since he hit the preacher's house." Marshal stood up and tapped his finger on the map Friedrich had posted on the wall in the main office. "No other burglaries, murders, assaults—no crimes of any sort. At least none that we could attribute to Harry."

"Yeah, it's been awfully quiet these past few weeks." Friedrich glanced at Marshal. "But not so quiet that you don't need us both, of course."

Marshal huffed. "Don't worry about that. I'm not cutting either of you any time soon. I can't afford to lose the manpower. Besides, as far as I'm concerned, we're supposed to reduce crime. If we don't have much to do, that means we've already done our job."

"Ain't *that* the truth." Jenner smiled and reclined in his chair, his hands behind his head, elbows up. "Not bad for my first two months in the county, huh? As soon as I showed up, all the crime stopped."

"Don't get too excited, Jenner," Marshal said. "Harry Deutsch is still out there. We just don't know where."

"I say good riddance. I hope we never see him again." Friedrich folded his arms. "Maybe it's time we stop looking for him altogether. We've got better things to do."

"I disagree. Harry Deutsch is still the greatest threat this county has ever known, and we're the only thing keeping him from harming anyone else. He doesn't care who he hurts, so we have to care extra." Marshal pointed to the map again. "So as far as we're concerned, he's not gone until we know that for sure. We keep looking."

"I hope we *do* see him again." Jenner nodded when Marshal gave him a questioning look. "I hope we see him, bring him in, and the judge decides to hang him."

"That would be a day to remember," Marshal said. "I hope it happens too, but I don't think Harry would let himself get captured alive. I think he'd die first."

"Did you ever think that maybe the Zambini family wasn't being quite honest with us about the whole situation with Harry and his boys?" Jenner asked.

Friedrich wrinkled his nose as if he'd just caught a whiff of something rancid. "Where in the world did that come from?"

Jenner shrugged. "I don't know. Just been thinking about it recently."

"They're a pastor's family," Friedrich said. "If we can't trust them, who can we trust?"

"It's just that we haven't heard anything about Harry for so long. It seemed like all I ever heard when I first got here was 'Harry Deutsch did this,' and 'Harry Deutsch did that,' at least once a week. Now—" Jenner waved his hand, palm down, in an arc in front of his chest. "—nothing."

"And you think that Reverend Zambini and his family had something to do with that?" Marshal asked.

"Maybe they converted him." Friedrich hooted and slapped his knee. "Maybe he's in Africa, preaching to the Negroes right now."

"Or something else happened to him. Maybe he's dead, and they hid the body because they didn't want to get into trouble," Jenner said. "Even though it seemed like a pretty clear-cut case of self-defense. Plus, anyone who kills Harry Deutsch would be doing us and the county a favor anyway, right?"

"You really think the *Reverend* killed Harry Deutsch, and then hid his body somewhere?" Friedrich squinted at Jenner.

"You just said that's where Harry's trail ended. It's possible." Jenner shrugged again. "I don't know."

"Really? Because I disagree." Friedrich spat on the floor. "I don't think that man has a violent bone in his body."

"People react differently in tense situations," Jenner said. "Imagine how you'd react if you walked in on some guy trying to assault your daughter. I'd break his neck, if not worse."

Friedrich shook his head. "I'm sorry, but I just can't see the Reverend acting that way. I don't know him all that well, but he didn't strike me as that type of person."

Jenner leaned forward. "Well, what about that *vampire* they got living with them? He already killed Jim and broke Steve's arm so bad that he may never be able to use it again. He could have killed Harry. He said he survived a bunch of gunshots from Harry, too. Seems he knows what he's doing, if you ask me. Maybe he had something to do with it."

Marshal's gaze hardened. Jenner had a point. "Perhaps I ought to go back out there and have a talk with that kid again."

"And maybe I ought to go with you, Marshal," Friedrich said. "Last time you pulled your gun on him for no reason. What was that about?"

Marshal folded his arms and cast a glare at Friedrich that could have melted a boulder, but Friedrich didn't so much as blink.

"That's really none of your business."

How could he tell them what had happened and still maintain his credibility as their leader? He couldn't. Even if he could, what would he say?

A vampire bit my woman about 35 years back. She became one of them, and I had to finish her off after my crazy Uncle Murray put a stake through her heart. Good story, huh? Now, who's up for a drink?

"It *is* my business, Duke." Friedrich pointed a finger at Marshal and all four of his chair's legs hit the floor. "I'm second-in-command around here, remember? That means if you switch sides and start pulling guns on unarmed civilians—*vampires* or not—I'm going to have to relieve you of your command."

"So you don't believe he was a vampire?" Marshal added, "*Sam.*"

"Whether or not I believe it is irrelevant to our conversation right now. Frankly, so are whatever personal issues that led you to draw on him in the first place. I just need to know that you won't jeopardize the safety of any more civilians because of whatever it was that—"

"Enough." Marshal held up his hand. "It was a one-time incident. I admit that I let my emotions get the better of me, but I reeled them back before anything happened."

"You did, but we don't know how that's going to play out next time," Friedrich said.

Jenner glanced between the two of them, his eyebrows up

and his mouth open slightly.

"There isn't going to be a 'next time.'"

"Sure, you can say that, but we really don't know if that's true or not, do we?"

Marshal stepped toward him. "I don't think I like your tone, *Deputy*."

Friedrich stood to his feet so fast that his chair tipped over and smacked the floor. He closed the distance between them in two large steps. "And I don't like you pointing guns at the people we're trying to protect, *Marshal*."

"You always were a power-hungry little weasel. Any excuse to get me out so you can take the reins. Is that it?"

"Some days I think I'd do a better job than you're doing."

"Maybe I should reconsider cutting some manpower after all."

"Actually, *most* days I think I'd do a better job than you. I wish you'd just retire already."

"That's too bad, because my succession plan doesn't include an old coot like *you*."

"You're calling *me* an old coot? You're ten years older than me, and that's about as long as you've been ineffective at your job!"

"Alright, take it easy." Jenner parted the fracas with his hands and wedged himself between them. "We're on the same side, here, remember? Now, both of you sit down."

"Don't you give me orders, Jenner." Friedrich pointed a finger at him. "I outrank you, remember? I have seniority by at least

20 years."

Jenner stared at him and squared his body. He outweighed Friedrich by at least forty pounds, some of it distributed in Jenner's extra four inches of height, some of it spread throughout Jenner's thick arms and barrel chest.

"I could care less about your seniority. You don't *ever* talk to the marshal, your *boss*, that way. You hear me? You respect his authority. *His* seniority. Now pick up that chair and sit down or I'll *make* you sit down."

Friedrich's jaw tightened. He glanced at Marshal as if he ought to intervene, but Marshal intended to do no such thing after their last exchange. Finally, Friedrich bent down, reset his chair and sat on it, his arms folded, his brow furrowed, and his lower lip jutting out.

Jenner turned to Marshal. "I'll go with you if you want to talk to the Reverend and his family again. And that vampire, too. It was my theory anyway, so I should have to be the one to prove it. I know you won't try anything with me along, because I trust you."

Marshal glanced at the clock on the wall. Slow by five minutes, but he knew what time it really was. "You want to go out there tonight?"

Jenner nodded. "Still early enough. Might as well. If we don't catch them off guard and I'm right, they might plan their responses for whatever time we might set a meeting. We'll get closer to the truth if they aren't expecting us to just show up. Besides, they're nice folks—if I'm wrong, that is. They'll probably welcome us in and feed us too. And I'm always up for good Italian cuisine."

"You really think they would plan their responses in advance if we set a time to meet with them?" Marshal asked.

"Well—" Jenner shrugged. "—that's what I would do."

Marshal looked at Friedrich. "Got any problems with this arrangement, Mister Second-In-Command?"

"Not in the least." Friedrich shook his head. "You know why? Because Harry Deutsch is not coming back. He's long gone."

"If I'm right about my theory, then that means you're right too, you know," Jenner said.

Friedrich tilted his head to the side and squinted at Jenner. "It does?"

"Never mind." Jenner nodded to Marshal. "Ready to go?"

"Just have to throw on my jacket." He glanced back at Friedrich. "You want me to rustle up one of the other deputies to come over and help you watch Steve?"

"No need. You know why?"

Marshal sighed. "Because Harry Deutsch isn't coming back?"

Friedrich winked and pointed a finger at him. "You got it."

"Have a nice night, Friedrich."

"I'll be here when you get back."

Chapter 32

"Who did you get to help you?" Calandra asked.

"I knew Vanessa would catch on to my plan if I wasn't careful about it, so I made sure not to break my routines or do anything different than I had been doing for the last several years. About three years before I actually enacted the plan, I established a trend of visiting Kristen's gravesite and her home at least once a week, sometimes more often," Raven said. "That way Vanessa would be acclimated to it for a long time and she wouldn't know what I was plotting."

Calandra nodded, then she moved the pillow aside and scooted closer to him on the couch. He hesitated at first, but she'd done it, not him, so he didn't say anything.

"I had originally wanted to spread all of this out by five years instead of three, but circumstances moved too quickly and I had to act sooner than I would have liked. In the end, it all worked out, though—I guess."

September of 1812

"Hello, Mr. Hannigan," Raven said from the shadows.

Patrick jumped back and clutched his chest. "Who said that?

Who's there?"

Raven stepped into the candlelight. "Don't be afraid. I'm not here to hurt you, and I don't want to take anything."

Patrick squinted in the darkness and extended the candle in his hand toward Raven. He tilted his head, still clutching his chest. "Do I know you?"

"Don't you recognize me?"

Patrick's eyes widened and he gasped, a stark contrast from the burly, rough-hewn man Raven had once known. "It can't be you, though. You've been dead for a decade."

"It's me," Raven said. "I know it's hard to believe, but it's me."

Patrick shook his head. "I—I don't understand."

"I'm about to explain everything to you." Raven motioned to the bed—Kristen's old bed. "Have a seat."

After Patrick complied, Raven leaned in close.

"How's your heart these days?"

Several nights later Raven's padded feet gripped the rough, uneven ground with ease as he chased Vanessa's grey tail through the forest. A gunshot snapped in his wolf ears. A sapling just ahead of him splintered, then dropped to the earth as he passed by it.

Some people from local areas had found out about them, thanks to Raven's doing. Patrick had helped fan the flames, of course, citing that his daughter had been killed by a vampire—but not by Raven. As far as he and Patrick were concerned, Vanessa shouldered the entire blame for her demise, along with Raven's.

Vanessa, of course, was unaware of his dealings and his plans—at least as far as Raven knew. So far the plan seemed to be coming together.

The lights from a half-dozen torches appeared in front of Vanessa and she skidded to a halt. Raven did the same not far behind. They both panted for air and transformed back into human form. Vanessa shot him a quick glare, as if this was somehow all his fault—which it was, but she couldn't have known that.

"We need to split up," she said, her voice unsettled. "I'll lead them away, and you head for the mansion. I'll meet you there later on."

"I really think we should stay together," Raven said. "We can overpower them. We're faster, stronger, and smarter than they are."

Vanessa hesitated, a reaction Raven had never seen from her. A moment of weakness, of vulnerability. "Are you sure?"

Raven nodded. "Think it through. If we don't kill them all now, they'll eventually find where we live and kill us in our sleep. We can't risk that. We have to end this."

"I was hoping you'd say that." Her expression shifted from concern to mischief. "You've finally learned what it means to be apathetic and cold. I'm proud of you."

"And with a hint of malice. It only took me ten years," Raven said. "Almost eleven."

"What matters is that you got there." She scanned the forest, including the approaching men and their torches. "Now, let's kill some people."

Raven examined the gathering crowd. Some of these men would die in order to accomplish his vendetta against Vanessa, but he knew they'd been made aware of the risks well in advance. Even so, he determined to avoid killing as many of them as he could.

A large man charged him, wielding a pitchfork in both hands. Raven sidestepped and whipped his right leg at the man. The blow both snapped the pitchfork's shaft and laid him out. Others stormed forward, each of them wielding makeshift weapons, mostly common farming tools with the occasional rifle or sidearm or sword mixed in.

Raven watched each blow come toward him at half-speed, then he reacted in double-time. A man swung an axe at Raven's neck. He ducked out of the way, lunged forward, and delivered a punch that sent the man flying into the forest.

Another attacker stabbed at him with a long, pointed wooden pole—a huge stake. Raven caught the pole just before it could reach his chest and anchored it in place with one hand. The attacker's momentum carried his body forward and he rammed his stomach into the pole's blunt end. He doubled over and wheezed until Raven whacked him on the back of his head with the pole. The attacker fell to the dirt, unconscious.

He fended off several more townsmen before they finally backed off, likely in an effort to regroup and plan a different strategy. Raven stole a glance back at Vanessa and the numerous bodies strewn around her feet. Unlike Raven, she'd killed the men instead of wounding or disabling them.

Pain dug into his torso and his eyes widened. He gasped, but the air didn't reach his lungs. He tried to clutch his chest, but something hard and rough pricked his hands.

A wooden stake protruded from the left side of his chest. Definitely not part of the plan.

His vision blurred, and he dropped to his knees as warmth leaked down his dark shirt.

"Raven!" Vanessa hollered. Everything went black, and the earth dropped out from underneath him.

A sharp pain ratcheted from his chest up his spine and jarred him back to consciousness. He screamed.

"You'll be fine. I took out the stake. Now get up and help me finish them off." Vanessa grabbed his wrist and pulled him to his feet.

Raven pressed the heel of his palm against his forehead. "Everything's so hazy."

"Don't worry about that. If it's not me, then kill it."

Metal flickered under the moonlight and slowly came into focus. A hatchet zipped through the air at him. He leaned back just in time and it thudded into a tree behind him.

A saber carved a gash in his left arm. Raven sprung forward and grabbed the saber man by his wrist, wrenched it the wrong way in a chorus of tendon-snapping pops, and sank his teeth into the man's neck. A few gulps of his warm, coppery blood soothed Raven's aching chest, sealed up the hole from the stake, and closed the laceration on his arm.

Raven wanted to drain him, but he didn't have time. Another man swung a thick club at his head, but Raven shifted his body and positioned the saber man's head in the way. The saber man wilted to the ground from the blow, and his companion stepped back, eyes wide and mouth agape. He too went down when Raven delivered a bone-cracking punch to his chest.

The rest of the mob faded into the woods in full retreat except for one large man who stood in front of Vanessa. He held a torch in one hand and a long wooden stake in the other.

Patrick Hannigan.

Chapter 33

"You killed my daughter." Patrick fixed his eyes on Vanessa. "And I'm going to destroy you for it."

When Raven stepped forward and stood next to her, he noticed a familiar cunning smile on her face.

"I've killed a lot of daughters," she said. "Which one was yours?"

"It was more than ten years ago, the night after you killed her fiancé, the man standing next to you. You went into her room and drank her blood just as you did to Raven, and she died."

Vanessa turned to Raven with a knowing look in her eyes. "So, you put him up to this?"

Raven nodded. "I knew I'd never be able to bring you down without help. I've never forgiven you for turning me, for killing Kristen. Tonight I will have my vengeance."

Vanessa's laugh echoed off the surrounding trees. "Oh, Raven. What am I going to do with you?"

"There's nothing more you *can* do to me that you haven't already done. Either you die tonight, or I do. There's no other way around it." Raven clenched his fists. The stake tucked in the back of his waistband would soon fill the empty spot in Vanessa's chest where her soul should be.

She smiled at him and shook her head. She turned to Patrick who had taken three steps closer. "You know he's lying to you, right?"

Patrick stopped, and his eyes darted between Raven and Vanessa. "What do you mean?"

"He told you I killed your daughter," she said. "But that's not true."

"What is she talking about?" Patrick asked.

Raven's eyes widened. "Nothing. She's trying to distract you from—"

"*Raven* killed your daughter. Not me." Vanessa smirked. "I'll take the blame for killing Raven, of course, but *he* killed your daughter. *He* drank her blood."

Patrick set his jaw and lowered the stake. "Is that true?"

"It's—" Raven hesitated. "—if she hadn't killed me, then I wouldn't have killed Kristen. Ultimately, it's still her fault, and—"

"But you're the one who actually killed my daughter?" The fury rising in Patrick's voice set Raven on edge.

He sighed. "Yes."

Patrick swore at him. "You lied to me."

"I'm sorry, I—"

"You told me she killed Kristen, but all this time—it was *you*."

"None of this would have happened if it hadn't been for her." Raven pointed at Vanessa. "She's the one responsible for all of this."

"We all make our own choices, Raven." Vanessa stepped toward him in her familiar sultry way. "You can't deny that."

Raven shook his head. "No. I promised myself that you would die tonight, or I would. That's how it's going to be."

Vanessa was in motion even before he yanked the stake from his waistband. She caught his wrist with one hand and the stake with the other, then she flipped him over her head and slammed him down on the hard earth.

When he finally opened his eyes, Vanessa stood over him, the stake in her hands positioned right over Raven's heart. "You've made your choice, Raven. It was fun while it lasted. I enjoyed your company, our long nights together, but I'll just have to find another toy tomorrow night."

"Go to Hell," Raven said.

"You first." She raised the stake into the air.

A roar split the night. Patrick charged toward her and jabbed his own stake at her torso, but she dropped Kristen's stake, caught Patrick's, and wrenched it from his hands.

"You foolish man," Vanessa said. "You thought you'd kill me while my back was turned?"

She delivered a whiplash kick to his face and Patrick hit the dirt. As he crawled away, Vanessa snapped his stake over her knee and flung the pieces into the woods.

"You're not a very good actor. I knew you were feigning surprise at the knowledge that Raven killed your daughter." She kicked him in his side. He rolled onto his back, clutched his chest, and gasped for air. "Now I'm going to kill you too."

"No—please!" Patrick cried.

Vanessa lashed down at him and cracked his neck with one quick motion. Patrick's motionless body slumped to the ground, and Vanessa turned back to Raven.

"No!" Raven yelled.

"You just lost your last friend on this earth, Raven. You really thought that you and a human man could defeat me by yourselves?" She shook her head. "I'm disappointed in you. I thought you were smarter than that."

Raven glanced at the stake—Kristen's stake—on the ground only a few feet away.

"I don't think so." She didn't take her dragon eyes off of him. "Try it and see what happens. You're so predictable, just like the night I turned you. Not much has changed, apparently. You might as well give up. You can't win. Come home with me and I'll forgive you one last time, alright?"

Raven stared steel at her. "I'd rather die."

Vanessa nodded. "If that's really what you want, then so be it."

A dark blur hit her from behind and she fell to the earth, tangled in her attacker's grasp. Raven stared at the sight, his mouth open.

Vanessa screamed and hollered and thrashed, but the thing restrained her. "Release me!"

The blur settled, and Raven saw the face of his last remaining friend, Patrick Hannigan.

"Your reign has ended, my dear," Patrick growled into Vanessa's ear. He lay underneath her, holding her arms in place. He anchored her whiplashing legs to the earth by locking her ankles down with his own. She writhed and wriggled, but she couldn't break free from his grasp.

"No!" she yelled. "This isn't possible—how are you still alive? How are you *stronger* than me?"

"I still don't quite understand it myself, but I suppose Raven has an answer for you," Patrick said between grunts.

Raven stood up, cracked the kinks out of his back and neck, and stalked toward them. "Isn't it obvious, Vanessa? I turned Patrick into a vampire."

She shook her head. "He still shouldn't be stronger than me, unless—"

"Unless I turned him, staked him, and kept him in stasis for a few days? You told me that vampires got stronger and more bloodthirsty from having to live in stasis. That's what I did with Patrick. That's why he's stronger." Raven bent down and picked up Kristen's stake. He held it in his hands and stared at it. "It's time, Vanessa."

"No, please—" Vanessa stopped writhing and flaunted those seductive hazel eyes Raven had grown accustomed to over the last decade, those same dragon eyes that had enslaved him again and again since she'd first attacked him. "Raven, you know you can't do this. You need me, and I need you. You love me. You can't kill me."

"Hurry up, son," Patrick said. "I'm stronger now, but I can't hold her forever. Do the deed. Stake this harpy and free us all."

"No!" Vanessa twisted and contorted her body with even more fervor, but she still couldn't escape Patrick's grasp. "Raven, don't! If you stake me, you'll stake him too!"

"Don't worry about me, my dear," Patrick said. "That was part of the plan all along. The last thing I want is to live like this forever. Raven, do it."

Raven raised the stake high above his head. "For Kristen."

Vanessa's shrieks filled the night sky, followed by a soft, sullen exhale from Patrick. Silence permeated the forest.

Raven picked up one of the swords left behind by the mob, lined it up over Vanessa's and Patrick's necks, and chopped down.

Chapter 34

Calandra touched Raven's hand. He raised his head and gazed into her deep brown eyes, now ripe with concern. Her voice quiet, she said, "I'm sorry."

Raven shook his head. "There's nothing for you to be sorry about."

"I know, but—" She glanced at her hand, and then pulled it away. "—I wish it hadn't happened to you."

"I ended up in that situation because of my own choices. If there's anything Vanessa ever told me that was true, it was that." Raven waved his hand. "Besides, that was 70 years ago. Ancient history."

"Still, something like that doesn't just go away, I'm sure," Calandra said.

He shrugged. "The pain is still there, but it has dulled over time."

Calandra just nodded and didn't say anything.

She seemed really afflicted by his stories, almost to the point of tears. Her reaction both puzzled Raven and filled him with hope—a hope forbidden to him by Garrett, and by himself.

Silence lingered between them like the palpable presence of a specter haunting the room until Calandra finally spoke.

"At least you got a mansion out of it, right?"

Raven tilted his head at her and tried to quell the smile breaching his cheeks, but failed.

"You smiled." Calandra's eyes brightened. "I don't believe it!"

"No—" Raven shook his head. He bit his lip to suppress a second smile. "No. I didn't."

"Nice try." She laughed. "But you smiled. I saw it."

"You saw nothing." Raven hoped he still had some hypnotic powers left. "*Nothing.*"

"That won't work on me. Just face the truth. You smiled, and I saw it." Calandra put her hand on his and grinned. "I knew I'd break through your dark, brooding façade one day. Your mysterious persona is no more, Raven Worth. I've found the real you."

When Calandra gave his hand a squeeze, Raven's heart leaped in his chest. She truly had found him. He'd shared his past with her, and she'd accepted him, the good and the bad.

For that, he loved her.

Raven stared into Calandra's eyes, and she returned his gaze. Her breathing quickened, and her face flushed.

She pulled her hand away and turned her head. "I'm sorry, I shouldn't have—"

"No, no. It's my fault. I haven't been discouraging you," Raven said. "You moved the pillow, and I didn't—"

"We're both at fault, then. I know I've been far too liberal with my affections toward you."

"Affections?"

"Holding your hand, especially," she said. "Long stares, being alone with you—it's all problematic for our friendship. If Garrett knew how much contact I've really had with you, he would—well, I don't know what he'd do."

Friendship? That was it?

Raven sighed. "I'm sorry. I don't want to jeopardize our friendship, or your relationship with Garrett. I'll wait outside until your family gets back."

As he stood up to leave, Calandra grabbed his hand. "Wait."

"I really should go."

"Wait. Please. Have a seat." She tugged on his hand. "We need to sort this out."

Raven locked eyes with her again, then he complied.

"If we don't talk through this, it'll just keep happening. We should—"

"I love you." It came out before Raven could stop himself. His heart hammered in his chest. "I—I didn't—um—"

Calandra gawked at him. Her voice soft, she asked, "What did you just say?"

Raven shook his head. "I'm sorry. I shouldn't have—"

"You—*love* me?"

"No. I mean yes." He sighed. "I don't know what I mean."

Calandra didn't move. She still held his hand in hers, still stared into his eyes. He expected her to break her gaze, to pull her hand away, but she didn't. What did that mean?

Raven placed his other hand on hers and relished her soft, warm skin. He closed the distance between them on the couch and touched her face with his fingers.

She didn't resist or recoil. Instead, she closed her eyes and leaned into his touch, then cupped his jaw with her hand. Calandra leaned forward, drawing so near that he could feel her warm breath on his lips.

Should he do it? Should he let his emotions dictate his future?

He'd considered such questions long before this moment, but now, in the midst of a dream come true, they no longer mattered.

Raven's lips caressed Calandra's. They shared a kiss, then another, then another. She wrapped her arms around him and pulled him even closer. He returned the gesture and pressed his chest against her warm body.

Incredible. He hadn't connected with anyone like this since Kristen had been alive. Sure, he'd engaged Vanessa hundreds of times during the decade he'd been her slave, but he'd never done it out of his own free will. Besides, Vanessa's frigid, dead flesh couldn't compare to Calandra's warm, healthy body.

When he separated his lips from hers, Raven focused his attention on her neck—not to bite it, but to kiss it. A small, persistent part of him still wanted to sink his fangs into her neck, but he restrained himself. Why drink her blood when he enjoyed kissing her so much?

Calandra knew she shouldn't be doing this, but it just felt right. Raven had enraptured her since she first laid eyes on him at the tent meeting a few months ago. Her attraction to him had only grown since then, and she'd found herself less and less interested in Garrett. After an incident like this, she knew she could never go back to him.

Raven's lips chilled hers, but in a way, kissing him refreshed her like a cool drink of water. She ran her hands over his arms, slim but strong and solid, and she reveled in his touch.

When Raven kissed Calandra's neck, her stomach dropped, and she had to fight against her instinct to recoil. Not only had she never engaged in such physical contact with a man before, but she also had to consider that Raven was still a vampire. Even though he no longer had to drink blood, that didn't mean he wouldn't be tempted to try.

She welcomed his second salvo of kisses and didn't suppress the satisfied breaths and moans that bubbled up from within her. Her fingers threaded through his long black hair and she kissed him again, and again, and again. She hoped it would never end.

Movement at the edge of her vision caught her attention. Dante had walked into the room, followed by Garrett.

She turned away from Raven, who started kissing her neck again, but Dante had already seen. He stood there, watching them both, as Garrett set two large bags on the floor. He too noticed the exchange.

She'd been caught.

Chapter 35

"Get away from her!" Garrett roared.

He traversed the distance in a flicker, grabbed Raven by his shoulders, and hurled him across the room into a small wooden cabinet with glass windowpanes on its doors. The cabinet—and its fragile porcelain contents—crumbled under the impact amid the sound of snapping wood and shattering glass.

"Garrett, stop it!" Calandra yelled. What had she done?

He didn't stop. Garrett blazed over to Raven, yanked him to his feet, and threw several brutal punches at him, mostly at his face. When Raven finally blocked one of them with his forearm, Garrett kicked the side of his knee. Raven crumpled to the floor again with a yelp and bared his gritted teeth.

Garrett's next kick hit Raven's gut, but the one after that stopped short. Raven caught Garrett's leg, lifted him off the ground, and dumped him on his back. Raven stepped back, dabbed his bloody lip, and held up his other hand in surrender.

Garrett sprung to his and plowed into Raven's torso like a rugby player making a tackle. They slammed into the wall so hard that three picture frames dropped to the floor.

"Stop it!" Calandra hollered again. Garrett didn't respond.

Raven shot her a desperate glance, then shoved Garrett back. "I don't want to fight you, Garrett. Don't come any closer."

Garrett slung a slew of profanity at him that made Calandra's jaw drop. "I'm going to put a stake through your black heart and end this once and for all."

He grabbed one of the small cabinet's legs and swung it at the mantle over the fireplace. A chunk of it snapped off, leaving a long, jagged spike in Garrett's hand. Raven caught him mid-lunge and anchored one hand on Garrett's wrist and his other on Garrett's forearm.

"Garrett, stop!" Dante shouted. "Let him go!"

At first Raven struggled to keep Garrett from advancing, but then the effort started to show more in Garrett's face than in Raven's. Garrett stepped back as Raven pushed forward.

"I *wasn't* attacking her, Garrett," Raven said, his voice unnaturally calm for the situation. "It's not what you think."

"I'm going to send you back to Hell where you came from." A vein bulged from Garrett's neck, and another from his forehead as he powered forward and forced Raven back a step, but no farther. Not two seconds after he'd advanced, Garrett took two steps backward, and then another. Now his face showed more than strain—it showed anguish.

The sight made no sense to Calandra: two grown men locked in a grapple, and the larger, supposedly stronger of the two now struggled just to keep the smaller from overcoming him. She refocused her attention. "Raven, stop! You're hurting him!"

Raven's jaw tightened, but he immediately relaxed his advance, even though he still held Garrett in place.

"What's going on here?" a booming voice filled the room.

Calandra swiveled toward the sound, her heart drumming in her chest. Her father had walked into the room, followed by her mother, sisters, and her other brother Anthony. Now everyone would know of her transgression. This couldn't be happening.

"*Raven*," Luco said. "Get away from Garrett *right now*."

Raven released his grip, then stepped back.

Garrett flung himself forward, his makeshift stake extended. Raven caught him again, but they fell to the floor, with Garrett on top, his eyes ablaze with rage.

"Garrett!" Luco bellowed. "Get off of him!"

"*No*." Garrett pushed his stake closer to Raven's chest. "He tried to bite Calandra. I *saw* it. So did Dante. He needs to die."

Luco hauled Garrett off of Raven with surprising strength and locked his arms in place under Garrett's armpits and around his chest. "You're *not* going to kill him, Garrett. *I'll* deal with it! Now stop struggling, put down the stake, and tell me what happened."

Garrett didn't calm down right away, but he couldn't break out of Luco's grasp either. When he finally calmed down, Garrett tossed the stake to the floor and watched it until it stopped against one of the walls. Deep, sharp breaths in and out.

He pointed a thick finger at Raven. "I walked in with Dante to set down the sacks of potatoes Mr. Johnson gave us tonight, and when I turned around I saw Raven's mouth on Calandra's neck. Ask

Dante. He saw it too. Raven was trying to drink her blood."

Raven stepped forward. "That's not what hap—"

"Please, Raven." Luco held up his hand and showed Raven a stern scowl. "You'll have your chance in a moment."

Calandra knew that look—one her father reserved only for the most heinous disobedience.

"Dante, what did you see?" Luco asked.

Dante studied Calandra for a long moment, one that unsettled her stomach. He'd seen them kissing. He knew the truth.

"Dante?"

"It looked like Raven was going for her neck. That's what it looked like, but I can't be sure." His focus flitted between Raven, Garrett, Luco, and Calandra. Every time Dante looked at her, a pang of guilt stabbed her gut.

"Of course you're sure." Garrett's eyes widened with fury. "What else could it have been? He's a *vampire*, remember?"

Calandra caught Dante's stare again. She hoped he would get the message in her eyes that begged him not to say anything more.

"He tried to bite her. We need to kill him before—"

"*Garrett*," Maria thundered. "Stop talking. *Tacere*. Let Luco handle this."

Garrett seethed at both her and Luco, but complied.

"Calandra." Her father's dark brown eyes locked on her, and she shuddered. "What happened?"

She hesitated. Her gaze bounced from Raven to Garrett to Dante, then back to her father.

"Calandra," he repeated, this time slower. "What happened?"

Calandra pinched her eyelids shut. If only she could wake up from this nightmare when she opened them. It didn't work. After a long pause, she said, "I—I was mesmerized, but—"

Everyone stared at her.

She looked down at her feet. Betrayal was easier that way. "I think he was trying to bite me."

Luco sighed.

When she garnered the courage to look up at him, Raven's expression had already turned to stone, and heartbreak burned in his eyes.

"Is that what happened, Raven?" Luco asked.

After a deadened stare that emptied Calandra of what little innocence and happiness she had left, Raven turned to Luco, stoic. "Yes. That's what happened."

Luco sighed again and looked at Maria, who nodded. "Then I'm afraid I don't have a choice. I need to ask you to leave. You can't stay with us any longer."

"What? You're not going to kill him?" Garrett stretched his arms wide.

Luco turned to him. "I said that I would deal with it, *not* that I'd kill him. He's leaving, and that will suffice."

"But—"

Luco slammed his palm on the wall and two more picture frames fell to the floor. "I said that will suffice, *Garrett*."

Garrett shut his mouth and continued to scowl.

Luco refocused on Raven, his voice much calmer. "Go now. Please."

"I understand. If you'll excuse me, I don't need much time to collect my belongings, and then I'll be gone." Raven glanced at Calandra. "For good."

"Here." Garrett's scowl shifted to a smirk and he dumped the potatoes onto the floor from one of the sacks. He tossed it to Raven. "You can use this to pack up."

Within minutes Raven returned with the sack, only about two thirds full, hanging from his shoulder. He cast another quick, cold glance at Calandra and then headed for the door, but Mina latched onto his right leg.

"I don't want you to go." Tears streamed down her pretty little face. Calandra's lie had hurt her too.

Raven lowered the sack to the floor and bent down next to her. "I'm sorry, but I have to. I did a bad thing, and I have to go."

"But I forgive you," she said. "I want you to stay."

Raven cracked a sullen half-smile. "I wish I could, Mina, but I can't. I'm sorry. Go back to your mother now, alright?"

She threw her arms around his neck and gave him a hug. Garrett gawked as Raven returned the hug with a gentle squeeze of his own.

Calandra wanted to spill her secret right then and there, when it would have been easiest. Even in spite of this situation, she knew her family, especially her father, didn't want to see Raven go. But in order to save herself some misery, she had multiplied Raven's. How could she be so selfish, so inconsiderate?

"Come here, Mina." Maria picked her up and approached Raven. She kissed his cheek and pulled him into a hug. "*Dio vi benedica*, Raven."

Raven didn't look at her. He just nodded to Luco and said, "I'm sorry, Luco. I'm sorry I let you down."

Calandra bit her tongue to keep from crying out the truth. She couldn't say it. She couldn't face the guilt of her actions.

Raven paused at the door, as if giving her time to do just that, but she didn't. He twisted the knob, walked out, and disappeared into the deep black night as he had so many times before.

Chapter 36

"I'm sorry, but there's just no way I can tolerate any behavior like that." Luco bent over and swept several shards of glass—large, small, and everything in-between—into a dustpan that Dante held in place. "We can't trust him anymore. I thought he was making real progress, but I was wrong."

Dante wasn't so sure of that, but he kept quiet.

"But he's never done anything like this before." Anthony collected potatoes from the floor and dropped them into a crate that Maria had found for him from the kitchen. "You told me that criminals sometimes don't go to jail for as long if it's their first time doing something bad."

"It's different when it's your family," Luco said. "And it's different when you try to kill or hurt someone, too. Penalties for those types of things are always much worse than penalties for stealing or property damage and the like."

"Think about it, Anthony." Garrett scooped up a few chunks of broken wood from the cabinet and dumped them into another box Maria had provided for the cleanup. He hefted a large picture frame that encased a colorful painting of a rugged Southwest landscape and hung it back on the wall where it belonged. "How would you feel sleeping at night while there's a vampire in the house?"

Anthony shrugged. "I've *been* sleeping while there's a vampire in the house."

"Yeah, but one who just attacked your sister?"

Anthony opened his mouth, but Luco spoke first. "We really don't need to dwell on this anymore, alright? Let's just finish our cleanup and go eat some dinner."

Dante just took it all in as he helped his father. He shifted the dustpan and Luco swept more pieces of broken furniture into it until Garrett nudged him with his foot.

"Wake up, Dante. I'm hanging this picture over your head. Care to move out of the way?"

Dante stepped back, and watched Garrett. He exemplified everything Dante had always wanted in an older brother: big, strong, smart, outgoing, handsome, even a little bit mean at times. But for all of those excellent qualities, Garrett still lacked one crucial element that Dante felt all older brothers should have: Dante couldn't talk to him.

He could talk to Raven, though. He had, many times throughout Raven's short stay with their family. They'd discussed everything from life in general to growing up to girls to faith and a variety of other subjects too, but now Raven was gone and Dante found himself stuck with Garrett again. He preferred Raven.

Garrett hung the next frame on the wall. "Back up a few steps. Does that look straight to you?"

Dante headed for the other side of the couch and stared at the painting of flowers on the wall. Normally it had a bit of sheen to it from the pane of glass overtop, but thanks to Garrett shoving Raven into the wall, the glass broke when the frame hit the floor. Now the painting looked flat.

"Hey." Garrett waved one arm. "Is it straight or not?"

"Yeah," Dante said. "It's straight."

"Good." Garrett turned to Luco. "Time to eat yet? I'm famished."

Dante definitely wanted Raven back.

Maria, Angelica, and Calandra served dinner once everyone had taken their seats. At first Maria had insisted that Calandra not help so she could take some time to calm down, but she did anyway. Helping did more to calm her nerves than sitting around.

That much, at least, was true. Activity helped take her mind off of what she'd done, how she'd betrayed Raven to save her own reputation and conceal her wrongdoing.

When Garrett pulled Raven's chair away from the table with a grin on his face, every ounce of guilt inside Calandra flared. Good thing it was dinner time. The emotion overwhelmed her to the point of wobbling her knees, but she could sit down and hide that easily enough. She slumped into the chair, her eyes closed as she breathed deep, deliberate breaths to quell the poison inside of her.

Luco led the family in a short, curt prayer of thanksgiving for their food, and also for their family to be comforted during this difficult time. He added in a quick "and be with Raven as well," probably for Maria's and the kids' sake.

Calandra opened her eyes and met Dante's scowl. She focused on her plate, a floral-rimmed white disc covered with red sauce, noodles, and meat. It might as well have been Raven's bloody heart laid out in front of her, there because she'd carved it from his chest. So much for eating dinner.

"*Oh.*" Garrett wiped his mouth with a cloth napkin and streaked a line of red sauce on it. "Maria, this pasta is delicious. Simply wonderful."

"*Grazie*, Garrett." Maria raised an eyebrow, then returned to her own plate.

As Garrett took another bite, Calandra arched her eyebrows and frowned at him. He slurped a long, thin noodle into his mouth, and it slapped his cheek on the way in, leaving a noodle imprint with red sauce where it hit him. He chuckled and deployed his napkin again.

Disgusting. Raven or no Raven, Calandra knew she could never marry Garrett, not after his behavior over the last few months. She had no reason to ever love him again. Maybe she never really had.

"Seriously, you have to teach me how to make this for when Calandra and I get married." Garrett raised a finger. "Or, even better, just teach *her* so she knows how to make it for me. I'm sure I'll be out all day ministering. It'll be nice to come home to dinner on the table and my beautiful wife waiting to greet me with a plate of delicious pasta."

When Garrett smiled at her, Calandra wanted to fling her pasta in his face, but she didn't. Instead, she turned to her father. "May I be excused, please?"

"You barely touched your dinner, Calandra," Maria said. "Aren't you hungry?"

"I don't feel well. I think I'm just going to go to bed for the night."

Luco didn't say anything, but he nodded to her.

"Thank you." Calandra stood up and headed to her room.

"Come in," Calandra answered the knock on her door. From her vantage point sprawled facedown on her bed, she couldn't see who it was, but when he spoke, she knew her brother's voice.

"We need to talk," Dante said.

Calandra released a deep, exasperated sigh. "I don't want to talk."

"I saw what really happened. I shouldn't have covered for you like I did, even though you're family and Raven isn't."

She rolled over on her bed and looked at him. Dante leaned on her doorframe and frowned at her.

"Don't give me that look," Calandra said. "You're not dad. And close the door if we're going to talk."

"You just said you didn't want to. Which is it?" When Calandra returned the frown he'd given her, Dante shut the door behind him and sat next to her on the bed.

"I know I did the wrong thing. I panicked, and blamed him

for…" She eyed Dante. "What exactly do you think you saw?"

Dante folded his arms. "Enough to know he wasn't biting your neck any more than you were biting his lips."

"Alright." She held her hands up. "Fine. You saw enough."

"You threw Raven under the carriage when dad pressed you. What's more incredible is that he went along with it instead of calling you out. He must really care about you."

"And I threw it right back in his face." Hurt pricked Calandra's gut, and her cheeks and nose stung with the beginnings of tears. She buried her head in her hands. "I loved him, Dante. What am I going to do?"

"You really messed things up. No matter what you do, someone's going to end up hurt, and bad too. You're going to lose Garrett for sure, and you've probably lost Raven as well."

Calandra sighed again, and tears formed in the corners of her eyes. She didn't fight them.

"You violated dad's rules, were unfaithful to Garrett, lied about it, and Raven was forced to leave as a result. Do you have any idea how much you could have damaged his faith because of that?" Dante asked. "I can't even imagine what he might be thinking about you, about us, about Christians in general."

Tears flowed down Calandra's cheeks. She leaned into her brother and wept, and he embraced her. He was right. This wasn't just a small slip—she had devastated Raven in doing what she did. Between sobs, she said, "I'm sorry, Dante. I'm so sorry."

"That's good." He gave her a squeeze. "Because you're

going to need to tell that to everyone else, too, including Garrett."

She nodded. "It's going to be so hard…"

"You have to do it."

"I know." She sniveled, then blew her nose into the handkerchief that Dante held out for her. "Would you mind gathering the family together for me? I'd like to tell them all at once, all together."

"That might actually be harder."

"It's the way I want to do it," she said.

Dante nodded, then stood up to go fetch them.

"Dante?"

He stopped at her door. "Yes?"

"Thank you for being a great little brother."

He nodded again. "I'll go get them. Come out when you're ready."

"I have a confession to make," Calandra said to her family, whom Dante had gathered in the family room. Garrett sat there too. He still wore a smug expression on his face, but interested tainted his narrowed eyes.

Calandra swallowed the lump in her throat. Her palms stuck against her fingers which she clenched into loose fists. She met Garrett's gaze. Despite her recent disinterest in him, they were still courting and she had still betrayed his trust.

She found her father's eyes next. She'd betrayed him too. She'd broken his rules and lied to him. Would he ever forgive her?

"We're waiting." Garrett folded his arms and reclined on his chair. He rocked it back so it balanced on its hind legs.

Calandra sighed. When she spoke, her voice quivered. "I've done something terrible."

A spell of quiet filled the room.

Tears pricked the corners of her eyes. She looked at Dante, who leaned against the wall, his arms also folded. He nodded.

"I—" She bit her lip.

"Calandra, whatever it is, you know that confession is the beginning of forgiveness." Maria's face showed concern, but love as well. "Just let it out. We love you no matter what."

She exhaled a breath through pursed lips and closed her eyes. Maybe her family wouldn't be there when she opened them back up. They were.

Enough stalling. She just needed to say it. "I lied to all of you."

Relief spread throughout her body, but it didn't last long. Sure, she'd confessed her transgression in its simplest form, but that didn't even begin to approach the breadth of the wrong she'd done. The relief faded, and the guilt returned.

"What did you lie about?" Luco asked.

Garrett yawned. He had no idea what was coming.

"I lied about what happened—" She swallowed again. "—between Raven and me."

"What?" Garrett's front two chair legs hit the floor. He sat forward with his hands on his knees. "What do you mean?"

"I mean that what I said happened between us—it didn't happen that way."

"Then what happened?" Garrett asked, his voice like hard, jagged rocks.

Tears streamed down Calandra's face. "He didn't attack me. He wasn't trying to hurt me."

"Tell me what happened, Calandra." Garrett glared at her.

"*Garrett,*" Maria said, her voice equally as firm. "Let her finish."

A shiver snaked down Calandra's back. Just a few more words and the burden would lift. "He—we were—"

Garrett folded his arms again.

"We—kissed."

"*What?*" Garrett's mouth hung open and his eyes widened. He clenched his fists.

"Garrett, calm down," Luco said.

"Did you do it willingly?" Garrett asked, his voice still on edge. "Or did he force himself on you?"

She shook her head. "I did it willingly. I—I'm very attracted to him."

"Oh, Calandra." Maria wrung her hands and started toward her.

Garrett just stared at her, his face sullen stone.

"So you lied about Raven trying to bite you to hide what really happened?" Luco asked.

Calandra nodded. "I'm so sorry."

Luco shook his head. "Do you have any idea what you've done to that poor boy?"

"I know. I really—"

"No, Calandra. If you knew, you wouldn't have done it," Luco said. "I sent him away because of what you said. I can't believe he went along with it without speaking up for himself."

"I know. I feel terrible." Calandra bowed her head and let the tears flow. A set of arms wrapped around her and pulled her close, followed by Maria's soothing voice.

"I can't even imagine the kind of damage you've done to Raven, and Garrett has no reason to trust you anymore either," Luco said. "You've broken your relationships with both of them, possibly beyond repair."

Calandra stole a glance at Garrett, who looked away. Her father was right. She couldn't fathom the depths of the profound harm she'd caused them both, not to mention her father and mother, whose rules she'd broken.

"I'm so sorry, Papa," she said between sobs. "I didn't know what I was doing."

"You owe Garrett an apology too. A sincere apology."

She looked at him again, and he met her gaze with steel in his eyes. Regardless of her lack of feelings toward him, she'd behaved poorly. Through more sobs, she said, "I'm sorry, Garrett. I never meant to hurt you or betray you."

Garrett didn't respond, except to maintain his glare at her. He stood to his feet, walked toward the front door, and slammed it behind him.

"Garrett?" Maria called after him.

"Let him go, Maria." Luco shook his head. "He needs time to be alone."

More teardrops poured from Calandra's eyes. She buried her face in her mother's chest and wept. Now she might never see either Garrett or Raven again.

Five minutes later someone knocked on their door.

Chapter 37

When Luco Zambini opened his front door, Marshal Flax noted how his countenance changed from a forlorn expression to one of confusion. His tone flat, Luco asked, "Can I help you, gentlemen?"

"You don't sound too enthused to see us, Reverend." Marshal's thoughts jumped back to Jenner's suggestion that everything might not be as it seemed in the Zambini household. "Everything alright?"

Luco sighed. "No, Marshal. Everything is not alright. We're having family issues right now. What brings you to our door—again?"

Jenner stepped forward. "Anything we can do to help?"

"Thank you, but no. It's a personal matter and we'll handle it ourselves, but it was kind of you to offer." Luco stood in his doorway and stared at them.

"That's not really the reason we're here anyway," Marshal said. "We're here about the incident. May we come inside, please?"

Luco closed his eyes and rubbed his forehead. "Forgive me, but didn't we already discuss this a few weeks ago?"

"We certainly did, but we haven't been able to locate Harry

Deutsch since. I just wanted to ask you and your family a few additional questions about that night to make sure we didn't miss anything on our end."

"This really isn't the best time, Marshal." Luco leaned against the doorframe. "Would you mind coming back tomorrow morning, or perhaps for lunch? We just aren't in any condition to answer questions tonight."

Marshal stole a glance at Jenner, who raised an eyebrow and gave him a faint smirk. "I'm afraid tomorrow isn't convenient for us. We came all the way out here this evening specifically to speak with you. I'd greatly appreciate it if you'd reconsider."

Luco shook his head. "No, Marshal. I'm sorry you took the time to visit us, but I just can't say yes. We've had a trying night and we need some time to sort out our own business before we can talk to you. This really isn't a good time. Thanks for understanding."

Luco stepped back inside the house and started to close the door but Marshal blocked it with his boot. "Forgive me for being so direct, but I must insist we talk this evening. It's imperative that we find Harry Deutsch, and your family is the only lead we have right now."

Luco's jaw tightened. "Marshal, you need to leave now. I want you off my prop—"

"We know you lied to us about what happened to Harry Deutsch, Reverend," Jenner said.

An assumption at this point, but it probably didn't hurt that Jenner had brought it up. Marshal grinned. Jenner continued to impress him.

Luco glared at Jenner. "I don't appreciate baseless accusations, Deputy."

Jenner glanced at Marshal. "We have reason to believe that you've withheld information about that night from us."

"And what might that reason be?"

"All I need to know is whether you *forgot* to tell us anything when we came over to investigate that night. You know, because sometimes people *forget* to include vital information that could lead to the capture, or at least to the close of a case involving a dangerous criminal." Jenner pulled out his pad and pencil, ready to write.

"I have nothing further to add to what I've already told you. Now, please leave."

"What about the young man living with you—the vampire? We'd like to speak with him as well, since he saw everything," Marshal said.

Luco shook his head. "He left. He's not here anymore."

So *that* was the family trouble Luco had mentioned. Marshal nodded to Jenner, and he wrote it down. "Where has he gone?"

Luco stared at the marshal. "I don't know. I have no idea."

"You don't know where he went? Did you ever find out where he lived before he started staying with you?" Marshal asked.

"No." Luco folded his arms again. "I've never been there. None of my family has seen where he lives."

"Is he coming back?"

Luco shook his head again. "I wouldn't count on it.

He…doesn't feel like he's welcome here anymore."

Marshal nodded. "I understand."

"Now, if you don't mind, I'd like to get back to my family in this difficult time."

"Of course. I'm sorry to have interfered with your evening. Please give our regards to your family. Have a good night."

Luco gave them a nod. "You too."

When Luco shut the door, Marshal stared at it for a moment, then grabbed Jenner's arm and pulled him away. "He knows more than he's telling us."

Jenner nodded. "So what do we do now?"

"I think we've done enough for one night. We'll come back and press him again in the morning." Marshal looked at their horses. "Let's get back to the jail."

No amount of water, wine, or blood could wash away the sourness in Raven's stomach—not that he had an appetite anyway. He felt empty, as if whatever had filled the once-vacant space inside of him had vanished. Maybe it had all been an illusion, a lie. Maybe he hadn't ever really changed—maybe God didn't care about him after all.

So this is what betrayal feels like.

There was no other term for it. Calandra had betrayed him. She had kissed him and then lied about it to her family and Garrett the next moment, all after he'd revealed his feelings for her and risked their friendship. Calandra was the first woman he'd truly loved since he lost Kristen so many decades before, and now he'd lost her too.

Still, though Calandra had wronged him, Luco and the rest of his family had only showed Raven kindness and love, all in spite of him being a vampire. But Garrett had never showed him kindness, or respect, or anything that even approached Christian love.

So which version of Christianity did they expect him to follow? Luco's and his family's version, or Calandra's and Garrett's version?

Maybe it was all for the best. It never would have worked between Calandra and him anyway. Raven was a vampire, and he knew now that he always would be.

But if that was true, then why didn't he crave blood anymore? He had earlier that night when he'd kissed Calandra, but now, nothing. The thought of consuming blood again sickened him.

Blood or no blood, he knew one thing was certain: he would no longer serve a God whose followers behaved like Calandra.

Thorns scratched at Garrett's ankles and snagged his pant legs as he stormed through the forest. The network of tree limbs thickened the farther he ventured into the woods, now a congested web that tried to hold him back. He threaded through them on an old path long overgrown with underbrush. Silver moonlight sliced through the thick canopy overhead at random intervals and cast eerie, dark shadows where it didn't.

In the distance a small, dilapidated shack draped with leafy branches awaited his return. Not much farther now. Garrett peeked over his shoulder for the hundredth time to make sure no one had followed him, and again he saw only the gaping chasm of the forest in his wake.

He pulled the shack door open. Its ancient hinges groaned against the chirping of crickets and the skittering of nature in the surrounding forest. A wretched plume of garlic and the stench of rotting flesh almost physically repelled him from the shack's doorway, but he steeled himself and stepped inside. Garrett lit a few candles scattered throughout the space and surveyed the shack's interior.

Layers of crosses, Bibles, and other Christian relics outlined a form in the middle of the floor—benefits of being a pastor-in-training. Cloves of rotting garlic hung almost to the floor from the hole-ridden ceiling, suspended by thin threads of string. In the center of it all lay a motionless human body.

Harry Deutsch.

Despite his best efforts to keep Harry's body safe from the elements by wrapping it in thick cloth, Garrett knew nature and time must have caused irreversible damage by now. At least no animals or people had discovered this hideaway and the body inside.

Garrett unwrapped the body, exposing Harry's darkened skin and decaying flesh, and the wooden stake through his chest. He covered his nose and turned away to keep from vomiting at the sight of Harry's blackened face, its bone structure now accentuated from the shriveled skin pulling against his eye sockets, his neck, and his mouth, which gaped wide open.

Revolting. Stomach-churning. Abhorrent.

He couldn't find words strong enough to classify the quality of the smell and the wretched appearance of Harry's corpse. The garlic didn't help, but Garrett had to leave it up there as a contingency in case something went wrong, as with all the crosses and Bibles.

Harry's clothes, though covered with dark stains and dirt, seemed mostly intact on his body. Along with the cloth wrapping, Harry's clothes had helped to keep most of the maggots and parasites from further destroying his corpse. His right wrist and hand lay at an awkward angle, still very much broken from whatever Raven had done to him.

Enough analysis. Garrett needed to move quickly if this was going to work. He produced a big, gleaming knife from a sheath on his belt, then knelt down and put it to Harry's rotted neck—another contingency. His fingers clasped around the wooden stake protruding from Harry's chest, and he pulled it out.

He braced himself for a struggle, ready to slit Harry's throat at the first sign of resistance or aggression, but Harry didn't move.

Nothing. No motion whatsoever, but the stench had intensified, thanks to the open hole in Harry's chest.

Garrett relaxed his grip on the knife and straightened his back. He dropped the stake and tucked his nose inside his shirt collar. Better to smell his own late-night body odor than rancid death seasoned with garlic. Even so, he battled another urge to vomit.

He waited a few seconds, both to calm his twisting stomach and to see if Harry would come back to life. A vampire could come back to life if someone pulled the stake out of his chest, right? That's what he'd been told. That's why staking them wasn't enough—decapitation made sure the vampire couldn't revive ever again. Garrett was supposed to have done that when Harry first died from Raven's bite, but he didn't do it.

Perhaps he'd allowed too much time to pass? Maybe Harry couldn't come back because he'd been dead for too long. Was there some sort of time limit?

Blood.

It splashed in Garrett's mind. That's what Harry needed to come back.

But how much? Not a lot, Garrett hoped. He preferred to keep as much of it in his body as he could. Perhaps a simple finger prick would suffice. If not—well, he had to start somewhere.

He picked up the stake in his other hand again, ignored Harry's repugnant smell and extended his index finger over Harry's open mouth. As he pressed the blade of his knife against his finger, Garrett stopped.

What was he doing?

Here, in the middle of the deepest, darkest part of the woods, he'd stashed the body of a thieving, murderous bandit-turned-vampire in an old shack and surrounded him with vampire anathema. Now, in the middle of the night, Garrett knelt there ready to practice amateur necromancy to bring Harry back to life, all so he could take revenge on Raven for ruining his relationship with Calandra.

How could he call himself a Christian, much less a pastor-in-training, and go through with this? In the beginning he'd felt called to minister to those in need, to help where he could. To spread the Word of God. But somewhere along the way he'd wandered astray.

No. He'd been *led* astray.

He'd exhibited wisdom and sound judgment when he told Luco to avoid Raven. He'd even warned Luco in advance that moving here was a bad idea because of the area's folklore, but were his warnings heeded?

Of course not. He was just Garrett, the evangelist-in-training. What did he know?

As if that wasn't enough, Calandra had disregarded his words as well. When Garrett recalled the sight of Raven kissing Calandra's neck and her subsequent admission of guilt, the last of his doubts about reviving Harry vanished.

"Ministry be damned," he muttered. God had never done anything for him anyway.

Resolute, Garrett pricked his finger. A single drop of blood fell into Harry's mouth and landed in the center of Harry's shriveled tongue.

Harry's eyes snapped open, two cloudy charcoal orbs filled with evil intent.

Garrett barely had time to move the knife up to Harry's throat before Harry flattened him on his back and pressed him against the floor with powerful arms. The stake clattered from

Garrett's hand just out of his reach.

"*Wait*," Garrett said as Harry leaned closer. There was no way he could physically push Harry off of him. He was too strong. "Wait, don't! I need to talk to you about—"

Harry hissed, and chilled flecks of saliva spattered on Garrett's face. His breath smelled like an open grave. He tilted his head and held up his right hand, still contorted, then he popped it back into place with a flick of his wrist and a chorus of cracks. He wiggled his blackened fingers for a moment, then clamped them onto Garrett's face.

"Please, stop." Garrett surprised himself with how calm his voice sounded, despite the situation. He pressed the knife against Harry's throat. "I can help you. We can help each other."

"I don't need any help," Harry said, his voice as dark and warped as his appearance. "I need—blood."

Before Garrett's eyes, Harry's fangs lengthened to twice their normal length.

"You need *revenge*," Garrett said. "And I can help you get it."

Harry's dead eyes flickered with an emotion, but Garrett couldn't discern what it was.

Still on his back, Garrett pulled a sheet of paper from his pants pocket, unfolded it, and held it up for Harry to see. Harry recoiled to his knees, then clenched his jaw tight.

That was Garrett's chance. He pushed off the floor, grabbed Harry, and pulled him down. Garrett scooped up the stake and plunged it through Harry's chest, deep into the rotted wooden floorboards again. Harry writhed and gripped his chest, but didn't die.

"I need you to listen to me." Garrett leaned his face close to Harry's. "I can leave you here with this stake in your chest forever, or I can cut off your head so you never come back, but there's a third option that suits us both better than either of the first two."

Harry hissed at him again and writhed, but he couldn't fight back.

Garrett sheathed his knife and backhanded Harry across his face. It felt like he'd smacked a dry skull. "Pay attention. You haven't got long."

"What do you want?" Harry gasped.

"Your partner, Steve, has betrayed you. You trusted him, and he ratted you out to the marshal." Garrett sighed. "I've been betrayed too, and I need your help to get revenge. In return, I've brought you back to let you take yours."

Harry arched his back and clenched his teeth shut. "Pull the stake out—please?"

"Not until you agree to help me."

"I agree—I agree! *Please.*"

Garrett pulled the stake out but kept it in his hands.

"Blood…" Harry wheezed. "Why do I want blood?"

"You're a vampire. The young man who killed you was a vampire also. He bit you and you became a vampire. Do you remember?"

Harry nodded. "Blood… I need blood."

"Lean back. Open your mouth." Garrett squeezed his finger and a few more drops of blood dripped into Harry's mouth.

When Garrett stopped, Harry grabbed him by the shirt. His charcoal eyes sparked with lust. "*More*."

Garrett pressed the pointed tip of the stake against Harry's chest. "I'll get you more soon, but first, I need you to promise to do something for me."

Harry growled and glared at Garrett, but he listened to every word.

Garrett concluded his scheme by saying, "Your friend has betrayed you. I suggest you start with him. Meet me at the house when you're done."

His eyes glistening, Harry licked his cracked purple lips and nodded.

Chapter 38

Steve Huggins sneezed twice then emptied his nose onto the jail floor.

"Shut up in there, will you?" Friedrich hollered from his chair on the other side of the bars. "I'm trying to read the paper."

"Not my fault you're illiterate," Steve said. Friedrich rapped the bars with the wooden switch in his hand, and Steve smirked. "You don't have to take it so hard. Lots of people can't read."

Friedrich muttered an obscenity.

"Not a very polite thing to say, Deputy."

"You really think I care?"

Steve chuckled, but stopped when his broken arm pinched with pain. "When it's all said and done, there doesn't seem to be much difference between you and me, except for that badge on your chest."

Friedrich scoffed. "Except that I don't steal, kill, and destroy like you do."

"That so?" Steve pressed his face against the cool iron bars. "You've *never* killed anyone? *Never* stolen anything?"

"I don't make my living off of that sort of behavior."

"But you *have* stolen. You *have* killed people."

"Only them that deserved what they got."

Steve chuckled. "What criteria did you use to determine who lived and who died?"

Friedrich stood and stared at Steve with cold, angry eyes. "I never once shot first, if that's what you're getting at."

"Never?"

"Never."

Steve leaned back. "I don't believe you."

"I don't care what you do and don't believe. If you recall, you're the one locked up, while I'm out here, free to do as I please."

"I heard you helped gun down a band of Apaches in the Arizona territory a few decades back, and more since then."

Friedrich raised his left eyebrow. "I don't know what you're talking about."

"Tried to kick them off their own land, I believe the story went. They wouldn't go, so you and the rest of the soldiers invaded and slaughtered the ones that resisted."

"Where'd you hear that lie?"

"Doesn't matter where I heard it. Is it true or not?"

Friedrich smirked. "Like I said before: I never shot first. Besides, that was war. War is different."

"So the women and children in that group that got killed, they were shooting at you?"

"No, they—"

"So you murdered them, then?"

"It was *war*. Things are different in—" Friedrich squinted at him. "You know what? I don't have to explain myself to you. You're in jail. *You're* the criminal, not me."

"I'm in jail, alright, but that doesn't mean you're not a criminal too."

Friedrich shook his head. "You don't know anything. Now shut up. I'm trying to read—I'm *reading* the paper."

Steve had a retort prepared but a strong wind whipped through the jail's barred windows and extinguished the flames in the three oil lamps mounted to the walls.

Friedrich swore. "Blasted wind. Sometimes I hate nature."

"I'm sure it hates you right back."

"Shut-up, Steve." Friedrich stood to his feet and patted his pockets, then swore again. "Forgot my matches in the office. I'll be right back."

"I'll be here."

More wind whistled through the jail and frigid air hit the back of Steve's neck. He shivered and rubbed his shoulders as best as he could with one damaged arm. He'd never liked being alone in the dark. A part of him hoped Friedrich would hurry up and get back to light the lamps again, though he'd never admit it.

A clatter sounded from the darkened office, followed by a string of expletives from Friedrich. Shouts. The blast of a gunshot ripped through the jail, then another.

Friedrich screamed and a sharp crack sounded from the office, then the thunk of a pistol hitting the floor. "You—get away from me, you *monster!*"

Friedrich screamed again, but something truncated it this time. Wetness spattered, then Steve heard the dull smack of a limp body crumpling to the floor. What in the—

More wind knifed through the bars and into his cell, but it seemed to originate from the office this time. It chilled his face and quickened the pace of his heartbeat.

Steve's heart rate multiplied. "Harry? Is that you?"

Footsteps, slow and deliberate, advanced toward his cell.

"Harry?"

A male silhouette materialized out of the darkness, hunched over and wearing a wide-brimmed hat on his head.

Steve swallowed and stepped back. If it was Harry, it meant one of two things: either he'd come to free Steve, or he'd come to kill him. "Harry, if it's you, I'm sorry. I—I didn't have a choice. They forced me to give up the locations of our hideouts, then they set me up as the one who betrayed you."

The man didn't move, except for slow, methodic breaths that heaved his torso up and down in silence.

"Friedrich—the one you just killed—he's the one who made me do it. He'd twist my broken arm to coerce me into cooperating. I had hoped for a chance to avenge myself, but you beat me to it, I guess. I'm fine with that, too, you know."

No response. Just breathing, nothing else.

"You're, uh—you're kind of setting me on edge, Harry." Steve swallowed again, but forced himself to take a step closer to the bars. "You're not mad at me, are you?"

A bit of moonlight crept in through the window at the end of the cell block, but not enough for Steve to get a good look at the man's face, but something on the man's stubbled chin glistened—some sort of dark liquid, perhaps?

The stench of rotten flesh, like meat that had sat out for several days or even weeks too long, hit Steve's nostrils. He staggered back and covered his nose, then coughed.

"What is that smell?" He rubbed his watering eyes. "It's horrific. Did you step in something?"

Still nothing. The form just stood there, breathing. Plotting. Scheming.

"Look, Harry, if it's you, then I need to know. If it's not, then I don't know who you are or why you're here, but you should either set me free or get out of here. You're stinking up the entire jail with—whatever it is that stinks so bad in here."

The form extended his hand toward the lock on the bars and inserted a key into it. One twist and the hinges droned like dying birds as the door swung open into the cell. The form stepped inside and the stench came with him. The wide-brimmed hat still covered most of his face, but Steve could now see that his darkened hands, almost as if they'd been bruised all over, matched the dark skin on his exposed neck and chin.

"Thanks." Steve would have left, but the form stood in the doorway, arms down and breathing just as he had before.

No way to get by the man except to push past him, something Steve didn't know if he wanted to try. After all, this man—Harry

Deutsch or otherwise—had just killed Friedrich without the aid of a gun.

"You, uh—you gonna let me pass or did you just open the cell for no reason?"

"Hello, Steve," the man said in a scratchy, gruff voice.

Steve sucked in a quick breath and shuddered. He knew that voice, distorted as it was. "Hello, Harry."

Harry took one step forward, the brim of his hat still shielding most of his face. "You betrayed me, Steve."

"I had no choice. You know that. I just explained the whole—"

"Spare me. You did far more than what's-his-name ever did. And you know how that worked out for him, don't you?" Another step forward.

"Mick," Steve said. "Mick had a choice. I didn't. Mick chose to try to turn you in for money. I only gave them information after they tortured me and—"

"*Shut up*," Harry said, his voice firm but not loud. He took two more steps forward, and Steve retreated an equal number to keep away. "Nothing you can say will change what happened. Nothing you can say will sate my thirst for your blood."

Steve had his answer, then. Harry had come to kill him.

Well, he wouldn't go down without a fight. He might have taken Harry with two functioning arms if he'd had to, but with one limb broken he could only hope to give Harry hell before he died.

The putrid odor swelled in Steve's nostrils and almost

clouded his vision. He stepped back again, but only managed a half-step before his back hit the wall of his cell.

His voice escaped as a whisper. "You don't have to do this, Harry."

Harry stopped, his fingers quivering at his sides, and he raised his head. "You have no idea how utterly wrong you are."

Steve stared at Harry's darkened, decrepit face. He eyed him from his head down to his feet, fighting to quell the sickness churning in his stomach the whole time. "What—what in the Hell happened to you?"

"Hell is the operative word." A twisted smile cracked Harry's bloodstained lips. "I died, and was born again."

Two long fangs emerged from the top row of Harry's teeth, and Steve's eyes widened. "God help me…"

"It's too late for that." Harry stepped forward.

Steve tried to duck under Harry's outstretched arms, but Harry latched on to his collar and thrust him back against the wall. By the time Steve recovered his cognition, Harry held him in place with one hand.

Steve pushed against Harry with his good arm, but to no avail. Somehow Harry had grown even stronger than before.

Harry lunged forward, and Steve's tortured screams split the night sky.

Chapter 39

"Marshal, the lights are all out," Jenner said as they approached the jail on horseback. "You don't think—"

"Quiet." Marshal skinned his revolver and held it in his hand. He glanced at the back of the cylinder to make sure all six chambers were loaded. "Keep your gun handy. If it's Harry Deutsch, he won't let us take him alive, and if he's set Steve free then there's two of them to worry about. We stick together, you hear me?"

"What about Friedrich?"

"Pretty sure we can count him out at this point." Marshal swung his leg over his saddle and hopped off his horse. His heart thrummed in his chest and his breathing quickened.

Jenner pulled out his pistol and dismounted. "Which way should we go in?"

"I want to get a look inside through that window first."

Five minutes later, after a cautious survey of the grounds and the building, they stood over Friedrich's lifeless body inside the office. He lay on the floor with his limbs sprawled out and a blank, wide-eyed expression on his ghost-white face. A small spatter of blood tainted the floor under his body, but not enough for him to have died from a gunshot or a stab wound.

Marshal knew immediately what fate had befallen him. "It wasn't Harry."

"What do you mean?" Jenner asked.

"I mean it wasn't Harry Deutsch. No gunshot wounds, no cuts. Only two bloody marks on his neck. See them?" Marshal holstered his pistol. "Our vampire friend from the Zambini household did this."

"Are you serious?"

Marshal nodded. "Go check Steve."

Jenner's voice carried into the office from the cell block. "Dead. Looks the same as Friedrich. His skin feels like an ice cube."

"Attacked by a vampire, like I said." Marshal noticed the remains of a splintered wooden chair next to his desk. He'd used broken furniture to do this sort of job before, and he would do it again tonight. He took two long shards of wood, probably two of the chair's legs at one point, and thrust one of them through Friedrich's chest. "Rest in peace, you old cuss."

"What in God's name did you just do?" Jenner asked from behind him.

Marshal turned his head. "I put a stake through his heart. If I didn't, then he'd come back as one of them." He stood and extended the stake in his other hand to Jenner. "And now you have to do it to Steve."

"What? No. You *desecrated* his body. I can't do that to another man, dead *or* alive."

"Then you're in luck," Marshal said. "Friedrich and Steve are now neither living nor dead, but both at once. They're *un*dead, just like the vampire who did this to them."

"I think you're letting your hatred of that boy from the Zambini house cloud your judgment."

Marshal stepped forward and locked eyes with Jenner. "And I think you have *no* concept of what we're dealing with here. Your job is to follow orders and protect the public from harm. I'm ordering you to put this chair leg through Steve Huggins's chest to keep him from coming back as a vampire and claiming even more victims than the two we've already got lying on our jailhouse floor."

Jenner's jaw tightened. "What happened to you? Why do you always behave this way when there's talk of vampires? They're not even real."

Marshal swore. "Are you kidding me? You've seen one with your own eyes, remember? The Reverend himself admitted that the kid was a vampire."

"I thought you guys were joking around. He's not *really* a vampire, is he? I mean, they don't actually exist." Jenner swallowed. "Do they?"

"They exist, alright. That boy got shot at least five times, two of them twelve-gauge shotgun blasts at close range, and he barely even had a scratch on him. How do you explain that?"

Jenner shrugged. "I just figured it was luck, or maybe most of the shot hit a piece of furniture or something. I don't know."

"He's a vampire. Bullets won't kill him." Marshal shook his head. He knew that firsthand. "That's why you have to put a stake though Steve's heart. It's the only way to be sure."

Jenner stared at the stake in Marshal's hand for a moment before he took it in his own. "Fine. I'll do it, but I want to know what happened to you. How do you know all of this?"

Marshal sighed. Memories of that night flooded him with anger and sadness. "A vampire killed my wife 35 years ago."

"Oh," Jenner said. "I'm sorry, Marshal."

"You still don't believe me, do you?"

Jenner shrugged again. "Sorry."

"I guess I can't blame you. I've been living with this for so long that I can't comprehend unbelief. I've seen it firsthand. You haven't. Until now."

Marshal leaned against the wall and fixed his eyes on his feet. The scene played out before his mind's eye as it had so many times before. Uncle Murray trying to warn him. Duke not believing him and shooting him. And it always ended with Elly dead on the floor next to him.

He exhaled a long breath and refocused on Jenner. "It's in the past. What matters now is stopping that kid from killing anyone else. Harry Deutsch isn't our problem anymore. It's Raven Worth."

"But we don't know where he lives, or how to find him. How do we stop him?"

"We head back to the Zambini house. They know more than they're letting on. We're going to find out where Raven lives one way or another, and then I'm going to drive a stake through his heart and end the killing." Marshal eyed the stake in Jenner's hand. "So put that through Steve's chest and meet me outside."

Silence surrounded Calandra. She lay in her bed, wide awake with thoughts swarming in her head and guilt churning in her stomach. Usually she had no problem falling asleep at night. After long days of setup, service, singing, ministry, and teardown at her father's tent meetings she would often drift off only moments after her head hit her pillow.

Tonight she couldn't fall asleep, though. Sure, she was tired, but the events of that evening wouldn't allow her any peace. Within an hour's time she'd ostracized herself from Raven, from Garrett, and from her parents, especially her father, all because of one terrible mistake. Now that mistake wouldn't leave her alone.

A tapping on Calandra's window startled her. After taking a few breaths to gather the courage to see what it was, she stood up, slipped a robe on over her nightgown, and headed toward the window. When she saw Garrett's sullen face through the glass her heart sank. She had hoped for Raven instead.

She unlocked the window and cracked it open, and Garrett helped her pull it up from the other side. She gave him a half-smile. "I'm glad you're back."

Garrett nodded. "I'm sorry I left in the first place. I was mad, and I behaved rashly. Will you forgive me?"

Calandra gave him a sad smile and touched the side of his face with her hand. "You don't have to apologize. I'm the one who owes you an apology. I shouldn't have betrayed your trust, but I did."

"Can you come out here?"

"Why?" she tilted her head.

"I'd like to talk to you for awhile, but I want to do it outside so we don't raise any suspicion of inappropriate behavior." Garrett rubbed his nose. "I don't want any more confusion tonight if we can avoid it."

"Why don't we just sit in the living room and talk instead? It's getting chilly outside and I'm underdressed."

Garrett shook his head. "I'm not comfortable going back inside yet. I just want to sit on the porch and talk for a few minutes, then I'll go."

"You mean you're not staying here anymore?"

"No. Not tonight, at least. I don't know if I'm coming back or not," he said.

A fresh pang of guilt stung her gut.

"Will you come outside with me?"

"I don't know if I should."

Garrett touched her hand and asked in a soft voice, "Please do this for me. It's the least you can do in light of everything else that happened tonight."

Another stab. He had a right to ask, and she should oblige him. How could she refuse after how horribly she'd hurt him?

"Give me a moment to put on some warmer clothes. I'll meet you at the front door."

Two minutes later she stood on the inside of the front door

with a hand on the knob, second-guessing the situation. Something felt off, but she couldn't pinpoint what it was.

It didn't matter. She owed this to Garrett for what she'd done, and if she could get him to stay by having an honest conversation with him, she would do it. She turned the handle and opened the door.

Garrett stood beyond the edge of the porch, his big frame illuminated by the moonlight. He almost looked like a ghost glowing in the darkness. He showed her a faint smile, nodded, and held out his hand.

A chilled puff of wind whipped her face, and she reconsidered. Maybe they should go inside after all. Maybe she could convince him if she went outside for a bit. Once they were inside she could get him to stay with her family again.

She stepped outside and a whiff of foul air stunned her. What—

Something hooked around her waist and yanked her to the right, and a frigid hand clamped over her mouth before she could scream. The last thing she saw was a pair of dead charcoal eyes, both familiar and frightening, and then everything went dark.

Chapter 40

"Dante, wake up." A man's voice wrested Dante from his slumber. "It's me, Garrett."

"What do you want?" Dante rubbed his eyes and glanced at the window. Still dark outside. "Why'd you wake me up? It's still nighttime."

"Calandra's gone. She's been taken, but I know where she is."

Dante blinked at him. "What are you talking about?"

"You need to wake the rest of your family and have them meet us in the dining room," Garrett said. "Now."

"What?" Dante jerked upright. Was he still dreaming? "Are you serious?"

"I'm afraid so," Garrett said. "It's up to you to get everyone together."

Within a few minutes Dante had his sleepy-eyed siblings and his frantic parents gathered in the living room.

"What's going on here, Garrett?" Maria asked. "Where's Calandra?"

"Where is she?" Luco squinted at him.

Garrett stood there with a smug smile on his face. "Have a

seat, will you?"

Luco stepped forward. "I asked you a question. Where is my daughter?"

"Take it easy." Garrett put his hands up. "She's fine. She's not hurt. Please, sit down."

Luco complied and took a spot next to Maria, who held his hand and asked. "What happened to her?"

Garrett smiled. "She was taken."

Maria clutched Luco's arm. He squeezed her hand and asked, "By whom?"

"By me."

Luco got to his feet faster than Dante had ever seen him move, but Garrett produced a revolver and pointed it at Luco's face. Luco froze mid-step.

Maria gasped and put her hand to her mouth. "Have you lost your mind, Garrett? Come to your senses!"

"I wouldn't do that if I were you," Garrett said, his focus set on Luco.

"What are you doing?" Luco growled. "This is *madness*."

"I have no intention of harming her. I kidnapped her to use her as bait to bring out Raven. He's the one I want."

Dante glanced at Anthony, who wore a sullen expression on his face.

"You're making a mistake, Garrett. Revenge won't give you fulfillment," Luco said.

"Don't tell me what will and won't make me content."

Garrett pointed a finger at Luco along with the revolver. "I warned you early on that this would happen. I knew he would try to make a move on her, but you didn't listen."

"Garrett—"

"*Enough.* I have her. If you want her back, find Raven and get him here in one hour."

"One hour?" Luco put his hands out to his sides. "That's not enough time. I don't even know where he lives, and if I did there's no way of knowing he'd even be there."

"That's not my problem. Either get him here within that timeframe or lose Calandra forever."

Dante knew his father wanted to tear Garrett apart, revolver or no revolver, but then they'd never get Calandra back. They had to find Raven, or Calandra would be lost.

"What do you mean we'll lose her forever? You promised you wouldn't hurt her."

Garrett shrugged. "I guess I lied, then."

Luco clenched his fists and set his jaw, but Maria stood to her feet.

"Stay back, Maria." Garrett pointed the revolver at her. "I don't want to have to use this on you either."

"I am ashamed of you, Garrett." Maria continued forward.

"I said *stop.*"

"You do this, and you're going against God. Revenge belongs to Him, and Him alone."

"What makes you think I care?" Garrett asked. When Maria

stepped even closer, Garrett raised the gun to her forehead. The room stilled. "Do *not* come any closer, Maria."

Maria glared at him, her eyes more volatile than Dante had ever seen them before. "This is not the Garrett I knew. Not the Garrett I helped to nurse back to health when my husband found you on the street."

Garrett returned her scowl, but said nothing.

"We took care of you, and this is how you repay us?"

"I'm done with doing things your way," Garrett said. "Once Raven is dead—for good this time—you'll never see me again. We'll part ways and you won't have to worry about me *or* Raven anymore."

"I wasn't worried about either of you in the first place. My only concern is that you live well and love the Lord. It's the same desire I have for all of my children, all of my family," Luco said. "You're still a part of that family, Garrett, if you want to be. You don't have to do this."

Garrett squinted at him. "Is Raven still a part of this family too?"

"Don't concern yourself with him. What matters is—"

"Answer the question, Luco."

Luco sighed. "He is if he wants to be."

Garrett shook his head. "Then your family can go to Hell for all I care."

"You need to leave my house now, Garrett." Maria's eyes narrowed. "Or I'll *make* you shoot me."

He glowered at her. "Get Raven here. You have one hour, and you'd better find him sooner than that. Sunrise is barely two hours away and he can't go out in the daytime."

Garrett backed toward the door, and Dante hoped he'd trip over something on the way out. He imagined Garrett falling to the floor and the revolver flying into the air. Luco would pounce on him and throw punch after furious punch at his face, and then he'd step aside so Dante could throw a few of his own.

No such luck. Garrett knew the house too well to make a simple mistake like that. He made it to the door, his revolver still trained on an unmoving Luco, and stepped into the night.

As soon as the door shut, Luco sank to his knees, his hands on his face, and uttered unintelligible prayers through his sobs. Maria came to Luco's side and wrapped her arms around him, followed by the rest of the kids, except for Dante.

"Dad?" he said.

Luco didn't respond. He just kept weeping and praying with his family. Mina clung to Angelica and buried her face in her chest, and Anthony clutched Maria's leg.

Dante felt like crying too, but he couldn't, not when there was still hope. Not when he had a role to play in saving his sister. "Dad, I know where Raven lives."

Luco's head popped up. "How? Where?"

"I followed him one night." Dante hesitated. "I can't tell you where, but I know how to get there. I can show you."

Luco put his hands on Maria's shoulders. "I'll bring her back,

Maria. We'll get Raven and we'll bring her back."

Maria nodded and put her hand on Luco's face. "Be careful. I love you, Luco."

"I love you too." He turned to Dante. "Go get the three rifles and my revolver from under the bed in my room. Make sure they're loaded. Anthony, help him."

"Can I come along?" Anthony asked. "I want to help Calandra."

"No," Luco replied. "You need to stay here and protect the house and the rest of our family. One of the rifles is for you. You remember how to shoot it?"

Anthony nodded.

"Good. Then make sure you learn from Dante how to reload it in case you need to. Go now and do it, then help Dante get the horses ready to go." He focused on Dante. "How long will it take to get there?"

"On horseback? Probably a half hour. Longer if we go on foot."

"Good. I want to be out of here in five minutes, then." When they stood up to fulfill his mandates, Luco said, "Wait."

Everyone stopped.

"Let's pray together first, as a family."

They formed a circle and clasped hands.

The front door to the Zambini home opened before Marshal Flax could knock on it. Luco Zambini, dressed for some sort of excursion into the wilderness, mirrored the surprise that Marshal wore on his own face.

"What are you doing here?" Luco asked.

Marshal eyed him up and down. "Going somewhere, Reverend?"

"Just—" Luco hesitated. "—have to run an errand."

Marshal glanced at the night sky. "At this hour? It's almost 4:15 in the morning."

"I don't have time to explain. Excuse me." Luco pushed past him and Jenner.

"Reverend, we need to find your young vampire friend. Do you have any idea where he might be?" Marshal asked, following Luco.

"I'm sorry, Marshal. I can't help you. I don't have the time."

Marshal put his hand on the saddle of the horse that Luco was loading up. "What kind of errand makes a man leave his family in the early hours of the morning with such urgency in his eyes?"

"It's a personal family matter."

"Does this involve Raven?"

Luco stared at him. "My daughter is missing. I'm going out to find her."

"Which one? The oldest?" When Luco nodded, Marshal said, "Perhaps we can help you in your search. Is there any chance she's with Raven? Perhaps if we find one, we'll find the other."

"I appreciate the offer, but we haven't seen Raven for hours, and I know for a fact that Calandra isn't with him. Thanks, but no thanks." Luco tied a bag onto his saddle.

"How do you know she's not with him?"

"I'm sorry, Marshal, but I don't have time to explain. Would you please excuse me?" Luco mounted the horse and it clopped back and forth a bit then re-situated itself.

Luco's two sons came out with a gun in each hand, the older one dressed like his father. He handed Luco one of the rifles and slung the other on his back, and then the younger son handed his father a revolver which Luco holstered at his hip.

"You're pretty well-armed for a simple search, don't you think?" Marshal asked.

"You've made it very clear that one of those bandits is still out there. Can't be too careful. Besides, you never know when you might run into a bear or something," Luco said. "Mount up, Dante. We're heading out. Anthony, go back inside, please."

"*Something* is right," Jenner muttered as the younger son headed for the door.

"Marshal, if you don't mind, I'd appreciate it if you and the deputy could stop by an hour from now to check on my family. Can you do that for me?"

Marshal smirked. "I'll see what I can do."

"Thank you." Luco tilted his wide-brimmed hat forward, then kicked the sides of his horse and galloped into the forest, followed by Dante, also on horseback.

As he watched them go, Marshal said to Jenner, "If we give them a head start, can you follow their trail through the woods?"

"No problem," Jenner said. "They're not even trying to be subtle. Should be easy."

"Get the horses. We're going after them."

Garrett's head continued to swivel and he scanned the surrounding forest. Harry should have been back by now. If Harry had violated the terms of their agreement then Calandra could already be dead. That's not what Garrett wanted. Perhaps he should have known better than to trust—

"Garrett."

He whirled around. There, in between two towering oaks, Harry stood with Calandra draped over his shoulder. She no longer kicked her legs as she had when Harry had first grabbed her on the Zambini family's front porch. "You didn't—"

"She's alive." Harry set her down on her rear end and leaned her against the tree as if she weighed nothing. Her arms were tied behind her back and a bandana stretched across her mouth. "Any longer and I'd be hard-pressed not to bite her. I'm still thirsty."

"Thank you for your discretion and patience," Garrett said. "We have a problem."

"What?"

"Luco and Dante rode into the forest on horseback, presumably to find Raven."

Calandra squirmed against her bindings, but she wasn't going anywhere.

"So what's the problem?"

"The marshal and one of his deputies showed up at the house asking questions. They're following Luco and Dante toward Raven."

"That's not a problem." Harry smirked. "That's a solution to my thirst. I'll drain them dry just like I did to Steve and the other deputy at the jail."

Garrett shook his head. Speaking of dry, he sure could use a drink to calm his nerves and stabilize his resolve. Still, it was too late to go back now. He would press onward, whiskey or no whiskey. "I don't want to know. I don't care what you do as long as you kill Raven and don't harm the girl. Got it?"

"Yeah." Harry gave Calandra a long stare. "I got it."

"I mean it, Harry. I gave you new life."

"I'm not arguing with you." His cloudy dead eyes twisted Garrett's stomach.

"Good. Pick her up. Let's go."

Chapter 41

"That's it." Dante pointed to the towering old mansion drenched with moonlight in the clearing. "That's where he lives. I followed him here early one morning and watched him go inside."

"You're sure?" Luco asked.

"Positive."

"Then let's not waste any more time." He rode his horse up the path to the front door and dismounted with Dante close behind. "You packed the crowbar, didn't you?"

Dante pulled it from his saddlebag and handed it to him. "Here."

Luco worked on the front door lock, which squealed against the crowbar's leverage and then snapped. He turned back to Dante. "Get the rifles, tie the horses to a tree, and meet me inside."

Screeching metal and snapping wood seized Raven's attention. Someone had found his home. He stole up the stairs from his basement in silence.

Marshal and Jenner arrived at the edge of the clearing in time to see Dante head inside the mansion and close the doors behind him.

"Leave the horses here."

"You ever seen this place before?" Jenner asked.

Marshal shook his head. "Never even knew it was here. We left our county about ten minutes ago, and this place is so isolated, I never imagined anyone would live out here."

Marshal dismounted and checked his pistol, then tucked a wooden stake he'd fashioned from one of the broken chair legs in his coat pocket. He hoped he wouldn't have to use it, but after what had befallen Friedrich and Steve, he decided he'd better bring one just in case.

"Go around the back and see if you can find a window or another way to sneak inside," Marshal said. "I just need enough of a distraction to finish him off. Take your rifle and try to find an elevated position inside the house to give me cover fire. A place this big has to have at least one balcony inside, if not more. I'm going to try to find a way in on one of the sides."

Jenner nodded and headed along the side of the mansion with his rifle slung over his shoulder.

The monstrosity carrying Calandra set her down again, this time a bit rougher than the last. She'd been terrified of him at first, mostly because of his hideous appearance. When she realized that he was Harry Deutsch, the man who had tried to rape her in her own home, now back from the dead as some sick, twisted form of vampire, her terror multiplied.

"See?" Garrett said from ahead of them. "It's just like I promised you. You get this new, permanent home once we kill Raven. You can live here for the rest of your life in perfect solitude, going out at night for whatever you need or want, blood or otherwise."

Harry nodded. "We still have to deal with the marshal and his Deputy."

"That's your prerogative, not mine."

"And we have to kill the father and the kid brother, too."

Garrett stopped, turned around, and faced him. "No. I don't want any part of that."

Harry squinted and stepped into Garrett's space. "You really think we can let them live after all they've seen? After they see *me*? They're a liability now, just like she is."

Calandra turned away when Harry's hellish eyes locked onto her.

"Everyone here tonight must die."

Garrett shook his head. "I can't let you kill them. Calandra has to live, and so do her father and her brother."

"They *must* die. They know where this place is. Even if you're not concerned about retribution, I am. They'll come back and kill me in my sleep. They must *all* die." Harry's tone resembled that of distant thunder. He stepped forward again and leaned his rotted face close to Garrett's. "Or I'll kill you first and kill them anyway."

Garrett hesitated, then finally nodded.

"Good. It's a shame that you'll be without the girl." Harry

stepped toward her and bent down. "But at least I can make her my slave for all of eternity."

He stroked Calandra's face with his decrepit hand and she recoiled.

"I wonder if her blood tastes as delightful as she looks," he said. "I'm going to enjoy this night very, very much."

Calandra cast a desperate glance at Garrett. Surely he wouldn't allow such a travesty to befall her? He would intervene and stop this monster from having his way. He would find a way to spare Calandra and her family. Or even better, she would wake up from this nightmare any second now.

Garrett met her desperate gaze with a look of apathy, cold and devoid of any remnant of the love he'd expressed to her so many times in the past, and then he looked away from her altogether.

In that moment, Calandra knew she would die that night.

Chapter 42

"Raven?" Luco called. "Raven, are you in here?"

Dante echoed his father's calls for a few minutes. He scanned the dark interior of the mansion for movement of any kind, and his heart jumped when a voice sounded from the shadows behind him.

"Why are you in my home?" Raven stepped into a shaft of silver moonlight. Colossal windows that stretched from waist-height almost all the way up to the lofted ceiling allowed the moonlight to stream into the foyer. "You are *not* welcome here."

Luco positioned himself between Dante and Raven. "Raven, I—"

"You invited me into your home as a guest, knowing I couldn't cross a threshold without an invitation. Now you come into my home unannounced, uninvited, and unwelcome. I want you to leave. Now." Raven advanced toward them, his fists clenched as tight as his jaw.

"I'm sorry. Calandra lied to me and I made my decision based on false information. I never should have sent you away," Luco said.

Raven shook his head. "It's too late for that. I'm done with you. Done with your family, done with your God. I don't ever want to see you again."

"I understand. It's just that—"

"It's just that Calandra's been kidnapped, and they were hoping you'd help get her back," a voice behind Raven said.

Dante looked past Raven and saw Garrett standing inside the mansion's front door.

"We finally know where you live," Garrett said, a big smile evident on his face even in the low light. "And now we're going to kill you."

Raven faced Garrett and stared ice at him. "You're welcome to try it."

"Interesting." Garrett rubbed his chin. "You're back to playing the bloodthirsty, soulless vampire. Perhaps your approach will change once you learn that *I* kidnapped Calandra."

Though Raven's fists loosened and his jaw went slack, his rage didn't subside—it intensified. "*What?*"

"We have her right here." Garrett reached outside and pulled a bound and gagged Calandra into view. She looked horrified. "So, no harm done, really."

Raven started toward them.

"Ah, ah, ah—not so fast." Garrett put a revolver to her head.

"If you hurt her, I'll—"

"You'll do what? Kill me? Turn me into a vampire, like you?" Garrett laughed. "I don't think so. No, you *love* her, don't you?"

Raven ground his teeth. Garrett was right. He did love Calandra. Even though she had lied about their kiss, Raven still loved her.

"I can see it in your eyes." Garrett's smile hardened into a cold, stoic glare. He looked at Luco. "See? It's exactly what I warned you about. If you had only—"

"Save it, Garrett. You told me once what I should have done. Once is enough to know that I need to admit I was wrong, and I was." Luco stretched his left arm toward her, his palm up. "Now will you please let her go?"

"Can't do it, I'm afraid. I'm already committed this far. I might as well go all the way."

"You don't have to do anything you don't want to. This can all end right—"

"This can all end when Raven is dead on the floor in front of me." Garrett said. "I want to stake you myself and watch you die. I want to send you to Hell where you belong."

Raven shook his head. "Not a chance."

"Then Calandra dies." Garrett pulled the hammer back on his revolver.

Both Luco and Dante took a step forward from behind Raven.

"No, don't!" Luco's firm tone shifted to pleading. "Don't kill her, Garrett. Please. Take me instead."

"No deal, Luco. I don't want you."

"Please, Garrett—don't do this."

"All Raven has to do is give himself up."

"If I don't, and if you kill her, nothing will keep me from ripping you apart," Raven said.

"But she'll be dead. You lose either way." Garrett glared at him. "Which is it going to be?"

"You won't do it," Raven said. "You may have killed vampires, and you may have it in you to kill in self-defense, but you don't have it in you to kill an innocent person. Especially not Calandra. You were going to marry her, remember? You love her just as much as I do."

Raven stepped forward. If he could close enough of the distance between them then perhaps he could reach them before Garrett pulled the trig—

"Take another step and I do it *right now*." He jerked her even closer to him and pressed the revolver's barrel against her head. She whimpered. "I *did* love her, but not anymore. She broke my heart by betraying me with you. With a *vampire*. A demon in human form. A monster."

"You still won't kill her. Killing me is what you really want. You've wanted that ever since I saved you and everyone else that night when the tent pole collapsed. If you kill her, you won't get me. Dead, alive, or otherwise, you'll never be satisfied knowing that you didn't get your victory." Raven took another step forward.

"I said *stop* coming at me." Garrett shook Calandra with one twitch of his burly arm, and Raven stopped. After a moment, he nodded. "You're right. I won't kill her. I want to kill you far more than I would ever want to kill her."

A foul odor tingled Raven's nose. Death—old death. Rotten flesh.

"That's why I brought along a contingency plan. I knew I couldn't match your strength or outmaneuver you, especially in your own home, so I had to recruit help."

Heavy boots thumped on the wood floor behind Garrett and a dark silhouette filled most of the massive doorframe. The stench of rancid meat intensified.

"God Almighty—Garrett, what have you done?" Raven asked, even though he already knew the answer.

"I'd like to formally introduce you to Mr. Harry Deutsch, the county's newest vampire."

When Harry stepped around Garrett and into the moonlight, Raven couldn't help but recoil a step. Harry was a vampire alright, but he'd been dead at least two weeks before he'd turned. Maybe longer. His skin had darkened with decay and tightened on his face and fingers, but he moved with the gait of a healthy being—perhaps *strong* was a better word to describe it.

Harry had been a monster when he was alive. Now, undead and decrepit, he was an abomination, not just to humans, but to vampires as well.

Raven eyed Garrett. "Do you realize what you've done?"

Garrett didn't look so sure of himself anymore. He didn't say anything, but he eyed Raven.

"The longer you delay a vampire from making his first

change, the more insatiable his thirst for human blood becomes, and the more powerful he is. How long after I bit him did you keep him from turning?"

Garrett swallowed. "About three weeks."

Raven's eyes widened, and he shook his head. "You fool. You stupid, stupid fool."

"What? What did I do?" Garrett tightened his grip on Calandra.

Raven focused his attention on Harry. "How many people have you killed tonight?"

Harry smirked. "Seven."

Raven shifted back to Garrett. "A normal vampire who turns the night after he dies is usually satisfied by the blood of one living person each night, and most times we don't even drink all of it. A vampire like Harry will consume anywhere from ten to fifteen times that amount *each night*. He has to in order to survive."

Harry showed a big, twisted smile.

"Garrett," Raven said. "You may have just created the single greatest threat to human life in history."

Garrett didn't say anything. He just stood there, his mouth open in shock.

"It's even worse than that," Raven continued. "He has the ability to go out in the daytime without fear of the sun. You've created the perfect killer, a devil that's almost invulnerable to any harm whatsoever. The only way to kill him is to stake him, cut off his head, and stuff it with garlic."

"Good luck with that," Harry said.

"Seven victims tonight, and I bet you're still thirsty, aren't you?"

"Parched," Harry replied. "But I know a nice Italian family that should fill me up for the evening. Here's hoping they don't have too much garlic in their blood."

"That isn't going to happen while I'm alive." Even as Raven said it, he wondered if he was really even alive or not. Had his time with the Zambini family and with God even meant anything?

Harry smiled. "I was hoping you'd say that."

He vaulted toward Raven with death in his eyes.

Chapter 43

Raven dodged Harry's first attack, then tried to block his second, but the force of the blow sent him reeling back into the wall. Harry swung his fist, but Raven ducked and it plunged into the plaster where his head had just been. He delivered two quick blows to Harry's exposed gut and rolled to avoid a wild kick that snapped a wooden banister to his left.

A gunshot split the air. Harry clutched his chest and staggered back into the wall he'd just put his fist through. All eyes landed on Dante, whose rifle still smoked from the shot.

Harry looked at Garrett, who still held Calandra close, his revolver to her head.

"You're a vampire, remember?" Garrett shouted. "Gunshots can't kill you. It doesn't matter where or how many times they shoot you. Only a stake through your heart will do the job."

Harry glanced at Raven with a sneer on his face and started toward Dante. Raven intercepted his route and drove his shoulder into Harry, who skidded across the smooth floor and smacked into the base of a thick marble pillar.

"Dante, Luco." Raven turned to them. "Get out of here. You can't do anything to help me. He's too—"

A boulder struck Raven's back and pieces of grey marble crumbled to the floor along with him. No, not a boulder—the marble leg to one of his statues. He recognized the heel of a sculpted boot on the floor just beyond his chin. Harry must have swung it at him.

His back ached with fresh pain, but he rolled to one side to avoid a second thundering blow from the rest of the statue's body, which Harry slammed down onto the floor where Raven had just been. It broke into hundreds of pieces.

Still on the ground, Raven grabbed a jagged melon-sized chunk of marble and whipped it at Harry's face. The marble struck the left side of Harry's forehead and he toppled to the floor.

Back on his feet, Raven quickly stretched out the kinks in his body. Everything felt tighter than normal, as if his resilience to physical trauma had diminished. Perhaps he wasn't still immortal after all.

Harry rose. Blood so dark that it could have been black trickled down his face, but the cut on his forehead had already started to seal up. He bellowed a roar that shook Raven from the inside out and stepped forward.

A salvo of gunshots rang out from behind them. Harry's body convulsed as multiple rounds thudded into his torso, and he dropped to the floor. He wouldn't be down for long, though. Raven had to make his move before—

A bulky form tackled him to the floor. "*Stay down*, Raven."

Raven twisted his body around and found Marshal Flax on top of him, pressing a wooden stake to his chest.

"Don't move, or I'll stake you!"

"But—"

"Why did you kill Steve and Friedrich?" Marshal asked. "Why did you target them? Were you working with Harry Deutsch?"

"What are you talking about?"

Before Marshal could answer, his eyes locked onto something behind Raven. "Impossible…"

Raven craned his head and saw Harry rising to his feet, as expected.

Marshal shook him and pressed the tip of the stake into Raven's chest. "What did you do to him?"

"He made me immortal, Marshal." Harry smiled, and two elongated fangs framed his yellow-brown teeth. "*Invincible*. He perfected me. *I* killed Steve and your deputy, not him. Their blood tasted wonderf—"

Marshal skinned his revolver and fired. The round struck Harry between his eyes, and he staggered back with his hands on his face.

When Harry moved his hands away, he dropped Marshal's bullet to the floor and smiled. The wound on his forehead sealed up. "Nice try, Marshal, but you can't kill me with bullets."

Raven shoved Marshal Flax away. He backed up, ready for the next attack, whether it came from Marshal or Harry. "That stake in your hands would do the job, Marshal. If we work together, maybe we can defeat him."

Marshal started to say something, but Harry launched

forward with tremendous speed and leveled him in one solid blow to the side of his head.

"You're alone again, Raven." Harry cracked his knuckles.

Alone.

Was he alone? He felt weak, much more like a normal human than a vampire. God could have picked a better time to allow *that* to happen. Either that, or Harry's vampiric strength dwarfed his own by so much that he just seemed weaker.

If there was ever a time where Raven needed God's help, this was it.

Harry lunged toward him, his arms outstretched, and Raven met him in the fray.

As Raven and Harry continued to battle, Garrett saw Deputy Jenner run over to the unconscious marshal to pull him away from the fracas. Luco and Dante had taken cover behind a large marble pillar, leaving Garrett alone with Calandra, who was still tied up and gagged.

Harry didn't fully understand the extent of his new powers, and as such, Raven continued to outmaneuver him in the fight. This wouldn't end in Garrett's favor unless he intervened. Besides, he wanted to finish off Raven himself.

He holstered his revolver and shoved Calandra to the ground, then pulled one of the stakes from his waistband.

Raven absorbed a ferocious blow from Harry with his

forearm, then drove the heel of his right foot into the side of Harry's knee. Harry buckled, but caught Raven's next punch with his hand and delivered a fierce head-butt to Raven's face. He recovered his footing and began to hurl blows at Raven.

The only things that kept Raven from submitting to Harry's superior power were the vampire-on-vampire training he'd received from fighting Vanessa and the knowledge that if he failed, Harry would kill Calandra, Dante, Luco, and the rest of the Zambini family. For them, he fought hard, despite what Calandra had done to him, despite how Luco had thrown him out based on false information. For their sakes, he couldn't give in.

Harry hefted a marble boulder the size of a horse above his head and hurled it at Raven, who dove out of the way. The boulder smacked through one of the mansion's marble support pillars, but didn't stop there. It continued its trajectory and tore a sizable hole in Raven's wall, and wind breezed inside the mansion through the fresh opening.

From a furtive glance outside, Raven knew that night would soon end. He needed to finish this fight quickly.

Harry's zeal and zest for taking revenge on Raven seemed to have dwindled since the marshal went down. Perhaps he had begun to deplete his energy. His attacks grew sloppy and inaccurate, his movement hampered and slow. Harry needed more blood, as any abomination would, to keep going.

Either way, it was a weakness Raven could use to his advantage.

Raven allowed Harry's next punch to make contact. It hurt, but it was a necessary price to pay for the advantage. The second punch came faster and harder, but this time Raven caught Harry's wrist with both hands, spun around, and wrenched Harry's arm behind his back at an awkward angle until a loud snap sounded.

Harry dropped to his knees and bellowed, but Raven didn't relent. He planted his foot on Harry's back and pushed down.

There, on the ground not three feet away from him, lay Marshal Flax's stake. If he could reach that, then he could—

Fire seared the center of Raven's back and burst out of his chest. Sticky warmth oozed down his stomach and weakness seized his body. His grip on Harry failed first, then his legs wobbled and gave out. Raven lay on the cool marble floor and clutched the pointed tip of the stake that protruded from his chest.

Two dark forms stood over him. One was Harry, who popped his arm back into place with a loud crack and flexed his blackened fingers. Garrett joined him and wiped his bloody hands on his trousers.

Both of them wore twisted smiles on their faces.

Chapter 44

Marshal's vision refocused and his cognition returned just in time to see Garrett plunge a stake into the center of Raven's back.

"*No!*" he cried as Jenner helped him to his feet.

"What are we going to do now?" Jenner asked.

Marshal shook his head. "I don't know if there's much we *can* do anymore."

Luco's heart dropped when Garrett stabbed Raven in his back, but in doing so he'd left Calandra alone. Luco turned to Dante. "Go get your sister as soon as you have the chance. Whatever happens, you need to get her out of here."

"What are you going to do?"

Luco sighed and cupped his son's face with his hand. "What I can, son. I love you. Now go for Calandra."

Dante eyed him, then nodded and scampered toward his sister.

Luco set his rifle down, darted over to the broken chunks of the marble pillar in the foyer, and hooked his hands underneath the largest of the pieces. He closed his eyes, and with a long exhale, he heaved against the stone.

Garrett leaned in close to Raven. "I told you I'd put a stake through your heart if you went near her."

Raven swallowed and clenched his eyes shut. He could care less about Garrett's taunting, or the bloodlust in Harry's eyes. He gasped, but even breathing hurt. *Everything* hurt.

This was it. This was the end. He'd finally figure out whether or not a vampire's soul could be restored, whether or not he'd face eternal damnation.

"Time for you to die, Raven," Garrett hissed into his ear.

A primal roar filled the mansion. Raven's eyes opened in time to see Garrett drop to the floor next to him. A gigantic white-grey mass struck Harry and pinned him between the floor and the wall—a piece of one of the mansion's marble pillars. From the size of it Raven guessed it had to weigh close to a thousand pounds, maybe more.

But…how?

A form leaped into view, grabbed Garrett by his shirt, then hurled him across the room. His body smacked into a wall, and he dropped to the floor and squirmed as he tried to get to his feet. Raven looked up at his savior in desperate disbelief. Was he hallucinating?

No. He wasn't.

It was Luco.

His eyes wild with fury, Luco reached down and wrenched the stake from Raven's chest. Pain spiked in his veins, but then a wave of relief flowed through Raven's entire body. He felt his strength starting to return, and the wounds in his chest and back began to seal up.

"Get up, Raven. This isn't over." Luco extended his hand.

Marshal couldn't believe his eyes. Luco Zambini, unaided by anything or anyone else, grabbed a colossal chunk of the destroyed marble pillar from the ground and hurled it across the room at Harry and Garrett. Then he soared through the air, grabbed Garrett, and flung him against a wall like a child discarding an old rag doll.

At that moment, it all made sense to Marshal. He knew why he had recognized Luco that first night he came to investigate Raven living with the Zambini family: Luco was a vampire too. And not just any vampire—a vampire with dark brown eyes and dark hair.

Luco was the vampire who had bitten Marshal's wife Eleanor 35 years earlier.

"Take my hand, Raven. Let's end this and get out of here," Luco said.

Raven, still reeling with disbelief, clasped his hand, but before Luco could pull him up, a jagged chunk of wood burst through his chest.

"*Luco!*" Raven yelled.

Luco dropped to his knees and slumped over, his eyes wide with shock.

He wasn't moving.

Chapter 45

Calandra was helpless to stop Harry from impaling her father from behind. She tried to yell to warn him, but the gag in her mouth muffled her voice. That same gag kept her from crying out when it happened, but it didn't stifle the tears in her eyes.

This couldn't be happening. It was all a bad dream, a horrible nightmare. She needed to wake up. Wake up.

Wake up.

Harry dropped the plank and staggered backward. He caught himself on the banister of the grand staircase that emptied into the mansion's cavernous lobby. Rage still burned within him, but his body couldn't fulfill his mind's desire to continue fighting, to continue attacking.

To kill them all. He could do it—he *would* do it.

But not without blood.

"Luco?" Raven said. "Stay with me, Luco. Stay with me!"

Luco shifted and blinked, and he turned to look up at Raven.

"Stay with me Luco. *Please!*" Movement flickered to his left. It was Dante, running to Calandra. "Luco?"

"Raven," he said, his voice weak and faint. "I'm sorry."

Raven shook his head. "What's going on here?"

"Isn't it obvious?" Luco gave a forced smile, then coughed. "I'm—"

"He's a vampire," a voice behind them said.

Raven turned and saw Marshal Flax standing there, his revolver in one hand and a wooden stake in his other. Jenner stood behind him, but his focus vacillated between Harry and Luco. Raven looked back to Luco, who nodded his head.

"And he turned my wife 35 years ago." Marshal stared steel at Luco, who clenched his eyes shut. "Eleanor. That was her name. I knew I recognized you, and it wasn't just from the mercantile. You look older now than you did back then, and that's what I don't understand."

"I'm sorry, Marshal," Luco said.

Marshal glared at him. "Sorry won't bring her back."

"It's true? You're a vampire? How come you never told me?" Raven didn't know whether he should be happy or furious. He felt some of both.

"I may be a Christian, but I'm not perfect."

Raven looked at the wood sticking out of Luco's chest. "If you're a vampire we can pull the plank out of your chest and—"

"No," Luco said between coughs. "It's too late. I'm not truly a vampire anymore. It won't have any effect."

"What are you talking about?"

"My strength was the only vampiric attribute I had left. I

gave up everything else to serve God, but I never gave up my strength. I thought I needed it." Luco looked at the marshal. "That's why I aged. I'm not immortal anymore. The best I can hope for is eternal life."

Raven shook his head. "I don't understand."

Luco coughed. "I never fully surrendered my life to God. I never surrendered my strength, so I kept it. But now—now it's all gone. I'm going to die."

Garrett pushed himself up to his feet. Not twenty feet from him, Dante cut the last of Calandra's bonds and set her free.

"Hey, stop!" Garrett started toward them, but he ended up flat on his back again. Had he slipped? No, something had caught his collar and pulled him down.

A dark, decrepit face loomed over him. Harry.

"Hello, Garrett."

Garrett's eyes widened. He reached for the last tent stake in his belt but Harry's bony hand clamped down on his wrist and crushed it in a cacophony of cracks. Garrett screamed, then pleaded, "No, Harry! *Noooooo!*"

The last thing he saw was Harry's fangs extending from his blackened gums.

"Papa?" Calandra skidded to a halt at her father's side as he lay with his head on Raven's lap. "Papa, don't leave me!"

Luco reached up and touched her face. "My sweet, beautiful

daughter. I'm proud to have seen you grow into the strong young woman that you are." He looked at Dante, wheezed, then said, "And you, son. You're a courageous young man with a bright future. I love you both."

"No, dad…" Tears rolled down Dante's cheeks. "You *can't* die."

"Marshal." Luco turned his head toward him. "I'm so, *so* sorry for what I did to you and your wife all those years ago. I don't deserve your forgiveness, but I pray that you will find relief through my death."

Marshal still just glared at him, not saying a word. Jenner picked up a stake and started toward Harry.

"Raven." Luco coughed again and dark blood tainted his lips. "I gave up my life to save you. 'Greater love hath no man than this, that he lay down his life for his friends.' I know now that God will grant me mercy for all of my years of concealing this dark sin. I believe God wants you to know that he is still the same God you met that night at the tent revival, a God capable of forgiving anyone of any sin, even yours. Even mine."

"I don't—" Raven shook his head. "I don't even know what to say."

"Don't say anything. Do what must be done. *Finish* this."

The old thirst flared in Raven's gut. He'd need blood if he was going to fulfill Luco's final mandate. Harry had already latched on to Garrett, who now lay motionless in his arms.

Luco took Raven's hand in his own and gave it a weak

squeeze. "Don't give in to the hunger, Raven. You're a new creation. The old man is dead and gone. The new man lives. If you rely on blood for your strength, I know you won't be able to defeat him. Substitute Christ's blood for the blood of the living. Blood for blood, Raven. Blood for blood."

Raven didn't know if he should believe Luco or not, but he nodded anyway.

Luco closed his eyes and whispered, "Trust me."

He fell limp in Raven's arms.

Chapter 46

Harry was already finished with Garrett and had begun to stalk Jenner by the time Luco died. A part of Marshal wanted to celebrate Luco's death, but another part wanted to forgive him for the past. Either way, they still had Harry Deutsch to deal with.

In the end, Luco hadn't been an evil man. He'd done wrong by Marshal 35 years ago, but the Luco that Marshal had gotten to know as of late had been decent, hardworking, and a flawed but generally good Reverend. Certainly better than any other preacher Marshal had known. He could forgive a man like that. He *should* forgive a man like that.

But a man like Harry Deutsch who had preyed on others even before he became the monster he was now? Well, that was entirely different.

Harry had been evil from birth, evil in life, evil in death, and now had grown even more evil beyond the grave. If Marshal couldn't avenge his wife's death on the vampire who had turned her, he'd have to settle for slaying Harry, the real enemy, instead.

He abandoned Raven and the two Zambini kids, scooped up one of the stakes from the ground, and charged toward Harry Deutsch.

Raven laid Luco on the floor and pulled the plank from his body. His legs wobbled, but he forced himself to stand. If he couldn't drink any blood and still hoped to fight Harry, he'd have to do it while he still had some strength left. Besides, the only blood he could drink would be that of Marshal, Jenner, Dante, or Calandra, and he couldn't do that to any of them.

"Raven." Calandra grabbed him by the wrist. "I'm sorry. I never should have lied."

Raven stared deep into her brown eyes, and they overflowed with hurt and anguished tears. She undoubtedly knew that her actions had contributed to this mess. Her apology signified her last attempt to make things right, not just with him, but for the entire situation. His response would either exonerate her from the wrong she'd done, or stamp her out completely.

"I forgive you." He didn't fully feel that he meant it, but he knew he had to say it in order for the process to begin.

She nodded. "Be careful."

"I will."

A stunning backhanded swipe sent Jenner sliding across the slick floor, but he still gripped a stake in his left hand and a revolver in the other. Jenner reacted as if the blow hardly fazed him, but Marshal fired off a few quick shots at Harry to give Jenner time to recover. Marshal emptied all six chambers then lunged forward with the stake in his left hand.

Harry caught his wrist with one hand, and the tip of the stake stopped just short of touching Harry's chest. He smiled at Marshal and bared his yellow-brown teeth. "Nice try, Marshal."

Marshal spat in his face. "Go to Hell, Harry."

Harry's smile warped into a snarl. He gave Marshal's wrist a sharp wrench down, and a sonata of snaps filled the air, dissonant against Marshal's cries. The stake clattered to the floor. Harry opened his mouth wide and bared his elongated fangs.

Marshal's life was over. He'd die at the hands of Harry Deutsch, now a vampire, and he would soon become a vampire himself, just like Eleanor. His last memory of her, of what she'd become, churned his stomach.

Even as Jenner screamed from behind them, Harry aimed his fangs at Marshal's neck.

A loud smack split the air and Harry released his grip on Marshal's obliterated wrist. It was Raven.

He'd delivered a deadening blow to Harry's cheekbone with his fist. Harry staggered back, then anchored Raven's entire body in place as he tried to tackle Harry to the floor. In one powerful motion, Harry hurled Raven across the room, then charged toward him.

Marshal held his crushed wrist with his other hand and looked at Jenner. He bent down and picked up his revolver with his good hand. "Go after him. I'll take some shots to see if I can distract him so you have a chance to stake him."

Jenner nodded and charged after Harry.

The impact from that last toss sent Raven's vision into spiraling swirls. He wanted to vomit, but Harry quelled the urge for him by delivering a brutal kick to his face. Raven lay on his stomach, unable to see much of anything. He clawed at the cool marble floor to try to buy himself some time, but it didn't afford him much of a break.

The next thing he knew, Raven launched through the air again and landed on prickly grass this time. He looked back and saw Harry stalking toward him from the massive hole in one of the exterior walls of his mansion.

Harry approached an ancient oak tree growing 30 feet from the mansion's perimeter and reached for one of its thicker branches. He ripped it from the tree and held up the sharp, jagged end for Raven to see. "This is going through your chest, kid. Then I'm going to kill your four friends. Better say your goodbyes now."

A battle cry sounded from inside the mansion. Harry whirled around, swung the large branch, and leveled Deputy Jenner to the earth. Jenner stopped moving.

Harry shook his head and released a warped, guttural laugh. "I don't know why you all keep trying to kill me. It should be obvious by now that it won't work."

From just inside Raven's mansion, Marshal Flax fired six more rounds from his revolver at Harry. Every one of the bullets hit Harry's back, but he didn't even bother to turn around. He just kept stalking toward Raven.

Calandra had to do something. She couldn't just watch Harry kill Raven. She grabbed a stake in her hands and started toward him. "Dante, start shooting at him. Get in front of him, alright?"

Dante nodded and cocked his lever-action carbine. "Alright."

She hid just inside the mansion on the other side of the broken wall near the marshal, ready to do what she had to do, while Dante ran outside and fired three shots at Harry.

"Hey, over here!" He cocked the lever action and fired another round, this time at Harry's face from the side.

When Harry turned his head to face Dante, Calandra stepped out and ran toward him. As she expected, he turned his entire body toward Dante, which exposed his back to her. Raven still lay on the ground to Harry's right with a dazed expression on his face.

Dante only got one more shot off before Harry grabbed the carbine from his hands and laid him out on the ground just as he had done to Deputy Jenner. Her brother had bought her enough time, though.

She leaped forward, raised the stake high above her head, and drove it straight into Harry's back. He writhed and flailed, and Calandra staggered away from him. Harry dropped both the tree branch and the carbine and tried to reach the stake in his back, but couldn't. After a few moments of thrashing and roaring, Harry dropped to his back and the tip of the stake broke through the left side of his chest from the impact of hitting the ground.

He convulsed for a moment, then lay there, still. Calandra stared at him for a long time before she finally felt at peace. A sigh escaped her lips and teardrops from her eyes followed. She ran over to Raven.

She bent down to check him. "Are you alright?"

He rubbed his eyes. "Everything's hazy. I feel dizzy, confused."

"Harry's dead. I staked him," she said. "If you're going to be alright, I need to go check Dante."

Raven nodded. "Go. I'll be alright."

She turned and started toward Dante, but a black viper latched onto her ankle.

It was Harry.

Calandra screamed, then twisted her foot out of his grasp. She fell to the earth and stained her hands with green grass streaks, then stumbled up to her feet to get away from him.

She watched in horror as Harry pushed himself up to his feet, grabbed the stake with one hand and pulled it all the way through his torso. He dropped it to the ground with a devious smile on his face.

"*Impossible.*" She gawked at him.

"You're next, cutie." Harry stalked toward her with murder in his eyes.

Chapter 47

The combination of Calandra's shrieks, Marshal Flax's yells, and a glint of sunlight creeping over the horizon snapped Raven back to cognition, but it was too late. He'd failed to defeat Harry before sunrise.

It wasn't too late to save Calandra and Dante, though. Luco's final message to him resurfaced in his memory: *Greater love hath no man than this, that a man lay down his life for his friends.* Raven forced himself upright.

There wasn't even a shred of a question in his mind. Raven knew what he had to do.

He charged toward Harry from behind, launched into the air, and drove his fist into the back of Harry's head as hard as he could. Harry toppled forward and landed face first on the ground, even as the first rays of hot sunlight touched Raven's skin.

He had to hold Harry in place, no matter what. Raven delivered a merciless blow to the center Harry's spine, then linked elbows with him back-to-back and pinned him facedown to the earth. Harry twisted and contorted his body to free himself, but Raven held on.

Please, God, if you want them to survive, help me to hold on.

Harry managed to get his legs underneath him and he stood up, bringing Raven with him. Raven refused to let go even as Harry tried to fling him off.

Come what may, he would hold on until it was over.

"Fine. You wanna go for a ride?" Harry couldn't move his arms above his waist because of Raven's elbows. "How about this?"

Harry kicked his feet up and dropped back, this time pinning Raven to the earth instead. He pushed down with his shoulders and ground Raven's face against the dirt and the grass. He lifted his shoulders up and then slammed them—and Raven—back into the earth for extra effect.

"How does that feel?" Harry asked, his eyes on the rising sun. "I'm going to keep you here until the sun burns you alive, boy."

Raven mumbled something unintelligible.

"What was that? Speak up, will you? I think you've got dirt in your mouth." Harry laughed.

"I said, 'that's what you think.'"

Harry twisted his body and drove Raven's face into the dirt some more. "What are you talking about?"

After another few jerks from Harry, Raven replied, "Remember how I said you have to consume ten to fifteen times more blood than a normal vampire?"

Harry let up on the face-grinding for a moment. "Yeah? So?"

Raven grunted, then said, "Vampires who need that much blood are also ten to fifteen times more susceptible to sunlight than regular vampires."

Harry didn't move. Terror seized his chest, reminiscent of the fright he'd felt when Raven came at him the night he'd tried to rob the Zambini house. "But—but you said I'd be *invulnerable* in the sunlight!"

"I lied," Raven said. "I may be a Christian, but I'm not perfect."

His eyes wide, Harry wrenched and contorted and tried to escape with every ounce of strength he had left. All the while he tried to grind Raven so far into the earth that he wouldn't have any skin left on his face by the time Harry finished with him.

None of it worked. He couldn't break free, and he couldn't get back up on his feet.

When all of his efforts failed to get Raven to let go, Harry hissed, "You'll burn too! Let me go!"

"I may burn with you here—" Raven's voice hardened. "—but you're going to burn alone when this is over."

Harry kept struggling, kept pleading for Raven to release him, but the kid was just too strong, too determined. It didn't make sense. Harry was more powerful, but now he couldn't break free?

Sunlight washed over him and one of his fingers caught fire. Harry screamed.

Calandra watched with wide eyes as Harry's body erupted in flames. It started with his fingers and toes and slowly worked toward his torso and head. His wretched wails filled her mind with sounds of agony she knew she'd never forget, but she refused to look away.

This was justice for her father's death.

Raven didn't open his eyes until Harry's screams and his writhing ceased. Until Harry was gone. A blanket of black ashes covered Raven, and weakness racked his body. He too would burn at any moment.

Time to die.

Chapter 48

It never happened.

Instead of burning, a comfortable warmth washed over Raven, reminiscent of a loved one's touch. He stood to his feet with some difficulty, and ashes fell to the dirt at his feet. As he touched his face, the raw, exposed flesh sealed up under his fingertips. All of his other wounds, including his aches and pains, evaporated in the sun's warmth.

Calandra ran over to him, her mouth open and eyes wide.

"Your skin," she said. "It looks—perfect."

Raven tilted his head. "What do you mean?"

"I mean *perfect*. There's not a blemish or a scar on it. You're not pale anymore. You look healthy—almost glowing."

Wonder filled Raven's heart. Could it be?

Marshal leaned down to Jenner and helped him sit upright with his good arm. "Take it easy, there, Deputy. No reason to over-exert yourself. The deed's done."

"Harry's dead?" Jenner rubbed an obvious lump on the side of his cranium.

Marshal nodded. "Wish you could have seen it. The sun

came up and burned him away. Finest piece of God's vengeance I've ever seen. Would've proved to you that vampires are real, too."

"After what I saw over the last few hours, I think I'm in your camp on that issue now."

Marshal grinned. After 35 years, maybe he could finally discard his memory of what Eleanor had become. Seeing Harry Deutsch burn up like that would more than replace it.

His wrist throbbed with fresh pain. Too bad Harry had gotten ahold of it before he'd gone up in flames.

He gave Jenner a pat on his back with his good hand. "Couldn't have done it without you, Deputy."

"Thanks, Marshal."

"In fact—" Marshal plucked the brass star from his chest and examined it. "—from now on, just call me Duke."

When Marshal dropped the star into Jenner's hand, Jenner eyed him. "I don't understand."

"You're the marshal now, Jenner." He sat down next to Jenner and leaned back against the outer wall of the mansion. He propped up his damaged arm on his knee. "I've had enough excitement for one lifetime. It's your turn to keep the peace. I'm retired."

Dante came over to Raven and Calandra, his eyes fixed on Raven's hands. He rubbed his head where Harry had struck him with his own carbine. "What happened to you?"

Raven shrugged. "I don't know."

"How are you able to tolerate the sun?" Dante asked.

Raven shrugged again. "I don't know that either."

Yes he did.

"That's incredible," Dante said.

Raven smiled, and recited the words Luco said to him just before he died. "Greater love hath no man than this, that a man lay down his life for his friends."

"Blood for blood?" Calandra asked, a faint smile on her face.

Raven nodded. "Blood for blood."

He put his arms around both of their shoulders and took in his first sunrise in almost a century.

The Lord is my shepherd; I shall not want.
He maketh me to lie down in green pastures:
he leadeth me beside the still waters.
He restoreth my soul: he leadeth me in the paths
of righteousness for his name's sake.
Yea, though I walk through the valley of
the shadow of death, I will fear no evil:
for thou art with me; thy rod and thy staff they comfort me.
Thou preparest a table before me in the presence of mine enemies:
thou anointest my head with oil; my cup runneth over.
Surely goodness and mercy shall follow me all the days of my life:
and I will dwell in the house of the Lord for ever.

Psalm 23

Epilogue

Twenty years later

Raven first noticed the young man lurking near the back of the chapel when he took the stage to open the revival service with prayer. Even from a distance Raven picked out his elongated fingernails, his mangy, overgrown hair, and his furrowed brow.

He stalked along the fringes of the crowd and his eyes darted to and fro like a nervous animal's for most of the service. Though the young man didn't respond to Raven's call to repentance at the end, Raven felt an urge to approach him.

He kissed Calandra's cheek. "I need to go talk to that young man over there."

Calandra smiled at him. "Take your time, sweetheart. I'll be here when you get back."

Raven walked over to him and extended his hand but the young man hesitated, much as Raven had so many years earlier.

"What's your name?" he asked.

The young man studied him for a moment, then answered in a shaky voice, "Ron. Ron Chaney, Jr."

"I'm Raven, the pastor here." He knew how this poor kid felt. He'd been there. "Do you need help, son?"

Ron glanced around as if someone was watching him. He ran his gangly fingers through his scruffy mane and nodded. "Yes, sir. Yes, I do. You see, tonight there's supposed to be a full moon, and it's almost sunset, and—and—"

"Easy, Ron." Raven placed a gentle hand on Ron's shoulder. "Everything will be alright."

"No, Reverend. It won't. It won't." Ron's whole body quivered. "You have no idea."

Raven smiled. "Actually, you might be surprised. I know almost exactly the type of anxiety you're feeling right now, and I have a solution for your problems."

Ron didn't smile, but he stopped quivering and straightened up from his hunched-over posture. "You—you do?"

Raven smiled. "Have you ever read Psalm 23?"

Thanks for reading **BLOOD FOR BLOOD.**

If you enjoyed this book, please help me produce more great fiction.

Here are 7 WAYS you can support me in my writing journey:

1. Sign up for my newsletter. If you enjoyed *Blood for Blood*, please sign up for my newsletter right at the bottom of my website's homepage: **www.benwolf.com**. You'll only get emails on an occasional basis and/or when I launch new novels, stories, products, or other content.

It's free to join and when you sign up, I'll send you four **FREE** short stories and two **FREE** issues from two of Splickety Publishing Group's killer magazines *Havok* and *Splickety Prime*, both of which feature stories written by me.

Again, please sign up at **www.benwolf.com**.

2. Tell your friends about this book. Lend it to someone. Buy it for someone as a present. If you're interested in doing something like that, contact me at 1BenWolf@gmail.com and I'll sling some bonus goodies to you for helping me out, including a free subscription to any one of Splickety's magazines.

Are you a blogging machine? Interview me about my book. Do you rule Facebook? Talk my book up to your friends. Have you conquered Twitter? Spread the word to the masses.

Whatever your medium of choice, feature a post about *Blood for Blood*, tag me in it (my social media info is below), and if I see it (you can also email me to let me know you wrote it) I'll comment on your post and engage with your readers.

Please also recommend this book on Goodreads.com and Amazon.com, and give it a great review (if you agree that it deserves it). If you know me, don't review the book as a friend or acquaintance—just review it as if we don't know each other.

3. Book me to speak at your event. I travel from coast to coast every year speaking on a variety of topics both related and unrelated to *Blood for Blood*. I'm not super expensive, and in most cases I'm happy to work within your budget when possible. We can also arrange for online speaking and presentations via video conference.

If you want to book me to speak at your event, shoot me an email at 1BenWolf@gmail.com. Be sure to put the words "Speaking Invitation" in the subject line.

4. Subscribe to Splickety. Do you love flash fiction? Subscribe to Splickety's magazines at **www.splicketypubgroup.com/subscribe** to read the best flash fiction in the world.

Email the code **B4B** to subscribe@splicketypubgroup.com when subscribing to get discounts and FREE bonus content.

5. Chat with me about the story. Want to chat about *Blood for Blood*? I'd be honored if you would "like" my Facebook page at **www.facebook.com/1BenWolf**. If you have business-related things to discuss, please email me at 1BenWolf@gmail.com instead of contacting me through Facebook.

6. Follow me on Twitter: @1BenWolf

7. Buy my next book. The best thing about reading my stories is that there's always another one coming out soon. If you want a sneak peek at some of my forthcoming works, circle back to #1 on this list and sign up for my newsletter at the bottom of my homepage at **www.benwolf.com**.

About the Author

Hey, all. I'm Ben Wolf. I write speculative action/adventure fiction. I live in the Midwest and have two gorgeous kids, Liam and Violet, whom I adore. I also love to swordfight, play video games, and play volleyball.

I have recurring dreams of being chased by dinosaurs in Jurassic Park and by secret service agents through hotels and movies theaters. The thought of drowning or being eaten or killed or dismembered by something in the ocean or a big lake frightens me, as do most spiders and insects. I wish I could be a cage fighter sometimes, but then I remember how much that would hurt my face.

I am harassed daily by ideas for stories, by characters who want a story of their own, and by the misery of everyday life's demands, so I keep writing. In my early school years I was tested for ADD but was never diagnosed with it. To this day, I still wonder if I

As someone who knows how hectic life can get, I founded Splickety Publishing Group in 2011 to meet the needs of busy folks like me: people who appreciate great fiction but don't have a lot of time to read. If that describes you, you should consider subscribing. Visit **www.splicketypubgroup.com/subscribe** for more information.

The sum total of all of my parts is as follows: I'm a driven, strategic, crafty troublemaker with a big mouth and an even bigger personality. Check me out at **www.benwolf.com.**

P.S. *Please* keep reading my books—I'm going to keep writing them whether you read them or not, so we'd all be better off if you just gave in already.

CPSIA information can be obtained at www.ICGtesting.com
Printed in the USA
LVOW01s1754280415

436415LV00022B/1561/P